CRIMSON OBSESSION

DEANA JAMES

ZEBRA BOOKS
KENSINGTON PUBLISHING CORP.

ZEBRA BOOKS

are published by

Kensington Publishing Corp.
475 Park Avenue South
New York, NY 10016

First printing: February 1988

Printed in the United States of America

To
Barbara O'Brien and Janice Pace—
Together we have enjoyed the lovely things of the past.

Prologue

. . . *and so, my dear Fitzwalter, I have no choice left. Absolutely none. No help for it.*

Regret much, of course, but too late. Much, much too late. All is irrevocably lost. I would stay and face it, but health gone too. No more than a few months left in the old ticker. Only be a burden to complicate the situation.

Now comes the purpose of this letter, Fitz. Will you take Cassandra? Don't know how to ask it other than bluntly. She's a great girl. A wonderful girl. Never one to fuss or complain. Smart as a whip. Just seventeen but not a bit silly like so many girls. Not exactly long on looks, but perhaps that's a all to the good.

Don't be alarmed, now, Fitz. I don't ask for marriage. Too much to ask even of an old friend. No — all I ask is that you find her a decent place. She could teach in a school for girls where she could have her room and board if you'd give her a recommendation. I'm sure you see it would be no good for me to write her one. No good at all.

Coming to the end now, Fitz. God bless you for reading this, and thank you from the bottom of my heart—for what that's worth to you—for granting me this one last request.

So will put down the pen—pick up the pistol. Neatly and decently without fuss.

As ever,
Scotty

The Honorable Cassandra MacDaermond, only child of the Earl of Daerloch, struggled to swallow a sob. The effort almost strangled her, yet in the silent room she dared not make any noise.

The earl lay sprawled on his side across the hearth. Near his right hand lay the antique pistol with the silver crest of MacDaermond embossed in the ivory handle. He had stuck the pistol in his mouth and squeezed the trigger. Blood from the back of his neck where the ball had passed through had coagulated in the cold gray ashes. When he had fallen, he had smashed his temple on the andiron, so that wound, too, had bled.

The ugliness of his death, the grotesqueness of his posture made Cassandra ill. The paper crumpled in her hand as she spun away. *Decently,* he had written in the letter.

She closed her lips firmly to stifle hysterical laughter as well as sobs. In all her young life, she had never beheld a more indecent thing. Added to the hideousness of the earl's face and the twisted shape of his limbs was the nauseating odor whose source was a pool from under the lower part of his body.

"Neatly and decently." The words quavered in the chill silence. "Dear God!"

The blood drained from her face as she swayed in

distress. Staggering from the room, she leaned weakly against the scarred kitchen table. She closed her eyes but opened them immediately as her father's body materialized in her mind. Her nostrils dilated with the memory of the awful smell in that quiet room. The gatekeeper's cottage suddenly became much too small.

Snatching a cape from a hook, she flung open the back door. Rain-laden wind froze the tears on her face and tore the pins from the bright red hair of her unprotected head. Ordinarily, the elements would have daunted her, but at that minute she welcomed their punishing force. Dragging the heavy cape around her shoulders, she burst out onto the sodden path.

With no destination in mind, she walked rapidly across the field. The drops spattered against her cheeks, washing away the salt tears as fast as they fell from her eyes. Far from ducking her head to avoid the stinging blast, she welcomed it in the vain hope that it might cleanse her senses of the grisly memories.

Something under an hour she walked, until her hand clutching the cape at her throat was blue with cold, until the tears of grief and despair had all fallen to be replaced by natural tears shed to protect her eyes from the temperature. The tumult of her blood that had forced her to flee exhausted itself and she staggered to a halt, one shoulder leaning against the bole of a tree.

How had she gotten so far? She could not remember.

Bewildered, she gazed dully around her. The rain had slackened to a heavy mist, but the wind still blew.

She could not make out a single familiar landmark. She was not even sure she stood on Daerloch land.

She gave a wild laugh. Of course, nothing belonged to Daerloch now, nor ever would again. The land, the tradition of the clan, the pride of place, all were gone. Consumed in gambling by the man whose distorted remains lay face down in the gatekeeper's cottage on what had been his estate. Only she remained of the name.

And she was nothing.

The paper crackled under the folds of the cloak. Only when she drew out her hand did she realize that she was still clutching the last words of her father upon this earth. Stiffly, she spread the paper, hunching over it to shield it partially with her body. At intervals from the black branches above her, gigantic drops fell on her bowed head.

For the first time she read it with comprehension: shame heated her cheeks. *Take Cassandra* . . . Not even *Take care of Cassandra*, but *Take Cassandra*, as if she were a parcel or a trusted hound, for heaven's sake.

The wind gusted suddenly; a drop of water splattered on the paper in front of her. The ink ran, instantly blurring the letters of her name. She watched it happen as more cold rain began to fall on her bare head.

More drops fell on the paper, until it was a streaked and illegible mess. The name *Fitzwalter* disappeared as *Cassandra* had already done. She felt no fear. Fitzwalter could not have helped her. Only when she let go all but one corner did she feel a stab of remorse. Then the close, *As ever, Scotty,* flowed away, leaving only gray blurs behind.

Directing her brain to make her numb fingers act, she watched them do her bidding. Stiffly they moved. As the opposing thumb opened to a right angle from her small palm, the rain drove the sodden sheet to the ground. There it slipped into a puddle between the exposed roots of the tree.

Suddenly she shuddered violently. Pulling the cape together, she hunched her shoulders. Angus, the groom at the stables, would ride for the constable and the minister. Perhaps he would smuggle her into the kitchen at Daerloch. There she could wait by the great black range until they arrived.

A wave of homesickness swept her, self-pity for her plight, grief for her father, longing for the girl she had been only a few months before. The pain was too great to be borne along with the cold. Sternly, she forced her mind to concentrate only on picking her uneven way toward the house. For the last time she would avail herself of someone's help in the name of the Earl of Daerloch, but only because her physical strength was not sufficient to take care of what lay in the gatekeeper's cottage.

When her father's body had been decently disposed of, she stood with Mr. MacAdam on the platform at the railway station. The butler's impassive visage that had greeted visitors at Daerloch for so many years was twisted into a tragic mask of grief. "Now, lassie, don't be thinking of the dead," he counseled, his voice stammering slightly over the last word. "You know you cannot change them. You'll only waste your sweet life and in the end they'll still be dead and will not know."

Cassandra shook her head. "I don't dare forget my father, Mr. MacAdam. If I forgot him, I might make the same mistakes he did. False friends led him until his body betrayed him. Then his weaknesses killed him. I'm not trying to change the past. I only want to avoid it."

"You'd best be forgetting the whole thing."

She said nothing. Her green eyes slid past his shoulder to stare down the track. Faintly came the distant chuffing of a locomotive. A plume of gray smoke rose in the sky.

"Lassie?"

She stooped to pick up her handgrip. "I'll write, Mr. MacAdam. In the meantime, I'll pray you soon find work."

"I'll find something." He raised his voice over the noise as the southbound train pulled into the station. Even before it stopped completely, people were opening carriage doors. As it braked, MacAdam climbed into an empty compartment with Cassandra's small trunk. Depositing it safely, he turned to give her a hand up.

They had time for nothing else. A quick press of his hand and then he was back on the platform, closing the door. The whistle blew and the train shuddered.

"Good luck and good fortune, lassie."

"Good luck to you."

The train began to move. She lifted her hand as she watched him change from familiar face to stick figure and then disappear completely as the track curved slightly.

"Luck," he had said. But luck had no part in her

father's tragedy. He had played a game in which there were only winners and losers. Predators and victims. She stood at the window a long time telling herself that MacAdam was right. She had no hope that she could ever extract vengeance. She would not purposefully set out to achieve it.

She lifted her eyes to catch one last glimpse of the craggy hill above the town. Her ancestors had built a fortress on that hill, so legend had it. The blood of the clan had run into the earth time and again when feuds had sprung up between the MacDaermonds and their neighbors. If wrong were done, it must be avenged.

Her blood heated in helpless anger against those who had destroyed her father. They were nameless and they were probably legion. Dispiritedly, she sank down on the train seat, her back to the locomotive. So long as she could, she would look back at the land she loved. A lump rose in her throat. She could not pray, nor would she cry. So she made a silent vow. She would put aside the old ways and the old traditions. At the end of this line of wood and rock and steel lay a new country. She would enter it a new woman.

Chapter One

Lady Constance's superb white bosom heaved and quivered with indignation. "How dare you, Sir? Command this brute to unhand me!" she cried.

Lord S— threw back his leonine head. His cold laugh echoed in the dark hall. "No, M'lady. Oh, no. When you denied my suit, I determined you should pay the price for your pride."

Despite the tight grip exercised by Odo, his lordship's cloddish manservant, she drew herself up haughtily. "My pride shall sustain me. My father shall hear of this."

"Ah, no, my fair beauty. You will tell him nothing. When you have acceded to my demands and satisfied my desires with your delectable body, you will have but two choices." He paused to run his eyes over her disordered loveliness. "You must either marry me—or—retreat to a nunnery to spend the rest of your days in penance and prayer."

"No!" She flung back her head in defiance. "You would not dare. If you go through with this you are no gentleman."

Lord S— laughed again softly as Odo tightened his

fierce grip. His lordship's eyes glittered in anticipation. Stepping forward, he thrust his hand into the cleft between her alabaster breasts. Her expression changed to one of terrified pleading but to no avail. With a sweep of his hand, he split the heavy mauve silk to the waist. "I am not gentle," he agreed with deceptive politeness, "but you shall acknowledge me your lord and master."

Edward Sandron yawned widely as he stabbed the nub of the pen into the inkwell. Tea. He needed something to wake him up or he would never finish the first three chapters by Monday.

Groaning, he massaged the back of his neck in an effort to loosen the stiffness that came from holding his head at the same angle for so long. When the muscles protested, he rolled his head on his shoulders and arched his back. The movements brought a measure of relief but not enough. At last, grumbling inaudibly, he pushed himself out of the straight-backed chair and moved stiffly across the room.

Lifting a cozy from the teapot, he touched his hand to the porcelain. "Stone cold! Damn!" He tossed the ineffective square of quilted cotton down on the table and lifted the lid. Almost empty anyway. Nothing but a sludge of tea leaves in the bottom. At this hour of the night there was nothing for it. He had to make his own tea.

Barging out of the lighted library into the darkness, he closed the door behind him to conserve heat. Slowly, he walked down the hall, counting the steps until he came to the top of the back stairs. His toes in the soft-soled leather slipper curled over the edge of top step. A tiny smile curved his lips at his own cleverness as steadily, with the confidence of long practice, he descended.

" 'But this place is too cold for hell,' " he muttered softly to himself, sharing Shakespeare's porter's heartfelt observation. The total blackness of the narrow staircase and the awesome chill into which he descended made him think of tombs. He paused once, debating whether he should abandon the idea of tea and return to work. Or better yet, abandon the idea of work and go to bed to start fresh in the morning.

Then his feet touched the flagstones of the main floor. The kitchen was to his right. He fumbled for the doorknob, turned it, and entered, the door grating noisily on its hinges.

By the time he made his uncertain way to the center of the room, the cold rising from the flagstones made his feet and ankles begin to ache. Grumbling and shuffling from one foot to the other, he fumbled for the lamp on the table. Lifting its chimney, he struck a match and held it to the wick. The flame rose readily, creating a pool of light that increased as he raised it to shoulder height and peered around him hopefully. The kitchen was empty.

He sighed, then shrugged. He had not really expected that his cook would be up at this time of night preparing culinary delights. The man's execrable concoctions were hardly edible. If the fellow actually were to take time at his work, the results might be poisonous.

Prominent on one wall loomed the great black castiron range. Carrying the teapot in one hand and the lamp in the other, Sandron approached it determinedly. But when he poked around inside, a string of oaths fell from his lips. No fire had been banked within it. The ashes were gray and chill.

He clenched his fist and shook it in the direction of the kitchen door through which the cook had made his exit for the night. "Damned lazy incompetent!" Irritably he regretted not having a new Bunsen burner installed now that he had gas piped into the house.

No tea! No more work! Suddenly, he began to shiver convulsively, his teeth chattering noisily. No tea! No stimulant! What was more, if he stood here much longer, he would die of double pneumonia. The muse or whatever stepsister of hers moved him had departed. Probably she had fled to some place warm. His shins began to ache. He would swear he could feel his kneecaps stiffening. Another few minutes here and he would freeze to the spot.

Leaving the useless teapot on the table, he turned out the lamp. All around him the silence was as impenetrable as the darkness. He closed his eyes. His mind pictured the arrangement of furniture perfectly. Out of long practice he found the door without incident. Arms extended slightly in front of him, he counted back the number of paces to the foot of the stairs. His hand rested on the railing and guided him up rapidly until he stood on the landing, where he again opened his eyes.

Far down the hall, he could see the sliver of light under his door. Bed suddenly seemed like a very good idea. He took one step. He could feel his foot slip sideways. He gasped incredulously as his balance started to go. Too late he tried to shift his weight back onto the leg behind him, but that foot was already off the step. He cartwheeled his arms striving for balance, but the sole of his carpet slipper might have been planted on ice.

Backward he fell, crashing downward into the darkness. The edges of the risers hit him at his hips, waist, and shoulderblades. The breath jolted out of him in a whoosh and he could not suck it back in. He clawed for the rail, but his fingers had not the strength to stay his plummeting body. He slid and bumped toward the bottom, scraping his spine and bruising the masses of nerves. Then the back of his head smashed into the flagstone floor at the foot of the steps. Most of his body weight crashed down on top of it. His neck bowed forward until his teeth clicked together by the force of his chin being driven into his chest.

His brain registered a moment of terror that his neck might snap, before his body somersaulted over itself. The pain lashed up from the strained tendons to his overcharged brain. A flash of dark light was his last impression before the pain and everything else was snatched away by impenetrable darkness.

"If you must walk around in the dark, old chap, you must expect these kinds of accidents."

Sandron opened one eye cautiously. He closed it quickly when the light assailed his traumatized nerves and added to his agony. Besides he needed only one glance. He was still alive, although the grating voice of Nash, his publisher, would certainly not be out of place on the devil himself. Infinitesimally, he began to shift his weight. First, his arms. The left one seemed in good working order, but the right hurt from wrist to shoulder when he flexed the muscles. The pain was to be expected, he reasoned. He had strained it in his futile grab for the dowels of the bannister.

He took a deep breath, released it on a sigh, and moved his legs. No problem. Then he shifted his hips. The dull ache at the back of his waist burst into a purgatory of pain. His whole spine must have been scraped raw. He did not need to make another move to confirm it. Now he needed to lie very still to keep from fainting or doing something much more embarrassing over which he would have no control.

His publisher's voice whined in his ear. "I say, can you lift your head, old chap? The cook has sent up a kind of a thick white paste that smells like a couple of fish died in it. Let me ladle a bit of it into you. You're probably too bunged up to taste much anyway."

Edward opened the eye again. "Nash," he murmured, "go to hell."

Eyes sunk in shadows beneath overhanging lids regarded him stoically. The sandy muttonchop sideburns twitched as Nash's thin lips spread back from his small sharp teeth. "Will soon, old chap. Will soon. But for now, need to suffer a bit more. Get in training, so to speak."

Edward experimented with another shallow breath and tried to raise his head. The muscles in his neck simply refused to work. The pain was so bad that he sank back blindly, nausea rising in his throat. He must get himself under control. If he started vomiting now, when he could not turn over, the results would be most unpleasant. ". . . doctor . . ." he murmured.

"Been and gone, old chap. Been and gone. Poked and prodded around on you for a few minutes, made you groan, charged me a guinea, and left."

"What . . . ?"

"Left you some medicine here. Laudanum. I could have sent someone round to the apothecary for it and saved the doctor the trouble and me the guinea." His voice took on a more aggressive note. "D'you want to take some now?"

Edward considered his options. "Yes," he muttered. ". . . head . . . pounding."

"Not surprised, old man. Cook found you crumpled up on your neck at the bottom of the back stairs when he came in to prepare this Lucullan delight."

"Slipped . . ."

Nash regarded him sternly. "How much did you have to drink?"

"No . . . Goin' to fetch tea . . ."

Nash snorted. "Surely. Do it all the time m'self. Often in danger of losing m' balance fetching more tea. Devil's own brew. Preachers rail about it from pulpits all the time."

Edward was in too much pain to argue. "Laudanum . . ." he whispered.

Nash rose and slipped his hand under the patient's neck. Almost as his fingers touched the spine, a guttural groan escaped from between Edward's teeth. Before the medicine could reach his lips, he slipped back on the bed unconscious.

"The cook has given notice, sir."

Edward leaned his head back against the chair and sighed. "God has seen fit to be merciful," he intoned.

The valet did not respond to his master's doubtful

whimsy.

Edward lifted an inquiring eyebrow.

Glumly, the man set the highly polished boots inside the wardrobe. His voice sounded muffled from its interior. "Fact is, sir. I'm terribly sorry, but I'm no hand to cook at all."

Edward shifted cautiously, hoping to find a more comfortable position for his only half-healed bruises. "Well, good lord, Parks, I didn't hire you for that. Why should you be apologizing?"

The valet straightened and closed the door silently. He cleared his throat awkwardly. "For no reason, sir, except . . ."

"Yes."

His face set in funereal lines. "He was the last one, sir."

Sandron looked blank. "The last one what?"

"The last of your servants, sir."

For a minute Sandron sat silent. Then he tugged at his ear thoughtfully. "I see people in uniforms running to and fro everywhere I go. Surely . . ."

Parks tilted his head back. The movement had the effect of raising his aquiline nose into even higher prominence. "None of them are yours, sir. They all work for Mr. Nash in the casino. There's not a one that'll set a foot back here."

"But surely—"

The valet slid the breakfast tray from in front of his master. "No, sir."

Sandron looked exasperated. "Then I suspect you'd better hire someone." Considering the subject dismissed, he pulled the sheaf of papers from the shallow drawer of the desk and picked up the one on top.

The valet lifted the breakfast tray with a long-suffering air. "Whom do you suggest, sir?"

Sandron laid the paper down with barely controlled irritation. "I'm sure I do not know. I hardly include the domestics in need of employment among my circle of friends. However, I have been given to understand there is a surplus of servants."

"Well . . . sir. There is . . . in a manner of speaking."

"*Fraser's Magazine* carried a long article about it just the other day. Something about 'What Should Be Done to Give These People Bread?'—or some such thing."

"Yes, sir."

"I should imagine if you went round to an employment agency, you'd be able to bring home an even dozen servants for every vacancy we have and then some."

"But—"

"How many vacancies have we?"

"Six, sir."

Sandron raised a dark eyebrow. "And how many servants do we regularly employ?"

"Six, sir, counting the cook."

"Why do we have no servants?"

"They won't work in this house, sir." The valet's expression did not change. "They don't like the surroundings."

Edward pressed the tips of his fingers to his aching temple. "For God's sake, this is just a house," he whispered.

Parks did not reply. Considering that he had stated the situation clearly, he took the tray away in ominous silence.

Edward Sandron looked around him at his study. A tiny grin twitched the corners of his lips. Perhaps it was just a bit theatrical. Most studies contained a bust of Caesar crowned with a laurel wreath. However, he had to admit that few sported one with a grinning golden skull in place of the face.

He shifted his chair around toward the fire. The tiger skin rug with three-inch fangs bared was not really unusual. As for the Great Pentacle drawn around it, he doubted that any of the servants had any idea what it signified. The ancient book of alchemy was open on its stand, but everyone he had ever hired had been illiterate.

Edward's faint grin became a frown. Probably Parks was just not trying. The valet had always been too amiable. Still he could not allow the man to do all the work. Keeping up with his master's things was a sufficient task. The pain eased somewhat in his temples under the gentle massaging. Promising himself to begin his search for help tomorrow, he returned to the work at hand.

The afternoon waned as he wrote on. Four pages became five and then six as he alternately stared into space and scribbled. Someday he should hire a secretary who could take down his words as he spoke. Nash laughed at him for not already doing so. He could turn out twice the work in half the time. Still, he preferred to do it himself. He had, after all, an ideal working arrangement. He could work on first drafts, second, and third drafts of his books in the quiet of his library with its shelves of books from floor to ceiling. A secretary would disturb his peace.

When Parks knocked at the door at the appointed hour, he frowned unhappily. Sometimes the Devil's Palace was a crashing bore. Sighing, he put down his pen and reluctantly slid the pages into the drawer. Then he gingerly stretched his back and neck. A good hot bath would take much of the stiffness out. For the last hour he had been supporting the weight of his head on his doubled fist. The sprained muscles of his neck began to tremble if he forced them to function for more than a few minutes.

Suddenly, he dreaded the night. Nash had made excuses for him for over a week. Tonight, they had agreed, he would put in his appearance, but he could not think that he would be able to stay for very long. Damn and blast! A real writer would not have to do this sort of thing.

Lifting the seven-foot staff topped with a gigantic silver ankh, the huge black majordomo struck the floor of the little stage three times. His deep bass voice thundered out over the assemblage. "Baal comes. Baal comes. The envoy to his satanic majesty has arrived."

Sandron barely controlled a wince as the noise intensified the throbbing in his temples.

People at the card tables and the roulette wheel stopped their play to look expectantly at the curtains of midnight black velvet. The majordomo signaled to two small black boys, who grinned, bowed to the audience, and drew the curtains aside.

Applause rippled among the tables as Sandron dressed as Baal stepped forward to the edge of the small stage. Flinging his arms out, he made the crimson lining of long black cape billow dramatically against the midnight curtain. "Sinners! Welcome to Hell!"

A general burst of merriment and more applause followed his shout.

He had dressed as usual in formal black evening dress. His perfectly cut tail coat accentuated his width of shoulder. His waistcoat, also black, and slim black trousers fitted neatly over his flat stomach. In a departure from fashion he wore boots, shined to a patent gloss with heels sporting silver spurs.

Arms akimbo, he glared out over the gambling tables with what he hoped was a devilish expression. From his temples, silvery white streaks of hair carefully combed to present the appearance of horns drew a gasp from several first-time visitors. His smoky gray eyes and otherwise dark hair, slicked down and shiny with Macassar oil, presented a stark contrast to the unusual pallor of his skin. Tonight he had not needed to add smudges of mascara beneath his eyes and in the hollows beneath his cheekbones.

The majordomo thumped his staff again and Edward swayed slightly. If the man had brought the end of the damned thing down on top of his head, he could have caused him no more pain. Wincing visibly this time, he deepened his frown, hoping that the expression on his face looked like a demon's anticipating the damnation of a group of lapsed mortals. Slitting his eyes against the agony, he spoke the next line. "Eat, drink, and be merry! Lose your money! Lose your property! Lose your souls!"

At this point in his speech he was supposed to throw back his head and laugh satanically. Instead, he managed only a weak chuckle. Swirling the cape again, he turned aside to descend the seven steps to the floor of the casino.

As the more ardent gamblers turned back to their games, the curious watched a woman in a black sateen gown sway forward to place her hand on his arm. Impossibly black hair was swept high into a knot on the crown of her head. From the center depended strands of jet beads so long that they brushed against her neck. He covered her hand with his and smiled coldly.

The croupier spun the wheel calling for bets. The last of the gamblers turned back to the tables and Edward began to move among them. "For God's sake, find me a drink," he muttered out of the side of his mouth.

"Head still hurting, darling?" the woman in black whispered back, her eyes scanning the tables rather than her companion's face.

"*Hurting* is too mild a word," he groaned, and signaled to a waiter, who stepped forward with a tray of wine goblets.

"If you had been in bed as you ought—"

"Spare me." He held up his hand imperiously. The effect was somewhat spoiled by the decided tremor in his fingers. He made a fist.

The two approached the first table, where the baccarat dealer stopped the play. "Come around to watch the suffering, Baal, old fellow?" one of the guests sneered.

"Your choice, Parkington." Sandron smiled thinly. "Don't notice any pitchforks stuck in your back."

The man called Parkington hooted before turning

back and gesturing impatiently to the dealer.

"Baal, I'm having a run of luck," one thin-faced woman whined softly. "Don't come around and stand too close."

Purposefully, the tall man in black moved away from her end of the table. "Wouldn't think of it, Sybil. I'll move on instantly." He stopped and chuckled as she swept up the card just dealt her. "Just remember. I'll get you eventually. Your luck never lasts forever."

And so it went as he moved round the room. His face grew whiter and whiter until finally he leaned against the wall, his hand supporting his face in what he hoped was an insouciant air. "Time to leave you all," he called. "Most of you are doing remarkably well ruining yourselves. However, a few are not plunging deep enough."

A laugh greeted this mock reproach.

"Empty your pockets, my friends. It's only money. Made to be spent. So place your bets. The excitement is what you live for, after all." As he made the last statements, he mounted the little stage again.

Ashtaroth remained at the foot of the stairs, her eyes following him upward. Her jet beads swayed gently with the nod of her head. The little black boys swept back the curtains. "Bad luck to you all," he called.

And then with a swirl of crimson satin, he was gone.

The players laughed as the croupier spun the wheel and the dealers slid the pasteboards across the green tables.

Edward Sandron stumbled to the wall and leaned against it, his face white, his forehead clammy. "God," he murmured in a voice that quavered with weakness.

"A woman has come from the employment agency," Parks announced gently.

"At last." Edward made no attempt to lift his head from the back of the chaise longue.

"Are you sure you're up to this, sir?" Parks asked doubtfully. "What if I interview them all then choose one?"

The prone man raised one eyebrow. "May I remind you that this is the first one we have had to interview."

"True enough, sir, therefore—"

"It has been two weeks since the employment agency was contacted."

"Yes, sir."

"Therefore, it might be fair to say that this woman may very well be the only one?"

Parks inclined his head. "That might be fair, sir. I had thought of that."

Edward looked at him suspiciously. "Is it then the idea of my interviewing this creature that bothers you?"

"Well, sir, you just might create . . . that is . . ."

Chuckling suddenly, Edward managed to push himself up and swing his legs stiffly over the side of the lounge. Gesturing his hand to the valet to show the woman in, he stood gingerly and tottered to the chair behind the desk. "I promise I shall be the soul of discretion. Under no circumstances shall I so much as hint that anything improper will be expected of her."

Parks sighed softly. He had caught the sparkle of interest in his master's eyes. Edward Sandron never could resist a challenge, nor let slip an opportunity to tease someone. "Sir," he admonished.

"Parks. I swear—"

"Very well, sir." He bowed slightly.

"You can even cover the bust of Caesar."

"Yes, sir."

"Mrs. Fitch?"

"*Miss* Fitch, sir. Miss Cassie Ines Fitch."

He could not quite repress a smile at the name. Lips quivering ever so slightly, he studied the small woman who sat bolt upright on the edge of the chair across the desk from him. If ever a name told the tale of the person to whom it was attached, Cassie Ines Fitch did. Only an inch of iron gray hair showed beneath the edges of a plain black poke bonnet. The bonnet itself, like the dress of rusty black wool, the shawl, the black gloves, the parasol, all were the style of some thirty years before. Her only adornment fastened the neck of her dress, a purple cairngorm set in an ornate silver mounting.

The skin of her face, the only portion of her body exposed to his gaze, was surprisingly smooth but pale to the degree that he wondered briefly at the state of her health. Her forehead was creased with fine gray lines above eyebrows so light they were almost invisible. Deep gray shadows stained her cheeks beneath her eyes and in the hollows beneath her cheekbones. Indeed, if not for the bright green eyes, he would not have been surprised if she had fallen over dead. Could the agency not find a housekeeper in better health?

He blinked suddenly as he realized he was staring.

Those green eyes were staring back at him with a startling flash of defiance. Then the pale lashes swept down to conceal the expression.

He cleared his throat. "So, Miss Fitch . . . you have excellent references."

"Yes, sir." Her voice had more than a hint of Scottish burr.

"And you have worked for these people?"

"They would not have written references for me had I not worked for them." Her black-gloved hands tightened in the black reticule.

"Of course." His eyes skimmed the three letters. Each spoke in glowing terms of Cassie Fitch's dependability, her cleanliness, her honesty. Each declared the writer sorry to see her go, but for one reason or another each had no further need of a housekeeper.

He looked at her again. She had not moved an inch. Indeed, she sat so still, so straight that she might have been a statue balanced on the edge of the chair by some clever sculptor. He looked at the letters again. At last he laid them down with a smile. "Everything seems to be in order."

She allowed her lips to part slightly in what might have been a tiny sigh. "I can assure you, sir, that it is."

He smiled then. "Very well, then, I suppose you can start to work immediately?"

"Yes, sir. Immediately. What are my duties?"

Her question stopped him cold. He looked hopefully toward the door. Now was Parks's cue to enter. Unfortunately, the soundproof study precluded the valet's having eavesdropped on the conversation. Edward ran his hand over his smoothshaven chin. "Why, er, the normal — ordinary — everyday, er, housekeeper things. I leave that to your experience to, er, decide."

She set her mouth in a straight, tight line. "Then I am to have charge of the staff?" she prompted.

He stirred uncomfortably, busying his hands on the desk by folding the references and stacking them neatly. "Well, yes. The staff to be sure. The fact is that I don't have—that is, I am understaffed at the moment."

"How understaffed, sir?"

He smiled offhandedly. "Well, actually my valet, Parks, is the only one. Of course, the servants in the other part of the house . . . but they are not your concern. Nor is the rest of the house," he hastened to add.

She looked puzzled. "I am not to be the housekeeper for the entire house?"

"Look here," he began. "What did they tell you at the employment agency about this position?"

"Just that it was a position for a housekeeper."

"They didn't tell you anything about what I do for a living?"

"They told me that my prospective employer was a writer."

"Er—yes. That's what I am. A writer."

She looked at him. "Do you not own the entire house then?"

"Oh, no. I do lease the entire house, though." He took a deep breath. "I just don't—live in the entire house."

She looked perplexed.

"I operate a gambling casino in the other part," he said baldly, then tensed, waiting for her to rise and leave.

When she made no move, he studied her closely. Her face remained impassive. A trick of light might have made it appear paler, but he could not be sure.

He relaxed slightly, then drew a deep breath. In for a penny, in for a pound. "It's called the Devil's Palace." Involuntarily, he hunched one shoulder preparing for the exclamation of outrage.

She raised those clear green eyes, such a contrast to the rest of her face. The eyes expressed no concern. Absolutely, none at all. "Yes, sir," was all she said.

Chapter Two

Believe me, my dear Mr. MacAdam, your presence will be most welcome. I know you have suffered much since the Earl's bankruptcy. I only wish I could find work for all those who were put out without a roof over their heads. But at least I can help you.

The position of butler will be waiting for you because the house is what you would call "a house o' the de'il." All God-fearing servants here in London have heard of the place and shun it. I myself was the only person the employment agency sent and they did not tell me what they were sending me to. I admit that I should have left immediately, but beggars can not be choosers. I had to have work and quickly.

If you have been able to find employment in the weeks since I left, why then I am pleased for you and wish you good fortune. If you have not, then I beg you to come as quickly as you can. Ask for Miss Cassie Fitch at the back of the house at 29 Regent Street.

Yours,

C.

"Brought you a cook, old boy," Nash announced grandly as he strode past Parks and into Edward's study. "Smelled that awful stuff the monster belowstairs was sending up for you. Thought about how you couldn't write if you was weak from hunger."

"Ah, Nash, your solicitude for my welfare moves me. I would be in tears if you had not interjected the idea that your concern is over my writing."

Nash shrugged cheekily, helping himself to a cigarette from the box Edward kept on the desk for him. "Best kind of charity is when you can help a friend and your own interests at the same time. Now ring for tea. There's a good chap. I'm absolutely parched and you'll see that I've done right by you."

Miss Cassie Fitch stared critically at her reflection in the clouded crazed glass. Although she hated to part with money for such a thing, among her first purchases with her first quarter's wages would have to be a mirror.

And a kerosene lamp. She cast a disgusted glance at the tiny gas jet beside the door. The flame was so small that its light was barely sufficient for performing the most common acts of dressing, much less for making up the face. She had moved the narrow chest of drawers and mirror to the wall beside the door. Nevertheless she feared the results when she rose to dress herself each morning before dawn.

The bell beside the gaslamp jingled peremptorily. She lifted both palms and ran them over the smooth iron-gray hair. Not a wisp escaped the tight bun at the back of her neck. She glanced once more at the reflection in the mirror and set her mouth in tight disapproving lines.

"Good God!" Nash exclaimed. "What was that?"

Edward eyed the laden tea tray with anticipation. "What was what?"

"That woman. I suppose it was a woman. It wore skirts."

"Miss Fitch?" Edward bent forward to help himself variously to a slice of jelly roll and a soda water biscuit topped by a thin slice of Gloucester. He arranged each on his plate, then took a spoonful of nuts and a pale green mint. "She's the new house-keeper." He bit down into the roll and sighed as currant jelly ran into his mouth.

"Surely you could have chosen someone a bit more prepossessing, Edward?" Nash complained, still star-ing at the closed door. "Suppose some of the guests caught sight of her?"

Edward popped the rest of the roll into his mouth and grinned. "They'll just think she's a witch. Right at home in the Devil's Palace."

Nash turned back around and helped himself to tea. "Witches ought to cackle and writhe. This one's so silent, I could have sworn she was dead. Almost fell out of my chair when she moved—or crept. Wouldn't be hiring someone that looked that bad myself. Are you sure she hasn't got consumption? In which case you're in danger of catching it too."

His host smiled cynically. "Still worrying, Nash. If I died, who would write your novels for you?"

"Right. Damned inconvenient."

"Right." Edward polished off a cream bun and licked his fingers with gusto. "God! That's good! Much as it distresses me to do so, Nash, I have to thank you. But where did you find this cook? Parks sent round to agency after agency. No luck. The only one who came near the place was Miss Fitch. She's from Scotland, newly arrived in the city. Didn't know what she was getting into. But she's worked out just fine. I've got clean sheets regularly again, not just when Parks could get to them, and—"

Nash held up his hand. "Spare me, old chap, the dreary recital of your domestic joys. Where are the next chapters?"

Edward groaned. "By the end of the month. Have mercy, Nash. You can't possibly have to rush the bloody thing into print before next year."

"Need the money to cover investments and notes coming due, old chap. We both do. We're in this together, you know. It's a crucial time in our program. Stocks and bonds. Notes coming due. Big push coming soon. Must give it all we've got. Biggest gamble ever."

Edward's eyes narrowed as he bent a critical gaze on his publisher. The muttonchop sideburns twitched with each staccato phrase that fell from his lips. Nash's hand on the teacup was not quite steady. "Are you telling me that we are in financial difficulties?"

"Oh, no. Not at all. Not at all. Never meant to give you that impression at all, old chap. Far from it. Extended to the limit is all. Takes money to make money, you know. We need every one of those beautiful golden guineas the chaps part with to buy each copy of your book."

Edward drew in a deep breath and released it with particular slowness. Never had he seen Nash look so upset. Usually coldly sophisticated, a man who jested in the face of calamity, the publisher now seemed fairly to seethe with nervous anxiety. "Nash, if you've ruined us with your bloody speculations . . ."

Not quite meeting Edward's eyes, the publisher set the teacup down and pulled his watch from his waist-coat pocket. "Must rush now. Finish the chapters like a good chap soon as ever you can. I can't stay longer. Enjoy your tea." He practically loped to the door.

"Nash . . . !"

The very best Darjeeling suddenly left a foul taste in Edward's mouth. He set the cup down clumsily, rattling it against the saucer. Taking another deep calming breath, he looked around him. The room, so warm and cheerful, so secure, seemed suddenly cold. The house on Regent Street, while not the best address, was a far way upward from where he had begun. Could it all be taken away from him so swiftly? Had he denigrated himself and pandered his talent for nothing?

His smile was rueful. What talent? His writing filled a niche. It could never be dignified by the title of literature. Leagues of decency marched against it. No one actually admitted to reading it. The critics did not even look at it. Not that they would find it worthy of their time. Yet it was profitable. Thanks to it and the gambling, he and Nash . . .

Nash. His publisher knew all about Edward Sandron, about Baal. He had helped in the creation. Or damnation.

Parks's entrance interrupted his grim musings. "Shall I collect the tea tray, sir?"

Edward looked at the array of delicacies he had not yet tasted. Nash had so upset him that his appetite was almost gone. Almost. But not entirely. He grinned mischievously up at the valet. "I know what you want." He wagged his finger at the impassive face. "You intend to carry this tray out of here and into your room. There you'll devour everything on it except the plates."

Parks looked uncomfortable. He opened his mouth to speak, then closed it with a sheepish smile.

Edward gestured to the chair Nash had vacated. "Sit down! There's more than enough here for both of us."

At that moment the door opened. Miss Fitch took two steps into the room. Her hands came out from under her white apron. "Shall I take the tea tray, sir?"

"No." Edward laughed, reaching for another jelly roll. "Parks and I were just getting ready to help ourselves. Come and join us, Miss Fitch."

She looked from valet to master then to the tray before them. Her amber-green eyes sparked with interest as she stared at the food. Then she shook her head. "No, thank you, sir."

"Oh, come on . . ."

But she backed toward the door. Before he could finish his invitation, she was gone.

"Perhaps I should go too . . ." Parks began.

"Nonsense. I meant what I said. I'll be damned if I'm going to let the first tempting food I've had in weeks be taken away and eaten by you. But I'm not such a pig that I don't remember that you haven't had any decent food in weeks either. So let's sit down and eat in company." Edward popped a butter sandwich into his mouth and refilled his teacup.

Parks hesitated only a moment before taking Nash's chair. He waited politely for Edward to finish piling his plate.

"How is she working out?"

"Mrs. Fitch, sir?"

"*Miss* Fitch. Yes. How is she working out?"

Parks poured himself a cup of tea. "She's a quiet bit of a thing, sir. Never says a word. Never stands around gossiping the way most housekeepers do. I wouldn't know she's around but for the amount of work she does. Marketing and cooking and cleaning. Of course, now that you have a cook, she can get on with her regular duties."

"Of course."

At last Edward sat back replete. He and Parks had polished off the entire contents of the tray. Every crumb of food and every drop of tea had disappeared down their throats in record time. Then Parks had picked up the tray and departed.

Edward sat back, a satisfied smile on his face. The light coming in through the windows was more direct. The afternoon was waning. Time for a quick nap before he bathed and dressed.

His last thoughts as he settled himself more comfortably in his chair were of Miss Fitch. He wondered if she had gotten anything to eat from the new cook. She should have stayed.

Cassie Fitch closed the door to the master bedroom. She slipped her hands under her apron and clasped them over her concave stomach. All that food! So beautiful! So rich! So elegantly prepared! Her stomach rumbled at the very thought. She pressed her palms against it and sternly bade it be quiet.

How she had longed to accept her employer's invitation. She had eaten sparingly of the very plainest foods for over a year. Nevertheless, if he ever found out that she was much younger than she appeared, she would probably be dismissed without a reference. She shivered at the thought. She could not even go back to the same employment agency. They would want to know why she had not given satisfaction.

Worse than the prospect of dismissal was the thought that he might wish to continue to employ her but in a capacity not to her liking. She shook her head. Faced with those alternatives, how could she even consider sitting down to tea with him. Still the temptation had been there.

Even as her stern moral principles prevented her breaking bread with a man so steeped in corruption as Edward Sandron, she was not so far removed from the luxury of her former existence that she did not hunger for the things that she had once known.

Like jelly rolls! She moaned slightly, remembering how she had eaten them as a child, light airy sponges, thick with currant jelly and lavishly dusted with sugar.

"Stop that!"

Her voice echoed in the empty room. "You're being foolish." Get to work and stop thinking about things that can never be again. You were lucky to have had them. Thousands and thousands never have them at all.

The thought failed miserably to bring her any comfort as she picked up the first linen from the pile of mending.

The next day Edward saw her black-clad figure disappearing into the room at the end of the hall. "Miss Fitch," he called.

Rather than stop and wait for him, or come toward him as he had imagined she would, she stepped into the room and closed the door behind her. Perhaps the housekeeper had not heard him.

Once in the room, she dashed across it and out the other door, closing it firmly behind her also. Her heart pounding, she leaned against the wall. If only Mr. MacAdam would come, then she could work here without fear of discovery. The old butler would act as the buffer between her and Sandron as well as Parks and the cook.

Her hand not quite steady, she touched the wig. It had not been dislodged. Even if it should be, she really had no fear on that score. Many men and women, particularly old ones, wore wigs. If it slipped, her employer would suspect nothing, unless of course, it were jerked off completely. Then he might suspect something at the sight of her own hair. She should have dyed it or shaved it off.

Tears pooled in her eyes. So much had been taken from her she could not bear to part with her hair also. To cut it would have been to cut away her own identity completely. She had changed her name, changed her age, changed her clothing. Sometimes she felt herself dissolving into the person that was Cassie Fitch. She shuddered. Her fingers slipped under the wig just behind her ear. The soft feel of her own hair was reassuring. She was still there under all the rice powder and ash.

He found her the next day in the dining room as he was returning from his morning "constitutional." He had exchanged his usual more conservative dress for stout walking shoes, a heavy Macintosh cape, and a plaid cap with earflaps. She knelt half under the dining room table, furiously running a polishing cloth over the rungs of a chair. "Miss Fitch."

His deep voice came unexpectedly from behind her. Startled, she spun around on her knees. With the folds of her black dress entangling her, she lost her balance. Even as he sprang forward to try to avert the fall, she caught at the chair. It came over on top of her, tumbled her to the hardwood floor, and narrowly missed striking him in the side of the head.

For an instant she lay stunned. Edward went down on one knee beside her. "Miss Fitch!" His voice was sharp with alarm as he slid his arm under her shoulder. "Miss Fitch, are you all right?" Her eyes flickered open. "Miss Fitch, are you all right?" She stared up at him blankly.

He had never noticed that her eyes were such a light bright green. In fact he had never seen eyes of that particular shade in his life. "Miss Fitch?" He pushed the chair over. It tilted off her and thudded onto its side. "Miss Fitch?" Was she injured seriously? He ran his hands down her arms and over her hips.

His unfamiliar touch had the effect of galvanizing her into motion. She rolled away from him and tried to clamber to her feet. He reached for her as she swayed back. Clumsily, she fended him off with her arm, but her action only succeeded in unbalancing herself again. They fell together, sprawling on the floor, her on top of him. Instinctively, his arms closed round her.

"Let me go! Damn you!" Like a cat she twisted in his grip. Suddenly, instead of her on her back on top of him, she had both hands braced on his chest and was pushing with all her might. "Damn you!" she repeated furiously. "Take your hands off me."

Instantly, he released her and fell back in amazement. The words themselves did not shock him. He heard much worse than this during his tour of the floor every night. What shocked him was the housekeeper, whom he would have sworn was a sheltered lady, letting fly with such language. "Miss Fitch!" he chided, a grin curving his mouth. "Temper. Temper."

Far from being intimidated, she shot him an angry look before pushing him away and springing to her feet without a bobble. He remained on one knee grinning while she backed hastily along the side of the table, her breath coming hard and fast. He slowly rose, tilting his head to one side as he studied his surprising housekeeper.

She was amazingly agile. As he stared, she all but skipped around the table. "Miss Fitch!" he called again. "I want to apologize to you."

She hesitated at the door. Her face was completely turned away from him. "It's not necessary, sir," she murmured.

He came slowly toward her. "Oh, but I'm sure that it is. I frightened you, by sneaking up on you like that. So I apologize most humbly for startling you so that you were overset." Reaching her side, he bent to study her face. "Am I forgiven?"

"Yes, sir." She reached for the knob.

"Good." He grinned. "Now you may apologize to me for cursing me."

As if the doorknob were hot, her hand jerked away from it and back under the fold of her apron. "I'm sorry, sir. I pray you forgive my ungovernable temper. It has been the cause of many of my problems. My father used to say it would be the ruin of me."

Sandron chuckled. "Oh, I hardly think it would be that. If a fit of temper would ruin a person, the world would be nothing but ruined people."

She reached again for the doorknob. "I'm sure you're right, sir."

"Stay a minute."

She rocked slightly on the balls of her feet as if she longed to go. "I really have duties, sir."

"Your duty is to me. Please come away from the door and give me a minute of your time away from your duties."

Silently, she turned back into the room as he took a seat. "Are you happy here?" he asked.

Keeping her head bowed, she nodded slowly. "As happy as one may be, sir."

"Ah, yes. In this vale of tears, et cetera."

"Yes, sir."

"Please sit down, Miss Fitch. You've been shaken up. You've taken a tumble that stunned you for a moment. I insist. Can't have you passing out in the middle of the stairs and falling down, head over heels. I've done that. It's worse than painful. It takes a long time to get over."

As he spoke, he indicated the chair at the opposite end of the table from him. Reluctantly, she perched on its edge, her hands clasped together in her lap.

They stared at each other in silence while her breathing returned to normal. Beneath the heavy black wool of her dress, her heart was beating from nervousness now rather than from the accident. Beneath the gray wig, her scalp began to itch. She laced her fingers together and clinched them tightly.

He smiled ingratiatingly. "Miss Fitch. I'm not going to leap upon you. You can relax. This is a very informal household as you should have guessed by now. I'm just an ordinary man. Not the character my publisher has painted me to be. In fact, I'd rather be writing than parading around in a black suit every night."

Color had flooded her face underneath the rice powder. What did she look like? Was he looking at her suspiciously? She longed to touch her cheeks, but feared that to do so might reveal her disguise.

For his part, he scanned her face for some sign that she was softening.

She inclined her head slightly, but her posture remained as tense as ever. "Yes, sir."

"Don't believe me, eh?"

Her head snapped up. For a moment the amber-green eyes flashed full in his face. Then they fell, her lashes carefully shading them. "I hardly see how that can make any difference, sir."

He stared critically at the top of her gray head. For

a moment there she had looked much different from her usual self. Then he shrugged. "I would like my household to be congenial."

"I will make every effort to be so, sir."

He was feeling a bit irritated with her response. "I'm a writer, you know."

"Parks told me I was not to clean the library unless he was present to direct the work and to keep anything from being disturbed."

"Is that why nothing has been cleaned so far in there?"

She faced him without flinching. "I thought to get the rest of the house in order, while Parks caught up on his duties. We'll get right on it, sir, if you desire us to."

He drove one fist into the palm of the other hand until his knuckles cracked. Her attitude was irritating in the extreme. "Suppose I really were the devil himself," he challenged her suddenly. Swiftly he rose from the chair and came around the table to loom over her.

Her eyes locked with his for a long moment. She had not had a chance to notice that his were a dark gunmetal gray. The blush which she had felt subside rose to her cheeks even warmer than before. "But you're not, sir," she replied positively.

"Ah, but how can you be sure? You are a Christian, aren't you?"

"Yes, sir." She pressed her hands together nervously.

"Then you learned that the devil has power to assume a pleasing shape?"

"Yes, sir."

"And am I not pleasing?"

For the second time in the interview, she allowed herself to look at him. Her eyes scanned him from the polished pumps on his narrow feet over the straight legs clothed in black trousers to the flat stomach to the pristine white shirtfront and the clean-shaven face. Her fast-beating heart, impossibly, stepped up its pace. "Yes, sir."

He grinned. "Then mightn't I be the devil sent to work you to damnation?"

He was teasing her now. She looked away in the direction of the door. "I hope you are not."

He took a quick sidestep into her line of vision. "Look at me when I speak to you, Miss Fitch."

She raised her eyes to meet his unflinchingly.

"You do not mind working for the devil himself?"

"Needs must," she replied staunchly.

"Ah, yes. 'When the devil drives,' " he finished for her.

"Yes, sir."

"Then you shouldn't run and hide," he admonished her sternly. "You are working for the devil himself. You shouldn't mind sitting down at tea with him. After all"—he flung out his arms in the theatrical gesture he used on entering the gambling casino each night—"the Prince of Darkness has no earthly rank. No, nor heavenly one either. You are above him by virtue of your unblemished soul. You are not violating any rules of society by supping with him."

She shook her head adamantly. "He's my employer, sir. Servants do not dine with their employers."

He dropped his arms. "You're a stubborn woman, Miss Fitch."

"May I go now, sir?"

He stepped back. "Yes, go. Go about your menial little tasks and keep dodging out of my way. Just as you've done for years, I would guess by the looks of you. Condemned to dodge and hide for the rest of your life."

The Scots temper rose again in her breast. She turned back to face him bravely at the door. "You are cruel to bait me, sir. I didn't wish to be a servant. Circumstances forced me . . ." She stopped aghast. She had told too much in too determined a voice.

He grinned. "Ah, Miss Fitch. More of that spirit you try so hard to conceal."

She covered her mouth with her hand. Then dropped it to her side. "May I go on about my duties, sir?"

He bowed nonchalantly. "Of course."

She opened the door, but he stepped forward to put his hand on the facing beside her face. His long fingers curved over the edge.

He held the door immobile until she was forced to face him again, struggling to still her bottom lip lest it betray her nervousness. "Sir?"

His lips pulled back from his white teeth in a sardonic grin. "I believe you were working in here, were you not?" He swept his arm toward the dining room table. Then he was gone, leaving her alternately fearful and angry.

Chapter Three

"Have I not told you, my fair beauty, that escape is impossible?"

Lady Constance could not suppress a cry of desperation as the ironhard arm of Lord S—caught her about her slender waist and pinned her against his muscular frame. Furiously, she struggled, but her frail strength was as nothing. Chuckling, his breath hot in her ear, he slid his other hand lazily across her white shoulders until it dipped beneath the silken folds of her gown.

The feel of his hand, hot, strong, rude, closing over her soft white bosom, sent a jet of fire through her veins. Paralyzed with shock, she sighed as her trembling knees buckled.

Feeling her resistance ebb, he lowered her pliant body, conscious but unable to resist, to the divan. "Now," he gloated. "Now! You will acknowledge . . ."

" . . . that this is the most miserable drivel you have ever written." Edward Sandron wadded the paper in his hand and tossed it in the direction of a basket at the end of the desk.

It bounced off the rim and landed among others littering the study. Edward sank back in his chair, hands shading his eyes. "Drivel! Drivel, drivel, drivel!"

A knock interrupted his critical analysis.

"For God's sake, come in!"

"Sir . . ." Parks barely stepped back out of the way before the entry of the woman known to the habitués of the Devil's Palace as Ashtaroth. Her black veils swirled round her shoulders and hips as she swept into the room.

"Eddie, why aren't you dressed? People will begin to arrive soon."

He glanced down at his rumpled appearance, noting a spot of ink on the linen just above his left cuff. One side of his mouth twisted upward as he raised a critical eyebrow in her direction. "You don't look particularly stylish yourself," he drawled. "Unless what passes for a set of widow's weeds is what we're adopting for the casino. Lord, Sally, were supposed to be entertaining the souls that come our way, not mourning their passing."

She peeled the veil back over the brim of her hat and made a face at him. "I'm going to change upstairs. My maid left me without a word. Disloyal slut! You have a housekeeper so I'm given to understand. I have to have help to dress. She can help me."

"So polite of you to ask." He grinned mirthlessly. "Same gutter manners, Sally, old girl. No matter what the fancy dress, they're always there."

She glared at him. "You're not so far away, yourself, Eddie. The language may have cleaned up a bit, but you're still clutch-fisted." The glare changed to a satisfied smirk. "I had a hard job convincing Madame Elise to give me the new dress. She was ruder than hell, mouthing about how you'd closed the account. That wasn't nice, Eddie. I have to have a new dress."

Edward slapped his hand against the desktop as he sprang up. "Blast! Sally, you don't need a new dress. You've got dozens. Wear one you've already worn. I'm not made of money. All your clothes look the same anyway. Tight and flashy. The customers can't tell one from another."

Her retaliation was as swift as his. "My clothes are all the pleasure I get out of this," she snarled. "You live in a fine house with a valet and housekeeper and cook . . ."

"And a gambling casino in the front."

"And gaslights and a bathroom with hot running water."

"And I'm supporting you and Nash. And God knows, who else he's keeping on the side."

"I could live with you, Eddie."

He shook his head. "Sally, I put you in the flat and made you part of this deal for old time's sake. Don't push."

Eyes so black the pupils were indistinguishable from the irises flashed angry dark fire. Placing her palms on the desktop, Sally thrust herself toward him. Her long polished nails clicked against the wood. "I'm part of this show, Eddie. Don't expect me to beg and plead for anything. The customers don't mind losing their shirts, so long as they can paw me."

He waved a deprecatory palm. "Nobody said you weren't part of the show. You can work here as long as you like. Just remember that our relationship is as business acquaintances. Nothing more. I don't arrive at your flat expecting to get dressed. And I don't harangue you when I don't get a new suit."

She did not retreat. Anger roughened and deepened her voice. " 'Harangue' is it? Don't 'harangue' me, Sally. Better than the likes of Sally from the streets, ain't you? You with that eye that don't forget a thing it's ever seen. Ha! What works for you don't make you any better. It's just your trick. It ain't no more nor less than my color and shape. The same customers buy 'em both."

Edward shrugged. "If you don't like selling, Sally, maybe you should get out."

"Not me. Not bloody likely. Where would I go? To the streets."

"You might be on the lookout for someone to marry."

"Some rich old man who'd drop dead and leave me a million." She made a disgusted sound. "That only happens in fairy tales. And any way, that's not for the likes of me. No, I've worked for what I have. And I don't intend to give it up. This club suits me fine."

He stared at her, wondering as he did so at the ill-assorted trio that were he, Sally, and Nash. If the devil had plucked at random from his legion of souls destined for damnation, he could not have chosen a stranger group.

Under his calculating gaze, the woman the world knew as Ashtaroth drummed her nails once on the desktop before she straightened. "Just so's we understand each other," she insisted.

"I understand you, Sally," he replied.

"Then *may* I borrow the services of your housekeeper," she sneered, her voice assuming its educated accent as easily as if she were donning a cloak. Without waiting for permission, she flounced out. "I'll ring for her."

"I shall need this pressed while I bathe. Let a maid run the bath water while you help me out of this dress." Ashtaroth leaned closer to the full-length mirror to inspect her face. When the woman behind her did not move, Ashtaroth met her eyes.

Cassie Fitch's thin lips were even thinner. "I'm the only maid in the house, miss. Which shall I do first? Unfasten you, or run the bath water?"

"Run the bath water, fool. And be quick about it. Then come right back and unpack that box." She indicated a long blue-striped box on the bed. "The dress in it must be pressed before I can wear it tonight. As to unfastening me, I suppose I'll be able to get out the dress myself since I got into it."

"Yes, miss." Miss Fitch moved toward the bed.

Ashtaroth swung around. "I told you to run the bath water first. Are you so simple that you can only remember one thing at a time?"

"I can take the dress with me on my way down to the bathroom."

" 'Down' to the bathroom?"

"Yes, miss. The bathroom is down the stairs."

"I can't go down the stairs."

Cassie Fitch shrugged. "Then shall I take the dress away and press it?"

Ashtaroth shot her a withering look. "I wish to bathe. Bring hot water, towels, and a tub upstairs."

The housekeeper picked the box up in both arms. "I don't think there is a tub, miss. I can bring you a pitcher of hot water and a basin."

An angry flush mottled the white, white skin. "Lazy slut. There must be a tub somewhere."

"Not to my knowledge, miss. Shall I send Parks to you? He's been here longer than I have and doubtless knows what arrangements are to be made."

At the mention of Sandron's valet, Ashtaroth subsided somewhat. "Never mind. Just press my dress and be quick about it. Those idiots in the casino would never know whether a woman bathed or not. I don't know how they stand the smell of themselves."

"Yes, miss." Outside in the hall, Cassie Fitch tucked the striped dress box carelessly under her arm and strode down the hall. Her own temper flared so hot that she trembled. If such treatment of servants were a common practice, she could not endure it. Another minute and she would have slung the box in the woman's face.

In the laundry room, still shaking, she flung the dress across the padded board and went to fetch the irons from their accustomed place in the fire in the kitchen. As she ironed, she felt herself growing calmer.

The dress was magnificent in a theatrical way, a rich emerald green brocade for the overskirt with pale green tarlatan underskirt. In order to press it properly, three dozen ribbon flounces around the bottom of the skirt had to be untied and then retied.

Her back was aching and her hands were red and swollen from lifting the heavy irons that were hot even through the pads around their handles. Ruefully, she admitted to herself that hard work cooled the hottest temper. At the same time, a tiny niggling pain grew in her brain. When she had worked for many years at this job, she would not have the strength nor the spirit to lose her temper.

Bleakly, she stared at the beautiful dress. Tears of self-pity were burning her eyes as she carefully gathered it up to carry it back up the stairs.

Answering a command to enter, she beheld Ashtaroth clad only in ruffled silk pantalettes and corset. Unconcerned that her generous breasts were bare, she glanced at the housekeeper. "Where have you been? I rang your bell at least a dozen times."

Instantly, Cassie's anger rekindled. With difficulty she managed a tight-lipped answer. "I was in the laundry, miss, pressing your dress." She held it out with what she hoped was a show of deference.

"Forget it. My new one has been delivered after all. I need you to lace my corset tighter."

The housekeeper looked doubtfully at the corset pinching the slender waist. "Are you sure, miss?"

"Of course, I'm sure, idiot. This lacing would have been all right for that green rag you're carrying, but that is the newest style." She gestured to a dress of magenta taffeta, the color so strident that the material seemed to fairly vibrate against the white bedspread.

Her face carefully impassive, Cassie Fitch spread the green dress on the other side of the bed. Then she wrapped the silk strings around her hands and pulled. As Ashtaroth gave an agonized gasp, the housekeeper allowed herself a tiny quirk of a smile.

"What shall I do with the green dress, miss?" she asked when the magenta taffeta was fastened and draped over the elaborate bustle.

"Pack it back in its box." Ashtaroth surveyed herself from the side. The bustle jutted out a full twelve inches from her waist in back. In front she was perfectly flat from floor to bosom. There the low neckline combined with the upward thrust of the corset to present an almost indecent amount of white full breasts. "No. Never mind." Her lips curved into a defiant pout. "Get rid of it."

Her statement prompted a gasp from Cassie Fitch. "Miss, are you sure?"

"Of course I'm sure, you fool." Ashtaroth rapped the housekeeper on the arm with her fan. "Edward Sandron paid for it. And for this one. He can pay for another one like it. Any way, it's old and out of style." So saying, she twitched her train around behind her and strode to the door.

The housekeeper stared at the green dress for a long time. The flickering gaslights gave the emerald brocade flowers incredible richness. It was a dress that would never grow old. As if of its own volition, her hand rose to slide beneath the coarse gray wig and touch her own hair. The real Cassandra MacDaermond would look superb in that dress.

Cassie Fitch might never have a chance to wear it, but she would not get rid of it. Cradling it in her arms as if it were a child, she carried it from the room.

Edward managed to keep his mouth closed although his eyes watered with the effort of suppressing the most monumental yawn of his life. Before him and surrounding him on either side were avid faces.

Stretched on an altar covered with black velvet, the body of a woman writhed suggestively. She was clad in a diaphanous series of veils, none of which concealed her darkly rouged nipples. Although her eyes appeared closed, he could see the candlelight glinting from beneath her lashes. Counting the house. His mouth curved upward in a sardonic smile as she arched her spine and took a deep breath.

The crowd gave a collective sigh of anticipation. "Baal! Baal! Baal!" The chanting began low, most likely initiated by Nash, who moved around the back of the room. Edward could see the publisher dressed in a monk's costume, the hood pulled forward to conceal his features. The brown peak bobbed constantly among the bizarre headdresses of glittery false jewels, feathers, and fur.

The kaleidoscope of colored glass and shiny fabrics presented a brilliant theatrical contrast to the basement's black walls and the velvet-draped altar. In the beginning Edward had been enthralled by the scene. The feeling of power at being the center of attention, the star performer in the drama, had been heady.

But the excitement had turned to boredom all too soon. The cast changed every night except for the star performer, who now found his part unchallenging. Perhaps if he could really believe that any of the participants was sincere? But the girl on the table tonight was a bird from Mrs. Emma Lee's in Margaret Street. The money she would make tonight in addition to what Nash paid her would keep her for months, plus the connections she hoped to make might lead to something permanent.

A whiff of incense, perhaps stirred up by the

general increase in movement in the crowd, made his nose burn. He was going to sneeze. Not any effort on his part would stop it. Hastily, he swept wide the great crimson wings of his cape and spun round to face the candlelit wall behind him. More crimson satin padded its surface around a great black mask imported from Africa. Ivory antelope horns—an addition from Nash's theatrical brain—curved up and over a full three feet above the carved brow. Around the mask were thirteen gold sconces from which candlewax dripped. The candles, too, were scented so that he sneezed not once but twice.

When finally he had gotten himself under control, the chanting had grown in volume. Plastering a scowl on his face, he swung round again, making the candles flutter wildly with the wind from his cape. Brows drawn together, he scowled at his "subjects" while the females in the audience murmured softly in the ears of their escorts.

Dropping the edges of the cloak, he stepped up to the altar. The girl writhed earnestly, drawing up first one leg and then the other, twisting her hips, arching her back. Her long blond hair spilled over the black velvet. Idly he wondered if it were real or a wig. Probably a combination of both.

With a theatrical gesture copied from a magician he had seen draw a rabbit from a hat, he caught hold of the first veil, a long strip of rose tulle and plucked it from her body. It came away easily, as the costumer had basted it with a few strategic stitches to the collar around her neck.

The audience cheered delightedly as he swirled it in front of his face before tossing it into their midst. As rehearsed, Nash caught it and pulled it beneath his garb. Veils were expensive. If several of them could be retrieved a night, then the cost of these little private productions could be much reduced.

A strip of gold tulle followed. Another man, an employee of the casino who was dressed in the costume of a bishop, caught it.

So far, so good. The girl had opened her eyes and was staring at him in pretended fear. The side of her face away from the audience quirked upward in a grin. He plucked a strip of sky blue tulle from her body.

"Just like plucking petals from a daisy!" a man's voice from the crowd called out hoarsely.

The comment broke the tension. Men began to joke among themselves, laughing, making obscene comments, drawing their partners close.

Must hurry it up now, Edward realized. The pink veil and the violet followed in quick succession. Only two more remaining.

Acolytes, actually waiters from the casino dressed in their evening dress with half masks of horns, slipped out of sliding doors on two sides at the back bearing trays of champagne and black cakes.

Sandron tossed the white veil to the "bishop" and raised his arms. The crowd tensed expectantly. "Drink and break black bread with the devil," he intoned, almost tripping over the tongue twister. "Drink and eat, and abandon your immortal souls."

Obediently, the paying customers accepted the tall glasses of champagne and the flat black circles.

"Eat and drink," he commanded again.

Ashtaroth, clad in magenta taffeta so bright that

the candles fairly blazed off it, knelt before him and offered a cake and a silver beaker of champagne on a silver tray. He seized the cake and tossed it into his mouth. A couple of quick chews and then he brandished the beaker.

Prompted by Nash and his men, the crowd cheered.

With both hands Edward raised the beaker above his head and poured the contents down his throat.

From long practice he managed the whole process without choking. The first time he had tried it, he had almost died, but now he could do it with aplomb that even the Prince of Darkness himself would have envied.

"Now!" he boomed. "To your own damnation." With a quick twist of his wrist he whipped away the black tulle veil leaving the figure on the altar totally nude.

The blond girl on the altar sat up, gathering her legs under her in a pretty pose and holding out her arms to him. "Baal," she called. "Master!"

The crowd cheered. "Baal! Baal!"

The "bishop" who also worked as a bouncer to handle obstreperous guests, swept her up into his arms and hoisted her over his head, one hand on her ankle, one on the small of her back. Her long blond hair streamed down behind him as she arched her breasts toward the ceiling.

The guests quaffed their champagne recklessly, as "demons" passed among them with more full glasses. The "monk" swept Ashtaroth into his arms, laid her back against the altar, and began to reign passionate kisses over her face and breasts.

In the background could be heard the beating of

drums as the musicians from the casino picked up his cue.

All around him people were living life to the fullest — or imagined they were. Edward Sandron watched feeling nothing. Suddenly, a sharp pain hit his stomach. It was so intense that he lost his breath and had to gasp to draw it back in.

Sweat popped out on his forehead. Grimacing, he took a deep breath and waited. Nothing happened.

Perhaps he had merely pulled a muscle switching his cape around and trying to suppress his sneezes. Another whiff of incense drove him to swirl the black and crimson cape around him and cover the lower half of his face like a devil in a Breton drawing.

Ashtaroth stared up at him, her eyes slitted, her hands limp at her sides as the "monk" trailed kisses down her back and across her bosom. She did not appear to see him. Her eyes were unfocused, glassy. All around the altar people swaying, drinking, laughing, embracing. More waiters dressed in the same costumes, formal evening dress with devil masks passed among them with trays of wine.

The naked girl had been borne back to the altar after being carried like a trophy of war around the room. Placing her so that her blond hair mingled with Ashtaroth's black, the "bishop" raised the skirt of his robe and fell upon her.

From behind his cloak, Edward grinned wryly. Many of the guests, their inhibitions released by darkness and by alcohol, were turning to their partners, who led them away into the darkness of the cellar. There they might do whatever their abilities and the accessibility of their dress might lead them to.

Nash and the "bishop" were part of the show, not a realistic part at all. And over it all to the beat of drums and more drinking, Baal presided.

His head began to pound in rhythm to the drums. Would the evening never end? He really wouldn't mind it so much if it weren't for his having to stand around at the end like some graven image. He had thought about participating in the orgy from time to time, but the doubtful cleanliness of some of the girls from Mrs. Emma Lee's put him off.

Another pain lanced through his stomach. One so fierce that he groaned aloud. Hastily, he glanced around him, but no one appeared to be paying the slightest attention to him. Would anybody really care if he slipped off the dais and trotted off to his room?

The candles in their scources around the room seemed to waver slightly before his eyes. What was wrong with him? Another pain. This time it staggered him. Willy-nilly, he stepped off the dais, one hand clutching at the altar for support. The other was clamped tightly across his middle.

Sweat, cold and sickening, bathed his body. His vision wavered and dimmed. Half-blind, he staggered toward the door.

Where was the bloody thing? Couldn't find it in the darkness. Why was it so dark? Grinning broadly, a fat man in a red devil costume stumbled across his pathway.

He reeled away only to find himself accosted by a Punchinello in a Venetian larva. A huge mouth opened beneath the plaster nose and laughed uproariously. "Baal! Old fellow! Great party! Great party!"

"Glad you're 'joyin' y'rself," he managed to mutter.

What was happening to him? His tongue would not shape itself for the words.

"Never had so much fun," the larva acknowledged. His velvet cap adorned with a pair of long slender plumes swayed from side to side as he nodded.

"If you'll 'xcuse me . . ." Edward tried to step round the man, failed dismally as one leg buckled under him. He went down on one knee, catching himself and doubling over. The pain in his gut was excruciating.

"Baal," a feminine voice trilled waspishly. "A little too much drinkie, sweetie?"

He managed to lift his head to stare upward over a front of silver-green damask to a powdered face in the center of a bright red curled wig framed by a ruff. Good Queen Bess? He was losing his mind.

He put both hands flat on the floor and pushed off. Stumbling, staggering, his shoulder banging into something that grunted then cursed angrily, he finally found the door.

The stairway mounted before him, lighted brightly by gaslight. He breathed a prayer of thankfulness. If he had stepped out into darkness, he would have fallen down and died.

The pain was so bad that tears began trickling down his cheeks. His breathing was labored. On hands and knees, he mounted the steps. One flight. Two flights. He was in the back hall now. The back hall where he had fallen, almost died before. His room was up another flight of stairs.

He slumped on his stomach. He could not make it. He could not. So cold. So cold. He was sweating, yet he was so cold. Bitter in his mouth. Bitter. He could not see. He hurt so damn badly.

Terrified and pain-wracked, he began to sob. He was going to die here in the back hall. What was the matter with him? Why was he dying?

"Mr. Sandron," a voice called out from somewhere above him.

He rolled over on his back. Even then he could not sprawl. His stomach hurt too much. He pulled his legs up to his chest and groaned. As bad as the pain was the cold. His feet and hands were going numb. He tightened his arms around his knees.

"Mr. Sandron, sir. What's wrong?"

He tried to speak, to answer. No sound came. Then he tried again. "Sick."

He felt a hand on his forehead. "Are you feverish?"

"N-no. Cold."

"Let me help you to your room."

He opened his eyes, tried to focus them, failed, tried again. "M-miss Fitch."

"Yes, sir."

"Sick. Sick at my stomach."

"Roll over, sir."

"Can't . . ."

"What have you eaten?"

"Nothing." She grasped his shoulder to turn him over on his side. "No . . . hurt . . ."

"You can't lie here. You must get up." Inexorably, she managed to turn him. Although he was slender, his body was large in comparison to hers. The shifting of it caused him greater pain, then suddenly nausea.

The bitter taste that rose in his throat was indescribably foul. It galvanized him into action. Violently ill, he scrambled to his feet and plunged for the bathroom. He barely made it.

There he hung over the basin, retching and retching, until he had no more left to give and still the vile liquid came. Acid so bitter he thought he would lose consciousness. And then he prayed that he would.

After a time he was dimly aware of Miss Fitch beside him, a wet towel pressed to his forehead. "Drink this, sir."

"What?"

"Just a little baking soda in water, sir."

He was too weak to resist her. At her behest, he managed to straighten enough so she could pour a little down his throat. "Now rinse your mouth with the rest, sir."

"My god, I don't think—" He could not keep it down. In a moment he was sick again. Foully so.

For over four hours, Cassie Fitch worked over Edward Sandron. At first, he could not protest. He did what she told him to do, drank what she told him to drink. And then she held his head.

Toward the end of the time he recovered himself sufficiently to feel acute embarrassment at his loss of control. By that time, Miss Fitch had seen him at the lowest ebb of his life. She had done for him what no lady should have to do for a gentleman. Once he had whispered to her to fetch his valet, but she had shaken her head. "I dare not leave you, sir. You are too sick."

And truthfully, she was right. Another bout of nausea racked him and he almost lost consciousness.

Finally, he was able to keep a little soda water on his stomach. She stepped back from his side. "I think the worst is over, sir."

He barely managed a nod as he slumped back in

the chair she had dragged next to the toilet for him.

She leaned back against the lavoratory, head bowed, hands curled in the pockets of her apron. Wisps of hair hung down on either side of her face. She heaved a sigh. "I'll get you some water, sir. I think now you should drink quite a bit of it. If there's any left of what made you sick, it will dilute it."

When she returned, she found him just as she left him. She held his head against her breast while he drank some water.

His tired eyes closed as she brushed the hair back from his damp forehead. "How can you stand to hold me this close?" he whispered hoarsely. "I must stink worse than a sewer."

She was silent for a minute. "I've grown used to you," she said at last.

"I need a bath. I'll be all right while you get Parks."

"Are you sure?"

He straightened away from her. Sitting erect in his chair, he only had to lift his eyes a couple of inches to look into her face. The deep shadows around her eyes and the lines in her face looked almost painted on. He blinked at the illusion. He frowned and blinked again. Hardly aware of what he did, he raised a hand slowly to touch her.

Hastily, she backed away toward the door. "I'll summon Mr. Parks."

Chapter Four

Outside the bathroom Cassandra collapsed against the wall and pressed her trembling hands to her cheeks. Edward Sandron's smoke gray stare had seemed to pierce right through her disguise. She had made a mistake in letting him get that close to her, but he had been so sick. She had never seen a person so sick before.

If she had not happened to find him and helped him to his feet, she could not doubt that he would have died. Unable to rid himself of whatever was bothering him, he would have lain there on the landing and lost consciousness. The substance would have shocked other parts of his body and the cold would have done the rest.

Suddenly, she began to shiver. Where was Parks? Her employer needed care that she was unprepared to render him. For a terrible minute there he had been close to penetrating her disguise. Probably he was too sick to remember anything about this whole episode tomorrow. But Parks had to be located so that Sandron would no longer require her attendance. Casting a hasty glance to be sure that the hallway in which she stood was deserted, she hiked up her skirts and dashed up the stairs.

"Mr. Parks! Mr. Parks!" When he did not answer her knock, she slapped the wood with her open hand. Where was he?

When he did not answer, she tried the knob. The door opened easily but a quick glance inside assured her that it was empty. On the dresser top lay a comb and brush, the teeth thrust neatly into the bristles. From the pegs on the wall hung a jacket and vest.

"Mr. Parks?"

She shut the door and hurried to the next room. It, too, was empty as well as the next. Finally, she pushed open the suite that comprised Sandron's library, dressing room, and bedroom. "Mr. Parks?"

The sound wave bounced faintly off the paneling. The thin echo raised the hair on the back of her neck. Fearfully she spun around in the doorway. An icy draught slid under her skirts and penetrated the thin material of her stockings.

The hall was empty. Suddenly she became aware that the entire upper story of the house was empty. The flickering gaslights did not seem so warm or cheerful. The shadows were deeper, more menacing. Phantoms might be lurking in the darkness in each draped alcove.

With hands suddenly clammy, she clutched her skirts, unconsciously hoping the feel of the stout-woven material would give her courage. Rapidly, she walked down the shadowy hall to the back stairs. Her hand on the newel post, she paused. Mr. Sandron had fallen here and almost broken his neck. Mr. Parks had told her the story.

The stairs looked uncommonly steep. Gingerly she ran the sole of her shoe across the wood of the landing. It was smooth as all steps come to be after thousands of footsteps, but not unnaturally so. Certainly not enough to cause a man's foot to slip out from under him and pitch him back.

A cold chill ran up her spine. Truly, she worked in a house of the devil, where men took sick enough to die all of a sudden and servants disappeared in the middle of the night. Keeping a firm clasp on the bannister, she hurried down to the bathroom.

He was just as she had left him, except he sat with head hanging down. When she entered, he lifted a face so gray with pain and illness that he might truly have been a corpse had he not spoken. "Where's Parks?"

"Running an errand," she replied.

Too weak to question her, he merely nodded.

"Let me help you to bed. Then when Parks returns, he can undress you and bathe you."

"No." He shook his head stubbornly. "I'll do it myself. I can't stand to go to bed the way I am." Rising unsteadily, he laid one hand flat on the washstand for support while he tugged at the fastening of the cape with the other.

Despite her fear that he might penetrate her disguise, she stepped forward and brushed aside his fumbling fingers. "You're too weak, sir."

"I can do it," he protested, but he submitted quietly now that he was getting his way.

He sighed and stretched his neck as she undid the fastening of the cape. Its full weight, a good twenty pounds, surprised her. The edges of it must have been weighted and the collar wired so the points would stand up on either side of his face. While she hung it on a clothes tree, he shrugged out of the formal evening coat and began to unbutton the black vest. "Just run the water, Miss Fitch, and leave me alone."

She lighted the gas heater and bent over to put the stopper in the tub. "Sir, I don't think this is a good idea. You're weaker than you think."

"Where is Parks?" he asked again, ignoring her comment. Doggedly determined, he slipped the suspenders over his shoulders and pulled his shirt from his pants.

"He's on an errand, sir." The warm water began to pour into the tub.

"Oh . . ."

She turned back to him. Both of his hands were pressed against the washstand. His skin had a gray-green hue around the mouth. "You're being ridiculous," she scolded.

"N-no. Good for me. Get clean, go to bed. Sleep off whatever made me sick."

"Sir, you can take a bath tomorrow."

He struggled at his boot. "No. I promised myself" — he let his foot drop to the floor and wiped the sick perspiration from his forehead — "promised myself I'd never go to bed dirty again. I never had a bath in a bathtub until I had that one installed. Swore I'd use it every night." He lifted the leg wearily.

Pitying his determination, she stooped and linked her arms under the heel. "Sit back down then and let me help you, sir."

His eyes thanked her as he gripped the edge of the spindly bath chair and held on while she worried the boot off. When his feet were bare, she stepped back, hands on hips, and surveyed him accusingly.

He pushed himself up and staggered slightly. "I know I must seem crazed to you, but that's the way I am."

"I'll wait outside for you."

Once outside the door, she regretted her decision. The hallway was dark and cold. Huddling against the paneling, she heard nothing at first, then the water sloshed as he stepped in.

After many long cold minutes, he called to her. "Miss Fitch."

"Yes, sir."

"Has Parks returned?"

"No."

From behind the door came the sound of splashing, then a helpless sigh.

"Miss Fitch. I can't get up."

She closed her eyes and took a deep breath.

"Miss Fitch?"

"Yes, sir." She could feel a hot flush rising in her cheeks. She had never seen a naked man before, much less been called upon to touch one. "He's sick," she whispered to herself, and opened the door.

He rested with one arm draped over the side of the high enamel tub. Its lip was a good four feet off the floor. His black hair curled in fishhooks around his pale wet face. His eyes were sunken and his lips pale. "I'm sorry," he whispered. "I've been a fool."

Keeping her eyes firmly on his face, she snatched a towel from the rack and flung it around his shoulders. "You should certainly be sorry," she scolded. "You could have drowned in there. What if you passed out?

I couldn't have lifted you out. I don't know that I can do anything for you now. Shall I summon some servants from the casino?"

He appeared to consider that for a moment. "No. Just give me a hand."

In the end he thoroughly dampened her dress and she had seen rather more of his long, lean body than she should have, but he managed to climb out and sit down in the chair. "Let me rest for a minute before I climb the stairs."

She sank back against the washstand again. Her embarrassment had been replaced by exhaustion. Would this night never end? "Surely, I should summon someone?"

"No." He was firmer this time. "I'll just rest a minute." He ran a shaky hand through his hair. The white streaks above his temples were more obvious wet than dry. They must have been real rather than powdered or dyed.

She shook her head wearily. "You can't go up the stairs, er, like you are. You'll catch your death of pneumonia."

Suddenly, he chuckled. His gray eyes looked into her own, inviting her to share his irreverent humor. "This is getting funny. Here am I, sick as a dog, naked in the bathroom of my own home, with only a Scottish maiden lady to help me." He cocked his head to the side and gave her a cheeky grin. "And what does she do? She concentrates on a spot on the floor by my bare feet and warns me about pneumonia."

Cassie Fitch drew herself up tall. "I told you not to take a bath," she huffed.

He nodded. "I deserve to be scolded, ma'am. Now

throw that stupid cape around me and let's go."

"The cape, sir? The water on your body will stain the satin."

"Too bad. Can't be helped."

"What about your feet?"

"When I get into bed, you can bring me a warming pan."

"Yes, sir." Her mouth tightened.

It was the strangest procession. Clearly, he was out of his head as they began to mount the stairs. "Thanks for the use of your body . . ." he whispered in her ear, his mind wandering in delirium. His hand gripped her shoulder, and before they were halfway up the narrow, steep flight, he was leaning his whole arm on her, his body trembling with cold and weakness. "Your body is just the right size. Why didn't a man ever find out, Miss Fitch? Why didn't a man carry you off?" His hand slipped down over her breast.

"Mr. Sandron," she gritted. "Behave yourself, or I'll throw you down these stairs."

He waved his hand in front of her face, the hand that had been cupped over her breast. "Don't believe a word of it. You'd never hurt me. Too good. That's why you'd never throw me down the stairs. That's why you didn't run screaming when I started undressing in front of you."

"Save your breath," she cautioned.

They came to the top of the stairs. "Careful here," he murmured as a caution to himself. Then they were in the hallway. He swayed against the wall for a moment to get his breath. "I've never been so sick in all my life."

Somehow she got him into his room. No fire had

been laid in the hearth. The bed covers were like wrapping him in a sheet of ice. His teeth were chattering so that he could no longer speak when she tucked him in.

Then suddenly they ceased. He relaxed into unconsciousness.

Horrified, she caught him by the shoulders and shook him with all her strength. "Mr. Sandron. Mr. Sandron. Edward!"

He did not move. His head rolled limply; his blue lips parted laxly. She slapped his face lightly, to no avail. His weakened body had given up the fight. "Mr. Sandron!" she called. "You must wake up. You're too cold."

She took his face between her hands. His pallor was alarming. Somehow she must get him warm and quickly or he would never recover. His body was too debilitated by the vomiting to have any reserves with which to fight.

Hastily, she scrambled on top of the bed and pressed herself upon him, the covers between them. No help there. He could not feel her warmth through the layers of quilts.

Sliding down from the bed, she looked helplessly around her. A man was dying. Her employer. She owed him whatever she could do to help him. But the risk.

"Damnation!" She chafed her cold upper arms. What risks was she running? If he died, she would be out of a job. She could warm him, then slip quietly away. He would slip from unconsciousness into sleep without ever knowing.

Even as she consoled herself, she locked the door.

When he was warm, she would creep downstairs with no one the wiser. Her decision made, she turned the gaslight off.

The wig was driving her crazy. She set it on the desk. Slipping out of the black dress and taking off her shoes, she slid beneath the sheets wearing only her undergarments. Sliding one arm around his neck, she stretched herself on top of him. Her head nestled just beneath his chin, the fragile pulse of life in his neck beating against her temple. He was so cold that she began to shiver herself at first.

Gradually, his body began to return to normal. Her own shivering stopped. She shifted to a more comfortable position where his ribs did not dig quite so painfully into her breasts. In a few minutes she could get up and dress. He would be warm enough to sleep alone.

Just a few more minutes.

His hands moved over her curves. A warm, softly female shape pressed him down into the mattress. Her breathing matched his. One hand slipped up her spine to encounter a skein of silken hair. "Who're you?" he croaked.

Still befuddled by sleep, she barely had the sense to respond. "A friend. Go back to sleep. You've had a hard day."

"Yes. All right. Just give me a kiss."

The shiver that ran through her then was not from the cold. She should get up immediately and leave. She should tear herself from his arms, snatch up her wig and dress, and run. She should . . . But exhaustion kept her limbs leaden.

He patted her rear companionably. "Nice," he murmured. He heaved a deep sigh. "Sweet dream," he whispered. "Come give me a kiss."

He shifted her so that her body curled more atop his. His head dipped, touched her forehead, her temple, her cheek, then found the corner of her mouth. His tongue circled that sensitive crevice. She squirmed and turned her head away. "No."

"Come on," he whispered plaintively. "Just one. Then I'll go back to sleep. I promise."

Trembling, her body burning with what she knew must be embarrassment, she turned her face. He rolled over on his side and curved himself under her buttocks. She lay in the cradle of his body, their heads side by side on the same pillow. Her legs dangled limply over his hip. The nest beneath the covers was suddenly too warm.

"Now, just one kiss."

His lips were warm and firm. She had never had a kiss before. At first, it seemed to take an inordinate amount of time. Then suddenly it turned to fire and was over much too soon. With a sigh he relaxed. "Thank you, sweet," he whispered. His hand caressed her thigh, her waist, her breast, then drifted back to her waist. His breathing evened almost immediately.

In the darkness, she lay quiescent, her thoughts confused. Now was her chance. He had slipped back into a natural sleep from which he would not awaken for hours. She could get up immediately, dress, and return to her own room.

At that moment a chill wind moaned against the windowpanes. She shivered in response. Perhaps it would do no harm to pass the remainder of the night here. With the door locked, no one would disturb them. Her soul quailed at warming another bed tonight. She would only get it warmed before she would have to get out of it and begin the day. Moreover, she would likely contract pneumonia if she got up now. Her dark thoughts went on and on. At the same time her body cuddled and shaped itself against him, her muscles relaxing until all thoughts were dissolved beneath the pressure of his warm skin and the gentle thud of his heart beating in time to hers.

After a long workday had come this fearful night. Her eyelids were so heavy and her eyes were burning from the strain of keeping them open. She blinked.

"Why are you wearing so many clothes?"

The words did not disturb her, but the sharp rip of her petticoat popped her eyelids open.

"Drawers, too?" he rumbled. "At least you don't have on one of those damned corsets. Hate the things."

"Wait!" she gasped. "What are you doing? Stop!"

The chill of his body had been replaced by a fever so hot that his skin burned next to hers. His head moved heavy between her breasts. His hands slid up the outside of her thighs, past the tops of her stockings, under the thin lawn of her chemise. His thumbs brushed across the flat plane of her stomach.

"Skin like satin," he murmured as he nuzzled the ribbon strap down and kissed the top of her breast.

"No-o-o-o," she begged, setting her teeth against the fire that leaped through her veins. He was suffocating her, burning her. His hands were everywhere on her body, and where his hands swept, the nerves under the skin began to tingle. The pleasure was like nothing she had ever felt before. Relaxed in sleep so profound as to be half-sister to unconsciousness, her muscles were slow to respond. "Oh, no," she whispered.

"Yes-s-s-s," he hissed, closing his mouth over her nipple. "What a beautiful, soft, tempting young woman you are!"

She grabbed fistfuls of the thick black hair and pulled.

"Stop that," he commanded, his mouth still on her breast.

"Damn you. Stop it yourself." She tightened her hold and jerked.

White hot pain shot through her left breast, making her cry out. She released his hair and tried to thrust her hands in between his face and her breast.

He drew back, snarling softly. "I told you to let go. Hurt me and I'll hurt you."

"You bit me."

"Damn right I did."

"You . . . you cursed." Her voice betrayed her shock.

He chuckled. "You cursed me first, remember. Now lift those beautiful breasts again, sweet."

His palms left her belly and slid under her body, one under the small of her back, the other cupping her buttocks. She gasped in shock as he lifted her even more tightly against him.

He was over her now, his legs spread on either side of her own, pinning her down, while the muscles of his lower body, hard and insistent, pressed against her belly. He kissed her face and then her breast, gently laving it with his tongue in penance for the cruel nip.

She shivered and sighed.

"I love a gentle woman," he whispered, shifting to the other breast. "You'll like this, sweet." He sucked the nipple up into his mouth and pulled on it strongly. At the same time the hand under her buttocks moved gently, then more insistently. His long fingers brushed the depths of the crease between them.

With a sharp cry of embarrassment, she squirmed frenziedly.

"Easy," he whispered. "Easy. Don't worry. If you don't like that, we don't have to do it." He pushed himself up on his knees.

"Please," she begged, almost sobbing, her body on fire, her mind whirling. "Oh, please . . ."

"Surely, sweet." He lifted her legs from between his own. Her knees fell back with very little pressure. One hand slid under her knee, the other stroked the inside of the thigh to the warm, damp secret of her body.

She shuddered as his fingers combed through her silken hair, parted her body even more, and touched the tiny bud of pleasure at the very core of her. "Please," she murmured mindlessly. "Please please please please . . ."

"I know what you want," he teased. His hand slid along her side, feeling each delicate indentation of her ribs, under the swollen curve of her breast. Smoothly, he cupped it, then closed round the nipple, squeezing it delicately.

Embarrassed again that he should find her breasts so swollen, she tossed her head restlessly on the pillow.

The darkness was complete. Did he know what she felt? No man had ever touched her before, but he had touched many women. He must know a great deal, but was her body different from or like the others'? The room was chill as the tomb, yet her body blazed with its own fire.

"Put your arms around me," he commanded. "You're going to have to do some of the work."

As she obeyed, he left her breast to splay his hand across her belly. Its smooth strength and burning heat made her dig her heels into the mattress to press herself against it.

"Shall I make you happy?" His fingers dipped lower, found the narrow opening, pressed against it. "You're very small. Have you used alum?"

She shuddered again at the intrusion. Was she too small? What was he talking about? Alarm sobered her for an instant, then the hand on her belly slid up again to tighten over her breast.

"You're ready," he whispered. His fingers left the opening of her body to be replaced an instant later by something much bigger. He pressed forward gently.

And the pain began. "No, stop!" Terror and intense agony blended together in one voice.

"Spare me the game," he grunted softly. "It's not necessary. Really it's not. You'll be paid without play-acting." Grasping her buttocks, he thrust himself forward.

"No!" Her protest ended in a scream, high and keen as the blade of a fresh-whetted knife.

Sandron's delirium was such that he could not distinguish her pain from her pleasure. As she twisted and fought, he pulled back and drove into again, reveling in her tight, enclosing flesh, the heat, the warmth, the delicacy of her. "My, God," he crooned. "You're tight. So good. So hot. It's wonderful. Beautiful."

In agony, trapped beneath his body, she could make no impression on him with her struggles. When she swung wildly at his head, her blows landed on his shoulders and the stiffened biceps of his upper arms.

Dimly Edward realized that all was not well with the girl beneath him. "Sorry," he murmured. "Usually have better control than this." Deliberately, he slowed his movements, leaning his weight on his elbows. One hand clasped her breast to play with the hardened nipple while he held himself still inside her.

Cassie whimpered softly, drawing a deep shuddering breath. Her nipple grew rigid between his finger and thumb. As his clasp tightened, her whole body tensed in response.

"My God," he groaned through set teeth. "I can't—" His pleasure grew with each passing minute while she lay pinned beneath him. Her body writhed and twisted beneath him as he cupped and squeezed the small firm breasts. He wished suddenly that he could see the satiny contours that his fingers traced. He bent to kiss her lips, sliding his tongue into the warm recesses of her open mouth. The muscles of her sheath tightened unbearably even as she lunged upward, her hips twisting. His head whirled dizzily as a kaleidoscope of color exploded in his eyes. At the same time he thrust deeply into her. Dimly he was aware of a shriek of pain.

And then he heard nothing more. His whole being was concentrated on the devastating release that far surpassed any pleasure he had ever known in his life.

As he eased back on his heels, he heard her sobbing, felt her writhing and twisting even as he slipped out of her. He must have been too fast for her. She had not achieved her pleasure. She had been most wonderful for him; he must return the favor.

"Ss-sh," he soothed, sliding over on his side and gathering her into his arms. "I'll take care of you."

His hands slid over her body then, working magic, soothing her at the same time they excited her. The warmth in her lower belly turned to a flame. His fingers slid through the silky curls at the top of her thighs, parted them, and found the throbbing bud that lay between. Leaning above her, he kissed her face, her throat, her breasts. As his mouth moved, his voice soothed her. "You're beautiful," he whispered. "Beautiful. So soft, so smooth, so eager. You were made for love."

Exhaustion deadened the fear. Pain ebbed and gave way to pleasure. The nerves in every part of her body focused on the center of feeling between her legs. She sank her teeth into her lower lip and moaned.

"Oh, yes," he whispered. "Oh, yes, sweet. That's the way. Go with it. Don't fight it. Don't be shy. You deserve pleasure too. Perhaps you've been misused in the past, but that's not the way it should be. Relax and let yourself go."

He really is the devil himself, she decided, her last conscious thought while she could still think. Then he rolled the core of pleasure between his thumb and third finger. At the same time he kissed her, thrusting his tongue deep into her mouth, meeting her tongue, running along the edge of her teeth.

She went out of control then. Her mouth sucked at his tongue as if it gave her life. Her breasts swelled as she rubbed them against the rough hair on his chest. Her belly muscles quivered and jumped as his hand rubbed hotly against its base.

Something happened then. Something wonderful and every bit as terrifying as the first thrust of his body had been. She arched wildly, striving for she knew not what.

Her efforts were those of a body that has been imprisoned for years suddenly breaking free. Then the feelings burst within her. She gasped for breath as he thrust hard with fingers and tongue.

His mouth caught the helpless wail of surrender and swallowed it along with the knowledge that her pleasure had been as intense as his own. Finally, her response ceased. Unconscious of self, she curved her body to his and sank into warm slumber where he joined her a minute later, his breath hot in her ear.

A faint grayness slid beneath the draperies. Dawn was breaking. And Cassandra pushed herself up from a drugged sleep, haunted by strange dreams. So much was not a dream. She was in bed with Edward Sandron.

No longer cold, his body was instead much too hot. Undoubtedly, he was running a fever after his terrible ordeal. She pushed herself up on her elbows. She had not meant to fall asleep at all. How fortunate that he had not awakened.

Then she tried to move her legs. Her breath escaped in an agonized hiss too late for her to stifle.

Hastily, she glanced in his direction, but he did not move. Summoning all her courage, she crawled from the bed. Her petticoat hung in two pieces, like a robe instead of a covering. The front of her body was nude except for her black stockings rolled to just below the knee and gartered there and her chemise that fell to the top of her thighs.

Fumbling about the floor, she managed to find her clothing and then the wig. Her own hair was a tangled snarl, but she stuffed it up under the wig. Throwing the figure on the bed one last look she fled from the room.

Chapter Five

"Mr. Sandron, sir, you won't remember this, but the night you were too sick to climb the stairs, the night you almost died, you gave me a baby."

"Nonsense, Miss Fitch, you must have mistaken me for someone else."

Lying on the narrow bed that belonged to Cassie Fitch, Cassandra MacDaermond gave a watery chuckle. Her pillow beneath her head was wet with tears that would not stop. She had long since given up trying to wipe them away. Exhaustion coupled with the trauma of the physical experience had dropped the barriers of control. Nevertheless, a small part of her stood back, helplessly acknowledging that she no longer cried for the single act of possession that might very well have changed her life forever.

Unknowingly, Edward Sandron had ruptured a dam inside her. The loss of control of her body had resulted in a loss of control of her emotions. Once in her room, the tears had begun to fall. She wept for things she had never wept for before. She shed the tears she had not shed when the pride of Daerloch had been humbled in the dust, when she and her father had left their home forever to reside in the miserable cottage while he drank by day and staggered away to gamble by night. The tears she should have shed at his graveside and later upon leaving Scotland followed the first gush in a briny waterfall that cleansed and left her too weak to remember what had happened to her last night.

Considered in the cold morning light, her employer's possession was no more than an accident. Cassandra was too much of a realist to think that Edward Sandron had wanted the body of his housekeeper. He had sought release in the aftermath of his own shock and exhaustion; she had been there warm and female. It had all happened quite naturally. She, an earl's daughter, had lost her virginity as a result of an accident.

Again the watery chuckle.

From the floating fantasy of his lovemaking she had awakened to a painful real world. Exercising all her will, she had managed to pull herself from his warm arms. The pain of strained muscles in unaccustomed places had made her groan. Only with much stumbling and holding on to the furniture had she managed to gather up her dropped clothing and step into it. Even now, her legs felt stiff as she imagined a very old woman's must feel. Moreover, she still felt a burning rawness between them. Furtively, she reached her hand down to touch herself. Only yesterday she had been inviolate. Now . . . She squeezed her eyes tightly against more tears.

Why could she not have fought him? Why had she lain passive, almost hypnotized by his demanding male touch? No, not passive. At the end she had been swept away by sensations frightening and at the same time altogether wonderful. Indeed, almost from the very beginning, she had not been able to refuse him.

She closed her eyes. She should have left him to die in the hallway outside the bathroom. If her tender heart rebelled at that, she might have left him to take his damned bath all night long and gone to her room. She might have thrown his robe around him and left him to climb up the back stairs on his hands and knees. And frozen solid on the way. Above all, why had she foolishly climbed into bed with him to warm him? Surely she should have had better sense.

Of course, he had been shivering, convulsions racking him, his teeth chattering uncontrollably. She closed her eyes in self-disgust. She sounded remarkably like her father excusing his gambling and drinking forays that drained the family fortune away.

Even she could not excuse the last. Given that she had climbed into bed with him to warm him, she should not have stayed. As she valued her honor, she should have stayed awake and left the bed the minute his trembling ceased.

The fact remained that she had chosen to make each step in complete possession of her faculties and knowledge of the consequences, in all except the clinical practicalities of how a man made love to a woman. She had no one to blame but herself. With that thought the tears ceased. Rolling over on her back, she lay quietly, watching the light of the morning filter through the tiny window. She should be up and about her business as housekeeper.

Should she continue in her position? What would be Sandron's reaction to the events of the night before? Would he dismiss her without a character? Would he expect to take her into his bed again?

She chuckled again a little sadly. Baal was a handsome devil. He could have much better than the likes of Cassie Fitch, housekeeper.

Oh, how she dreaded seeking a job again! She did not fool herself. No fewer than half a dozen domestic employment agencies had merely shaken their heads when she had approached them. Only this one with its position as the Devil's Palace had been able to send her out. Only the unsavory reputation of the Devil's Palace had allowed her to step into this job. No other domestics had been desperate enough to apply.

If she went out again where unemployment was high, she would most likely face starvation and homelessness. Furthermore, references from the Devil's Palace would not favorably impress any decent person who might be looking for a dependable housekeeper. Edward Sandron was infamous as a lecher and gambler . . . but she had food and shelter, a warm bed.

Resolutely, she forced herself to look at the truth. She liked living and working in the Devil's Palace. She liked Edward Sandron. Beneath the pose of the devil himself was a man who she suspected was kinder and more considerate than most.

When he had reached for her, like a heroine in a novel, she had fought for her virtue. But before she had truly awakened, he had been on top of her. The pain had been real and without respite. Between fear and befuddlement, she still did not fully comprehend how he had done what he had done. Beneath his lean, strong body, she had moaned and struggled against the pain.

He had finished and rolled off her. Even as he had finished and she lay in sorry amazement at woman's lot, his hands had touched her and soothed her. She had been tight-lipped, stiff, shivering slightly, every nerve screaming in resentment. Then everything had begun to change. Her body had responded of its own volition.

As the pain left her, so did the sense of self, of control. It had been stolen from her. Now her hands followed the path his had taken. Her breasts and belly had felt the stroking of his fingers — his clever, hot, intruding, mesmerizing fingers. And his mouth had kissed her face, her lips, had nibbled at the lobe of her ear, had breathed hotly over the curve of her throat.

A fiery blush rose in her cheeks at the memory of her responses. Reaching for her robe, she began to move carefully about the room. She was certainly sore, but how much of her soreness was the direct result of his lovemaking and how much the result of struggling to hold him in his illness and weakness? He really was a devil. She should be hating him as the personification of everything evil, everything that had ever hurt her.

Instead, she thought about him with pity. Edward Sandron had almost died. Whatever had brought on the violent illness had come very close to killing him. No matter that he and men like him had provided the opportunity for her to lose her home, her fortune, her father's life. She was not her father and he had made his choices as well.

She stared at herself in the mirror. Why wasn't she dead? Critically, she touched her cheeks, her lips, her breasts. The most horrible thing that could happen to a woman had happened to her and yet she lived and breathed. In the books she had read, women died. They died of shame or, at the very least, pined away to a listless shadow. And then the hero, humbled, repentant, weeping . . .

She had thought of Edward Sandron. She could image him smiling, cynical, easygoing, even angry, perhaps a little concerned, but her imagination could not conjure up a picture of Baal of the Devil's Palace as humble. Nor repentant. Weeping? She made a disgusted noise. So much for fantasies.

Her eyes were deeply tinged with red, her lids, swollen; the skin at the point of her cheekbones, mottled. Weeping was a real exercise in futility, she decided. No, Edward Sandron would never be caught weeping. Furthermore, she felt a little foolish about it herself.

Dipping a washcloth into the icy water in the basin, she pressed it to her eyes. A good breakfast and she would be ready to face the morning. Already her movements were becoming less jerky, less painful as she dressed. The resiliency of her young healthy body asserted itself until the stiffness disappeared completely. However, the tight unhappy look about her mouth was very real when she stepped into the kitchen.

"Ain't seen no sign of Mr. Parks," the cook informed her as he stirred a small kettle of porridge. "He's usually down before you, Miss Fitch."

Cassie poured herself a cup of tea and warmed her hands around it. "He was not available to help Mr. Sandron last night. Perhaps you'd better check on him?"

"Me?" The cook shook his head. "I wouldn't even be knowin' where his room is." He dipped up a bowl of porridge and moved ponderously across the kitchen. His huge belly preceeded him, thrusting out over his feet and making his arms seem unnaturally short. He had to lean hard against the table to set the bowl in front of her.

"It's upstairs on the same hall as—"

"I don't climb no stairs." The cook shook his head adamantly. He did not bother to dip his portion up. Instead he lifted the pot by its handle and began to shove the contents into his mouth with the long-handled wooden serving spoon.

Cassandra blinked. Fascinated she watched his mouth stretch wide and his huge Adam's apple bob as he pushed the food between his lips and swallowed it in a steady efficient motion. When he was finished, he set the pot down and licked the back of the spoon. Hastily, lest he catch her staring at him, she bent over her own portion, which had not even had time to cool.

The cook drew himself a tankard of ale from the barrel in the corner. "May be you'd better go up and see what's wrong," he suggested, turning the tankard up and taking a gargantuan swig.

Parks's room was the only servant's room on the upper floor. It was located at the very head of the back staircase. The entrance to the master suite was at the opposite end of the hall with all its rooms—including the library—facing the front of the house.

Thoroughly convinced that Parks was not inside,

Cassandra nevertheless knocked. When no one answered, she opened the door. A glance showed her Parks's bed still made up neatly, his few personal items still as they had been the night before. She shook her head.

Times were hard and servants did not usually leave without a good reason. Moreover, Parks was a valet, a treasured position. He and Mr. Sandron had seemed very cordial. She had seen them about to sit down to tea together. Even the Devil's Palace could not be considered a good reason for his strange absence. Working for the devil had not seemed to bother Parks.

As she gazed around the room, hands on hips, the bell beside the door jangled imperatively.

Her nerves, which she had thought under control, sent frenzied messages to all parts of her body. Suddenly, her hands were cold and she had to clench her fists to still their trembling. What would he say to her? How could she go into that room again?

"Where the hell is Parks?"

"I don't know, sir."

"Parks! Parks!" Edward Sandron craned his neck to look around her toward the door.

Her hands gripped the tea tray tightly as she put on her most disapproving expression. "I wish you *could* summon him. I have knocked and looked in his room. I can't imagine where he's gone to."

When no valet appeared, Edward sank back on the rumpled pillows. His black hair plastered to his forehead made his face all the more pale by comparison. The smoky gray eyes appeared almost black. The skin around them, faintly bruised. "Damn . . ." He swiped a trembling hand across his eyes and frowned at the perspiration on the tips of his fingers.

"I've brought your tea, sir." She placed the tray on the table beside the bed and poured it.

When he took it from her hand, the cup rattled dangerously in the saucer. "Damn . . ." He muttered again as she hastily took it back.

They stared at each other. Then he closed his eyes weakly and turned his face away. Frowning, she stepped forward and slipped her arm under his shoulder. "You need liquids," she informed him sternly when his eyes flew open and he would have protested. "You were very ill last night."

"And you had to take care of me alone?" he murmured.

"Drink this," she instructed hastily.

He took a sip. "I can't remember a thing," he confided as he slipped back listlessly onto the pillows. "Only the pain. God! It was terrible. Like knives in my stomach. And then I was vilely sick."

"Don't think about it." She held the teacup to his lips.

He drank but would not leave the subject. "I vaguely remember taking a bath. Did I do that?"

"Yes, sir. You were filthy and had sweated your clothes down."

He shuddered. "Right." He lifted the covers and looked down then up at her. A speculative light entered his eyes. "How much do you know about me, Miss Fitch?"

She started, a slow flush climbing into her cheeks. "In what way, sir?"

"Did you have to help me undress?"

"Only your cape, sir. Here's another cup of tea. Drink it all. I'm sure your body craves liquids."

Obediently, he downed the tea in a couple of swallows. She slid her arm away so he could sink back on the pillow. Seeing that his eyes were closed, she began to move about the bed, straightening the tumbled covers, scooping up the crimson and black cape he had worn up the stairs. She hung it in the wardrobe and turned back toward the bed.

One step and an instant flash of embarrassment brightened her cheeks. Peeking out from under the edge of the bed's duster was a loop of white ribbon. With difficulty, she quelled her first impulse to dash across the room, snatch up the stray garment, and hide it beneath her apron. So sick he could not sit up in bed, he had not found it yet. She could casually walk across the room, stoop, and retrieve it.

She was suiting the thought to the action when he opened his eyes. "What time it is?"

She started visibly but he was too tired to notice. "Midday, sir."

"Has Nash come?"

"I don't know, sir."

He struggled up on the pillows. "Fetch him."

She stared at him, horrified. "How?"

He waved an impatient hand. "By sending a messenger for him. Most employees working in the casino should know the way to his digs."

"But . . ."

"Yes?"

"Should I just *go* into the casino?"

He looked at her amazed. "Of course. It's nothing

but a big room, after all. Lots of employees. If anyone annoys you, which they won't, just let out a yelp. We've got a bouncer who'll take care of him." He paused. "Do you know the way through my study?"

A thousand protests flashed through her mind, reasons why she could not, would not, should not go. All trembled on the tip of her tongue, but she grimly swallowed them. Curiosity coupled with a niggling desire to dare the devil, or at least dare to enter the devil's den, enabled her to shake her head a little breathlessly. "Yes, sir."

He lay back and closed his eyes. With her toe, she poked the embarrassing white ribbon back under the duster and quietly left the room.

The rain that had begun the night before still pelted the house. In order to reach the front of the house from the outside, she would have to walk past the backs of several more houses to the end of the alley, then down the other side. The way through the study was eminently more sensible.

The Devil's Palace was connected to the rest of the house by a sliding panel. Edward Sandron, dressed as Baal in black and crimson, could open a tall cabinet with beveled-mirror door, step inside, and close the door behind him. When the door was closed, the back of the cabinet would open from the inside at the slightest pressure. Once through, the door swung back behind him.

From a small landing a couple of steps long and no more than a yard wide, a steep staircase led down through Stygian darkness to another wall. There a system of weights and a pulley moved a panel to one side for him to step through into the back of the stage.

The curtain was kept drawn until it was time for Baal to enter the casino.

Of course, Cassie Fitch had not actually seen the system at the bottom of the stairs. Parks had led her onto this tiny landing while he delivered instructions to clean it of a thick layer of dust and festoons of spider webs. Hesitating skeptically, she had stared down into the dimness when the door had swung shut behind them.

For several seconds Parks had continued talking unperturbed, while she gasped soundlessly, her terror so paralyzing she could not speak. At last he had asked her a question. When she did not answer, he had touched her shoulder.

His hand released her catatonia. She began to scream, hysterically, blindly, unreasoningly. The terrified valet had fumbled badly for several seconds before finding the handle and opening the door. Through it she had fled, flatly refusing to stay in it let alone clean it. When Parks had suggested that she could take a lantern in, she had shaken her head adamantly. She had no fear of the dark. The walls had closed round her when the door had slammed shut. Never had she known such abject and dibilitating terror.

Now struggling with her panic, she thrust a book between the door and the jam to hold it open. Muttering unhappily and trembling with dread, she lifted her skirts and tested each step before she placed her weight on it.

Halfway down, a step creaked ominously underfoot and the faintest of skittering sounds reached her ears. Mice? Rats! Filthy furry beasts with fiery eyes and sharp-pointed teeth. She shuddered convulsively as her hair rose on the nape of her neck. What was she doing here? How ridiculous to be putting herself in this position for Edward Sandron. She half turned to go back up to the study.

Sternly, she locked her jaw. Baal came up and down these stairs every night. No harm had befallen him. Certainly, despite his dress, he was no supernatural being. She would not be stupidly female. Sucking in a deep breath, she continued her descent.

The system of weights and pulley was as Parks had described. Fortunately, it operated easily and soundlessly. When the panel slid back, she stepped into a small open area that had probably been intended as a musician's gallery in the original plan of the house. Directly in front of her was the curtain.

Gradually, her breathing evened. Her heart slowed its wild rhythm that sent the blood roaring in her ears. On the other side of the curtain, she could hear the faint mutter of voices. People were indeed working and playing beyond it. She passed her hand across the rough side of the velvet, finally finding the center. Her first impulse to pull back the curtain at its center, she discarded. Instead, she pushed the curtain aside at the proscenium and peeked out.

The decor was in sharp contrast to the rather ordinary furnishings and absence of bric-a-brac that characterized the rest of the house. Here every surface, whether floor, walls, or ceiling, was broken into small patterns of color, texture, and design. Beneath the feet of the gamblers was a thick black carpet. Almost like velvet, its plush was woven with a diamond-trellis design worked in antique gold and dark crimson the color of blood. The same dark crimson glimmered on the walls between the intricate patterns traced in black. A magnificent gas-o-lier, like a giant golden flower, blazed down on the players and lighted a ceiling of dark crimson between black stucco diamonds, each tricked in gold, repeating the design in the carpet.

The effect was more hot than warm, especially with the mirrors hanging on every wall, golden gas lights at regular intervals around the walls, and golden ornaments decorating every mantel. Indeed the flames along with the black carpet and writhing designs of the wallpapers created the traditional idea of hell. A very luxurious hell to be sure.

Shaking off the stunning effect of the room, she slipped down the seven steps and moved quietly along the wall. If Nash was here, she should be able to spy him without trouble.

He was not among the group at the roulette wheel. The rapt faces studying the race of the little white ball past the black and red slots paid no attention to her scrutiny. Likewise, she did not see him among the card players. Staring around her, she could see no one else. A series of private rooms, their entrances heavily draped in black damask, opened on both sides of the main room.

At that moment a servant in the black and crimson livery of the Devil's Palace came out of a door at the back of the hall and bore a tray with a steaming silver coffeepot and cups into one of the private rooms. She shifted from one foot to the other, then approached it. She would wait until the man came out, then ask him Nash's whereabouts.

Another man lunged out of the door, bumping her hard, and almost upsetting her. He cursed and caught at her arm. Face to face they swayed, then he straightened. His soft white hands came down on her shoulders, while his sharp black eyes looked at her with equal parts of dawning recognition and incredulity.

"Cassandra?"

Ducking her head, she tried to draw back from him. "You're mistaken, sir," she mumbled.

His hands squeezed her shoulders harder. "No. No, I'm not." He shook her gently. "Cassandra MacDaermond, 'tis you."

Stubbornly, she kept her head down, showing him only the top of the gray wig. "Begging your pardon, sir, but my name is Fitch. You've no cause to lay hold of me. I'm just a poor woman running an errand."

His grasp loosened. "I could have sworn—" he began.

"No, sir."

She turned away only to be confronted by a tall man in livery. "What're you doing in here?" he demanded gruffly but taking care to keep his voice low. "You can't just come in off the streets . . ."

Cassandra stumbled back, shaking her head, her hands fluttering in an ineffectual effort to make him listen to her. "I didn't. Believe me. I've come on an errand—"

Fitzwalter caught up with her. "You are Cassandra," he said positively. "Of course you don't work here. Scotty's daughter in a place like this." He shook his head sadly. "Then he smiled. "I've been looking everywhere for you."

"You're mistaken . . ."

"What's going on here?" At the sound of Nash's grating voice, Fitzwalter's smile disappeared. "I say, Fitz. I know you're a Puritan and all that, but ain't she a bit drab even for you?"

Hastily, Cassandra stepped out of his reach, keeping her head down against her chest. Her hands clenched under her apron.

Her father's friend Fitzwalter swung away from her to confront Nash. "Whatever I chose to do would be as the work of angels compared to the loathsome deeds of the occupants of this house," he sneered.

"Of course, of course," Nash replied blandly. "Loathsome deeds on every hand. Do at least one before lunch each day m'self. Ain't that right, Miss Fitch?"

"Fitch?" Fitzwalter sounded thoroughly confused.

"Mr. Nash," Cassandra kept her voice low and hoarse. Likewise she adopted a thick Cockney accent in imitation of the greengrocer who came by regularly in his cart. " 'Imself is took sic, 'e 'as. 'E arsked me to come fetch yew." With that, she curtsied, turned, and fairly raced for the stage.

Once safe behind the curtains, she leaned trembling against the wall. The man who accosted her had indeed been Mr. Fitzwalter, her father's friend, and the one who had been asked to take her. And he had recognized her. What if he told Nash?

She would have to lie again, to swear that Fitzwalter had been mistaken. He and Nash did not appear to be friends. Perhaps they would not even discuss her. With pounding heart, she peeked out between the curtains.

Nash and Fitzwalter obviously were arguing about

something. Nash's face was flushed with anger while Fitzwalter's hands were clenched together in back of him. The chubby knuckles showed white.

Fitzwalter finally turned on his heel. His dark eyes stared fixedly at the curtain. Fearful of discovery, she pressed her hands to her cheeks, willing him to go away and leave her alone.

Then Nash said something. Evidently, it angered Fitzwalter even further. His face burning bright red, he strode rapidly across the black and crimson carpet. A flunky handed him his hat and stick as he stepped into the curtained anteroom before the front door.

Nash watched his departure, then pulled a gold case out of his waistcoat pocket. Extracting a cheroot, he waited impatiently while the servant who had carried in the coffee tray lighted it.

Puffing until it caught, he nodded to the man, then strolled toward the stage. Joining Cassandra behind the curtain, he stared her up and down, eyes slitted through an exhalation of tobacco smoke. "Now, Miss Fitch," he asked after a brief pause, "perhaps you'd better tell me what's the matter."

Chapter Six

"Believe we've had this conversation before, old chap? Why can't you watch where you're going?" Nash cast a jaundiced eye at Edward's prone form.

Furiously angry yet physically exhausted from the ordeal, Sandron's hoarse whisper cut through the publisher's flippancy like a serrated edge. "Bloody hell, Nash! What was in those damn cakes?"

The publisher's mouth dropped open at the same time his eyebrows rose. He drew himself up huffily. "Same old stuff. Absolutely same old ingredients. What? I really can't say. Not strong on the things m'self."

"Then why did you put the damn things in the ritual?" Edward rolled his head irritably on the pillow. The single explosion of anger had brought the hideous taste of his illness back into his mouth. Perspiration sheened his upper lip and forehead.

Nash looked disgustedly around the disordered room. "Had to, old chap. Expected, you know. Black mass and all that has to have black cakes."

Edward felt his strength ooze away. The room seemed to tilt from side to side and Nash's body swayed like a reed. "Stand still, damn you!"

Nash bent over him. To Sandron's pain-distorted vision, his business partner was scarcely recognizable. The long nose sharpened and thrust forward like a beak. Its normally pale reddish-brown freckles stood out like plague spots on the white skin. "I say, Eddie," he whined, "are you all right?"

"Of course, I'm not all right. I'm sick as a horse." Edward turned his face into the pillow. For effect, his stomach groaned threateningly. The noise was accompanied by agonizing pain and nausea.

"Oh, I say . . ." Nash muttered, but Edward paid no attention. Flinging back the covers, he staggered to his feet. Reeling slightly, he made his way into his dressing room. When he returned, he was even paler than before.

In the meantime the publisher had regained some of his aplomb. "I rang for the valet," he offered helpfully. His pale eyes flickered over Edward's lean naked body. "Bit chilly for sleeping nude, I should think," he murmured.

"Damn you! I was too sick to put on nightclothes last night. I don't even remember how I got to my room." His explosion of ire trailed off to a disgusted grumbling. Edward slumped down wearily on the edge of the bed. His head was pounding so hard he could scarcely bear to touch it. Resting his forearms across his thighs, he stared down at the carpet between his bare feet. His heart thumped massively against his ribs.

Nash shifted uncertainly from one foot to the other. "Well, I only thought to offer a suggestion. Not good for a man to get a chill."

Edward did not raise his head in acknowledgment. Instead his attention had focused on streaks of brown marking the insides of his thighs. Curiously, his misery forgotten for a moment, he touched his finger to one of them. Blood. Had he hurt himself somehow?

At the same time Nash made a discovery. "Ah-ha! Is this all a hoax? Come now, old chap." Amazed at the man's sudden change of tone, Edward raised his head. Nash waved an admonitory finger at him. "Bad form to get drunk and spend the night carousing, then complain about it." He fished a scrap of white cloth from beneath the edge of the rumpled bed.

Edward gaped as the publisher twirled the bit of ribbon and white lawn around his index finger. "I never saw that before in my life," he swore solemnly.

Nash chuckled nastily. "Probably not if you're sick drunk when you take its owner to bed."

Sandron staggered to his feet, his hands doubled into fists. "Nash, damn you—"

Both men were distracted at that moment by a knock at the door.

"Come in." Sandron pivoted angrily just as Miss Fitch opened the door.

"Excuse me, sir . . . Oh!" Frozen in shock, she stared at his tall nude figure, her eyes flying from his pale face to his loins, then back again.

Likewise, the sight of his housekeeper, who insisted firmly on being called "Miss" in token of her maiden status, froze Edward to the spot. One shaking hand moved in some vague effort to hide himself. Then he made a dive for the bed, thrust his legs under the covers, and snatched the sheet across his loins in one smooth movement.

Nash clapped his hands noisily at the sight of Edward's retreat. "Timely interruption, Miss Fitch. Timely. Edward was just about to slam me a facer." He chuckled malevolently. "Not a white knight, but a virgin queen to rescue poor Nash. How appropriate! Considering the devil himself was about to strike me dead. Sorry, Miss Fitch. I rang for the valet."

Eyes on the floor, her lips all but disappearing, so tightly had she compressed her mouth, the housekeeper hesitated in the doorway. Finally she mumbled, "What did you need, sir?"

"Coffee. Plenty of it. Hot as fire." This from the publisher.

"N-no." The very thought of hot strong coffee made Edward's stomach clench.

Miss Fitch glanced in his direction. "I think cool tea might be better, Mr. Nash. His stomach might be too weak to tolerate coffee."

"Yes. Fetch me some tea," Edward agreed hastily as the housekeeper backed out the bedroom.

Nash scowled at the prostrate man. "I suppose this means that you won't be writing today."

His condemnation was too much. Edward sat bolt upright in bed. "For God's sake, Nash, I didn't send for you to rip me up about writing. I want to know what in hell you put in those cakes last night."

Nash managed to look more bored than ever. "I've already told you, I have no idea of the recipe."

"You furnished the cook. I naturally assumed—"

"The cakes did not come from your kitchen, old chap. Charley picks them up from a bakery across town. So no one knows where they come from. D'y'understand? Keeps up the appearance of mystery."

"Something made me sick as a horse."

Nash flicked open the case of his watch. "Must have been something else, Baal, old imp. Nobody else got sick. Most people stayed around till the wee small hours, drinking, eating, et cetera." He closed the timepiece with an authoritative snap and slipped it back into his vest pocket. "Must be off, old chap. Need to drop by the office for a few hours today."

"Damn it, Nash . . ."

The publisher smoothed a palm over his thin sandy hair as he regarded Edward calmly. "Can't you be a bit more selective about what you eat, old chap? Indiscriminate gorging is bound to take its toll."

"I didn't eat indiscriminately, Nash. What's more, I've been eating those damned licorice cakes for months. Apart from licorice being a taste I cannot seem to acquire, I have never felt a moment's twinge until last night."

"Well, there you are. Must have been something else that put you off."

"Excuse me, sirs." Cassie Fitch appeared again in the doorway, a tea tray in her hands.

"Thank God. Must rush." Nash stared hard again at the housekeeper as she passed. At the door he paused, following her black-clad back with his eyes as she carried the tray around to the far side of Edward's bed. "Do try to put this behind you as a thing of the moment and do some writing, old chap?"

"Nash . . ." Edward threatened angrily.

"I know. 'Go to hell.' " He shut the door.

Keeping her eyes firmly on the tea tray, Cassie Fitch set it on the bedside table. Edward pulled the covers up higher across his chest. Still his bare shoulders and arms were exposed.

Tension gathered in the pit of her stomach as she leaned above him. "Rise up, sir."

"Miss Fitch?" he began hoarsely.

Keeping her eyes firmly on his face, she pulled the pillows out from behind his back, turned them, plumped them, and replaced them. "Now, sir. You'll be more comfortable."

"Thank you." He sank back. A flush rose in his cheeks. He could hardly believe his body's reaction to her nearness. Despite his wretched weakness, he could feel himself tensing. He glanced up at her set face. When one of her small hands brushed his shoulder, he flinched in reaction to its icy cold.

Sternly, he reminded himself that she was dying of embarrassment as any maiden lady would be. Her sensibilities, her innocence, had been shocked by the sight of his nude body. He was surprised that she had not run screaming or swooned.

But perhaps she had seen him last night? Vaguely, he could remember taking a bath. Had she not helped him in and out of the bathtub? Perhaps she was not as shocked as he imagined she was. He glanced at her speculatively.

Despite the tension that made the muscles in her belly tremble and heat, Cassie poured his tea. While he drank it, she moved with what she hoped was a competent air around the end of the bed, straightening the covers as she went. At last she bent over to straighten the duster.

He cleared his throat nervously. "Miss Fitch, was there anyone here with me last night?"

She popped up from behind the footboard so fast

that he was startled. Her face, flushed from her exertions, looked younger and more attractive than he remembered. "Here, sir?" Her tone was lighter, less gruff.

He stared at her, momentarily distracted. If she were dressed in the proper colors, her gray hair arranged in an attractive style, she would be a handsome woman. "Yes," he said at last. "Here with me last night."

"Not that I know of, sir. Why do you ask?" She clasped her hands under her apron and put on her most disapproving face.

He felt the skin over his cheekbones heating. "Nash found an, er, lady's unmentionable garment beside the bed."

The housekeeper's color drained almost instantly. Her eyes, whose color he had noted before, now appeared extraordinary in her white face. Green as peridot or emerald, they stared at him in horror. Abruptly, she spun away and began to straighten objects on the table beside the chaise.

Embarrassed, he looked away. "Sorry, Miss Fitch," he mumbled. "I didn't mean to embarrass you with my"—he cleared his throat noisily—"peccadillos." He drank the rest of the tea down in oppressive silence.

"Will that be all, sir?" she asked when she heard the faint clink of the teacup in the saucer. She had worked herself around until she stood near the door, her hands clasped under her apron.

He lay back, his face creased by a frown. "It's no use. I can't figure out what happened to me. What's more I can't remember what happened after a certain point."

"Shall I leave you, sir?"

He shook his head. "No, come here. Pour me some more of that blasted tea and tell me what condition I was in when you found me."

She hesitated, then came back to the bedside. "I heard you moaning in the hallway outside my room, sir. I suppose the pain had made you draw up into a tight ball."

"Oh, God, do I remember that! It hit me right after I ate that cake and drank the wine."

"Did the others eat the cake, sir?"

He nodded and fell back on the bed. "Yes. That's the damnedest thing. The ceremony was coming to the end. Nash has it set up so that after we eat and drink that damned stuff, the girl gets off the altar and"—he flicked a glance at the housekeeper—"that is, the audience begins . . ." He ran his hand through his sweat-stained hair. "Ashtaroth handed me the cake and wine. I swallowed it and chugged the wine right down. It's the only way I can get by the damned licorice," he muttered in an afterthought.

Miss Fitch watched him thoughtfully, her smooth forehead wrinkling as she considered his words. "What did you eat beforehand?"

"Parks brought me a light meal. Just some fish and potatoes and peas. Simple. Tasted just fine." He shook his head. "No. The minute after I drank that wine I had this terrible pain."

"But your cake came from the same batch, didn't it?"

"So Nash told me." He rolled over in bed. "God. I can't figure it out."

She hesitated. "Perhaps if you were to just rest for

today. Sometimes things pile up. Maybe what made you sick was everything you'd eaten and drunk all day?"

"I need to get up. You heard Nash."

She shrugged. "Shall I get you some breakfast then? Perhaps a coddled egg and a piece of toast?"

He made a face. "I need a shave. Don't suppose you could oblige?"

"Sir, I'm not your valet."

He handed her the teacup. "Parks," he mused. "I can't imagine where he's got to. Been with me for several months now. Seemed like a good man."

"I was under the impression he had been with you for many years."

"No, acquired him just recently. Through an employment agency." Sandron smiled a sweet smile, only faintly incongruous shining out of his prickly blue-black shadow. His gray eyes turned soft and pleading. "Since I can't ask you to shave me, please bring me my robe, Miss Fitch. I don't want to stay in this bed all day."

He could have sworn her mouth twitched at the corners. Then her face resumed its disapproving mode. "Oh, very well, sir."

He watched her as she crossed the room to the wardrobe. From the side, her figure was quite passable, not like an old woman's with protruding belly and sagging breasts. No dowager's hump curved that erect spine. He blinked. Nothing looked right to him this morning. Nash had looked like some malevolent being and now Miss Fitch looked like a young girl. His illness must be affecting his mind.

He had certainly been sick enough. He could

remember the hideous pain. The cramps. The violent nausea. And this morning, the pounding headache. And the stains. He frowned. His hand dipped beneath the covers to touch the slight roughness where the smears of blood still clung to his skin. Possibly he had bled in some hideous way. He did not want to contemplate it. A shudder racked his body.

She brought both his robe and his slippers, then turned her back while he struggled into it and belted it tightly around his middle. "All decent." He managed to chuckle.

Miss Fitch turned back to him. He sat on the edge of the bed, his face pale as chalk, his eyes sunken in his head. The robe covered his knees, but his shins and ankles as well as his long bony feet were bare. She had set the slippers on the floor too near the head of the bed.

Hastily she went down on her knees to slip them on first one foot and then the other. The peculiar tension she had experienced ever since she had come into the room quickened until something akin to actual pain curled within her. His skin was very white in contrast to the sparse fleecing of curly black hair. Her fingers trembled as she slid them round his ankle and lifted his foot. Trying to control her breathing, she finished her task and rose. "What now, sir?"

He ran a hand around the back of his neck. "God, I don't know. Where in the hell can Parks be?"

"Shall I send for the police, sir?"

He gave her a fierce look. "For God's sake, no, Miss Fitch! To investigate a disappearance from a gambling casino. And the disappearance of a servant at that." He sighed. "No. I suspect that Parks just decided that he didn't want to work here anymore. Perhaps he got a better offer."

Miss Fitch shook her head doubtfully. "His bits and pieces are still in his room, sir."

Edward shrugged. "Probably nothing worth coming back to take with him." He stood up and stretched warily. "Damn. Ache all over. I don't care what Nash says. Something in that cake or that drink made me sick as a horse." With that he padded into his dressing room.

Cassie Fitch breathed a sigh of relief. He did not remember. Not anything at all about what he had done. She could go on being a housekeeper here, her disguise undiscovered. With a feeling of relief, she went for fresh linens. Of course, Fitzwalter *had* recognized her. But she doubted that he would pursue her, especially when she had so clearly shown that she did not want to be recognized. The possible consequence of her night spent with Edward Sandron, she did not allow herself to consider.

Returning to the room with the fresh linens, she heard the splash of water in the dressing room. While he made his ablutions, she would change the bed. Suiting her act to thought, she pulled the disordered covers from the bed.

With blankets and top sheet in her arms, she froze. Her throat swelled as she strove to suppress a sob. There in the center of the white bottom sheet were dark brown smears—her virgin blood.

A sound behind her made her whirl around. Edward Sandron loomed over her shoulder. His frown had deepened into a scowl. He had evidently washed his face and run his damp hands through his hair. It gleamed wetly, black as night except for the prominent white curls. Uncombed except by his hands, the striking horns hooked upward, all too true representations of the devil's own.

Unaware of her stare, he opened the huge oak wardrobe to select a pair of trousers. "I don't know what happened," he murmured. "But something did."

Hastily, she quit the room as his robe fell away from his long bare legs lifted to slip into them.

"Mr. MacAdam!" Cassandra's eyes filled with tears at the sight of his familiar face. Eagerly, she clutched both his hands in her own as if by doing so she could somehow transport herself back to Scotland and the past.

"Ah, lassie, 'tis a long journey I've made to see you looking like an old woman."

She laughed joyously, then leaned forward. "It's a good disguise, isn't it, Mr. MacAdam? You can't tell I'm wearing all kinds of makeup, can you?"

He shook his head sadly. "Aye, 'tis a good disguise, lassie, but 'tis a shame to make your blooming self up to be old. You'll be old soon enough."

She sobered. Dropping his hands, she turned away. "I'll be starving soon enough if I don't keep up this disguise. I suppose you've seen the front of the house."

They were standing in the entryway behind the door that led from the alley. MacAdam stared doubtfully down the short hallway that led past the kitchen. " 'Tis a house o' the de'il and no mistake."

"The Devil's Palace," she agreed softly.

"And do ye not fear to work here?"

She hesitated then shook her head stubbornly. In the light of day, her fears seemed groundless. Two weeks had passed since the night she had spent with Sandron. Her flux had begun only a week later, relieving her of the fear almost before she had had time to worry about it.

If Fitzwalter had returned, he had not found her in the gambling hall. Very possibly he did not know that Baal kept a house and servants in the same building as the Devil's Palace.

The mysterious disappearance of Parks had created a vacancy that so far no employment agency had been able to fill.

Suddenly, she realized she was staring into space while Mr. MacAdam watched her with a frown. She smiled up at her old friend. "You've come at a fortuitous time, Mr. MacAdam. Mr. Sandron's valet decamped without a word. The employment agencies haven't been able to find any ignorant little boys from Scotland to send around, so the job is open."

"Hold on, lassie, I'm not a valet. Neither am I sure I want to work in a place—"

"Mr. MacAdam, I've worked here for weeks. Mr. Sandron is a perfect gentleman at all times." She swallowed hard as a particular memory pricked her but she continued gamely. "He's really a writer. His publisher runs the gambling casino."

"I dinna think—"

She shook her head. "Believe me, Mr. MacAdam, the man you'll be working for isn't the devil. No matter what the name of the house is and no matter how he dresses, he's really playacting more of the time than not. Believe me." She clutched his hands tightly again.

The Scotsman shook his head. He looked around the bare entryway. "Not much to take care of here," he murmured.

She grinned. "The rest of the house—at least the part that we have to keep—is just the same. Plain furnishings without a lot of gewgaws."

His mouth turned up at the corners. "You've said the words that find my heart, lassie. The English and their gewgaws work the servants to death."

"Most of the rooms have hardly any furniture at all. And there's the most marvelous bathroom. And gaslights. In every room. And heat." She led him to the foot of the staircase. "Wait here. I'll go up and announce you. Mr. Sandron will want to hire you himself, I know. He hired me."

"Putting on airs, Eddie?" Ashtaroth remarked nastily. "A butler, for God's sake. In this firetrap."

Sandron had gone on working, paying little attention to Ashtaroth's gossip until she had made the last remark. At that he raised his head from the sheaf of papers he was correcting. The door was just closing behind Mr. MacAdam, who had brought the tea tray, poured, and disappeared. "What's wrong?"

"Nothing's wrong, except you," she snapped. "You used to be a regular sort of guy. None of this hoity-toity stuff. Now you've got a staff of servants, for God's sake."

"A butler cum valet, a housekeeper, and a cook hardly constitute a staff, Sally." Edward returned his eyes to the paper before him. Dipping his pen into the inkwell, he scratched through a word and wrote in another with a tiny satisfied smile.

" 'Hardly con-stee-toot a stoff!' " she mocked. "Quite a change of attitude for poor little Eddie Boggan. Eddie Boggan! Shinin' boots fer 'is ma's customers. 'E don't mind whut she does."

The pen spattered ink on the papers as it broke in Edward's fist. With an angry frown he stared at the mess, then at the woman taunting him. "Stow it, Sally," he warned.

" 'E don't mind whut she's done!" She laughed as she hiked her skirts up over her knees and splayed them lewdly. "Is this the way y'r ma used t' do it?"

"Damn you."

" 'E'll walk yer nag, sir, while you ride 'is ma." Pulling her skirt higher, she grinned maliciously at him, her face avid beneath the makeup.

"Damn it, Sally! Shut up!" He rose from behind the desk and came toward her. She sprang up and dodged behind the chair, still taunting. He came after her, arms outstretched to hem her in.

Ashtaroth laughed again and dodged from side to side, finally brought up short in a corner against the bookcase. "Eddie!"

Looming over her, he caught her by her shoulder. "This is my library," he growled angrily. "Don't come in here and disturb me by speaking of the past. It's over and done with."

"It's not," she panted. Her voice was shrill. "It'll never be. You think because you wear fine clothes and write those books, you've got rid of the stink of the streets, but you never can. You're still Fanny Boggan's son, just like I'm still a—" She uttered a foul name, then laughed.

Realizing she was fast becoming hysterical, he caught her by the arm and struck her sharply across the side of the face. Her corrosive denunciation ended in a shriek of pain, which changed almost instantly to a scream of anger. Ducking her head, she slashed her teeth across his wrist.

He did not let her go. Swearing himself, he buried his other hand in her chignon and dragged her head up. Her lips and teeth were smeared with blood. Her eyes were wild as a wolf's.

"Sally!" He shook her like a terrier with a rat between its jaws. "Sally. Be quiet." He dragged her out of the corner and across the room, where he stood her in front of the mirror. "Look at yourself," he commanded, brutally thrusting her face close to the glass.

She stared long at the tormented reflection, then covered her face with her hands. "Eddie," she groaned.

Instantly, his anger cooled. Even as he pitied her, he stepped back away from her, nursing his injured hand. It stung badly and blood smeared his cuff. Moreover, he resented her irrational baiting as well as the interruption of his work. He glanced over his shoulder, wishing wholeheartedly that she would be gone.

But she was not ready to go. "Eddie," she gasped. Her arms were clamped tightly around his waist as she pressed her cheek against his back and rubbed her lower belly against his buttocks. "Eddie. I'm so unhappy.

"For God's sake, Sally . . ." Caught off guard by the mercurial change in her, he tried unsuccessfully to prize her fingers apart. His hands fumbled and pushed, but she clung like a leech. Her avid mouth sucked against the side of his neck beneath his ear, bringing the blood to the surface where her teeth could bite painfully. ". . . Ow . . . Sally, damn you . . ."

Utterly revolted, he stopped fighting her. Standing stiffly in her grasp, he reached for the bellpull. Reinforcements were definitely the order of the day. Otherwise, he would have to kill her to get her off him. "Really, Sally, old girl, you must get yourself under control."

She scarcely heard him. Desire heightened by pain and anger made her deaf and blind to all except her own burning needs. No longer encountering resistance and believing him as aroused as she was, she unclasped his waist. Her hands tore at the front of his shirt, ripped it open. Her long nails scratched his chest, tore at his nipples.

He gasped as pain lanced through him. "Sally . . ."

The door swung open. "Sir? Oh, pardon me."

"Miss Fitch," he called. One broad sweep of his arm thrust Ashtaroth aside. "Miss Fitch, don't go."

"But, sir—"

"No . . . no." He hurried to the door.

Her green eyes widened as she stared at his bared chest, the curling black hair in sharp contrast to the white of his shirt. In even sharper contrast were the angry, bleeding wounds left by Ashtaroth's fingernails.

"Eddie," the woman snarled behind him. "Send her away."

Miss Fitch backed toward the door, but he caught her hands. "No. We need coffee, Miss Fitch. And brandy."

"I'll get it, sir."

He caught her arm. His expression pleaded for understanding. She tightened her lips in their most disapproving lines. Instantly, his hand fell away. "Take the tea tray first," he commanded, drawing himself up.

While Ashtaroth watched, panting, and Edward Sandron buttoned his shirtfront and restored some order to his clothing, Cassie Fitch glided across the room. Taking her time, arranging the teacups, saucers, and plates with painstaking care, she finally stacked everything to her satisfaction.

Several sheets of paper from the novel had slid to the floor. She stooped to pick them up. Only when they were carefully stacked and the pen was returned to the inkwell did she pick up the tray and depart.

At the door she paused. "Coffee and brandy, you said?"

"Yes, Miss Fitch, and some more of the excellent cake the cook made last night."

"Eddie," Ashtaroth whined. "We don't need anything."

"I say we do."

"Very good, sir." Exchanging a carefully bland expression with him, she left the room.

Ashtaroth started toward him, arms outstretched, but he held up his hand. "Take one more step, Sally, and I'll beat you senseless and throw you out into the street."

"You wouldn't dare."

"Try me." His eyes had turned to steel. He made a fist out of his right hand and polished his knuckles on the palm of his left.

Her black eyes flashed. "You're just the same as me," she insisted.

He shook his head. "No. That's where you're wrong. I've left it all behind me. The very fact that you're here testifies to how far I've left it. I'm willing to be generous to you even though you act like the worst whore in Cheapside. But, Sally" — he straightened the points of his collar and adjusted his cuffs — "my generosity is not inexhaustible. I'll be your friend and your banker. But you and I both know that I won't be your lover. You're going to have to find someone else."

She clasped her hands in front of her breasts. Her voice assumed a whining tone. "Oh, forgive me, Mr. Edward, sir. Forgive me. I swear I'll never dare to approach you again. Not even for old time's sake. Not even if you beg me to."

He shook his head. "I'll never beg you to. Just go, Sally. Be glad for what we've become. Forget the past. There's someone somewhere who'll take care of all your needs. But it isn't me. So don't ask more of me than I can give."

Her face took on a haunted appearance. "I need warmth and touching once in a while, Eddie. I've tried to go without it. But sometimes I . . ." She clamped her jaw tight against its quivering. "I can't let anyone else get close enough. I swear I can't." Her color was high, her voice, a grating snarl. "I don't dare. I couldn't face contempt or pity. They'd find out what I came from and despise me. With you I'd be safe."

"Sally . . ." He shook his head regretfully.

Carelessly, she flung the exquisite cashmere shawl

around her shoulders and caught up her purse. Her black eyes spat fire as she stepped close to him. " 'Generous' you call yourself. 'Clutch-fisted' I call you. 'Clutch-fisted' with your money and worse with your body."

Edward could feel her frustrated rage like heat from a fireplace. Ignoring it, he reseated himself at his desk and picked up the top sheet from the stack.

"Damn you, Eddie Boggan. I'll make you sorry if it's the last thing I ever do."

The door slammed behind her.

Chapter Seven

The wicked earl threw back his leonine head. The wind that tossed his thick mane of midnight black hair carried his triumphant laugh to her terrified ears. "How very foolish you are, my dear! You might have spared yourself this useless effort."

Lady Elinor, her slim figure clad only in the nearly transparent material of her nightrail, writhed futilely against the leather straps that bound her to the platform. "No! Let me go!"

The hunchback servant sniggered evilly. His bulging eyes rolled wildly as he limped away into the dark shadows. The wicked earl laughed again as one by one he mounted the seven steps to the platform. The many capes of his black greatcoat billowed about him. His black gloved hand carried a riding crop which he slapped rhythmically against his black leather jackboots.

"You will now be forced to submit, Lady Elinor," he laughed.

"Never, you beast. You may take my body, but never

my soul."

As he loomed above her, his eyes glittered as his blood heated. Her defiance despite her helplessness drove him mad with desire. "You should never have tried to escape, m'lady," he whispered silkily. "I have commanded you to acknowledge me as your master. You must be punished for your recalcitrance."

The color drained from her aristocratic features. "What do you mean?" she gasped.

"You will soon find out," he promised. His black-gloved hand stretched toward her . . .

The door to the study burst open. "Baal! Get dressed and come downstairs immediately."

Unperturbed by the anxiety in Nash's tone, Edward added a word to the manuscript. "For God's sake, Nash. Can't you see I'm writing. You hound me to death to get it done, then come interrupt me." He rocked the blotter back and forth across the last lines. At the same time he carefully avoided looking at the distraught publisher.

"There's, er, trouble in the casino."

The word "trouble" drew Edward's head up from his work. "What kind of trouble?"

"A young man, Viscount Caltharpe, is . . . drunk."

Edward's irritated frown deepened. He stabbed the pen back into the inkwell. "For heaven's sake, Nash, don't we have men to take care of that."

Nash wrung his hands, an uncharacteristic gesture, that made Edward raise his eyebrows. The publisher's air was decidedly not his usual languid facade. With hands that shook, he made a hurried dismissive gesture. "Not their sort of thing, really. We need you.

You just might be able to talk some sense into the young idiot." As Edward rose to come out from behind the desk, Nash gripped him by the shoulders. "Hurry! Get something on besides that moth-eaten smoking jacket and come."

In a matter of minutes they descended the stairs in the passage behind the wardrobe. His hand on the mechanism, Edward turned to Nash. "At least tell me what's going on?"

Nash shouldered him aside and worked the mechanism himself. "No time to explain. The idiot might do it any minute."

"What?"

"Squeeze the trigger."

Edward gaped at the publisher's back. "My God, Nash. Who is he trying to kill?"

"Himself."

"A drunken viscount? With a gun?"

"Frightening, ain't it?" Nash's cynical chuckle was a ghost of itself as he pushed aside the curtains. "He's in the card room."

Edward caught hold of Nash's elbow. "Then why are we going in there?"

Nash swung around. The light of the gas-o-lier revealed his forehead glistening with perspiration. "You must reason with him, old chap. You're the one he might listen to."

"Why me?"

"Symbol. Figurehead. Owner. He's intimidated by authority. They all are. Scared to death of the old pater." With any luck he'll think you're someone like his father. Right now he's too drunk and too upset to be reasonable."

A knot of men shifted nervously in front of the door to one of the card rooms. A short stocky man whose round face was all the rounder for his sidewhiskers turned as Nash and Edward hurried toward them. Immediately, Nash lagged behind. "Baal, old boy," the bewhiskered one squeaked, "jolly glad to see you. Kipple's gone quite off his rocker. Been losing steadily." He turned back and began to elbow the others side. "Clear the way there, chaps. Here's help."

Edward's cape flared out around him like wings as the men hastily gave way. On the threshold he paused, blinking as the thick cigar smoke stung his eyes. The room was empty save for the lone figure seated at a green baize table facing the door.

A young man lifted a glass to his lips and tossed a shot into his mouth. A decanter of whiskey, only a quarter full, stood at his elbow. As he set the glass down, he shook his head drunkenly. The fingers of his left hand curled loosely around the butt of an Adams Mark II revolver.

Fear—cold and horrendous—spread from the pit of Edward's stomach. Behind him, he felt Nash's hand at the back of his waist. "Situation doesn't look too bad," came the publisher's words.

Out of the side of his mouth Edward let loose a virulent curse. "Not too bad! Are you blind?"

At that minute the young man spied the dark figure in the door. He blinked owlishly. "Come fer m'sh-soul, B-Baal. Give it t' you, in jus' a minute." He lifted the pistol and wagged it back and forth. "Jus' lemme finish thish whisk-key."

As the mouth of the barrel swept across his body, Edward cringed. "Easy there, son. Don't let that thing go off. Sometimes they do, you know. When you least expect them to."

Kipple Caltharpe laughed mirthlessly. "Not a problem. Not a problem. Know how to handle 'em. Pater taught me. Dear old pater!" Tears oozed from his eyes and trickled down his plump cheeks. He snuffled noisily.

"Your, er, pater, er, loves you." Edward looked around helplessly, but Nash and the other men had ducked out of the doorway when Kipple had swung the pistol toward them.

The decanter clinked against the rim of the glass. "He'll kill me," Kipple mourned. "Lost everything. Lost m' quarterly. Lost m' team. Lost . . . lost . . ." The whiskey splashed into the glass, overflowing and spreading on the table. "Damme! Makin' a mess."

While the young man set the decanter down and mopped ineffectually at the green felt, Edward took a couple of quick steps into the room. His movement unfortunately did not go unobserved. The pistol wavered up again.

"Stay back," warned the choked voice. "Goin' to do the decent thing."

Edward held up his hands. "Careful, Viscount. This isn't the decent thing."

"Yes, 'tiz. Yes, 'tiz," Kipple murmured unhappily. He tossed the drink down with a sad hiccup. "Really can't face ol' pater and mater. Disgraced 'em. Gamblin' debts . . . affair of honor." He turned the pistol in his hand until the muzzle pointed directly toward his face. Mournfully, he stared at its black hole.

"No!" Edward cried. "No. For God's sake wait.

Kip— What's his damn name?" He flung the question over his shoulder.

Behind him he heard Nash's voice, shrill and stammering with nervousness. "Kipling Caltharpe, Viscount Lenley."

"Kipling!" Edward boomed in his most authoritative voice. "Put the gun down. Don't point it at your face."

Surprisingly, the young man replaced the gun on the table. His eyes slitted as he stared through the layers of the blue haze at Edward Sandron. Then he gulped. "The devil . . . !" he squeaked. "The devil's come to claim m'soul."

Edward's quelled the impulse to reveal his true identity. Instead, he spread the crimson wings of his cloak on either side of him, making them billow forward, then back. "Put down the gun. Satan doesn't want your soul yet."

"Awk!" the young man gabbled fearfully.

"Exactly." Sandron took a step forward, then another, slowly closing the distance to the edge of the table. His tall dark figure cut off the light from the gas-o-lier as he raised the wings of his cloak. "Drop the pistol."

"No! Goin' t'do the decent thing and end it." Kipple thumbed back the hammer. The barrel swung toward the ceiling, then swung around toward the center of his chest.

"No!" Edward thundered in his best theatrical voice. "Baal does not want your soul now. Wouldn't take it if it came his way." Sweat beaded his forehead as he sifted his imagination for lunatic reasons. "Er, it is too innocent, too, er, too immature, too good. It needs years of, er, black sins . . ."

"Really." The young viscount seemed to consider this. "You mean if I died right now, I might go t' heaven?" A beatific smile lit his face. He tossed another shot of whiskey down his throat. "Then now 'ould be th' time to die."

"For God's sake no!" Edward rolled his eyes heavenward. Trying to think in the face of a loaded gun was hard work. He spread the wings of his escape. "Er, you've already damned your soul. Stay and, er, enjoy the fruits of your labors," he finished lamely.

Kipple gaped uncertainly. The barrel of the revolver swung back around.

Edward dodged to the side.

"Stay back!" Kipple warned as the cape billowed. Nervously, he started up from his chair. The pistol jumped in his shaking hand. His hand tightened convulsively. The report was shockingly loud in the small room.

Edward Sandron felt the bullet tug the edge of the cloak from his grasp. Too surprised to be terrified, he could only stare at the viscount, who stood stupefied, staring at the pistol as if he had never seen it before, then fumbled with his thumb on the hammer.

Sandron sprang forward. His right hand closed over the young man's wrist and twisted violently at the same time that he threw his considerable weight behind his left fist. It connected solidly with the trembling jaw.

Kipling Caltharpe fell backward, taking the chair with him. His body slammed into the floor with a force that knocked the breath out of him. He lay groaning softly, his long legs tangled in the furniture.

Edward Sandron bent and scooped the gun into his

pocket before he turned to face the doorway. "Come in, Nash," he called. "You can stop cowering now. Come in and gather him up."

Led by the publisher, the other men crept around the edge of the door facing and stared fascinated at the scene. Nash walked cautiously to the table and looked over it at the groaning man. After a minute, he shuddered visibly. The next minute he had resumed his part. "Not dead," he remarked in a sardonic tone. "Just dead drunk. Definitely merciful on your part, Baal. Not a bit like you, old chap."

Another man came up to stand on Baal's left. "Bit of a near thing this," he remarked seriously. Edward stared where the man pointed. A blackened hole clearly showed in the crimson satin. It was the proper height but to the left of Edward's heart.

The hair on Edward's scalp prickled; his breath caught in his throat. The round had missed his chest by bare inches. Behind him the murmuring increased in volume as the man who had noticed the bullet held the cape out for the others to see.

Someone clapped him of the back. "I say, Baal. Good show. Knocked him over clean as a feather."

The viscount's groaning increased in volume as two heavyset men dressed in demon's costumes scooped him up by the armpits. His eyes opened. He managed a look around him. His eyes settled on Edward. He stared. "Am I dead?"

"No such luck, Kipple." One of his companions slapped him on the shoulder heartily. "Baal here kept you in the land of the living right and tight. Handed you a facer and you went over . . . Oh, I say!"

Viscount Lenley gave a soggy hiccup before slumping unconscious. His full weight mattered not in the least to the burly duo who supported him. At a discreet signal from Nash, they dragged him out, while another righted the chair and carried away the debris of whiskey bottles.

Hurrying to the door, Nash signaled to the musicians, who swung into a popular music hall tune. Waiters in demon dress bore in trays of sweets. An imp dashed around placing unopened packs of cards on the tables.

Through it all Baal stood still, his arms folded across his chest. Around him men praised him and looked at him with real admiration in their eyes. He smiled thinly while his heart thudded and leaped beneath his hands bruised from the blows he had dealt Kipling. His knees shook despite the long calming breaths he drew into his lungs.

In the next room the croupier spun the wheel and called for bets in his usual voice. The sound acted as a signal. Swirling the damaged cape around him, Baal strode from the casino.

In his library once again, he poured himself a liberal toddy and stared at the liquid vibrating in the glass. He was shaking badly. The difference between the boy he once was and the man he had become came home to him with shocking clarity.

Eddie Boggan would have faced such an opponent with a sneer and flung himself gladly into the fray. He would have welcomed the danger, reveled in the shock that jolted him to the shoulder when his fist struck his opponent's chin. Eddie Boggan had nothing to lose.

But Edward Sandron was another person entirely. He looked around him at the study. The dark red carpet beneath his feet, the gleaming mahogany furniture, dark red also, the fireplace with its mantel of veined black marble all seemed dearer than they ever had. He held his trembling hand before his eyes. The skin was white now, the nails neatly manicured. He laid it on the unfinished manuscript. Had Kipple's bullet been a few inches to the right, his novel would never have been finished.

Around him were the shelves overflowing with books. He let his eye wander across the titles with a quiet pride. Long before he had become acquainted with Nash, they had been quite literally dumped upon him.

From the back door of a shabby rooming house, a landlord had dumped them out into the alley. The first box had landed at the bare feet of the skinny urchin scanning the neighborhood for discarded items worth a few pence or for carelessly guarded items that might be stolen easily. It had tipped over on its side, spilling some of its contents onto the filthy cobblestones. The sight of them had awed him. He had never learned to read. Eddie Boggan from Cheapside had never held a book in his hands before, but he knew what they were.

He did not, of course, recognize leather-bound volumes of classics, cloth-covered backs of writers from the turn of the century, cardboard backs of contemporary authors. Their worth in terms of education was inestimable. A veritable library had fallen at his feet as the uncaring landlord, grumbling the while, tossed out box after box. A total of twenty.

Edward Sandron plucked the first edition copy of Lord Byron's *Corsair* from the shelf and ran his hands over the back. The blue silk binding was stained and rippled. Rain and soot had fallen upon the books before young Eddie Boggan could carry them all away.

For two days he had worked at carrying them off, sharing his own cubbyhole in his mother's rooms above the gin shop with them. At the time he had some idea of selling them for a few pence apiece.

With this thought in mind, the next time a drunken customer had had to wait while she worked with another, Eddie had thrust a volume in front of the man's face. The boy opened his mouth to ask how much the man would give for it. But his question went unasked. The customer had glanced blearily at the book shoved under his nose, straightened, and then begun to read in a clear deep voice.

To the young intelligent boy the words had been magic. In a few minutes he was hanging above the man's shoulder, watching as the page was turned, following the words as they crawled along, matching the sounds.

Remembering, he closed the volume with a snap. Everything he had, everything he was, was in this room. In a sense they were father, mother, lover. The manuscript beneath his hand was his offspring. The body of Eddie Boggan was nothing but the container to house the product of this room. Eddie Boggan no longer existed. The room with its original twenty boxes of books plus three times that number that he had added to their store was the womb from which he had come.

He had left Cheapside behind, had changed his name, his dress, his way of speaking. He was Edward

Sandron now. And suddenly the ephermeral quality of his life struck him strongly. He could have been destroyed by that bullet. And Eddie Boggan, the casing, the shape, the tangible form of Edward Sandron, was too young to die.

He did not want to die. Instead, he wanted to be Edward Sandron, writer. Not Edward Sandron, cheap pornographer and actor. Not Baal. He replaced the volume of Byron. His fingers caressed the gold letters on the spine. In his dreams his own name was embossed on that spine.

A knock at the door drew him from his dream. "Come in."

Cassie Fitch opened the door. "Mr. Sandron, shall I serve tea?"

He glanced at the clock over the mantel. Middle of the afternoon and already the viscount had been too drunk to know what he was doing. Edward shook his head in disgust. "By all means, Miss Fitch. I could use some refreshment."

When it was brought, she poured for him and stood back.

"Sit down," he commanded with a wave of his hand. "Too much stuff here for me to eat anyway."

She shook her head sternly. "Mr. Sandron, it would not be proper for me to have tea with you."

"Hang propriety, Miss Fitch. I need company. Someone who will be honest with me." He looked at her straight-backed figure. "You are honest, are you not?"

"I hope so, sir." The question made her feel decidedly uncomfortable. In fact she was not honest. She was living a whole series of lies not the least of which was her name. Rather than have him pursue the matter too closely, she sat.

Edward insisted that she take a cup of tea and help herself to some of the excellent jelly role. Satisfied that she was eating, he helped his own plate. The food caught in his throat. Abruptly, he set the teacup down in the saucer.

"Miss Fitch."

She raised her clear green eyes. "Sir?"

His fear clogged his throat. He pressed the heel of his hand against his forehead. "How do you like your work?" It was not what he had meant to say.

She tilted her head to one side, considering. "Quite well, sir," she said at last. "I do not find the tasks exhausting nor the hours overlong."

"Except when your employer keeps you up all night," he reminded her.

She nodded. "Except then." Hastily, she hurried on, not wanting him to dwell too long on that evening. "I thank you for inquiring, sir. You are an unusually considerate employer."

He heaved a deep sigh. "Meaning that I don't know how to treat servants." He stirred the tea slowly. His gray eyes soft as smoke searched her face to gauge her reaction. "But you see I haven't had them very long. I don't feel any class distinction."

Her eyes narrowed slightly. She would have sworn that this well-spoken, well-mannered man had always lived in comfort. "Truly, sir?"

"Truly."

He stared at her uncertainly. Her eyes were the clearest green. They looked young. The whole face around the eyes looked young, despite the fine lines emanating from it. "Why have you never married?" he asked suddenly.

"Sir!"

"Forgive me." He waved a hand. "I'm upset." He looked away. "A young man tried to shoot himself today in the Devil's Palace. Nash sent for me and I was almost killed."

He did not notice her stiffening. Nor did he notice her reaction until she rose abruptly.

"Excuse me."

He looked up into her face, surprised by her angry expression. "Where are you going?"

"Out of this room."

He rose too. "Miss Fitch . . ." he began uncertainly. He reached out; his hand touched her arm.

She shrugged it off angrily. Her quick-trigger temper flared. "A young man tried to kill himself and you're upset. In his anguish over losing everything he had in the world, he became frantic and almost shot you. He will be shamed and disgraced. His family will be impoverished. Innocent tradesmen to whom he owed money will not be able to collect. Their families in turn will suffer. And why? Because he gambled. And you're upset!" Her voice rose, shrill with fury, a hint of tears behind it.

Edward blinked. The unexpected onslaught drove him back a couple of steps. "I can't help it if young folks gamble."

"Young or old. Foolish or smart. You can help it," she snapped. "You can close down this—this—sty and get a decent job."

He drew himself up haughtily. "This sty—as you call it—pays your wages and provides you with the job you just admitted to liking very well."

She dug her doubled fists into her hips. "Don't think I wouldn't, if there were any to be had. But in case you haven't heard, there are very few jobs available. People are starving."

"I'm not to blame for the all the woes of English society," he shot back, his own temper heating.

"You are not helping them."

"And you wouldn't work here if you could work anywhere else. That's loyalty."

" 'Needs must when the devil drives,' " she flung at him. "And the devil drives here, harder than anywhere else."

He held out his hands palm up. With an effort he maintained a calm reasonable tone. "I'm not responsible for all the young idiots who come in here and want to throw their money around for a thrill."

"That's it," she accused. "You give them a thrill and it costs them everything."

"I don't lure them in off the streets," he insisted. "So many of them want to come in here that sometimes we have to turn some away. They come of their own free will, let me assure you."

"Oh, I know. I know. But you don't gamble yourself." Her voice roughened. "You don't know how it catches you by the throat. How it won't let you go. You win a little, lose a lot, substance you can't really afford to lose. But you keep thinking that you'll lose a little, then win a lot. Every bit you win encourages you, and every bit you lose challenges you. Until you don't think of wife, nor children, nor servants, nor land. You only feel your blood hot, until it cools off forever."

"Miss Fitch," he whispered, holding out his hand. "Control yourself." Her speech delivered with such eloquent sincerity cooled his anger.

She slapped his hand away. "I've been in control ever since I came here. Everytime I remember where I am, I get sick to my stomach. I try not to think about what goes on at the foot of those stairs." She gestured wildly toward the door of the bedroom.

Edward stared open-mouthed at her fury. The full sense of her words made no real impact on him. Instead, the high color in her cheeks, the animation in her face fascinated him. What had she been like as a young person?

"Was your hair red?" he asked suddenly.

She gaped. Her hand flew to the edge of her wig behind her ear. "Why . . . y-yes," she stuttered.

"I'll bet your temper was something when you were younger."

His reference to her youth rocked her back a step. She clapped both hands to her flaming cheeks as the extent of her revelations shocked her. "I'm sorry, sir." She spun away.

Her sudden humility returned to him the sense of injury. His mouth tightened. "Oh, don't go soft on me now," he drawled. "I was so enjoying being slashed to pieces by your tongue."

One shaking hand slid to her cheek, her forehead. "I'm sorry, sir."

"You forgot yourself completely, Miss Fitch."

She turned back. "Yes, sir." But the spirit of rebellion within her was not quenched. "I forgot myself, but what I said was true. If I had my way, every gambling hall in this city, in this whole world would be burned to the ground and all the gamblers with it." Her voice was low and flat, almost emotionless, yet with an underlying intensity.

His handsome face turned to stone, every trace of generosity, of whimsy gone. The gray eyes took on the intensity of steel. "Then we shall all be fortunate that you are not likely to get your way, Miss Fitch."

She clenched her fists at her sides, her blazing anger reduced to impotence by his refusal to feel guilt. "Yes, sir," she breathed. She turned on her heel and stalked toward the door.

His voice brought her to a halt with her hand on the knob. "Miss Fitch. You have stupidly forgotten your duties. Take the tea things with you."

He saw her shoulders slip back another impossible inch. The spine straightend even more. "Yes, sir." Her face white as chalk except for bright flags of color on her cheekbones, she walked back across the room and bent to pick up the tray. The china cups rattled in their saucers.

"You must be careful about your nerves, Miss Fitch," he jibed as she made her way to the door. "All that shaking and trembling might cause you to break something."

Chapter Eight

The wind whipped a fine mist into her face. Its coolness felt welcome to her flushed cheeks. With a feeling of desperation she realized her employment grew more precarious by the day. She had allowed her employer to get too close to her. How had he guessed about the red hair? Of course, it was supposed to go with quick temper, but she had felt his eyes staring at the wig, as if they could surely penetrate it. Then he had looked into her eyes. She shivered at the memory of her response.

So immersed in her thoughts was she that she did not notice the man sitting in the window of the small tea shop on the corner across from the Devil's Palace.

When his hand closed round the back of her arm, she started in alarm. "What are you doing? Let go of me, sir." She tugged violently as she raised her handbag to strike at her captor.

Ducking her blow, Fitzwalter pulled her into the archway of a building. There he caught her by the shoulder and pressed her back against the wall. His eyes narrowed as he stared into her frightened eyes.

"You *are* Cassandra MacDaermond," he said positively.

She had already recognized him and her struggles had ceased. She bowed her head. "Yes, Mr. Fitzwalter."

"Cassandra. Cassandra," he repeated softly, shaking his head. "Why did you not come to me when Scotty . . . when Scotty died?"

She shook her head, refusing to look at him. "I was not your responsibility."

"Not my responsibility?" he queried incredulously. "If not mine, then whose?"

"My own." With those words she raised her head. Pride had sustained her through the months in the Devil's Palace and the years before when her father's gambling had forced them first into straitened and finally destitute circumstances. Pride came to the fore now. The expression in her eyes made him drop his hands instantly.

He stepped back, glancing at the doorway, at the wet, black paving stones beneath their feet. "We can't talk here. Come back to the shop with me."

"I think not," she began.

"Oh, please." He laid his fingertips on her forearm. His plump red face curved and rounded like a cherub's as he smiled winningly. "The very least I can do is to buy you a cup of tea to restore your composure. Although I did not mean to, I fear I frightened you dreadfully."

She started to protest that she had not been frightened, merely annoyed. She needed nothing.

He read her thoughts. "Please, my dear."

With a weak smile, she capitulated. "Some tea

would be very nice."

"And scones. This tea shop serves real Scottish scones."

"Truly?" The thought of them brought their taste into her mouth and with it a lump in her throat. "In that case I accept with pleasure."

When they were seated at his table in the window, he leaned forward. "Why did you lie to me the day I thought I recognized you in that fearful place?" His eyes were black—both pupil and iris—peering out between the swollen folds of his eyelids. They had a piercing accusatory quality that made her shift in her seat.

Hastily she studied the swirling patterns she was creating with the cream in her cup of tea. "I have already told you. I have to work. You would have given away my identity, my age."

"You should not be there." He made a harsh gritting sound with his teeth. "You are an earl's daughter. You should be living in your ancestral home."

Her spoon rattled sharply in the saucer. "I have no ancestral home," she reminded him. The cup vibrated only slightly as she raised it to her mouth and took an experimental sip.

"You father would turn over in his grave."

This time she met him stare for stare, her eyes as hard as emeralds. "He put himself there. He has no right to criticize anything I do."

Surprise, too quick to be feigned, registered in his face. "What do you mean?"

"You have not heard," she told him flatly. "My father stuck his pistol in his mouth and shot himself."

"Dear God . . ."

"He left a note but it . . ." She hesitated. "The note was directed to you, but I destroyed it."

"My dear girl . . ." Her confession rocked him back in the chair.

"I was ashamed of its contents," she interrupted hastily. "He told you he was ill and was doing the decent thing."

"Then why—"

"He also admitted to being bankrupt. He left nothing to me. No word. Nothing but a blackened name and a drawer full of papers covered with pleas and threats for payments from all the poor tradesmen who supported him for the last years of his life."

Fitzwalter fumbled a kerchief from his breast pocket and wiped perspiration from his mouth and forehead. "I didn't know." He looked out the window at the sodden trees, the slippery pavement. A lorry drawn by heavy draft horses plodded by. Muddy water dripped from their manes and fetlocks. "I thought his heart stopped," he said at last.

"He mentioned his heart in the letter. It was his excuse for not staying alive to try to clean up the mess he left." She broke off a tiny end of scone and raised it to her mouth, then put it down again. She loved scones, but the recital of her father's end had taken her appetite.

Fitzwalter, too, seemed to have lost his appetite. "Scotty gone," he mourned. "And by his own hand."

Suddenly, she could no longer bear to sit there at that pretty table with the steam curling out of the spout of the teakettle and the warm stove radiating heat from the center of the room. She blotted her lips and laid down her napkin. "I must be going. Thank you for tea. It was delicious."

Her decision snapped him out of his reverie. "Wait." He reached across the table to catch her wrist. "You have eaten nothing at all. Eat. I insist. While you do, we will plan what to do."

She shook her head. "*We* will plan nothing. I must get back to work. I have a job. Honest employment in a comfortable warm house. The work is not too hard."

"It is not suitable. An unmarried lady alone in a man's house would be bad enough, but in that house." He shuddered. "The Devil's Palace."

"I am not alone. There is a cook and Mr. Mac-Adam, my father's butler, has gotten work there. I am not alone. And, of course, disguised as I am, no one bothers me."

His face darkened at her argument. "You are working for the man who ruined your father. Edward Sandron drove him to do the desperate deed that ended his life."

She shook her head. The walk had given her time to cool her temper. "My father gambled from the Land's End to John o'Groat's. His debts were legion. No single man ruined him."

"He gambled most here."

"I don't deny that he might have come to the Devil's Palace when he was in London. He might even have come every night. I cannot say about that. But he was home for many months of the year and still he gambled."

The black eyes gauged her narrowly. "You do not believe me." His voice was flat with accusation.

Her mouth tightened in disgust. His arguments all hinged on the personal. She regretted that she had come with him. "I have no reason not be believe you. I also have a job where I can be warm and dry."

"Warm and dry!" Fitzwalter's voice rose shrilly. "Indeed! Warm and dry in the Devil's Palace. Roasting and burning would be more like it. I tell you that den of iniquity was responsible for his death. Those men. Nash. Edward Sandron. Why he even calls himself Baal! The devil's own lieutenant. Those men drove your father to commit suicide."

She wavered then, remembering the reason she had come out for a walk. Again she heard her employer's confession that a young man had almost committed suicide today. "But what can I do?" she whispered.

"You could live with me."

A cold chill trickled down her spine. She was too intelligent not to understand the hidden implication of his statement. She shook her head swiftly. "I thank you very much, but I prefer to remain independent. I am young and strong. I can work for my living. There is no shame in *honest* work. Thank you, but I would prefer that." She started up, anxious to be away.

He reached across the table with the same square hands that had forced her into the archway. "Sit down," he commanded.

She looked around her wildly even as he overset her balance and she sat in the chair harder than she had intended. Across the street from the shop window, a man stared at the scene. She recognized him as Nash, Edward Sandron's publisher. Did she dare try to motion to him? Even as she raised her hand, he turned away and hurried on. With a sigh of disappointment, she subsided.

Fitzwalter reached across the table to shake her

wrists. "Listen to me. If you live in the Devil's Palace, you will be ruined sooner or later. You are a gently bred girl. My wife . . . my wife could tell you. She understands men's needs, my needs. She is an invalid. She has borne me several children and now feels that her obligation is done."

Cassandra stared at him with mounting horror. "Mr. Fitzwalter . . . you must not say these things to me."

"My dear, I have always loved you. As a child, of course. As a child. Your father was my best friend. As my mistress you could have many advantages. You could live in comfort. You would not have to work anymore. I would buy you a house, deed it to you. You could have spending money to buy clothes. Not these terrible old things." He rubbed his thumbs over the frayed white cuffs around her wrists.

"I don't want your money," she protested. "I don't want to live in a house that doesn't belong to me or where I have no right to be."

He hunched closer, his chest bunching up the tablecloth. His voice dropped to a husky whisper. "I can feel the pounding of your pulse beneath my thumbs. You are a young woman. Your lovely white skin would not have to be covered with gray powder and drawn lines. Your pretty red hair could hang down your back and over your white breasts."

"*Mr. Fitzwalter!*" With a violent movement she twisted her wrists from his grasp. Her elbow jostled against the table, causing the tea things to rattle and clink. The noise attracted the attention of the waiter, who looked sharply in their direction.

Fitzwalter shut his mouth abruptly when he saw the

man's look.

"I must leave," Cassandra gasped angrily. "Please do not bother to follow me. We have nothing more to say to one another." She rose and threaded her way between the empty tables.

The waiter held open the shop door. "Good day, ma'am."

Rising hastily, Fitzwalter threw down a couple of notes. In the street outside, he caught up to her. "Wait, Cassandra, I apologize."

"And so you should, but it is too late for apologies. I want nothing more to do with you."

"Good. Good." Stepping in front of her, he raised his hands in front of her face to applaud.

She shot him a disgusted look before she dodged around him and hurried on.

"You have passed the test," he called after her.

She did not look back.

He hurried to catch up with her. "I might have known you would. You were always a good girl."

She nodded her head shortly. "You have remembered that too late, Mr. Fitzwalter. I do not want your charity. Nor do I want to be paid for being"—she could feel the hot color rise in her cheeks—"your mistress."

"Your father would be proud of you."

"Would he?" She stopped in her tracks. Fitzwalter had to wheel around to face her. "Would he indeed? I don't know. He was a strange man in his last months. Often I caught him looking with a speculative eye at me. Perhaps he thought he would get little or nothing for me."

Fitzwalter's face was very still although redder color

suffused his plump cheeks. His gaze flickered.

She set her head to one side and studied him. "Is that where your offer stemmed from, Mr. Fitzwalter? Did my father offer me to you?"

He shrugged. "Let us discuss this painful subject no farther, Miss MacDaermond. Suffice it to say that you have passed the test. You may be one of us now and work for the betterment of all."

She looked beyond him at the skyline. A tiny ray of sun peeped beneath the lowering clouds just before it sank behind the horizon. She was heartbreakingly tired of the entire business. Her solitary walk to calm her spirit had resulted in a scene that had left her trembling and upset.

"I am going to walk on now, Mr. Fitzwalter," she told him coldly. "If you follow me, I shall go in the casino of the Devil's Palace and ask assistance from one of the men Mr. Sandron hires to handle men who are poor losers." Inwardly she trembled as she made her empty threat.

"Do you not want to help all those poor unfortunates who are inflicted with the same sickness your father was?" He raised his voice to carry after her.

She half turned. "I can do nothing if men gamble."

"Ah, but you can. You can help to rid England of all gambling casinos. Then the gamblers cannot gamble."

He came toward her, his smiling face round and cherubic again. "Become a member of the League for the Uplift of Moral Virtue."

"The League for the Uplift of Moral Virtue?"

"It is an organization I and others like me have formed to rid England of all distractions. You could be a great help to our organization. You actually work in the household of one of our targets."

She shook her head. "I am no spy. I won't take a man's money, live under his roof, and betray him to his enemies."

"I'm not asking you to spy." He came closer to her. "I may not ask you to do anything at all, except perhaps come to the meeting sometimes and testify to the need for uplift. From what you see you could—"

"A good housekeeper is discreet," she protested.

"At least say that you will give us moral support," he pleaded. "It would mean so much to me to know that my old friend's daughter was safe in the ranks of those who seek to uplift others." His face took on an exalted look.

She shifted uneasily from one foot to the other. What harm could agreeing do? His voice was light and soft. So an angel might have pleaded. "Oh, very well. But I will be of no use to you. My loyalty is to Mr. Sandron."

"Of course, my dear, of course. I would have expected that it would be."

"The damned League for the Uplift of Moral Virtue must have investigated our business," Nash announced, tapping the leather grip in his lap.

Sally tipped back her head and chuckled mirthlessly. "The League for the Uplift of Moral Virtue, Nash. Try another tale. No organization has a name like that."

"This one does," he retorted. "It seems to have a rather strong membership."

She snorted inelegantly. "I'll bet half of them sneak in here at least once a week."

He grinned. One pale eyebrow rose a quarter of an inch. "Where you can 'uplift' their — ahem — virtue, Sally, dear?"

"Swine," she spat. "No one nastier than Nash. A really sty for a mind."

"You were the one who said they sneaked in here. People who come in here to gamble don't bother to sneak. Only when they come in for other things . . ."

She started to her feet. "Shut yer trap, Nasty, or I'll shut it for y'."

Edward rapped on the desk with his knuckles. "If you two want to have this out, go elsewhere. I'm extremely bored. Everytime we try to talk some serious business, you go at each other."

Sally fastened her hands like claws around the arms of her chair. Her carefully whitened cheeks had heated until they glowed through the powder. "One day he's going to start something and I'm going to finish it."

Nash's eyelids drooped lazily. "Please, Lord, spare me," he intoned in an emotionless voice.

"Nash," Edward snapped. "Get on with it. You've upset her and we're both still here. Now explain what's going on that we need to get more money suddenly."

"Right-oh, tell us, y' bloomin' dandy," Sally called. Her tongue lanced out from between her teeth.

With a hard slap of leather, Nash set the grip on the floor in front of him and snapped it open. "I'll never understand how you became attached to that slut," he muttered to Edward through clenched teeth.

" 'E loves me cause I'm so refined," she sneered.

Edward motioned Sally to silence.

Nash, seeing he had no longer any way to delay, selected a paper and held it up ostentatiously, sighting it to the length of his arm, then taking out a pair of spectacles and hooking them over his ears. He peered over them at Edward. "Time's shrinking my arms," he chuckled ingratiatingly.

"Get on with it."

The smile thinned to a mirthless slit. "First on the list is seven thousand pounds invested in Bart's Limited. They were paying handsome dividends until the League began to protest them. As a result they have had to curtail some of their shipments and are consequently in need of capital."

"What is Bart's Limited?"

"A very fine little distillery in the Lowlands."

"Scotch whiskey?" Sally wanted to know. "Sounds good to me. People always like to drink."

"Exactly. This is merely a temporary situation. When all this Moral Uplift dies down, as it surely will, then they will return to full production. Unfortunately, they must pay their bills until such time." Nash shrugged. "The way of the world."

"How much would we need to contribute there?" Edward took out a sheet of paper and jotted down the name of the company and the amount invested with them.

"Oh, possibly ten percent. Say seven hundred fifty pounds."

Edward made a rude sound. "How many of those investments have you made for us?"

Nash ran his finger down the list. The paper rattled

nervously. "Twenty more or less."

"Fifteen thousand pounds!" Sally gasped at the amount.

"You have to think big, Ashtaroth, old gel," Nash snapped. "Leave the gutter mentality behind in the gutter. It takes money to make money." Reluctantly, he passed the paper over to Edward's outstretched hand.

"Railroad. Tramcar. Woollen mill. Florist shop."

"Some need almost nothing," Nash protested. "In fact some are turning a profit. That little florist shop, for instance."

"Electric Power and Light!" Edward snorted angrily at the next entry on the list. "What kind of investment is that?"

Nash stirred uncomfortably. "It's the new power of the future. Much cleaner and safer than gas."

"Than *that*," Sally hooted, pointing to the flickering flames in their glass chimneys. "Impossible!"

"Afraid you've got us a loser there, Nash," Edward agreed, sliding the list across to Sally, who took it but continued to glare at Nash.

Nash hunched his shoulders. "Some of these are gambles. I admit it." He reached for the list, but Sally held it out of reach, pretending to study it with great deliberation. He spread his hands. "We're all gamblers, after all."

"We gamble with the house odds," Edward reminded him drily. "That's really no gamble at all."

Sally leaned forward. Her face was only a couple of feet from Nash's. Her voice was as harsh as the lines that cut their paths through her face. "You're talking about the money I work night and day to get, Nash.

You throw it around as if it was water. If you end up cheating me out of it, I'll make sure you don't live to enjoy it."

He threw her an affronted look. "It's my money too, for God's sake, Ashtaroth. I stand to lose more than either of you if I make a bad investment."

"It doesn't mean so much to you, if you make a bad investment," she countered. "You've got more where that came from."

"Not so much that I can stand to throw it away." He sprang up and began to pace up and down the room. "For God's sake. You both agreed that I would do this since you knew nothing about it."

Edward regarded him steadily. "No one's claiming that you're dishonest, Nash. Sally and I just want you to understand the way we feel. We don't have anything to fall back on."

Nash swung round to face them both. "Don't you think I know that?" he exclaimed.

"Just don't forget it." The black-haired woman crumpled the paper into a ball and tossed at him. His face went carefully blank as it bounced off his lapel and fell to the floor. His eyelids drooped over his pale eyes. He struck a pose as he stared her up and down. "Well, if worse comes to worse, you can always get some old man to come through for us, Ashtaroth, old thing."

Hurling a virulent curse, she sprang to her feet and faced him, her chin thrust forward pugnaciously, her fists dug into her hips. "I'm no whore, Nash. I play a part the same as Baal and you do. But I don't whore."

While she was speaking, he pulled a cheroot from the case in his vest pocket. Rolling it back and forth between his thumb and fingers, he smiled his most unpleasant smile. "So you say."

"I say the truth. And don't you forget it. I'm no whore."

He walked past her to strike a match against the fireplace. "Might as well have the game as the name."

Abruptly, Edward Sandron pushed back his chair. "I think I'll take a long walk. You two don't need me here to referee this bout."

Nash turned hastily. "Oh, I say, my presence is required elsewhere, old chap. No need to leave your library. I'll be—" He choked on his words as the door closed behind the writer. Instead of turning back to face the infuriated woman, he made a grab for coat and stick, but Sally snatched them up and swung them behind her.

"Ashtaroth," he murmured, turning slowly and struggling to keep the irritation out of his voice. "Let me have my things."

Two bright spots of color blazed on her cheeks. "Not until you apologize for what you said."

He drew himself up tall. "I have no need to apologize."

Her breathing became harsher. She gave her head a violent shake. Pins flew from her long black hair. A loop of it slipped from its chignon. "Sure y' do, scutty. Y've insulted me, an' ain't nobody insults me an' gets away wiv it."

"Sally."

Flinging the expensive coat and stick to the floor, she lifted her doubled fist and danced toward him. "Apologize, y' damn pansy," she snarled.

He barely had time to raise his arms before she

flung herself at him, fists punching. He deflected the blows only by his superior strength of shoulder. "Ashtaroth, for God's sake!"

"Apologize," she panted.

"No."

One of her fists slipped in under his guard. A hard blow thudded into the hollow of his cheek.

"Ow!"

"That's got ye. An' there's more where that came from." She swung a powerhouse with all the length of her right arm, forgetting to keep her guard up with her list.

And Nash was ready for her. Blocking her blow neatly, he countered with the flat of his hand, a short hard slap. It cracked against her cheek and snapped her head on her shoulders. She did not cry out. Instead she danced back out of his reach. "Pansy bastard," she rasped.

"Bitch!" He followed her, cornering her.

She swung wildly, one more time. He slapped her again, this time with the other hand, reddening the other cheek. Her head snapped back against the wall behind her with a solid thud. Her vision blackened as streaks of light and color flashed across it.

Then his arms closed around her, pinioning her arms to her sides. "Sally, you damn fool," he snarled. He hugged her to him, so hard that her breath slid out hot against his neck. "You damn fool," he repeated.

She twisted frantically, trying to step on his feet. "No—"

He silenced her. His mouth came down hard on hers, arching the slender neck, tasting the sweet-salt blood where his blows had smashed the skin against her teeth. His tongue locked with hers, pushed until she gave back.

He heard her whimper, felt her body strain. Her breasts heaved for breath against his chest. And still her kissed her. Kissed her until her body went soft and still. Until she hung heavy in his arms.

Then his kiss gentled. His tongue touched the delicate membranes on the inside of her mouth, touched the sharp little teeth with caressing movements, until he heard her moan, tasted her passion rising. Then he withdrew.

She caught her breath in what might have been a sob. He could feel her breasts press harder against him as her laboring lungs expanded.

His lips moved on to kiss the corner of her mouth, to feel the heat rising from the blood close beneath the bruised skin of her cheek. He nuzzled that cheek before he moved on to her earlobe and then down the side of her throat.

When he had kissed her thoroughly, he raised his head at last. "I'm sorry, Ashtaroth," he murmured.

"You bloody—"

He kissed her again with great precision, using lips and tongue and body to chasten and subdue.

This time she could only manage to sigh his name.

At last, he set her away from him. His face was composed and still, without the slightest flicker of emotion. At the same time it was devoid of its usual cynicism. As she swayed where she stood, he retrieved his belongings. The coat he swung around his shoulders and adjusted it like a cape. From his pocket he extracted gray gloves and pulled them on with studied care, smoothing each finger. The stick he took from beneath his arm. He looked at her then. Lifting it, he slapped it smartly into the palm of his left hand before saluting her with it.

"Ta-ta, old gel. See you tonight."

He was away before she could move, and then her only movement was to totter unsteadily to a chair and sink into it. She pressed her palms against her hot cheeks and stared at the door.

Chapter Nine

"No matter how hard you struggle, my dear, you cannot escape these straps. Your will may be as strong as steel, but your strength is too frail, your body too fragile. And it is mine. Mine!"

Her voice had long exhausted itself in futile cries and pleas. Still Lady Beatrice shook her head. Her long silver-blonde hair swirled about her body as he chuckled diabolically.

His eyes never leaving her proud face, the duke slid his strong brown hand down the side of her neck and over her smooth white bosom. Beneath his questing fingers, it heaved and trembled, warm as a trapped bird.

"No!" she cried shrinking back to the limit of her bonds. "No! No!" But her voice was no more than a harsh rasp.

At the pain-filled sound, he scowled darkly. "Shall I lift the champagne to your lips, my dear? I fear your futile pleas have hurt your throat. Drink." He held the silver rim to her mouth allowing her to swallow thirstily. At the same time he stroked the firm softness of her breast. Beneath his fingers the roseate peak hardened and

158

throbbed.

She moaned and twisted gently in her bonds as . . .

His honest Scot's face grooved by lines of utmost seriousness, MacAdam tapped lightly at the door of his employer's library. When no answer came, he opened the door and peered in obsequiously. "Mr. Sandron . . ."

"For God's sake, MacAdam. Can't you see I'm busy?"

"I would not have disturbed you, sir" — MacAdam's apology was in his tone — "had this person not seemed most determined."

"Who is it, damn it?"

"A police inspector, sir."

A drop of ink blotted the manuscript. Edward stared at it incredulously, then muttered a curse. Angrily he recognized the unreasonably alarmed response his whole being made to authority. In his youth the mere sight of a blue uniform and helmet had been enough to send him scurrying into hiding in the crannies of whatever alley he had been pilfering. Now despite his middle class status, the old habits died hard.

Drawing a deep steadying breath, he replaced the pen in the inkwell. "Fetch me my coat, MacAdam. Then show him up."

"Mr. Sandron. I'm Inspector Revill." The heavyset man tucked his bowler military-fashion under his arm and extended his right hand.

Edward suppressed a wince at the force of the policeman's grip. Refusing to be intimidated, he clenched his jaw and counteracted the grip with answering pressure.

Their arms vibrating slightly, the two men stood toe to toe. Revill's eyes flickered, then narrowed as he took the measure of his opponent, noting his host's piercing eyes and superior height. He cleared his throat. "Sorry to interrupt your, ahem, your . . ."

"My writing," Edward supplied drily. "What can I do for you, Inspector?" He released the inspector's hand to step back. The backs of his thighs touched the edge of the desk. He teetered once, then stiffly righted himself. If he did not get hold of himself, he would be cowering at the man's feet in a couple of minutes.

Intently studying his host's face and the movement of his hands, Revill cleared his throat again. With just the tiniest smile of satisfaction at the younger man's discomfiture, he pulled a tiny notebook from the breast pocket of his coat.

"You are Mr. Edward Sandron, operator of the gambling casino called the, ahem, Devil's Palace?"

Edward felt the palms of his hands begin to sweat. "Yes." His voice croaked huskily.

The inspector studied the little notebook again. He looked up at Edward and then down at the page. "And you are also a writer of, ahem . . ."

"I am a writer," Edward managed the answer in his most normal voice.

Revill shot him a piercing glance before flipping over the page. "Right. And did you have in your employ one Georgie Parks, medium height, medium weight, brown eyes, gray hair with a bald spot on the crown?"

Edward nodded. "I employ a man named Parks as my valet. He fits that description. Come to think of it, I didn't know that his first name is Georgie."

The inspector's eyes were wide and clear although of a rather nondescript color. They scanned Sandron's face minutely as Revill turned the page. " 'Tisn't anymore. That is, he's dead."

Faint sensations of nausea and cold started deep in the pit of Edward's stomach. Suddenly the light in the room seemed dim as if his own dread had cast a gray shadow. His mouth thinned to a tight line as he stared at the inspector. "How did he die?" he asked at last.

Another tiny page flicked over. "Now that's the interesting thing. We had a little problem with the cause of death. First, tell me if you're familiar with an establishment called Mrs. Devaney's Bakery near the East Street Market?"

"No, can't say that I am. Should I be?"

"According to Mrs. Devaney's son, who now owns that bakery—Mrs. Devaney being deceased—he delivers a rather large order of aniseed cakes to this address every month. The man you identify as your valet was found dead in the alley behind the shop."

Edward shook his head. "I can't imagine why Parks should be there, Inspector. As it happens, I do know that an order of cakes is delivered to my house every month, but I didn't know where they came from. My business manager places the orders for all the comestibles that come into the club. My cook handles the personal shopping. To my knowledge, Parks had nothing to do with either."

The inspector appeared to consider. "Could be a

coincidence. But it's very unlikely. Very unlikely."

Edward shifted his weight uncertainly. "How did Parks die?" he asked again.

"Strange thing. The officer who found him didn't know. No wounds. No bruises or other marks on the body. He put down natural causes in his initial report. If the fella hadn't been dressed so nicely, the case would have probably ended right there. But he looked like a gentleman, don't you know? Or in this case a gentleman's gentleman." He looked around him at the library, taking in the numbers of books untidily shelved, the shuffle of papers on the desk, withal the air of order beneath a surface of chaos.

"I see." Edward waited but the inspector seemed to be making a mental inventory of the room's furnishings. "You were saying . . ." he prompted.

"Er, yes. Then there was some question when the coroner was looking over the body." Revill turned back a page in his book. "Coroner called in the forensic surgeon." He looked at Edward as if gauging a reaction. When none was evident, he continued. "No doubt about the cause of death. Poison."

"Poison?"

"Right. Terrible stuff. No doubt about it. The forensic man found traces of it in his stomach." He flipped the page in his notebook, turned the book upside down to read the back of the page. "Arsenic. Black arsenic it was. Terrible stuff. Terrible stuff."

"Arsenic?" The nausea in Edward's stomach intensified. He could feel cold sweat film his upper lip. "Black?"

"Maybe you'd better sit down, Mr. Sandron," Revill suggested.

Edward shook his head. "I'm all right. But I don't understand."

"Neither do we, Mr. Sandron. We hoped you might be able to give us some idea of how your valet might have got there and who might have killed him."

"Killed him?"

"Right. The only only other substances in his stomach were alcohol and traces of aniseed cakes."

Edward carefully lowered himself to the edge of his desk. His mind worked furiously as recalled the night of his illness. He had eaten aniseed cake and washed it down with wine. It was the same night Parks had disappeared. Parks often ate the same things he did. He had frequently invited the man for tea. Likewise, if he left something on a tray or was served something he did not eat, he did not doubt that Parks as did most other servants ate after his master. "Good lord!" he gasped.

"Had a thought, have you?" Revill stepped closer. Extracting the stub of a pencil from the same pocket, he turned to a blank page in his notebook.

Edward nodded. "What are the symptoms of arsenic poisoning?"

Revill looked disappointed. "Vomiting, pain, chills, fever," he supplied grudgingly.

"My symptoms exactly."

"When?"

"The same night Parks disappeared. I thought I was going to die."

The inspector gave him a skeptical look. "But you didn't."

Edward shook his head. "My housekeeper found me and helped me. I was almost paralyzed by that time."

The inspector did not exactly sniff the air like a hunting hound, but he lifted his chin and drew in a quick breath. "May I talk with her?"

Edward shrugged. "Of course." A tug on the bell-pull brought MacAdam, who went for Miss Fitch. "She can't have any information about Parks's death. She was the one who searched for him to help her get me into bed."

"Indeed?"

"Yes, she couldn't find him. The woman's not large. She had a devil of a time getting me up the stairs . . . Ah, Miss Fitch. Inspector, Miss Cassie Fitch."

Revill nodded, briefly preoccupied with writing down Sandron's information in his little notebook.

Edward gestured to a chair. "Please sit down, Miss Fitch."

Her eyebrows rose in unspoken question as Cassie looked from one to the other. Keeping her hands underneath her apron, she perched on the edge of the seat.

The inspector came to stand on her right. "Now, miss, tell us what you know about the disappearance of Mr. Sandron's valet Georgie Parks?"

She licked her lips. A tiny frisson of fear skittered down her spine.

"Inspector Revill is from Scotland Yard," Edward supplied.

She raised her hand to tug at the gray hair behind her ear. "I don't know anything, Inspector. I only know he's been gone for several weeks."

Revill bent over, pitching his voice directly to her right ear. "He's been lying in the morgue for several weeks, miss."

Cassie winced to the left, clasping the chair arm tightly with both hands.

"Inspector," Edward objected, "there's no need to frighten Miss Fitch."

Revill ignored him. "He was poisoned, Miss Fitch. Poison is a woman's weapon. Men don't use the stuff. Not manly. Not square. No, poison's a woman's weapon."

"Inspector!"

Cassie raised one trembling hand toward her forehead. "I—I—"

"When did you come to work here, Miss Fitch?" The policeman's face was only inches from hers.

"Two months ago."

Edward Sandron took a step forward, but the inspector waved him back. "And soon after your arrival both your employer and his manservant became deathly ill."

Cassie shook her head. Tears formed in the corners of her eyes; her lips trembled. "I didn't poison anyone."

"It looks bad for you, Miss Fitch." The detective rapped out the words like bullets. "Best make a clean breast of it all."

"But I didn't—"

"Denying it now will only make it go harder for you later."

"The cook is also new," Edward interrupted.

Revill snapped up. His scowl deepened. "Oh, he is, is he? And I suppose the butler is too?"

Edward hesitated, a tiny shadow of suspicion flickered in his mind. "Well, yes, he is. He came here after

Miss Fitch . . . at her recommendation."

Recognizing the change of tone, Revill pounced triumphantly on that piece of information. "At her recommendation . . ." He bent again, this time putting his hand on the back of her chair, hovering over her like a hawk ready to stoop. "I suppose you and he have pulled this before."

"What before?" Cassie's voice broke helplessly. "What do you mean?"

"You go ahead and poison the servant, then your husband gets his job."

"Mr. MacAdam is not my husband."

"So you say."

"It's true. I am *Miss* Cassie Ines Fitch." Her face was white to the lips. Watching her, Edward clenched his hands. He took a step forward, prepared to call a halt to the browbeating.

"Did this MacAdam move the body for you?"

Before Sandron's eyes, Cassie Fitch changed. Green fire flashed from the drowned depths of her eyes. "No!" Her head came up. Furiously, she sprang to her feet, almost oversetting the inspector, who had to draw back hastily. "Mr. MacAdam is completely innocent of all of this," she declared. "He was in Scotland when Mr. Parks disappeared." She looked at her employer for confirmation.

"She's right about that," Edward put in dutifully.

"Can he prove that?"

"I wrote letters to him after Mr. Parks left. I naturally assumed that Mr. Parks had decided to work elsewhere. I knew that Mr. Sandron needed servants. Mr. MacAdam had worked for me all my life." She caught herself as Edward's eyebrows rose at the information. "I mean he had worked with me. That is, we worked together at my last place of employment."

Both men were staring at her, their faces grim. Revill spoke first. "And where might that have been?"

"At Daerloch Castle. He was the butler to the Earl of Daerloch for years."

"Then why did he leave?"

"The earl died." Her voice faltered dangerously.

The Inspector made a note in his notebook. "The Earl of Daerloch, you say. Died. From natural causes?"

She clenched her hands at her side. "No. He committed suicide." Those words dispelled the righteous wrath from her body. She had not thought about her father's death in a long time. Suddenly it seemed horribly real and frighteningly recent. Her thoughts, nervous and confused by the inspector's questions, conjured up sights long-suppressed. In her mind's eye her father lay crumpled on the hearth. The depth of her loss hollowed the pit of her stomach.

Forgetting herself and her disguise entirely, she put a trembling hand to her mouth. She took one step toward Edward. Her eyes uttered an unspoken plea even as her legs trembled beneath her.

He caught her as she stumbled. His strong hands clasped her, supported her, guided her back to the chair. As his fingers molded the slender shoulders, he marveled again at how she had been able to get him up the stairs the night of the mass.

Once again in her chair, she drew a calming breath and let it out slowly, "Mr. MacAdam was the most loyal of men to the earl," she declared in a flat voice. "He and I have worked together for many years."

Inspector Revill made a note in his tiny notebook. "Someone murdered the valet," he insisted.

"Miss Fitch was with me after the Black Mass—"

"Black Mass!"

Edward turned away toward his desk with an off-hand gesture. "Not really a Black Mass exactly. Just theatrics." He backed up against the desk again and shrugged. "Just playacting. People having a little fun dressing up in costume, don't you know?"

"Not really." Revill's attention now concentrated on Edward. Miss Fitch was forgotten for the moment. "Perhaps you'd better tell me about it."

"Nothing to tell that would have any bearing on Parks's death. Just a little theatrics. I dress up like"—Edward felt his ears grow hot with embarrassment—"like a devil, and guests of the casino get involved in a little playacting."

Revill's mouth curled contemptuously at the corners. "Is that why this place is called the Devil's Palace?"

"It's just a show," Edward repeated for the third time.

"And these aniseed cakes, could they have a part in this *mass?*"

"They're part of the communion."

"And you got sick off them?"

"Yes."

"But you didn't die? Although your valet did."

The cynical tone of the inspector's voice irritated Cassie. "Mr. Sandron would have died. When I found him, he could scarcely move."

Revill pivoted. He swung his head from one to the other as if they surrounded him. His mouth opened, then snapped to after expelling a quick exasperated breath. "But you managed to get him up to bed?" He shot the question at the housekeeper. Before she could answer, he fired another at Edward. "I thought you said she was too frail to take care of you."

"She took care of me," Edward insisted. "She helped me to the bathroom, then helped me up the stairs to bed. I'd have died in that hallway without help. I was so sick I couldn't move."

"So, evidently, was the deceased," Revill inserted cynically. "But he was dumped in an alley and left to die."

Edward straightened. "So you've told us, Inspector, but you haven't told us anything else. I'm sorry that he's dead. He was an excellent valet. I shall miss him. If he got the arsenic here, then I am more sorry than I know how to say. Still you cannot be sure that he got the poison here. After all, he was found dead a long way from here."

"He was last seen alive here," Revill insisted.

"That may be. I don't doubt it, but the fact remains that neither I nor Miss Fitch can help you more than we have said. Mr. MacAdam can have absolutely no information at all since he was in Scotland when Parks disappeared."

"That's as may be, but we only have her word for that, don't we? And right after your loyal man disappears, her old friend appears. Don't that stretch the coincidence a bit far?" Tenacious as a bulldog, the detective directed the question at Cassie.

"But I knew that Mr. Sandron needed employees," she protested. In her desperation, she twisted her hands about the carved arms of her chair.

"And so I did." Edward confirmed. "I believe that will be enough, Inspector. You have no reason to continue to browbeat the woman."

"I'm here to get proof."

"In that case you have failed." Edward informed him in a chilly voice.

"I've just begun the investigation," Revill protested.

"Then, since we've told you all we know, perhaps you'd better be on your way conducting your investigation in other settings." Sandron crossed to the door and stood waiting.

Revill closed his tiny notebook, closing his blunt fingers over it and pressing it tightly in the heel of his hand. "You're taking a chance, Mr. Sandron," he warned. "You admitted to me that you almost died. And who's the one who found you?" The hand that held the notebook thrust toward Miss Fitch an index finger aimed like the barrel of a gun. "Her. That's who?"

Cassie shook her head agitatedly. "I did find him. I did. But I only wanted to help him. He's an employer. I owe him so much. So very much." Her control broke. The last word quavered and cracked.

Revill, scenting a possible revelation, plunged on. Thrusting the notebook back into his pocket, he spread his hands. "I'm sure your employer's a very generous man. If you gave him a mild dose of arsenic and nursed him back to health, he might be even more generous than he is. You might even keep him crippled with it, so you and the butler could run the household while he lies a helpless invalid at your mercy."

"No. For God's sake, no."

"But you had to get rid of the valet. He'd throw a spoke into your wheel. While you take care of the master, MacAdam, him that everyone believes is still in Scotland, comes down on the quiet and poisons the valet. Gets the valet to drink and eat with him, most likely. Then dumps his body in an alley in a cheap neighborhood. All neat and tidy. With a little luck no one finds it." Revill's thick jowls had darkened with passion as he fairly spat out the words at the shuddering housekeeper. "Am I right? Confess. I'll see you get a light sentence. MacAdam did the murder. Right?"

Edward Sandron snapped out of his trance. "That will do, Inspector. Miss Fitch is not under arrest. Leave her alone."

"Mr. Sandron, you don't understand—"

"I understand that all that you have said is mere speculation. You should have been the fiction writer, not me. You found the body of my valet in an alley miles from here. Instead of combing the alley for witnesses, you come back here and accuse my employees, one of whom saved my life, the other of whom was in Scotland." Determined to end the unpleasant scene, he walked to the door and opened it.

The inspector's mouth snapped closed like a sprung trap. He stared first at the man, then back at the woman. His frustration permeated the charged atmosphere. At last he let out his breath in a sigh. "You're taking a chance, Mr. Sandron," he counseled sorrowfully.

Edward blinked at the sudden change in attitude. Then his mouth twitched at the corners. Revill was obviously a master player. As another actor of sorts, Baal paid respect to the man for his craft. "My chance, Inspector." He inclined his head slightly.

Revill positioned his hat carefully on his head. At the door, he measured Sandron. "You're the one in danger here. Not Parks. Parks got in the way. He saw something, overheard something, learned too much." He paused.

Edward remained silent.

The policeman shrugged. "Good day to you, sir." He ignored the frightened woman clinging to the chair.

When his footsteps had faded down the hall, Edward crossed to his desk. Opening a small box, he extracted a cigarette. As a matter of course, he did not smoke them regularly. He kept them there for Ashtaroth and for Nash. Today, he could think of nothing else to do with his shaking hands. He lighted it and dragged the smoke into his lungs, waiting for its calming influence to take hold.

As an afterthought he held out the box to Miss Fitch. "Care for one?"

She shook her head warily. "I'd best leave."

"A good idea. Go back to your room and rest."

She kept her head down. Her hands twisted around the chair arms. "I mean leave."

He stared at her. "Where would you go?"

"I'd find work. You'd give me a reference, wouldn't you?"

Taking another drag on the cigarette, he coughed slightly and stubbed it out in the little brass tray beside the box. He shook his head. "I'd never give a reference to someone who left on such short notice." He smiled suddenly. " 'Specially some 'un who'd skip off like 'at from a copper."

Her head snapped up. Frowning, she stared at him, unable to believe the accent he had adopted so easily. "I don't understand."

He crossed the room to her and held out his hands.

Her own were ice cold as she placed them in his and allowed herself to be drawn to her feet. "Miss Fitch, I don't have any use for the police. Surely you must have realized that the Devil's Palace as well as its operators don't work within the limits of the law."

"But—"

"This place is a gambling casino, Miss Fitch. While gambling in itself is not against the law, it comes under considerable fire from various do-gooder groups. Worse than that. On the side we do a little amateur theatricals to please some of the bizarre tastes of the guests. Once in a while we give a little costume party where everyone does what he pleases protected by the anonymity of masks."

As he spoke to her, he drew her toward the door. She was so small and he so tall. In a natural gesture of comfort, he put his arm around her shoulders. Cassie felt the warmth of his body through his clothes. The feeling made her skin prickle at the same time that her trembling eased.

He still held her right hand in his. Now his thumb rubbed over the back of it. "You've had a bad experience this morning. Your hand is cold as ice."

She sighed. "No one has ever talked to me the way he did."

"Coppers are good at that," he observed drily. "It's their stock and trade. And more besides. I've seen them . . ." His hand tightened around her, drawing her closer to his body.

Suddenly, he was all around her. His strength, his heat, his scent. Her head swam dizzily with the sudden memory of that night with his warm hands caressing her body, parting her thighs, probing. His naked body pressed tightly against her own, the clean smoothness of the skin of his flanks contrasted with the roughness of the hair on his chest. And the pleasure he had brought her cuddling against him almost as he was cuddling her now.

Shameful, exciting memories stirred too. Of pain and pleasure intermingled. When she had pulled his hair, he had bitten her in instant savage retribution, then his mouth had laved the hurt with exquisite sensitivity until it had begun to ache again, but in a different way.

As she recalled that way, a warm languorous feeling seemed to settle at the tops of her thighs. His hands had touched her there, cupped her buttocks, and stroked her in the most embarrassing places. As she felt the heated blush rising in her cheeks, she looked up hastily.

He was looking down at her, a strange expression on his face. A shudder ran through her. Did he pierce her disguise? What condition must her makeup be in? In her hysterical denials to the policeman, she had wept. The tears were still damp on her cheeks.

"I . . ." she began. Her voice failed her. Her heart sped up until she was certain he could feel it pounding against his own rib cage. "I'll go lie down for a few minutes, then be about my duties."

"Do that," he replied, his voice oddly harsh.

She slipped out of his arms and closed the door behind her.

He turned around, running his hand through his hair. What was wrong with him? He had actually been aroused by his proximity to that aged housekeeper. Alone at last, he adjusted his clothing, which had an unaccustomed tightness over his loins.

He had responded to her distress in such a natural way, placing an arm around her shoulder, offering comfort as he would do for any old lady. Then something had hit him. Her scent, her warmth, the shape of her.

He cursed mildly as he lighted another cigarette, noting that his fingers fumbled with the small cylinders and the tiny pieces of wood. A good thing the All Hallows' Eve masque was next week. He must be more desperate for a woman than he had ever been before. It came of working too hard. He really should take more time off for the simpler pleasures.

Chapter Ten

"Those arrogant swine! Those stupid, blundering, insolent, arrogant swine!"

"Who?"

Nash was panting, his face livid with anger, his eyes flashing blue fire. Edward leaned back in his chair amazed at the extraordinary sight. His publisher was a man who normally maintained an appearance of ennui as a point of honor. "The police. Damn them!"

Edward slumped forward, forearms resting on his desk. Again he felt the thrill of fear that he could not suppress. "What have they done?"

"They've been all over the casino. Disturbed everyone. Everything. Customers positively fogged out of there. It'll be days! Days before they come back." Nash fairly spat the words as he paced swiftly up and down the room. He had pushed his coat back and thrust his hands into his trouser pockets, where he jingled his coins and keys furiously.

Edward hunched his shoulders protectively. "Did they find anything?"

Nash stopped short in front of the desk. "No." He flung his fists over his head in a violent gesture. "No, damn them. That is, I don't think they found anything. What would they be looking for?"

"Arsenic!"

"Arsenic?"

"Black arsenic. It was found in Parks's stomach."

The publisher thrust his hands back into his pockets. "Good lord," he breathed. His air of grievance evaporated.

"Exactly. An Inspector Revill from police headquarters came here this morning. Told me all about it. Seems Parks's body was found in the alley behind Mrs. Devaney's bakery. Sound familiar?" Edward inquired nastily. His black eyes searched Nash's face.

The publisher gaped in what was obviously unfeigned surprise. "Perhaps you'd better tell me what the hell is going on," he demanded.

Edward shrugged. "Parks is dead," he said unnecessarily.

"Who is — was — Parks?" Nash flung himself into a chair and pressed his fingertips together in a steeple before his nose.

"Parks was my valet. My manservant. Surely you remember him? He's been missing since the night I got so sick."

"Can't say that I do, old chap. Noticed an old woman one time. Looked like she's been dead at least a dozen days and dug up. But not a manservant." Nash closed his eyes as if trying to picture the servants in his mind. When he opened his eyes, he tilted all eight fingertips in Edward's direction. "And the police think he was deliberately poisoned. By you?"

Edward nodded glumly. "Probably thought so at first. But I told them I had had a dose of the same stuff."

The publisher nodded slowly. "So now whom do they suspect?"

Edward stirred uncomfortably, unwilling to name Miss Fitch. "My new staff."

Nash closed his eyes, again conjuring a picture of Mr. MacAdam and Miss Fitch in his mind's eye. His mouth twitched, he chuckled, then threw back his head and laughed. "Oh, that's rich. Rich and famous." He flung up his hands. "Lord, thank you for the incredible intelligence of the London law enforcement officials."

"Nash," Edward chided wearily, "this is no laughing matter."

"Sorry to contradict you, but it is, old chap. Don't you see? Your valet disappears. Later found poisoned. Who did it? The servants you hired to fill his position."

Nash waved his hands in the air delightedly. "Makes perfect sense to me. Must happen all over London all the time. Perfect answer to personal unemployment problem. Man wants job. Poisons the man who has it. Never has a question in his mind but that he'll be hired over all other applicants for the vacated job. Surprised employment agencies don't do it as a matter of course. So many more fees that way." He sprang up and began to pace again, laughing to himself. "Silliest damn thing I've ever heard."

Edward allowed himself a thin smile as he stretched his neck. At the base of his skull, the tension eased slightly. Put in that frame, the whole thing sounded more than ridiculous. He could dismiss the tiny niggling doubt the inspector had managed to plant in his mind about Miss Fitch and Mr. MacAdam. Of course, it was silly. He shook his head, still chuckling with relief.

Suddenly, Nash whirled with a great shout of anger. "But!" he thundered. "That still leaves us with the problem of no customers in the casino. Damn! Just when we need extra money, we have a lot of bad nights. Damn!"

"Nash." Edward smiled. "Settle down. You're letting this excite you too much. You know they'll be back in a day or two. They can't stay away from the excitement for very long. And certainly not everyone was run off. Only the most timid or the most guilt-ridden ducked out. Most of our customers'll regard it as a lark anyway. Some of them are probably back already."

His words struck the right note with the publisher. As if he had donned a cloak, the man shrugged into his cynical pose. "You know you're right, old chap," he murmured. "Got myself all lathered up for nothing. Must be getting old."

"Or worried about money?" Edward suggested.

Nash's left eyebrow rose sharply. "That's probably it. Worried about money." He heaved an exaggerated sigh. "Ah, yes. Money has changed the personality of many a ne'er-do-well like m'self. Made him forget himself and the correct proportions of things."

"Glad you're back in form again."

Straightening his embroidered waistcoat and shooting his cuffs, Nash strolled to the door. "We'll doubtless make up most of the loss at the Devil's Masquerade on All Hallows'. Understand lots of people have had costumes made especially for the party. Should be quite something." His eyelids drooped. "Can't imagine what I became so excited about," were his parting words.

Edward chuckled to himself. Rising from his desk, he stretched his tense back and shoulders, then strolled to the window. The rain of the night before had washed the sky to a clear blue. A warm autumn sun managed to raised a gentle mist as it evaporated from the pavement. Suddenly, he found the day much too nice to pass inside. A quick stroll through the park would be just the ticket to ease the lingering traces of his visit from Inspector Revill.

Turning away from the window, he surveyed his library with inordinate pleasure. The advent of the police inspector followed by the investigation downstairs had cast a pall over him. He shuddered as his imagination conjured a great threatening cloud suspended above him and all he had managed to acquire. He closed his eyes, then opened them. The familiar books were all around him; the mahogany desk was still littered with his work. Like him, they had escaped again.

Yes, everything appeared as always, yet it was better. Since Miss Fitch had come into his life, the place was sparkling clean. The chaos of his creative activity no longer operated above a thick layer of dust. With surprising intelligence and sensitivity, his housekeeper had set about cleaning his library when he was out of it. Everything she picked up to dust, she replaced in exactly the same position. Everything she took away to polish, she restored to its former luster before replacing it. He fancied that he worked better in those surroundings.

He smiled, relieved to find that he no longer entertained the slightest suspicion about Miss Fitch. Nash's good sense had reduced the inspector's accusation to the realm of the impossible. He could relax in perfect charity with the world.

Humming tunelessly, he exchanged his slippers and velvet jacket for a wool sack coat and jockey boots. Donning a top hat, he strolled down the alley and out into the sunshine of Piccadilly.

Both the Green Park and St. James Park awaited him. He could see the tops of their trees as well as glimpses of green between the buildings as he walked along. A stroll was exactly what he needed. He would walk along the Green Park up the Mall to Trafalgar Square. Perhaps he would drop in at his favorite bookseller. His library could always use another volume. Perhaps a history or a new novel?

The streets were relatively deserted at this time of day. Up ahead of him, he caught a sight of a woman in a bonnet and dark unfashionable dress. The very lack of fashion of the garment was what drew his eyes to it. It lacked the popular bustle, thrust out behind it. Instead the woman's hips, uncamouflaged, swayed seductively from side to side.

A tiny smile lifted the corners of Edward's mouth as he strolled along. The waist was willowy slim, the frame delicate. The shoulders were square, the spine straight. Indeed her entire figure except the limbs was clearly outlined.

Idly, he began to speculate on her appearance. Undoubtedly her face would be fair with a delicate blush in her cheeks. Such an attractive, slender figure would have a sculptured bone structure.

His curiosity increased as he enjoyed his picture of the unknown woman. The black bonnet topping the ensemble completely screened the wearer's head. She was young, he decided. Her figure and the lithe rhythm of her walk identified her as a young woman. Her stride was firm and springy as she walked briskly along ahead of him.

Edward increased his pace. What would she do if he caught up to her? Greeted her? Would she be afraid? Would she be offended? Probably a combination of the two, he reckoned. She was surely no prostitute.

Coincidentally, a couple of·the "soiled doves" could be seen entering the Burlington Arcade. Their dresses made of the brightest moiré taffeta covered enormous bustles, projecting fully twelve inches from the waist in back. Likewise, the feathers on their bonnets, dyed to match their dresses, danced wildly about their faces in the breeze.

No, the woman ahead of him was no prostitute.

Suddenly, he determined to catch up to her. He could almost count the times on the fingers of one hand that a young woman had smiled at him out of a fresh face bare of makeup. Perhaps that lack explained his unsettling attraction to Miss Fitch. She probably looked much prettier and younger that she really was because she was innocent and pure. The whores on the steps of the Burlington Arcade and the women who came to play at the Devil's Palace at night, one and all, covered their faces with makeup. And one and all they had the same wrinkled, burned-out look. Their eyes looked dull and lifeless.

Taking a deep breath, he extended his pace. He

would at least look into her face beneath the broad brim of the bonnet. No one could object to his looking.

Cassandra MacDaermond stared out the window of her tiny room. Despite the chill, she had opened it for the first time since she had come to the Devil's Palace. Arms folded on the sill, she drank in the cool afternoon air. Scotland had never seemed so remote as now. The last walk when she had been accosted by Fitzwalter had alarmed her, so she had not been out of the house since. Now she felt she would suffocate if she did not get away.

Staring up at the patch of blue sky she could see between the houses, she sighed eloquently. No, she could not bear to remain in this room a minute longer. She was not a prisoner after all. Since her employment she had taken no time off. Her spirit cried out within her. Surely, she could at least take a walk.

Green trees above the tops of the houses bespoke some kind of a park to the west. Tying her bonnet firmly under her chin, she stepped out into the alley. Once out on Piccadilly, she kept her eyes on the tops of the buildings, beckoned onward by the nodding greenery of the trees.

She heard footsteps behind her, a man's by the length of the stride and the speed at which they approached. She did not look around, expecting that he would walk by. He did so, but turned and looked at her full on.

"Miss Fitch!"

"Mr. Sandron!" Immediately, she ducked her head in alarm.

"I didn't recognize you from the back," he began lamely, then realized his statement would not explain why he had turned around. "That is, I didn't know it was you, but I knew that you weren't. . ." He faltered to a stop. he could not very well say that he had turned around and spoken to her because he knew she wasn't a prostitute.

"I was just out for a walk," she replied nervously, as though he had demanded an explanation. "I haven't taken any time off since I've been working for you."

He stared at her bemused, again taking in the slender figure that seemed to belie the gray hair that framed her lined face. "You are entitled to an afternoon a week, Miss Fitch, more if you like, so long as your work is performed smoothly."

She nodded, keeping her head turned slightly to one side. "I just thought I'd walk to those trees over there. Perhaps there's a park there."

He did not bother to look over his shoulder. "There is indeed. Two parks as a matter of fact." He did not move but continued to stare at her face.

She fumbled in her handbag for a handkerchief, found it, and raised it to her cheek. 'I. . .On the other hand, perhaps I'd better go back to the house. It is rather warm today." In the act of turning away from him, she felt his hand on her arm.

"No. There's no need for you to go back so soon." When he felt her stop, he instantly dropped her arm. "That is. . . why not continue our walk together?"

"I'm your housekeeper, sir."

He looked around him with exaggerated secretiveness. "I won't tell a soul, and since you don't wear a sign around your neck, who's to know?"

"But, sir. . ."

He cast a look at the sky overhead, then smiled ingenuously. "Come on. We can't depend on this sort of weather lasting in October."

Run, her brain counseled. Make any excuse, but leave him. But he doffed his hat and bowed gracefully. Despite her better judgment, she found herself placing her hand lightly on his forearm and allowing him to lead her down the street.

As they entered the park, the wind through the wet trees cooled them. The smell of rain-washed grass pricked sharply at her senses too long shut within the walls of the house on Regent Street. Suddenly, her eyes brimmed with tears as her senses evoked an overwhelming wave of nostalgia.

Scotland! Daerloch! All that she had held dear for most of her life. All she had lost, swept away from her. She wanted to cry bitterly. She wanted to do worse than cry. She wanted to strike and scream. She wanted to curse and rant at the faceless mass of people who had taken her fortune at the same time they had taken her father's. She was the innocent party here deprived of home and hope, of youth and gaity.

"Miss Fitch?" The man at her side was bending, staring into her face, which had gone quite white. "Miss Fitch?"

"Oh, sorry, sir. I do apologize." She blinked rapidly. Her lips felt strangely stiff as she spread them in the least of smiles.

"May I get you a sweet?" A seller of confectionery

pushed a small cart along the way.

She shook her head.

"Please. I insist."

She smiled. "Perhaps a peppermint then."

He bought mixed candies, hard bright sugar bits, in orange, yellow, red, and green. Holding the bag out, he smiled and watched her select the green, her face serious in her decision. She certainly did not look like an old woman despite her sallow skin and gray hair.

He offered his arm again for them to walk along together in companionable silence. The oppression of the Devil's Palace lifted and lightened.

As her senses cleared, Cassandra found herself becoming aware of Sandron's warm arm beneath her hand. His upper arm brushed against her shoulder. She could feel a blush starting in her cheeks at the memory of his arm and hand in much more intimate contact with her body. She took a deep breath, but that served only to make her aware of her nipples tingling as they rasped slightly against the fabric of her chemise.

She let her breath out slowly. "I must return, sir," she said, taking her arm from his.

He had been smiling at a child rolling a hoop toward them on the footpath. Abruptly, his smile faded. He shook his head. "I'm your employer. I haven't set a time for you to return."

She kept her tucked head down, so that all he could see was the shake of her black bonnet. "I have duties, sir. I must return and do them, otherwise you'll be uncomfortable tonight. And then you'll be angry with me and with yourself."

"No, I—"

But she was gone. Hurrying away, her skirts swinging with the rhythm of her walk, her spine straight, her shoulders back.

He stared after her. She had no call to be afraid of him, and yet she seemed to be. He shrugged. Probably the investigation had upset her, but he certainly did not blame her for that. Indeed, he admired her for defending her friend MacAdam. He wondered about them. Despite a seeming diversity in their ages, they seemed devoted. Perhaps they were more than friends.

He turned away to star unseeingly at a patch of autumn crocuses. Why did that thought bother him?

"Sinners! Welcome to Hell!" With real enthusiasm Baal swirled the brilliant crimson satin over the glittering heads of the masquers. Hands outstretched to their full length, he swirled the cloak again before letting it settle at his sides. His black eyes sparkled and the white horns at his temples gleamed like molten silver.

Unlike the sea of people before him, he wore his regular costume, his suit of formal midnight black. In place of his usual cloak, however, he had donned a full-length crimson cloak with collar that stood about his head like a high ruff, its points raising at five intervals like the web of a spider.

"You do me good tonight," he called. "All dressed in your best, I see. Each revealing the person he would most like to be. And an evil lot they are." He set hands on hips and laughed theatrically. The crowd led by several waiters joined him.

Abruptly he stopped his laugh and swept the room with a long arm, his index fingers pointing in air of accusation and command. "So tonight until dawn we leave our masques on. No unmasking tonight. Everyone is what he has secretly desired to be."

The assemblage cheered noisily.

Ashtaroth came forward to the foot of the stairs, dressed not in her usual black dress but a dress of Egyptian cotton so sheer that the outline of her nipples and the dimple of her naval showed plainly through the fabric. Around her brow was a crown of gold with cobra and falcon faithfully represented. From her hips at back and front dropped panels of jeweled fabric that partially concealed the tops of her thighs and the curve of her buttocks. About her ankles and upper arms were bracelets shaped like snakes. Her feet were bare except for jeweled sandals.

Because of a concealing cloak, her costume had drawn no comment before. But as Baal swept the room with his commanding finger, she stripped her covering away to hand it to one of the blackamoor attendants. Now her shadowy near-nudity drew first gasps and then loud raucous comments.

She remained unperturbed. Her pale skin and heavily painted eyelids might have been the masque of a graven image. Seemingly oblivious to the sensation she was causing, she moved to the foot of the stairs. There she waited calmly to place her hand on his arm.

"So your secret desire is to be Cleopatra, Queen of Egypt?" he jibed out of the side of his mouth.

She shrugged one smooth shoulder. "At least it's a

step up from the Devil."

A King Charles II pranced by on red high heels. His curled wig hung down his chest like huge spaniel ears. He laughed uproariously as he palpated the ample breast of a woman in peasant blouse and plaid skirt.

"Great party, Baal." The woman, who only vaguely recalled Flora MacDonald, gurgled as she slapped coyly at her escort's hand.

"Oh, yes. Great party," Charles called.

A headsman bare to the waist, his head completely covered by a black hood, stood in the doorway of one of the private card rooms. He held his axe across his thighs. Queen Mary Stuart in her red petticoat tugged at his arm. "Come on, Drexie. You don't want to play cards tonight. They're tuning up the orchestra for the dance. Have something to drink, Drexie."

She gestured to a passing demon, who immediately brought a silver tray of glasses each filled with dark ruby port.

A man in dark Italian velvets bowed low to Ashtaroth and extended his arm. His face was darkened beneath a dark curly wig. *"Madonna."*

"Nash," she breathed, recognizing the pale blue eyes, so startling in the darkened face.

"Caesare Borgia, old gel." Nash's snide voice sounded odd coming from the Italian face.

She studied him, her head tilted to one side. With the pale freckles concealed beneath the dark makeup and the dark curly wig lending width to his thin face, Nash looked almost handsome. She blinked in astonishment.

His lips spread over his sharp teeth in a mirthless

answering smile. "Cleo, old gel, I've always wanted to see more of you. Now I have the chance. To see 'more' of you, that is." He leered suggestively at her unencumbered breasts.

She moved uncomfortably. "Nash . . ."

Edward disengaged his arm from under her long red nails. "If you two are going to fight, I don't want to be in the vicinity. Nash, I'd advise you to let well enough alone. Sally is dressed in a costume; you are dressed in costume. All around us people are dressed in costume. Let's remember that we work here."

"Why, Baal, old chap, I never have the least intention of stirring up trouble. I was merely on the verge of complimenting Miss Atkins on her choice of dress. So startling. Although a bit chilly." Nash laughed gently. His fingertips trailed up Ashtaroth's arm to her shoulder, then down across her back. Beneath his sensitive fingers, the smooth skin prickled.

His pale eyes stared into her own dark ones, reading there her anger and something more. When he dropped his eyes to her full breasts, the nipples were stiff, clearly turgid through the thin cotton. His eyelids drooped. "Ashtaroth, old gel, or is it Cleopatra? You look superb."

"I'll kill you for this," she gritted back.

"So delighted to know my enemy." His hand slid around her upper arm, coming in contact with the side of her breast. Purposefully he moved his fingers, pressing their knuckles into her soft flesh. "What a lovely enemy it is," he declared. He smiled maliciously, his teeth very white in a vulpine smile.

Her breath caught in her throat. "Damn you!"

She tried to lift her arm to twist it out of his grasp,

but his hand clamped tightly. "Lovely breasts, my gel. Beautiful, soft, yet firm." His knuckles rubbed suggestively again. "You really do have a superb figure." He turned her to survey the room. "I cannot think of another woman here who has anything to compare with yours."

Liquid warmth curled low in her belly. He was arousing her deliberately, torturing her with her own sensuality. Though she hated him with all her heart, she could not control the traitorous impulses of her body. She swayed slightly, her thighs pressing together beneath the apron of bejeweled fabric.

"Are you faint, Cleopatra?" he inquired maliciously. "Shall I conduct you to some private chamber where you can . . . lie down."

"Damn you, Nash. Let me go." Her face was pale except for two bright spots of color on her cheekbones. Her breath hissed between her bared teeth. Her hands clenched, burying the nails in the soft flesh of her palm. If she had possessed a dagger, she would have thrust it into his heart.

He shrugged. "Not before I steal a kiss, Egypt." His other hand cupped her shoulder. He pulled her about to face him. He stared into her eyes. The light from the gas-o-lier made them luminous as passion which she could not control brought tears to them. His sardonic grin faded as he studied her. Her anger stirred him in a way he did not understand. He was tempted to let her go. Then his eyes dropped to her breasts, to the slender waist, to the swell of her thighs clearly outlined beneath the sheer fabric.

Conscious of his eyes as if he had touched her, she whimpered faintly. Desire tightened the muscles of her belly until she shuddered.

Enjoying the tension, he moved closer, enveloping her with his heat. In ruthless fascination he observed his own invasion and conquest of her senses. "One kiss, Cleopatra," he murmured. "I promise you, I am no asp."

Around them, Genghis Khan, Diane de Poitiers, Nicolo Machiavelli, and Marie de Medici laughed uproariously and pointed as Sally Atkins of Cheapside flamed helplessly in Trevor Nash's impassioned embrace.

Cassandra decided that no one was paying any particular attention to the stage. She could step from behind the proscenium arch and stroll unhurriedly down the steps. The few who saw her would probably think she had merely been confused, or curious, or was returning from an assignation. They would never believe that she was slipping into the party from the back door.

She touched the edge of the black mask with cold fingers. Besides the traditional covering shape, it had a black lace veil gathered over the lower half of her face. When it was in place, she had stared at herself for long minutes in the mirror. Miss Fitch had completely disappeared. No one would even think about the sedate middle-aged housekeeper, much less associate her with the creature in the elaborate emerald brocade.

She had washed her red hair and brushed it until it shone. The sides she had braided into a little coronet across her crown, but the back she had left loose, long and wavy, almost to her waist. The style was wrong. Indeed, it was no style at all and totally inappropriate with the beautiful formal dress. But she did not know how to dress her own hair. Another failing of her pampered youth that came back to haunt her. How could she have had so little training in the business of living an independent life?

One step. Two. Alexander the Great in his battle regalia accompanied by Aphrodite in diaphanous Greek chiton reeled toward her. In stepping forward to avoid their lurching passage, she moved easily into the crowd.

To her relief no one paid the slightest attention to her since the masquers were comprised of almost as many lone figures as couples. A demon eeled by with a tray of champagne. Determinedly, she accepted a glass and took a generous swallow.

The musicians struck the first chords of the dance, a Viennese waltz, and a general movement of the crowd cleared the dance floor in front of the stage. Several couples began to dance immediately. Hastily, she backed against the wall opposite the stage, where she could watch among the others.

So far, so good. She took another swallow of champagne. And then another. Her glass was empty. She looked at it in astonishment. These little stemmed glasses certainly did not hold much. A demon materialized at her side and she exchanged the empty glass for a full one.

Feeling somewhat confident that she would not be discovered, she began to look around her. The brilliance of the costumes, the dazzling display of light and movement beneath the flickering gas-o-lier made her feel almost dizzy.

She took another sip of champagne. How glad she was she had dared to come! All her fears seemed groundless now that she was actually here among the masquers. No one would even notice her. She could move among them all evening, delight in the glorious costumes, eat the delicious food, drink the champagne. The rhythm of the music caught her. She lifted her glass in a toast to her own daring and smiled over the rim of her glass.

The idea to attend had occurred to her as she hurried home from the park. The taste of freedom coupled with the courtesy of Edward Sandron had reminded her focibly of what she had been. Her father's fortune had been lost before she had been introduced to society. He had had barely enough money to buy simple day dresses, much less a ball gown. The idea of a debut had been unthinkable with creditors camping on the doorstep.

Now there would never be a chance for any of that. The Earl of Daerloch's daughter was no more. But these people did not know her. Probably some were as deeply in debt as her father had been. With that thought in mind, she had convinced herself that she might mingle in their midst and enjoy if only for the one time a gala ball. Feeling like Cinderella, she had cast aside her black dress and gray wig.

She did not seek a prince, she told herself sternly. She only came for the festivities. Long before the dawn, she would be snug in her bed, the brilliant green brocade hung away. But for just a few hours she would do something more than imagine.

More couples were joining the whirling dancers.

The space along the wall became more crowded. At a leisurely pace that would draw no attention to herself, she moved in the direction of an archway. The music in her ears was familiar. Unconsciously, she began to hum, marking time gently with her glass. A woman gave a screech of laughter behind her. She glanced aside, hoping to find the source of the merriment.

Only for a second, but out of the crowd a figure loomed before her. A stiff white shirtfront dazzled her eyes in the V of a formal black evening jacket and vest. Her head tilted back on her shoulders to look up into the face of the man blocking her way.

"Where did you come from?" asked Baal.

Chapter Eleven

Cassandra clutched the stem of the champagne glass with both hands. While she did not actually shrink back, she could feel her legs tremble beneath the emerald green skirt. "I, er, that is, we . . ." Her breath hissed out between her lips as her brain refused to function.

Baal regarded her, one saturnine eyebrow quirked upward toward the silvery lock of hair. His black eyes bored into her until she could not have told him her name if she had been of a mind to. In his full panoply he might very well have been the devil himself. At that instant a passing masquer jostled against her. Shifting her weight from one foot to another, she took another swallow of champagne and shrugged helplessly.

He did not ask again. Instead he reached out with infinite grace to lift a lock of hair from her bare shoulder. "I don't remember ever seeing hair this color among my guests," he mused.

Her skin tingled where his fingers touched. Her quick backward step tugged the lock from his fingers as she pretended to look around for a partner. "I came with, er, Percy," she murmured. "But somehow we got separated. I'd better see where he's gotten to. If you'll excuse me."

Her voice trailed away, as he continued to stare at her. His black eyebrows drew together as a crease appeared between the piercing eyes. "Percy who?"

She took another step backward, treading on a long train of fuchsia satin. The woman to whom it belonged gave a squawk and jerked on it angrily. Cassandra staggered sideways.

Baal's hand shot out to steady her. Retaining his grasp on her upper arm, he led her aside. "Percy who?"

"Oh, Percy, er . . ." Her thoughts whirled frantically. She dared not give a last name. Baal undoubtedly knew the names of his customers. She gave a nervous wave toward the couples on the dance floor, now dancing enthusiastically to the quick rhythms of a country dance. "I don't really know his last name. We're all just part of a party, you know."

He stared at her, his interest piqued. "I can't see your face, nor recognize your hair," he murmured. "I can't see the color of your eyes, but your voice . . . I've heard your voice before."

Hastily, she bounced on tiptoe, waving to someone over Baal's tall shoulder. "Oh, there he is. Excuse me, but I must join him. So nice to talk to you." She darted into the thickest part of the crowd.

In the center of the room, she took a quick left turn and then slipped into another room, this one decorated with profusions of green plants. Lighted only by sconces on the walls, the tall potted palms cast shadows. Into the midst of them she darted and crouched down behind a magnificent iron plant.

He followed her to the door. She heard the click of his heels, saw the flash of crimson satin, but then he passed on.

After several minutes she crept out and drew a deep steadying breath. The evening was becoming too dangerous. She had best take herself back up the secret stairs as soon as she could make her way through the crowd. Much as she hated to leave, she dared not jeopardize her job. She had not only her own self to provide for, but Mr. MacAdam as well.

She sighed regretfully, looking around her for the first time at the pretty room. She would have liked to linger here to give Baal time to forget her. However, from somewhere in a far corner, she heard a faint scuffle followed by a slap and a mild curse. Several couples were taking advantage of the seclusion afforded by the palms. If she did not leave immediately, she might see more than she wanted to. Cheeks burning, she hurried to the door.

"Wait!"

She froze momentarily, then started forward again.

"Wait, I said," a woman's voice commanded imperiously.

Reluctantly, she halted and turned.

"Where did you get that dress?"

Coming toward her from out of the shadows, an irritated-looking Bacchus in tow, was Ashtaroth. "Where did you get that dress?"

"This dress?" Cassandra squeaked.

Ashtaroth pointed rudely at the emerald brocade. "I

had a dress exactly like that. It was supposed to be an original."

Cassandra drew herself up, haughtily surveying the rumpled state of Ashtaroth's Egyptian costume. Clearly Bacchus's sweaty hands had a deleterious effect on its condition. "I'm sure you didn't have a dress like this one," she replied in her most aristocratic voice. Even if she were no longer a countess, she had not forgotten how one should sound. "My dressmaker assured me that it *was* an original. Besides she does not take anyone but the finest class of clientele." With a little surge of satisfaction she watched angry uncertainty play across the features of the Empress of the Nile.

Into the tiny uneasy silence, Bacchus whined, "Come on, Cleo. What difference does it make? You've got on all the dress you need." He tugged at her arm impatiently.

Cassandra turned her shoulder to the couple. "Excuse me," she intoned icily. "I shall return to the dancers. I had no wish to interrupt a business transaction."

In the main rooms of the casino, the noise and excitement of the party swelled. The musicians sawed away furiously at their instruments. The croupiers spun the wheels, the dealers dealt the cards, and gamblers, their minds dulled by champagne and distracted by the frenzied pace, bet higher and higher stakes. The masquers hurried to and fro in their bright costumes alive with spangles and sparkles. Feverish with excitement they sought pleasure after pleasure, their glasses ever replenished by the demons with their trays of champagne.

Her blood tingling, her mind exhilarated by her meaningless triumph over Ashtaroth, Cassandra leaned against the wall giggling softly. Had her father felt the same way? The thought of her father saddened her immeasurably. All around her the party whirled, but suddenly it was damnable. Her father had felt as they were feeling. No wonder he had bet. In this atmosphere all control, every inhibition was gone. The masquers, cloaked in anonymity, must feel powerful and immortal as gods.

A demon bowed at her elbow. In a sort of daze, she took a glass of champagne. Her thoughts bitter, she grimaced as she stared into the tiny froth of bubbles erupting in the center of the liquid. How she wished she had not come down. Her own recklessness in coming to this decadent place appalled her. She had been near disaster twice tonight. Ashtaroth had recognized her dress, Baal had . . . what had Baal thought?

Anxiously, she took a swallow. She must get back to the stairs.

Over the rim of her champagne glass, her eyes met his. He had completed a half circuit of the room. Now he came toward her, his cape billowing out behind him. With a smothered exclamation, she fled in the direction of the dance floor. Surely, she could lose her pursuer in the maze of dancers.

She might have made good her escape had not Julius Caesar chosen that moment to execute a complicated turn with Messalina. Cassandra had to skid to a halt and duck beneath the swirl of yellow drapery that was part of the empress's costume. In that moment, Baal caught up with her.

"If you want to dance, I'll be pleased to oblige you," he offered.

"No. Oh . . ."

His left hand clasped her waist while his right smoothly took the champagne glass from her and deposited it on a tray. "Come," he insisted. "Northumberland can find his own partner."

"Percy," she corrected.

"Same thing."

The music had changed to another waltz. His hand slid round her waist encircling it with his arm. Even as a frisson of alarm coursed down her spine, he drew her forward until their bodies touched. She should be pushing against him. She should be drawing herself up to her full height, holding herself stiff with affront, freezing him with a chilly stare.

Instead her breasts pressed warmly against his chest. Again she felt the tingling sensation in her breasts, except the sensation intensified as she took a deep breath. The gentle feeling changed to a peculiar ache as if he were holding her too closely.

He swept her in a circle within the circle. Like chips of glass in a kaleidoscope they turned. Instead of tensing her muscles and holding herself rigid, she clung to him, swayed with him, following his steps as if they shared the same body. His will was her will. The remnant of control regained after leaving Ashtaroth was swept away by sensual pleasure fast turning to desire.

Lulled by the alcoholic fumes, her brain refused to give warning. She tilted her head back. His face, although a long way up, was very handsome. She hummed softly along with the music. He did not look devilish at all. The white horns on his temples looked more like wings. The flickering lights above her whirled and dipped as her body pressed itself against Baal with a will of its own, giving of itself with natural sensuality.

For Edward Sandron the lady in his arms piqued his interest. Who was she? Why did she seem so devastatingly familiar? "What shall I call you?" he asked.

Beneath the provocative black lace veil, her mouth curved upward in a smile. "Cassandra."

"Cassandra what?"

"Just Cassandra," she chuckled. "Remember, noble Prince of Darkness, tonight the masks stay on. Isn't that what you said?"

He frowned as she silently congratulated herself on her witty answer.

She was sure she was flirting with him. She had read and heard about flirting but had never seen it done. It consisted of "behaving in a trifling manner without serious intent." It suited her mood exactly. Everything that she would do tonight would be done without serious intent.

"And do you foretell the future, Cassandra?"

She shook her head. "Never, sir, for you know no one would believe me."

He raised one satanic eyebrow. "Amazing. An educated woman."

"Sorry," she murmured.

"Oh, no. I'm pleased. A man gets tired of talking

with himself. So many women are like blank walls. Your own words echo back to you."

She shook her head in mock sympathy. "Poor fellow."

His broad grin made his face less austere and more approachable. "I need someone with intelligence to share my thoughts."

She glanced around her. "There must be any number of women here willing to share your . . . thoughts."

A particularly shrill laugh burst from the throat of the woman dressed as Catherine the Great. Napoleon's mouth moved against the side of her throat. Whether he was kissing her, biting her, or merely whispering in her ear was impossible to tell. Probably he was doing a combination of all three as his hands clutched her soft buttocks, crushing the elaborate train of her gown.

Embarrassed at the sight, Cassandra threw Baal a glance to judge his reaction. He gave no evidence that he saw the behavior going on around him. Or if he did, it merely inspired him to hold her a bit closer.

"What color are your eyes?" he asked softly.

She shook her head, dropping her eyelashes, thankful that the lights were neither bright nor steady. "You are trying to pierce my disguise, sir. That is against the rules."

"Since when did the devil ever play by the rules," he growled. His arm held her tighter. "What color are you eyes?"

She hesitated. "Brown."

"Is that the truth?"

"Why should I tell the truth to the devil? He does not deal in truth."

The music finished with a triumphant flourish. The conductor pulled a handkerchief from his pocket and wiped his forehead.

"More champagne?" Baal offered, signaling a demon.

"No, I've had more than my share."

"Nonsense. It's here to be drunk." Pretending to misread her meaning, he pressed a glass into her hand. "To masks," he toasted, holding her eyes with his own.

Reluctantly, she touched the rim to her lips.

He leaned down, his eyes even with hers, his mouth only inches from the rim of her glass. "Drink and enjoy it," he whispered. "Then we'll dance again."

He might not be able to see the color of her eyes, but she could see deep into his. Tonight they were black, deep, cavernous, with tiny flickering flames within their depths. With no will of her own she drank the champagne. Her heartbeat accelerated beneath the emerald brocade.

Over the rim of the glass, she watched him lift his own glass to his lips, watched the golden liquid flow into his mouth. Finished, he touched the bottom of her own glass, tilting it so she drank as deeply as he. Then he took her glass and set both on a tray for the demon acolyte to bear away.

"Would you like something to eat?" He stared into the shadow of the mask. Her eyes were wide, the pupils practically filling the irises.

Without waiting for an answer, he took her wrist

instead of her hand. He had to stifle a grin as his fingers found the furious thrumming of her pulse. The bright red hair was a sure gauge of a passionate nature. "Would you like to eat here, or would you prefer some place more private?"

The pulse leaped. "Here," she murmured.

"You can't escape me, you know."

She shook her head stubbornly. "No, I don't know that."

He made no effort to hide his smile as he led her into another chamber.

A long time before midnight, too early for most of the revelers to think about food, the board was still a delight for the eye. Over twenty feet long it was graced by five silver epergnes each with three tiers of delicacies. Between them were bowls of fruit and vegetables, trays of breads, standing plates of cakes and pastries, and four gargantuan platters of fish, ham, poultry, and roast beef.

Overawed at the sight, Cassandra stopped, her hands clasped together before her breasts.

"What is it, Cassandra?" Not Baal's voice but the voice of Edward Sandron came dimly as through a fog.

Hearing the familiar voice, she replied honestly. "I've never seen so much food."

At her admission his expression changed, but she did not notice. Avidly studying the various dishes, she let him lead her to the head of the table.

"Then let us not delay. Allow me to fill your plate."

She walked beside him as he indicated the portions to be placed on their plates. More demons with faces of icy hauteur sliced and spooned and forked tidbits. At the end Baal took her arm to lead her to a small supper table, lighted by a tall silver candle. A demon set their plates in front of them, poured wines both red and white into tall stemmed glasses, bowed obsequiously, and left.

Cassandra lifted her eyes from the plate to the face of the man across from her. His mouth quirked at the corner. Lifting one black brow, he gestured toward the food. "Please enjoy." His voice had a sarcastic tinge. "Perhaps this evening will mark an exceptional occasion in your young life."

Spreading a bite of pâté maison on a small crust of bread, she nodded. "I am sure it will. I've never seen people having so much fun."

"And have you never danced before? Nor played?"

"Never." She took a bite of the delicious meat concoction.

At her admission, his voice turned hard. "Then what did you come here for, my dear? What or who was your target?"

Suddenly chilled to the bone, she set her fork down. Bewildered she looked at him. "I don't understand your meaning."

He shook his head laconically, one arm slung over the back of his chair. "I think you do, my dear, but, of course, you won't reveal anything. After all, you came with Peregrine, did you not?"

She hesitated. "Percy."

"Oh, of course. Percy. Of Northumberland?"

With trembling fingers she refolded her napkin. Her brain was suddenly tired. What had gone wrong?

He had invited her to supper, after all. He had selected these foods. Did he begrudge her the meal? "Perhaps I should be finding him."

His expression did not change. "But you have never seen so much food before, dear lady. You have never been to a party before. You have never drunk champagne before, or danced before. Am I correct?"

Her heart skipped a beat. "Is that a crime?"

"No. But to use this party as a pretext for entering this house is."

He was not making any sense, but she realized that he was seething with anger. "I'd better go."

His hand snaked out across the table and manacled her wrist. "Don't." The word was softly spoken, but the grasp was steely. "Sit and eat."

She looked around helplessly.

"No one will come to aid you," he sneered. "You came to this party unannounced. Did you come to rob some of the more imprudent of my guests? Or perhaps you came for some more nefarious reason?" His grip tightened painfully. "Did you come perhaps to poison me?"

Horrified at first, she could only gape at an accusation she regarded as absurd. Then desperate to convince him of her innocence, she leaned forward over the table, ignoring his imprisoning hand around her wrist. "Oh, no. I swear. I came to see the party. That's all. You're right. I've never seen a party like this before. I should not have come, but I wanted to come so badly. Believe me, I only wanted to come." Her voice broke on the last words.

His grin was malicious. "A very convincing act, but

why should I believe you? You have been lying all evening. You tried to avoid me earlier. Don't lie."

"I'm not lying now," she protested, her voice quavering.

He held her tightly when she tried to twist away. "Furthermore, you are trespassing, madam. You are stealing my champagne and my food. This party is for regular guests at the Devil's Palace. By invitation only."

At the virulence of his last speech, she shrank back in the chair as far away from him as the length of her arm. "I can only beg your forgiveness. I didn't think I'd eat or drink very much."

Her words were uttered with such simplicity that he stopped his tirade. If she were a murderess, she was certainly in the wrong profession. She should be making her living as an actress. She could convince anybody of anything.

Slowly, he released her wrist. "Eat your food," he commanded shortly.

"I really don't think I want anything now."

"Eat it. You've drunk too much champagne for an empty stomach. You'll get sick or pass out or both."

She shook her head. "I'm not drunk. I don't feel sick."

He lifted his glass of white wine. "Drink then. You should perhaps be a little bit drunk. It might make the rest of evening easier." The implicit threat in his words appalled her.

"Please, I've done nothing."

"You're here. And you shouldn't be," he sneered. "You'll have to take what comes."

She shivered, her eyes locked with his, seeing again the flames reflected in their depths.

He sat forward suddenly. Reaching across the small table, he forked a bite of lobster pie and held it out to her. "Come," he coaxed, his sneer wiped away in a dazzling smile. "Eat."

Against her will she opened her lips.

"Good?"

She nodded, chewing slowly.

He watched until she swallowed with difficulty. "Now, feed yourself," he urged. "No one can bother you now. You're with the host." He attacked his plate with gusto, slicing off a bite of roast beef so rare that pinkish brown liquid ran across the plate.

She stared at her own food. A philosophical calm settled over her. He was right. She had nothing to fear any longer. She had been discovered. He was allowing her to eat before he threw her out onto the streets. She dipped a celery heart into mayonnaise.

As the supper room began to fill, he drew her hand through his arm and led her back to the dance floor. The orchestra, refreshed by its rest, was playing a waltz in a minor key. Without asking, he swept her into his arms. This time he made no effort to hold her in the approved fashion. His hand pressed against the small of her back to bring her against his moving body. Anger and excitement seemed to radiate from him as his hands moved her to his will. At the same time she could feel unmistakably the shape and hardness of his arousal.

Whirling breathlessly around the room, their bodies dipping and twirling in the eerie minor key, Cassandra could only stare upward into his cold smiling face framed in the ruff of crimson satin. By his hard dark eyes she recognized him for what he was. A devil, a very devil, a beautiful devil. For evil was beautiful. His face was flawless, as finely sculpted as a Renaissance angel's. His body, lean and tall.

Inherent in that beautiful face was ruthlessness that made her quiver. She had worked for him long enough to know that Edward Sandron was a complex personality. Vaguely she remembered his teeth at her breast. With all his culture, all his gentleness, all his cleverness, his soul also had its dark, unplumbed depths.

Looking up into the flames flickering in his smoky eyes, she pushed fearfully against his chest. His hands and arms only tightened. And perversely, her own body burned through the emerald brocade as his heat branded her.

The music came to a finish with a florish. Baal's red cape flared out from his shoulders and swirled round them, enveloping her. Taking advantage of it, he pressed her painfully tighter against him.

Suddenly, tiredness and excitement, champagne and rich foods, all came together in a crashing wave. Her vision dimmed. She swayed.

He felt the motion. His left hand came up to cup the back of head and guide it to his shoulder. "Come with me," he commanded.

"Where?" she whispered.

He laughed shortly. "You'll see." He guided her out

of the ballroom into a lighted hallway. Through another door they went and into a small chamber that was nothing more than a closet containing the foot of a staircase.

"Where are you taking me?" she begged.

He paused at the foot of the stairs. "You talk too much." He thrust her back against the wall then. His hands roved over her body, not roughly but not gently. They were firm, undeniable. His fingers traced her figure, her upthrust breasts, her slender waist, her hips beneath the drapery of her skirt. "You're very slim," he remarked. "That's good."

She shifted restlessly, her mind bidding her traitorous body to struggle. With a gasp, she tried to pull away the hand that dived beneath the décolletage of her gown and found her nipple. "Stop it."

"No," he chuckled softly. "If you really came with Percy—if there were such a fellow here by that name—then you must have come as his fancy piece. Well, I've taken a fancy to you. It's little enough to pay for your food and drink."

"No!"

"No?" He pushed against her, pressed his hips against her hips, moved meaningfully. "No?" he whispered. He fondled the nipple while she moaned helplessly, her belly muscles rigid, a terrible ache building at the apex of her thighs. "Oh, I think yes."

As he bent to kiss her, she made one last feeble attempt at reason. "I'm not a fancy piece," she protested hoarsely. "I swear I'm not. I'm sorry about coming to the party. Please let me go. I promise you'll never see me again."

He chuckled deep in his throat as he squeezed her nipple harder. "Sweetheart, at this very moment I don't care what you are. You're here and I'm here."

A bolt of raw desire shot through her. Its power frightened her. "Let me go," she demanded, feeling smothered between his body and the wall. "Damn you. Let me go."

"Such language . . ." he chided.

His laughter ignited her mercurial temper. She kicked him hard in the shin and darted back down the hall.

Grunting a foul expletive, he caught her in half a dozen steps. "Oh, no you don't." Before she could aim another blow, he scooped her up his arm and tossed her over his shoulder.

"Let me go."

"No." He headed for the stairs. "You need to be taught a lesson. You don't break into a casino and try to rob it."

"I didn't do it for that. Let me go!"

Inexorably he mounted the stairs, despite her curses and futile threats. "If you came to meet clients, you should know that each man was to bring his own escort. Your sort aren't allowed."

"I'm not that sort," she insisted.

"Oh, no, you came for the pâté maison?" he sneered.

"Partly, yes. Let me go." She kicked violently, but only succeeded in making him almost drop her on her head.

He swatted her on the rear. "Don't wriggle so. You're making a mountain out of a molehill. I'll not hurt you."

"No!"

At the top of the stairs, he carried her slowly down a narrow passage, counting softly. Soon he leaned against the seventh panel in the wall. It swung open with an eerie creak into another long dark hallway. "Discreet rooms in the next building. Nash doesn't know I know about these," he informed her.

"Let me go," she whispered fearfully. "Please let me go. I swear I'll leave. You'll never see me again."

Surprisingly, her captor let her slide down his body. "Let me think about that," he breathed. Cupping her buttocks, he lifted her to meet the sharp planes and taut muscles of his body. Her protest he cut off with a hard mouth.

She could not struggle. Her body recognized his. Despite the warning screamed in her mind, she could not help herself. The resisting muscles loosened, grew weak. Like a torch she flamed against him.

His kiss deepened. Then he tore his mouth away. Drawing her impossibly deeper into his arms, he groaned. "The truth. Tell me who you are and I'll let you go for now. I swear I know you. Yet I can't remember."

Breathlessly, she shook her head. He felt her movement. "Take off the mask."

"Never," she gasped. "Never."

"Are you a prostitute?" He ran his hands over her body. "You're young. Too young. If you're just setting yourself up with some pimp, your price shouldn't be too expensive. I'll buy you." He felt her shudder even as he sifted his motives frantically. His intention to frighten and punish, to perhaps extract a confession of intent from this girl faded. If she had not been so adamant, if she had made a clean breast of her reasons, he would have thrust her out into the street when she had done that.

But now he wanted her. Wanted her badly. Her body called to his in a way he found altogether alarming and unbearably exciting.

She twisted restlessly against him. "Let me go," she muttered. "I promise you'll never see me again."

Suddenly selfish, he held her tighter. "No. Not until you've satisfied me. You've aroused the devil. You have to meet his price." He hoisted her onto his shoulder and lugged her down the hall.

Chapter Twelve

A gaslight turned low flickered fitfully in a sconce by a door. Its etched glass chimney was so smoked that the light it cast revealed scarcely more than shadowy shapes.

Nash had planned the hallways in the adjacent building to protect the reputations of some of the guests. A man could even leave or enter by another exit in the front of a building on Margaret Street. More than a few men found the secret entrance prudent rather than gaining admittance through the well-known entrance at 29 Regent Street. In the further interest of these guests' sensibilities, Nash had installed minimal gaslighting, which incidentally economized on the amount of gas used by the Devil's Palace.

Opening on this hallway, rooms were maintained strictly for the convenience of clients who enjoyed female companionship while they gambled. These rooms were to be entered by prearrangement only. For a fee a demon with a candleabra would escort the guest and his lady to a room. The guest always supplied his own lady. The Devil's Palace had certain standards.

For a more generous fee, the guest and his lady would be served wine or champagne and an accompanying cold collation. The obsequious demons would then withdraw, leaving the couple alone to their own devices for an agreed-upon number of hours. All such business was conducted in discreet shadows.

Baal kicked the door to one of these chambers closed behind him. His burden had not moved since uttering her last plea. He suspected that the discomfort of being carried thrown across his shoulder a second time had made breathing difficult, but he did not pity her. She was only getting what she deserved. Once when he had paused to check his bearings in the dark, she had given a faint groan. Otherwise she might have been unconscious, her rapid breathing the only reassurance that she was not dead.

"Down you go, madam," he announced. His hands slid up the back of her legs under her voluminous skirts. Through the thin material of her pantalettes, he felt the shape of slender thighs and firm buttocks. A wave of desire tightened his belly.

Taking exquisite care that she should slide down the front of his body, he slowly lowered her to the floor until she stood upright within the circle of his arms. There he held her until she could regain her equilibrium. At last she took a deep breath that lifted her breasts against his chest. Again he endured an almost painful surge of desire.

His voice hoarse, he lifted his right hand. "Now,

madam, I will have that mask off."

"No!" She twisted violently out of his grasp. His back was to the door. She had no real hope of escape, yet she fled. In the darkest corner of the room, she spun to face him. "No. Please." She thrust her hands out in front of her to ward him off.

Like a great beast he stalked her. The cloak cast a huge malignant shadow that concealed them both. His strong hands caught hers, drawing her toward him. "Give it up, madam. You can't escape." Even as he spoke, he recognized his own words. His mouth twisted into a cynical smile.

"No. You don't understand. I really only came because—" She flung her head back as he twisted her hands behind her and locked them with his own to press against her buttocks. Protesting, gasping as the shape of his rampant masculinity moved against her body, she struggled to free herself. "No . . . I swear . . ."

The bar comprised of their arms pushed insistently at her back at the same time he ground his loins against her.

Her struggles ceased abruptly. She slumped in his arms exhausted by the effort and overwhelmed by memory. He had taken her before in the dark. He was going to take her again. At first he had hurt her, dreadfully, but later she had come to pleasure— exquisite, soul-wrenching pleasure. Her legs felt weak. A soft liquid tingling began at the bottom of her belly.

He bent to her, his breath warm on her cheek. She snapped her head aside trying to thwart him anyway she could. Without hesitation he accepted the place she offered him. Beneath the skin of her white throat, he could feel her frantic pulse beat against his lips. Suddenly she moaned and twisted, kicking at his shins. Her renewed struggle caught him off balance. He staggered a couple of steps before recovering. Muttering something unintelligible, he released one of her hands to wrap his arm around her waist and hold her even closer.

She clenched her free hand into a fist, beat his shoulder once, clutched at the fabric of his cape. Nothing worked. Defeated at last, she slumped exhausted in his arms.

He raised his head. "The mask," he commanded.

She hesitated. "No," she rasped finally.

He pressed her harder against him. Behind her back he still held her left wrist. "The mask," he repeated, tightening his grip ever so slightly.

She shuddered convulsively.

He could feel her vibrate all along his frame. His free hand left her waist, trailed up over the textured brocade to the side of her breast. He paused, enjoying the exquisite, almost unbearable tension he was creating in her body. Then his fingers hooked over the décolletage of her neckline, and slipped it down.

He expected her to renew her futile struggles. Instead, she went still in his arms, no breath or motion, as if she anticipated what was to come. He grinned faintly. She was a whore after all. For a moment there he had begun to believe that he might somehow be wrong. A real lady would be fainting, dying to protect her virtue.

His fingers touched the nipple, pushed against its hardness. She moaned, undulating her hips, conscious of his male shape, helpless to control the wave of desire that swept her.

With exquisite care he held the nipple on the tips of his second and third fingers. Bending his head he touched the aroused flesh with his lips. His tongue laved it. His teeth caressed it warningly.

She gave a small cry. Was she afraid or eager?

"Take off the mask," he ordered relentlessly.

Her fingers clutched once more at his shoulder, then relaxed. He had the power to remove it himself. But he demanded that she do it. Even as he bared her breast he would bare the rest of her body and take it. He would take his pleasure and then . . . she shuddered again at the memory. He would make exquisite love to her and drive her quite beyond herself. If she took it off herself, its removal would signify her surrender.

His teeth closed on the nipple, sending a tiny shaft of fire through her body. It should have hurt, but instead it only increased the pleasure. Her conscience deserted her with her fear. She lifted the mask from her face and let it fall to the floor.

Chuckling, he tugged harder at the nipple, laving it with his tongue. Then he straightened and began to kiss her face. Her forehead, her eyelid, her cheek. He touched the corner of her mouth, then drew back.

"Kiss me," he commanded as he released her other hand held so long shackled behind her back.

Her eyes had closed in the grip of emotions too strong to acknowledge. Now they flew open. His eyes accustomed to the dimness made out great dark wells in her white face.

"Yes, sir," she whispered.

He drew back slightly, disturbed by a certain familiarity of intonation. Did he detect an accent? A tiny trilling of the *r?* Then she was rising on tiptoe and he could not think at all.

Putting both arms around his neck, she lifted her lips to his. Her mouth was sweet, her lips soft at first. But quickly, the kiss became demanding. Her mouth opened to receive his tongue, then follow his into his mouth. The heat and perfume of her body were all around him. They swayed dizzily in the embrace, bodies tightly locked together, toes touching.

Suddenly he broke it with a muffled groan. "Turn around."

"What?"

"Turn around."

Shivering with aroused lust, she complied, folding her arms across her breasts, her breath coming in short quick gasps.

"Lift your hair." Before she had time to comply, she felt his hands on the heavy mane. Gathering it up, he draped it over one shoulder before attacking first the buttons at the back of the dress, then the ties on her petticoats.

She could only wonder at his experience when both her dress and underskirts fell away in a matter of seconds. Her corset cover came next, his fingers unerring as they found the tapes. The corset hooks beneath her left arm did not deter him. "Why do you wear this?" he complained, casting the whalebone shell aside contemptuously. "You don't need it any more than a child."

She shook her head mutely, shivering at his ruthless efficiency.

Last, his hands stripped her chemise to her waist and clasped her breasts. She gave a sound suspiciously like a sob as he squeezed them hard, concentrating on the nipples, using his thumbs to trap them against the sides of his index fingers.

He kissed her cheek, the corner of her mouth, the lobe of her ear, as his hands found the ties of her pantalettes. As they fell to the floor around her ankles, he caught her up in his arms lifting her out of them. She was nude except for her hose and shoes.

He stretched her on the bed, arranging her legs apart, placing her hands above her head. "Don't move," he cautioned. "I want to think of you waiting for me like this." His hand caressed the shape of her shoulder, down her breast, over her belly. He patted the soft curls of her mound. Reflexively, she drew up one leg.

"No," he cautioned. "Don't move." His hand encircled her ankle and drew it down.

"That's hard to do," she whispered between clenched teeth.

He smiled. The woman in the emerald brocade was surely no lady. Her responses were too sensual, too instantaneous, too violent.

Unaware of his thoughts, concentrating on the waves of desire spreading through her, she stared upward at the soft semicircle of light gradually diminishing into darkness upon the ceiling above the gaslight.

Baal tossed aside his cape and pulled off his clothes. When he was nude, he strode around the bed to stand looking down at her. The lack of light defeated him. He could see only her shape, the upthrust breasts, the narrow waist, the slender limbs apart as he had arranged them.

He could not see her face clearly. "Who are you?" he asked.

"You don't know me," came the soft reply. "I only came to see the party."

Darkness veiled the sneer that curled his mouth. Her lies refueled his anger. He waited no longer. With lithe grace, he put a knee onto the sheet between her legs and climbed into the bed.

She shivered in fear and desire not unmixed with some shame as she knew herself damned for the sin of lust. But she could not help herself. She had long been without affection, cast on her own resources, forced by the necessities of her disguise to lead an isolated life. She wanted him desperately to touch her and hold her in a warm embrace.

Kneeling between her thighs now, he ran his hands possessively over every inch of her skin, kneaded the firm breasts, traced the lines of her narrow hipbones with his thumbs. "Do you like this? This? This?"

To each question she replied, "Yes. Oh, yes. Yes!" Her words, little more than gasps of delight.

"And you liked to be touched there?" His fingertips delicately threaded through the soft curls at the apex of her thighs. Instantly, she arched upward, her tiny cry admitting her pleasure. "So quick," he murmured.

"You do like that. Such a passionate little thing."

She subsided. Her body throbbed even as her conscience berated her. "I'm — that is — I've never felt —"

He placed the tips of his fingers over her lips. "No lies," he admonished. "No more lies."

Stirring uncomfortably, she sought to defend herself. "But the devil deals in lies."

His hands stilled their caresses. After a moment's silence, he bent to her again. "Why you're right," he agreed. "Of course. The devil deals in lies and in evil of all kinds."

Then his hands moved again, a bit rougher, pressing against the tender skin of her inner thighs, forcing them wider apart. "Lift your hips."

"Please," she begged, a little frightened. "Don't hurt me."

He guided his shaft to the moist opening between her legs. His hands stroked once, twice, three times across the ultrasensitive nub of flesh at the top of the slit. She sucked in her breath in ecstasy. Then he slipped his hands beneath her hips. "Don't be afraid." His words believed the hint of malice in his voice. "A woman like you can't be hurt by this."

She shivered, then, knowing he might hurt her very badly. Her brief twinge of anxiety was groundless. His thick shaft slid into her easily, stroking her deliciously with its hot length. She moaned in mindless gratitude and excitement, clutching at the top of his shoulders. Her legs left the mattress and wrapped around his hips to drag herself up to him.

"My God! How can you be so perfect?" His question was little more than an ecstatic groan as he felt himself locked against her by her smooth thighs, his entire length clasped in hot velvet. She was so small, so delicate, so soft. His hands cupped her breasts, stroking the heated flesh even as he stroked forward and back inside her. His pleasure was so intense that it took him completely out of himself.

Cassandra wept, her tears streaming from her eyes, into the masses of hair on the pillow beneath her head. Her body was on fire, the flames fanned higher and higher until suddenly she could bear no more.

Pleasure became intense pain that turned to pleasure again, each sensation signaled by her high keening cries. Her body convulsed, throbbing, fairly clutching at him. With a shout, he exploded, every muscle bent on this wild moment of pleasure.

Cassandra had no clear memory of the next few minute or hours. Somehow, Baal must have moved and arranged her body and his. When she knew herself, they lay together still entwined. Her cheek rested on his chest, so that his heart thrummed rhythmically beneath her ear. With each breath he took, her pillow rocked her. Unfortunately the chill of the room had awakened her.

Or so she thought. Her consciousness returned when she shivered. Her feet and hands, her legs, her buttocks were chilled. And Baal was holding her tightly against him.

But something else disturbed her. Footsteps. A man. A heavy man was running down the hall. She heard a muffled shout. Then another set of footsteps, then two more. A couple of people hurried along.

Baal stirred beside her, sat up. "What the hell . . . ?"

"Someone is running down the hall," she whispered unnecessarily, for the hall outside was now fairly noisy. A whistle shrilled somewhere.

"My God!" He sprang off the bed, grabbing for his clothes.

"What is it?"

"A raid."

"A raid? What? Are you sure?"

"I'll never forget those sounds. Guests must be escaping through the discreet exit."

She sat up, crossing her arms over her naked breasts. "Who is raiding?"

"The police," he shot over his shoulder as he made for the door. "Get dressed and wait here. I don't think they'll come in here. It's technically a different house."

"But . . ."

He darted out the door, slamming it behind him.

She sat bemused for a full minute, thinking of nothing. Then common sense reasserted itself. "Dress," he had said. Dress she would. And disappear. A bit of luck had come her way. She had not had to waken to his searching stare in the morning. She would not be dismissed from her job.

Unfortunately, she was not free yet. She would need more than luck to slip back unnoticed to her room, change into Miss Fitch, and continue her job.

How many police were raiding as well as how long would be a determining factor. She had no idea. One step at a time, she cautioned herself. Swiftly, she tugged on her chemise and drawers. She bent to pick up the corset, then with grim satisfaction kicked it under the bed and stepped into the dress. Her fingers fumbled as more sounds alarmed her, but she managed to button at least every other button.

The black mask lay where she had dropped it. Never had she needed anonymity as she did now. Her hands like ice, she adjusted it on her face, then opened the door to a crack to peer out.

Two men and two women hurried past her, their faces masked. One man cursed loudly as his companion stumbled. "For God's sake, come on."

"It's these damned shoes," the woman replied.

"Then take them off, and be quick about it."

"Wait. For God's sake. Don't leave me." She hopped along on first one foot and then the other, hanging on to his arm and whining.

Cassandra smiled grimly. Resolutely, she slipped out into the hall as they passed. She did not waste a glance after them. As if by not looking at them she would somehow render herself invisible, she fled back along the hall toward the casino.

As she fled, Cassandra found cause to bless Nash's miserliness as well as his sense of discretion. At the top of the stairs, she halted, staring wide-eyed down into the darkness of the stairwell. Suddenly, the darkness was suffocating, the sense of looking down into a pit, stifling.

She looked fearfully back the way she had come. Should she follow those people? Obviously, they knew where they were going. They must be leaving the Devil's Palace by another exit. If she went outside, how would she get back in? Certainly, she could not return as the red-haired Cassandra in the emerald brocade dress.

She clutched at her throat. Somehow, despite her overpowering fear, she must get back to her room by the only way she knew. A whistle shrilled again somewhere beyond the stairwell. Somewhere in the light were people and space. She clutched the rough railing bracketed in the wall and put her foot on the first step. More noises, thuds, muffled voices raised in anger led her. She could make out a faint glow at the bottom. Light seeped in under the door.

Finally, panting, breathless, she flung herself down the last steps and flattened herself against the door. The ordeal of darkness with walls crowding in around her had bathed her skin with perspiration. No matter what scene lay beyond, she could not bring herself to remain in the stairwell a moment longer.

Jerking open the door, she eeled around the jamb into the light. To her surprise and intense relief, the hall was empty. At its end the door to the casino stood open. Bright lights and the sound of many voices assualted her senses. Perhaps escape would be easier than she had imagined—or more difficult.

She considered waiting where she was but instantly discarded the idea. She would not wait tamely for someone to come and drag her out. Moving on tiptoe, even though the noise that came from the outer rooms would have covered up any small sounds she might have made, she hurried down the hall.

The card room was also empty. One table was overturned. Cards, chips, paraphernalia of all kinds were strewn across the carpet. The draperies were ripped down off one window, which stood open. Had someone tried to escape? Had he succeeded or had he been dragged back by the police? She shivered.

Clenching her fists, she flitted to the wall beside the door that led into the ballroom. Huddled against it, she crouched low and peered around the corner.

The scene before her was chaotic. At least a dozen policemen herded angry people into two groups—guests and employees. The guests in disheveled costumes, many with masks still in place, argued, complained, and threatened.

Another small group consisted of the demon waiters and the musicians clutching their instruments. At their head stood Baal, his expression thunderous, his crimson cape enfolded behind him by his arms. Why was he standing with his arms behind him?

In a moment she had her answer. He turned slightly. Cold horror prickled her skin. His hands were shackled behind him. A sick feeling rose in her stomach. She sank back against the wall out of sight.

He had run out of the bedroom right into the arms of the law. But where was Nash? Where was Ashtaroth? Why was Baal the only one to be arrested?

"Let's move along 'ere, naow." she heard a man's deep voice, heavily accented with Cockney. Her curiosity would not be stilled. She peered around the edge again.

"You've no right to break up a private masquerade party," Baal protested.

"A private party, is hit?" the Cockney policeman replied. "Wal, that's not wot we 'eard. Our orders ain't usually wrong."

"You'll hear more about this in the morning," Baal argued frantically. "You'll be reported for exceeding your authority, for breaking and entering, for—"

"Save it." The policeman brandished his club. "Move out o 'ere. You're the leader. Since you speak so fine, you get t' move out first."

Baal bowed his head momentarily. Cassandra saw his shoulders swell as if he tested his bonds. He threw back his head then winced painfully. A wide red welt marred the side of his neck beneath his ear. They had hit him with one of their clubs. She clenched her hands until the nails bit into the palms. Again came the almost overwhelming desire to run to him.

But she could do nothing. If all the rich and titled people dressed in those elaborate costumes could not prevent this raid, then she would have no chance. She consoled herself that if she managed to get back into the guise of Cassie Fitch, she could perhaps present a voice of defense tomorrow at the Old Bailey.

Helplessly, she watched as the prisoners were herded out, Baal at their head.

Another policeman turned to the larger group. "Now, you people better disperse quietly. This place is closed until further notice."

A communal sigh of relief went up from behind the masks. Several people made a dash for the door, frantic to be out with their skin whole and their anonymity preserved. As they hurried out, four uniformed men pushed through. The axes they carried in front of them elicited a scream from one terrified woman.

"Wait 'til we get out, boys," the policeman commanded. "Then do a proper job of it."

Among those pushing to get out, Cassandra caught sight of a bedraggled Queen of the Nile. Ashtaroth had managed to convince the police that she was only a guest. Cassandra felt real regret that Baal had not worn a mask as well.

A small minority of guests still milled about ostensibly to collect their cloaks. In actual point of fact they were scooping chips off the abandoned tables. The Devil's Palace might honor them later when the night's unpleasant brush with the law should be forgotten.

Recognizing that she would never have a better chance, Cassandra slipped around the facing of the door and hurried across the ballroom.

"Where y'goin', lady?" A young man in a blue uniform blocked her way.

She skidded to a stop before him. "Oh, please," she begged, wringing her hands. "Please, just let me go behind that curtain. I'll be right back. I promise."

He looked in the direction she indicated, his eyebrows drawn together in a frown. "Why should you want to go there?"

She hung her head. "Please, sir. Oh, please." She lowered her voice to a conspiratorial whisper. "I really *have* to go."

He did not at first catch her meaning. Then a faint flush spread over his cheeks. "Oh, certainly, ma'am." He turned quickly away.

Quelling a desire to giggle, she scampered up the stairs and darted behind the stage curtain. As she pressed the sliding panel mechanism, the first axe splintered the center of the roulette wheel.

The door was propped open as she had left it at the head of the secret staircase. As the panel slid closed behind her, she felt the familiar twinge of panic, but it was only momentary.

Catching up her skirts, she raced up the stairs two at a time and bolted into the library. Her heart pounding, she pulled the books off the door sill. The panel slid to with an authoritative thud.

As if it had struck her, she swayed where she stood. Eyes glazed, she stared at it. Her whole body began to shake. What a fool she had been! What an utter and complete idiot! Emotionally and physically exhausted, she simply wilted. The emerald brocade dress belled out around her. The heavy books remained clasped in her arms as if they were some sort of lifeline.

Wearily, she rolled her forehead against them. The enormity of what she had risked hit her with terrible force. She could have been arrested for trespassing, for stealing, even for murder. She knew of the visit from the police inspector. She knew that everyone in the house was under suspicion.

Furthermore, she had behaved like a spoiled child, wanting to attend a party. And for what? She had attended a drunken revelry where she knew no one except the host, whom she had tried to avoid all evening. She had drunk too much alcohol, eaten too much rich food, and had ended by avidly participating in her own seduction.

She gritted her teeth at the shameful memory. Baal was the very devil himself. He had accused her of dreadful things. Yet in his arms, she had behaved as wantonly as any man might expect a loose woman to behave. Never mind that she felt herself coming to care for him. She blushed with shame at her response.

Edward Sandron, her employer, had made love to her again. She had made only half-hearted attempts to ward him off. Why? because she enjoyed his hands and mouth and body. She shuddered. After the delicious mind-numbing excitement, she knew again the hideous fear. Would she conceive his child this time? Surely she had taken a terrible chance. She could not hope to avoid pregnancy if she continued to put herself in his way and allow him to do as he would.

But she enjoyed it so. Tears welled from her eyes. She — Lady Cassandra MacDaermond — was a wanton disgrace to her class. She was not a gently bred lady at all, for no lady would or could enjoy that terrible act as she did. Everyone knew that ladies did their unpleasant duty in order to have a goodly number of children to carry on the family name. It was a duty. Not a pleasure.

Wearily, she wiped at the overflowing tears with the tips of her fingers. Climbing to her feet, she returned the books to the bookcase and staggered out. The hall was dark and empty. She had no need to hurry along. Edward Sandron was not in his house. Was he all right? Had he been thrust into a cold, dark cell?

She felt foolish for caring so much, but she could not help her feelings now. Perhaps that was where the problem lay. If one of her own class had made love to her, she would not have enjoyed it. It would have been a duty. Instead, she had been made love to by a person of a low class, a man who ran a gambling casino, a writer of low and filthy books. Of course, she had enjoyed it. If she had never met him, she would never have cared for him or enjoyed him the way she did.

Therein lay the problem. In her own small room at last she fell full length across the bed. She had associated with the wrong class of people. Now she very much feared that she would never stop caring.

Chapter Thirteen

Edward was not surprised to find the room empty. He had known it would be. He could not have expected her to remain here alone for eighteen hours. Still, as the hours had crept by in the Old Bailey's common cell, he had fantasized returning to find her lying naked in that bed, her red hair blazing in the light of day, her arms opening to him.

Damn the dim gaslight in these rooms! He had been able to see her body clearly, but her face had still worn a mask. He turned away from the door. How was he to find a woman whose face he had not seen clearly? He hoped she had gotten home safely.

Who was she? Whom had she come with? Ah, Percy. He shook his head. No one named Percy had been invited to the party. He had seen Nash's guest list made up weeks before. No one with the first or last name of Percy had been on it.

So she had been lying. Again he was not surprised. She had probably been lying about everything else too. And yet she had been so sweet. So very sweet. And passionate. He frowned. Somewhere in the back his head was the memory of another time. Another

234

woman whose body had pleased him as this woman's had. But he could not remember when. And now the woman in the green dress was gone.

To his exhaustion, his frustration, his very real anxieties, he was forced to add disappointment.

"Nash!" he bellowed. "Nash! Damn you!" He strode down the hall past the stairs toward the blank wall at the end. Coming right up to it, he pushed against a cherub's face in the stucco in the corner. The cherub slid back easily with a clicking sound followed by a faint rumble. The system of weights moved and a narrow panel opened, not at the end but at the side of the hall beneath the cherub.

Turning sideways, he edged his way through into the hall opposite the room that had belonged to Parks. The panel was so close to the back stairs that he had to step on the next to the top riser before he could continue down the back hall to the library. "Nash!"

The publisher lounged in the doorway. "No sign of her, Edward, old chap? Too bad." He gave an airy wave of his hand. "Well, you can't really blame the gel. After all, she is a busy woman, I'm sure. Probably had more to do last night than wait around for you to get out of gaol."

Edward shot him a withering look. "I wouldn't be searching for her now if you had taken care of the police."

Nash flipped open the carved box on the desktop and selected a cigarette with exquisite care. When he had lighted it, he sank into the wing chair opposite Edward's desk. "Did as I've always done, old chap." His expression was apologetic "Just failed to take into consideration that others are doing more. The League for Uplift of Moral Virtue gave some of our most sympathetic friends some money for their campaign. Then when the, er, unpleasantness with your valet came to light, well, it was all simply too much."

"Where were you when the police rounded us all up?"

The publisher raised one laconic eyebrow. "You couldn't expect me to wait around. One of us bursting in and protesting loudly was enough."

Edward ran a hand gingerly over the swollen bruise on the side of his neck. "Not one of my better choices I will admit. If you had been there to explain . . ."

Nash shook his head. "Not a chance. They were doing a job. They had their orders."

"They were very enthusiastic about them. A bit higher and that cockney bloke would have crushed my skull."

"Never," Nash replied with mock horror. "I would have had to find another writer."

The flames leaped in Edward's smoky eyes, making him look astonishingly like a Renaissance painter's rendition of the devil. "Nash, did you arrange this whole thing?" His question couched in the mildest of tones hung in the air between them.

Nash's thin lips tightened. His face took on a pinched look. The silence lengthened. Neither man dropped his eyes. At last Nash spoke. "I got you out, old chap."

Edward leaned back in the chair, regarding him silently. Nash never moved. The pale eyes met the dark ones with never a flicker. At last Edward let out his breath in a sigh. "Will we have to close down?"

Nash took a deep drag on his cigarette, then grinned through a cloud of smoke. "No chance. Too many people enjoy coming here regularly. Our absence makes them desperate. For a few days we'll lock up but not permanently. The time will give us an opportunity to replace the equipment. Damn vandals." He leaped up and began to pace. "Do they think equipment like that can be bought at the corner hardware store? That stuff has to be imported, y'know. That roulette wheel alone costs more than the whole lot of them makes in a year." He raved on and on, gesticulating wildly.

Edward slumped forward, his forearms on his desk, listening with only half an ear now to Nash's voluble complaints. "Did you see her?"

"Who?"

"The girl with the red hair. Cassandra, she called herself."

Nash rolled his eyes heavenward. "Sorry, old chap. Didn't pay much attention to any of the females. Took a general look. All too ill-dressed to be of much interest." He stubbed out the cigarette. "M'self I've always preferred a bit of mystery, don't y'know?"

"Nash!"

"Well, what would have me say? Didn't see the gel. Haven't the faintest idea whom you're talking about. Can't imagine what you're upset about. All cats, gray in the dark anyway."

His further musings were interrupted by a knock.

"Come in." Edward smiled with real pleasure at his housekeeper, who hesitated when she saw Nash. "Miss

Fitch."

"I didn't mean to interrupt, sir." She thrust her hands beneath her apron. "I just came to say how happy we all are that you're back safe and sound."

"Thank you, ma'am. I'm fine."

The publisher eyed her narrowly, a faint sneer on his lips. "So, Miss Fitch, you're happy that he's back safe and sound. Are you really?"

"Why of course, sir. When Mr. MacAdam told me what had happened, I was most upset. Gaol is a horrible place, I'm sure."

"But don't you believe that your employer is a horrible man?" Nash went on, his voice laden with sarcasm.

Edward rose from his chair, casting a puzzled look from Nash to Miss Fitch, who shook her head, her expression blank.

"He is my employer, sir."

"Oh, yes, your employer. And you owe him more than just housekeeping, don't you? You owe him loyalty, don't you?"

"Why, yes, sir." She took a step back, teetering on the threshold.

"Then why did you meet with that sanctimonious rat, Fitzwalter, just a few days after you went to work here?"

Later Cassandra realized she should have pretended to know nothing about Fitzwalter or the League. She would have convinced them if she had not protested her innocence.

"You actually met with this man, Miss Fitch?" This from Edward, who was regarding her speculatively.

"He was a friend of my—that is—a friend of a friend. I told him that I couldn't and wouldn't get involved in the League. I told him I owe loyalty to you." Color rose in her cheeks. "You've been more than considerate as an employer. Neither Mr. Mac-Adam nor I—"

"Of course, there's the butler. Hired at your behest." Nash raised a wicked eyebrow. "How convenient if the League knew just when the party was going to be, so they could inform the police. Then the raid could be staged at just the right time for maximum embarrassment."

Cassandra shook her head adamantly. "Neither Mr. MacAdam nor I would be disloyal. Mr. MacAdam worked all his life for the Earl of Dearloch. He believes, as do I, that the servants who live in the house owe the laird their fealty."

Nash threw up his hands. "Oh, the 'laird,' is it? Oh, of course. Forget about Bonnie Prince Charlie and Loch Lomond and all that sort of trash. Makes everything different."

Cassandra's face reddened with indignation. "Mr. Nash, neither Mr. MacAdam nor I would do anything to hurt Mr. Sandron. He has been everything that is kind to us. Besides, surely many people knew and discussed the party. It couldn't have been a secret."

Controlling herself with icy calm, she looked full in Edward's face. "I'm glad you're back, sir. I came to tell you that and to ask if there was anything I could do for your comfort, or any special thing that you might need or want."

Edward shook his head. "Thank you, no, Miss Fitch. I have everything I need."

"Then I'll be about my duties, sir. Cook is preparing a special dinner tonight to welcome you after your terrible ordeal." With her chin high, she closed the door.

"Nash," Edward began. "You had no call to do that."

Nash grinned a mirthless malicious grin. "Oh, but I might have shocked some sort of a revelation out of her, old chap. Servants are always up to something dishonest. Sometimes a good scare shakes 'em up. Makes 'em admit to things that you didn't have any idea about."

Edward scowled. "You did that because you were angry at me."

"True. Wanted to show you how accusations work, old thing. You make a plausible case against me. I'll turn around and make a plausible case against those two. Easy enough to do. That's the thing about cases. Everyone's guilty of something."

"I'll remember that the next time I try to make a case. For now let's get to why the bribes did not work."

But Nash persisted. "Did see her with Fitzwalter, you know. She sat down with him at a tea shop on the corner."

"Probably he was trying to get to know her better. Miss Fitch wouldn't be half bad if she were dressed up properly. Her sort of strict propriety might appeal to someone like Fitzwalter."

Nash snorted. "Never. He's too peculiar. Selfish. Greedy to a fault. For all that, he's half cracked on religion."

"The other half?"

Edward had never seen Nash so serious. "Who's to say? There's something slimy here. May not be able to stand his own hypocrisy. Greed drives a man to do things he knows are wrong. Then rather than let people know that he's committing one of the 'seven deadlies,' he turns into a rampant do-gooder, but the sin's still there. He'd probably do anything to keep someone from discovering what a fake he is." He shrugged. "What am I talking about? I don't know a damned thing about religion or religious freaks. Don't understand them worth tuppence. And care less."

Edward grinned. "I was enjoying the dissertation actually. I should have taken the whole thing down so I could recall it later."

Nash drew on his gloves. "Then I'll leave you with those illuminating thoughts. I have an appointment with a sympathetic ear down at Scotland Yard. The investigation into the death of the valet is going nowhere. No clues. Nothing. They probably never will know who did it. I'm going to suggest that they push it back into a file and forget it. With the least bit of luck, they'll do just that."

Edward shrugged uncomfortably. "Why do I get the idea that you're not nearly so worried about this as I am?"

"Why should you be worried at all?"

Edward ran his hand around the back of his neck. "Because I was sick too," he reminded the publisher.

"Coincidence." Nash picked up his stick and hat, preening in front of the mirror beside the door.

"The same night Parks disappeared."

"You weren't poisoned, Edward, old chap. You didn't die. You just threw up your guts and went to bed. That's all there was to it. The two things are unrelated."

Edward looked unconvinced.

Nash sighed with exasperation. "Listen here. No one sets out to poison a servant and accidentally poisons a master. It's not done, don't y'know? All the great tragedies have a villain who poisons a master and accidentally poisons a servant. The other way around won't sell."

"Nash, we're not talking about pulp fiction. And besides, what if someone really did intend to poison me and poisoned Parks as well?"

"Then you'd be dead, Baal, old imp, and gone to meet your master. But you're not. At least not yet. Ta-ta."

Clad in his usual mackintosh and cap, Edward strode briskly along the Bayswater Road. Head lowered, eyes slitted against the cold drizzle, he looked neither to right nor left. The dripping green around him, he had seen all too often. Hyde Park was one of his favorite routes, no matter how inclement the weather.

Shortly into the regimen of his life as an author and casino operator, he had discovered that neither profession provided fresh air or healthful exercise. He had toyed with the idea of joining a gym but had discarded it swiftly. Certainly, no gentleman's club would promote him to membership. Burdened with an acute sense of inferiority, he would not go where any would have a chance to sneer at his base origins or questionable profession.

In place of boxing or fencing, he had begun a practice that got him out into the fresh air and kept him trim. He walked five miles four mornings a week. One day he would walk along Bayswater Road to Holland Park, then back along Kensington Road onto Piccadilly. Another he would walk along the Victoria Embankment as far as Blackfriars. Another route would take him north around Regent's Park. A fourth he would walk down Whitehall past the Houses of Parliament and thence to Vauxhall.

At first, he had looked about him warily, sure that people would stare at him suspiciously. He had pulled the flaps of his cap down over his ears lest they recognize that he was from Soho and come out of their houses to drive him back where he came from. When no one paid the slightest attention to him he had relaxed and begun to take notice of the scenes around him.

Now he never looked where he walked at all. Instead, he used the time to work out problems in his books or in his personal life. Today as cold wind stung the blood into his cheeks and he flexed his chilled fingers around his walking stick, he brooded about his former valet.

Despite Nash's skepticism, Edward could not keep from dwelling on the night of the Sabbat. Parks's death was most surely attached to the Devil's Palace in some way. Furthermore, he was sure that a potentially lethal dose of poison had been given him. He had been saved only by the timely intervention of Miss Fitch. If she had not come upon him when she did . . .

Shivering, he flung up his head and shrugged his shoulders. Tiny drops of water flew from the edges of his cape as he paused at the corner of Portobello Road.

A vegetable wagon drawn by a heavy cart horse swung out of Notting Hill Gate. The driver flicked a whip over the horse's back and urged it into a stumbling trot. Another man beside him on the box lobbed a stone down onto the dappled rump. The animal threw up its huge head, whickering in pain. The trot increased to a lope.

Edward stared at the spectacle amazed, a frown creasing his forehead. In another instant, he gave a piercing shout and jumped back from the edge of the road. The driver snapped the whip again and the heavy Clydesdale lunged forward in its harness, galloping straight toward the street corner where Edward stood.

Dodging behind the lamppost, he sprinted back the way he had come as the iron-shod hooves struck sparks from the paving stones. He could not hope to outdistance the swift-moving horse. It would run him down in another second.

The driver on the box cracked his whip again. Edward could smell the hot breath blown from its flaring nostrils. Wildly, he dodged out into the middle of the street. He took one terrified glance over his shoulder, then flung his body from the path.

The curve shaft of the wagon sheared into the

flapping mackintosh and dragged Edward off his feet before it ripped. He landed on his back on the cobblestones as the heavy wagon swept by him, the ironbound wheels only inches from his head and shoulder.

Even as he struggled for breath, his keen survival instincts shouted messages to his limbs. He twisted himself over onto his hands and knees in time to see the driver pull the horse and begin to haul the big head around. At the same time, the other man on the box sprang down and came loping back down the street. At that moment the rain began in earnest. The skies that had been dripping all day suddenly opened up and poured forth a great deluge.

The cold rain splashing on Edward's head and neck helped the dizziness. His gold-headed walking stick had rolled against the curb. Instead of rising, he flung himself onto it as his attacker pulled a heavy knotted club from the front of this belt.

Edward rolled over, his back pressed into the angle between street and curb, the walking stick flung up to take the force of the blow. As it cracked, he kicked hard. The heel of his boot drove into his assailant's crotch. The man yelped and backed away, clutching himself.

Edward staggered to his feet, stabbing his broken stick into the man's face. The jagged end tore the man's cheek open below the eye. He screamed like a wounded rabbit.

In the meantime, the driver had managed to turn the wagon and come galloping back. Accurately gauging the situation, he leaned over the horse's rump, urging the horse to maximum speed. "Jump on, Jock!" he yelled.

Jock reeled away, one hand clasped to his cheek, the other clutching his privates. Shivering with shock, he nevertheless managed to fling himself onto the open tail of the empty bed. The driver whipped the horse, and the vehicle clattered away down Notting Hill Gate, weaving in and out among the carts of farmers coming early to open stalls in the market.

Edward stumbled out of the street and leaned against a wall. Now that the danger had passed, he shook his head, unable to credit what had happened.

" 'ere, now. You all right?" a cockney voice whined in his ear as a warm hand clasped his shoulder. "Saw th' 'ole thing. Them blokes was after y', sure as 'ell."

"I'm all right," Edward muttered.

"Figured y'were," the man chuckled. "Y'sure gave the one wot fer. Kinda surprisin' t' see a gent fight s' tough."

The rain slackened, and Edward managed to push himself away from the wall. "I warn't allus a gent," he informed the other as he flashed a cheeky grin.

The man blinked then burst out laughing. "Good fer you, Cocky."

Edward rubbed his shoulder where he had landed in the street. It would have a terrific bruise tomorrow, but otherwise he deemed himself all right. A few twitches restored his garments to some semblance of shape. Although they were filthy from the roll in the streets, they would clean. He looked around him for a cab rather than make the two-mile walk back home again.

" 'ere's yer stick." The cockney had retrieved the pieces. "Got a real gold 'ead on it. Be easy t' fix."

A cab rolled toward them. Edward straightened his garments again and stepped to the curb to hail it. 'You get it fixed, pal. And thanks for your help."

As the cabbie pulled his horse to a halt, the cockney hurried forward to open the half door and swing it open. " 'Ey, guv. I didn't do nothin'. It's a real gold 'ead."

Waving the thing away, Edward climbed in and sank back wearily on the damp leather squabs. His voice was hoarse as he gave the driver his address.

The cockney latched the door and grinned in the window. "Much 'bliged, guv. Don't worry none 'bout them blokes. They ain't from around 'ere." He slapped the side of the door and motioned the cabbie to pull away. "They'll be 'eadin' back where they came from right soon," he promised.

"Inspector Revill, sir." MacAdam's Scottish trill of the r's struck a strangely familiar chord in Edward's ear. Where had he heard that trill before?

Then his speculation was swept away by the entrance of the burly police inspector accompanied by a man in uniform. "Mr. Sandron."

Again Edward felt the nervous clench of his stomach muscles. Desperately, he schooled himself to nonchalance. "Inspector Revill. Just the man I wanted to see. The police are certainly efficient. How have you heard about the incident so soon?"

"The incident?"

"A couple of men in a vegetable wagon tried to run me down in Bayswater Road."

The inspector gaped. He pulled his notebook from his breast pocket. "No, sir, I had not heard. Are you all right?"

"Oh, quite. A bit bruised. A little shaken. But otherwise thankfully healthy."

"You're sure it wasn't an accident."

"They turned the wagon around and came back to finish the job. One jumped out and came at me with a club," Edward replied drily.

The inspector began to write furiously in his notebook. "Did you recognize them?"

"Never saw them before," Edward replied, then acted on the cockney's information. "They were not from London. The driver called the other Jock."

The pencil paused, then moved on. "Jock. A Scot's name."

Edward raised his eyebrows. "Possibly."

Revill took a deep breath, swelling his heavy chest. "Would you ask that man to step back in here?"

"Mr. MacAdam."

"The same."

Edward rang, then seated himself behind his desk, regarding the inspector warily. Surely the single word *Jock* could not be construed as evidence of anything. The name was common in every part of the British Isles as well as northern France.

Composing his features into their most serious cast, the inspector planted himself squarely in front of the door and waited.

When the butler entered, the inspector drew his

omnipresent notebook from his pocket, turned a page or two, then cleared his throat. "Where were you on the night of October first," he rapped out.

MacAdam's face remained impassive. "I was in Scotland, sir."

"No, sir. You were not."

Edward straightened in his chair. Would this be the confirmation of all that had been said before? Would the original idea be proved true? He could scarcely believe it.

"I beg your pardon." The butler's face paled slightly although his expression never changed.

"I mean you were already in London. We've checked with your sister in Scotland. You left there in response to a letter sent to you by someone who called herself Lady Cassandra MacDaermond."

At the mention of the name *Cassandra,* Edward raised a black eyebrow. Cassandra was the name of the girl with red hair, the girl in the emerald green dress.

MacAdam remained erect, his back ramrod straight, his shoulders well back. They might have asked him for the most mundane bits of information. Only his throat, working convulsively, betrayed his agitation.

Revill turned another page. At the same time, he took another step forward until he was only inches from his quarry. He was shorter than the butler. MacAdam's eyes remained level with the inspector's forehead. "What do you have to say for yourself, MacAdam? Were you in Scotland or were you not? If we searched your room, would we find a used train ticket among your belongings?"

The butler's voice was only a little hoarse when he answered. "Perhaps you might, sir, but I doubt that it would prove that I came from Scotland before October first."

"It would have a date on it," Revill informed him triumphantly. "The conductor's stamp with the date and time."

"There is no ticket." MacAdam insisted. "I came from Scotland a week later, on the fifth or sixth. I can't remember the date for sure."

"And what about your sister's story that you received a letter from your former laird's daughter that invited you to London to a place of employment? Where is this woman? Since the death of her father, no one has seen her."

Edward shook his head in wonder. How many pieces did this puzzle have? Where did the Lady Cassandra MacDaermond fit into this? She had written Miss Fitch's references as well.

MacAdam paused momentarily before he spoke in measured tone. "I did leave as my sister said, but I stopped off to visit a friend on the way to London."

"And what might the name of this friend be?"

"Er . . . Smith."

"And where might Mr. Smith reside?"

"In Y-Yorkshire." The butler's fingers twitched at his sides. He doubled them into fists and continued to stare straight ahead.

"In Yorkshire? Would you care to be more specific?"

"I'm afraid I can't do that, sir. He lives on a farm."

"On a farm. Near what town?"

"York."

Revill turned away. He motioned to the uniformed man who had stood at attention by the door. "Perhaps we'd better take this man into custody until we can corroborate his story."

Edward looked at the butler, whose forehead now glistened with a thin layer of sweat. "But are you sure that he's really guilty of anything?"

"Won't take more than a week or two to get information," Revill replied. He put his hands behind him and rocked back and forth on his heels. "Until then we'll hold this fellow for your safety, Mr. Sandron. Who's to say but what he might try again? The criminal mind is difficult to understand, don't you know? A man who'll poison another man." He made a clicking sound with his tongue. "Well, that fellow don't, er, doesn't think like the rest of us. Poison's not a man's weapon."

"So you've said." Edward felt his own body tense as the blue-uniformed man extracted a pair of light shackles from beneath his overcoat. "Just a minute, I can't believe that's necessary. He's not proven guilty of anything."

"Nevertheless . . ."

"No. He's not going to run off. Are you, Mac-Adam?"

The butler had heretofore managed to maintain his composure. Now it began to slip a bit. His mouth wobbled slightly. As the policeman moved behind him to grasp one of his wrists, MacAdam extended the other hand beseechingly. "I beg you, sir . . ." he began.

Edward stepped forward. "Hold up there, Revill. Call off your dog. You don't have anything against this man except that he left Scotland before October first. He'll go quietly."

Revill looked unconvinced. "You don't know these quiet ones, sir. Sometimes they'll be the quickest and the trickiest. Knock the officer in the face. Break and run. Dart out between carriages in the street, duck into alleys. Zip! Swish! They're gone! And you're left standing scratching your head."

The policeman pulled MacAdam's free hand behind him.

"Mr. Sandron, sir . . ."

"Really, Revill . . ."

Revill made a signal to the man in the blue uniform. At the same time he took Edward Sandron by the elbow and turned him around. "Mr. Sandron, there's no need to trouble your mind about this. This is routine."

Edward shook him off. "No! By God! No! This is too much. You don't even known whether he's guilty or not."

The policeman was already thrusting MacAdam out into the hallway. Revill stepped between Edward and the door. "He'll have a fair trial before a judge and a jury. Every Englishman has the right to trial by jury."

Edward glared at him.

Revill faced him firmly. "This is all for your safety and protection, Mr. Sandron. After all you were the one who told us that you nearly died. You can't deny that your life was attempted again today."

Edward pushed past the inspector to follow MacAdam and his guard down the hall. "I'll come in and post bail as soon as possible, MacAdam. You have nothing to fear," he called.

The butler gave no sign that he had heard. His proud head was sunk between his shoulders. He swayed away from the hand of the arresting officer.

Edward turned to confront Revill, who halted abruptly at the sight of the gray eyes and black eyebrows drawn together in an angry scowl. "For God's sake, let him loose. He's an old man. He's not going to hit nor run nor duck."

At the same moment, Cassandra met the party coming down the stairs. At first she could not see what had happened. She only knew she had never seen Mr. MacAdam's face look so gray. Then she saw the swept-back arms, the policeman at his back.

Horrified, she put her hand to her mouth. "Mr. MacAdam!"

Halfway down the stairs, the butler stopped. "Now, lassie, don't be upset . . ."

"Upset . . ." Her voice was the merest whisper. "What are you doing to him?" Forgetting her disguise completely, she drew herself up. Her next words were uttered in her most imperious tones. "You will let him go instantly. There has been some ghastly mistake."

Revill hurried down the stairs, responding without thought to the authority in her voice. "Beggin' your pardon, ma'am, but there's been no mistake."

"Oh, but there has. A terrible one. Mr. MacAdam would not hurt anyone. I've known him all my life.

He is kind and gentle."

"He'll have his chance to prove his innocence in a court of law."

"What is he accused of?"

"Nothing yet. We're just taking him in until he can prove his whereabouts on the night Mr. Parks was killed."

"This is the most ridiculous thing I have ever heard." Cassandra gave a grand sweep with her arm. At the same time she raised her chin another notch. Her green eyes flashed imperiously. "Even if Mr. MacAdam were capable of harming someone, which he is not, he could have no reason for harming a man he did not know and who had done him no harm."

She almost carried it off. The officer backed away from his prisoner with hands outspread to indicate that he was not to blame for any mistakes that might have been made. Revill swept off his bowler and thrust it beneath his arm military fashion. "Ma'am . . ." he began.

"You will release him immediately," she demanded. The ring in her voice, the authoritative sound of it was unmistakable.

Edward Sandron came down the stairs, suspicion darkening his countenance. When she raised her eyes to his, he noted the flash of emerald fire, the same shade as the dress of the masked lady the night before. Perverse as the demon whose name he assumed, he paused a couple of risers above their heads. "I think not. After all, Inspector Revill is merely doing his duty. He would not take up a man if he were not sure of a case against him. Isn't that so,

Inspector?"

Revill blinked. Then looked from one to the other. Suddenly, the appearance of Cassie Fitch, her frumpish clothes complete with white apron, her gray hair slicked back in a tight knot, her thin pale face, conquered the impression of the authoritative voice and the flashing green eyes.

He clapped his hat back on his head with more force than necessary. "Right you are, sir. Let's get a move on." He gave MacAdam a shove that staggered him into the officer.

"No!" Cassandra's voice was shrill with panic. "Oh, no. Don't hurt him. You mustn't."

"We'll take him along, sir," Revill continued. Even as Cassandra protested, the trio passed out the door and down the steps.

When she would have run after them, Edward caught her by the arm. "Not so fast, Miss Fitch." He gave the name a peculiar emphasis. "I want to talk to you."

She turned on him with a ferocity that astounded him. "Did you have good, kind Mr. MacAdam arrested?"

Edward shrugged. "I didn't have anything to do with it. Inspector Revill obviously thought he had enough evidence to at least take the man along on suspicion."

"But he didn't do it." Cassandra was almost sobbing now. "Mr. MacAdam couldn't do anything like that. And they'll lock him up in a cell." She clasped her hands around her arms, shuddering. "They'll lock him up." Her own terrible fear made her voice breathless as horrible fancies permeated every nerve in her body.

Under normal circumstances, Edward would have responded to her distress, but Baal was the master here. He ignored the obvious distress. "I was prepared to believe that until I learned that Mr. MacAdam had come to London on the advice of a letter from a certain Lady Cassandra MacDaermond." Again he enunciated the name with a peculiar clarity. "You wouldn't know anything about her, would you?"

At the name, Cassandra stepped back from the stairs. Her eyes searched his face frantically, then dropped away, veiled behind her eyelashes. Unless she thought very fast, she would be hustled after Mr. MacAdam with so many crimes against her that she would be sent to prison with no hope of ever being released.

And a stone and iron cell would kill her. She could never survive it.

"Lady Cassandra MacDaermond," he repeated, coming down to the landing.

She could feel his dark eyes raking her. Were they piercing her disguise? Somehow she must allay his suspicions. She cleared her throat nervously. "Oh, of course, I know Lady Cassandra MacDaermond. And a sweeter lady there never was. Poor little thing. To be left alone after the death of her father."

"Oh, so her father is dead?"

"Yes. And a terrible thing it was too. He had a terrible disease. He had kept it a secret from her. But when it got too bad, he ended it. He couldn't stand for her to be burdened with his suffering, don't you know? She took it terrible hard," she continued, trilling her *r's* for all she was worth.

"So the Earl of Daerloch is dead?"

Concerned with her own safety and with the ultimate safety of Mr. MacAdam, Cassandra did not wince. "Dead, sir. His household divided, his servants sent away to look for a new place, and Lady Cassandra, her that wrote me the letter of reference, left all alone in the world."

He moved closer. "And where is she now?"

"Well, sir, I dinna ken her exact address. She didna give it to me. She went to live with an aunt in the Highlands."

"I thought you said she was alone in world?"

He was sharp. She tucked her head down and twisted her hands under her apron. "Only in a manner of speaking, sir. She's got relatives. Of course, many people are kin to the MacDaermonds. But she has neither mother, nor father, nor brother, nor sister, nor husband, nor . . ." She swayed slightly with the rhythm of her speech.

He held up his hand. "I see."

She bobbed her head up and down. Her hand fumbled behind her for the doorknob into the kitchen. "Yes, sir. Now if you'll excuse me, I'll hurry into the kitchen and be sure that the supper is being prepared. I'll have so much more to do without Mr. MacAdam."

"By all means get to your work," he mocked.

She paused in the doorway. Her thick Scottish brogue that had become pronounced when he reminded her of it dropped away completely. "You will see to his release, Mr. Sandron. He is a good man. He didn't do anything to deserve being locked up in prison."

"That's for the law to decide."

"You know how terrible it is in prison," she reminded him haughtily. "Surely you wouldn't wish such a thing on your worst enemy. Let alone an innocent man. And be assured, Mr. Sandron, Mr. MacAdam is innocent." With those words, she left him.

Sandron stared bemused at the door. Miss Cassie Fitch had lost her accent again. She aroused his strong instinct for self-preservation honed on the streets of London. Whoever she was, whoever the unknown killer was, neither would catch him unawares a second time. Furthermore, he would solve the puzzle of her before he cast her out into the streets.

Chapter Fourteen

"Lady Beatrice pounded her tiny white fists against the iron bound oaken door. Her cries of rage ceased at last, but the Savage Earl knew it would be many days before the proud beauty imprisoned behind it would be tamed to his hand. He smiled as he thought of the pleasure he would obtain conquering both her body and her soul.

Mounting the spiral staircase that led to the balcony above the chamber, he leaned his elbows on the finely wrought iron railing and looked down. "So, Lady Beatrice, you have at last ceased your useless caterwauling."

She sprang back from the door to stare up at him. Her emerald eyes blazed in the light from the flambeaux placed at each corner of the cell. "Let me go, you fiend," she demanded imperiously. "Or surely I will see you hanged."

He laughed maliciously. "You are in no position to make demands on anyone, my lady. Did any come in response to your shrieks just now? No. You kept on and *on until your voice was exhausted. Even now I detect a certain hoarseness in your throat."*

"My father . . ."

"Your father has given you to me to tame as I will. I have paid him well for his daughter. You are totally alone and in my power."

He snapped his fingers. A small door opened in the cell. Ivan, his hunchback servant, limped in, shackles dangling from his hairy hands.

Warned by the clink of the chains, Lady Beatrice turned. At the sight of the man's scarred face and gaping eyesocket, she uttered a frightful scream of terror. Her overcharged senses could stand to more. She collapsed in a heap, her dress of emerald silk belling out around her like the leaves around the blossom of the rose.

Ivan twisted his head up out of the wreck of his back. "Shall I strip her naked, master?" he whined.

The Savage Earl nodded. "By all means, Ivan. And chain her limbs so that . . ."

The clock chimed the half hour after nine. Edward jabbed the pen into the inkwell. Miss Fitch would be leaving for market. His mouth set in a grim line as he pushed himself back from the desk.

Too long he had accepted this employee at face value. For forty-eight hours now, he had tried unsuccessfully to fit together the pieces of her puzzle. Her face was sallow and lined above a slender, willowy body. When excited or nervous, she betrayed strange peculiarities of accent. At such times, too, her humble aspect would be replaced by sudden flashes of aristocratic temper.

He had overlooked these discrepancies until Inspector Revill had taken MacAdam into custody. Now his curiosity was aroused. Sandron was determined to solve the puzzle of Cassie Fitch once and for all. Every puzzle had a solution. Since his life might depend on the solution, he would gain an added benefit from it.

The house was unusually silent. No servants were about. No bustling noises came from the gambling casino, temporarily closed while awaiting its new equipment. No sounds issued from the kitchen on the cook's day off.

With an anticipatory gleam in his eye, Edward Sandron thrust open the door to Miss Fitch's room. It was plain as her clothing, its furnishings meager. The narrow bed was neatly made, its coverings tucked beneath the thin mattress. Beside the bed was a stand with an old-fashioned oil lamp and a book. He crossed the room to check the title curiously. He found he held one from his own library. She had borrowed one of his books without permission.

Intrigued rather than angry, he rubbed his hand across the fine leather of the cover. Instead of getting closer to solving the puzzle, he had found another piece. Most housekeepers were probably minimally literate. Certainly he would not expect one to be reading Pepys' *Diary*. He put the book down, then stooped and ran his hands beneath the mattress. He found nothing there nor under the bed except an empty valise.

He clenched his jaw as he straightened. The room was depressingly bare. Only a couple of gowns and an apron hung on pegs beside the door. A feeling of frustration began to knot his muscles. He had devoted less than a quarter of an hour to his search and found nothing. The only thing left was the chest of drawers beside the door.

Moving in front of it, he saw his own face reflected in the crazed mirror. The sight of his stern expression made him smile. He felt increasingly foolish with each passing minute. Who but a fool would go through an old woman's things to finds clues to a murder? He was coming to believe he had exaggerated the entire thing.

With a resigned sigh he opened the shallow top drawer of the chest. A glance at its contents almost made him close it immediately. Neatly aligned were a comb and brush, a small tray of hairpins, a couple of lengths of ribbon rolled neatly, a graphite pencil, and three jars.

Expecting nothing, he nevertheless unscrewed the top of one. The heavy smell of greasepaint filled his nostrils. His flesh chilling, he stared down at the contents of the jar. It was theatrical makeup. He could not be mistaken.

His mother had used it on occasion to cover bruises left by particularly brutal clients. His mother's makeup, however, had been rosy flesh-toned. This paint was pale gray. The content of the second jar was darker. The third jar contained powder, again not a normal cosmetic color, but a dull drab shade. A sallow shade, in fact.

Suddenly, a piece locked into place. Miss Fitch was making up her face to look older. She was disguising her appearance. Her clothing was drab enough, but she had failed to disguise the willowy figure. She could not, of course, hide the bright green eyes.

The next drawer contained shifts and pantalettes, hose rolled in neat pairs, all arranged with careful precision. The third drawer contained a wool pelise, and several wool stoles and scarves, all of Scottish weave. The pattern was the same in all, a plaid of red, gray, and blue. He was unfamiliar with the clans of Scotland, but he would get a guinea that these were the plaid of MacDaermond.

The contents of the last drawer were covered with a sheet. Gently, he pushed it back. His first glimpse of emerald green brocade told the entire story. "So, Cassandra, here you are."

As if it were her body, he lifted the dress out. With the side of his leg, he closed the bottom drawer. Then with the dress still draped over both arms, he carried it from the room and up the stairs.

When Miss Fitch returned, the bell in the kitchen was jangling. She gave a withering glance at the ceiling as she set her parcels on the table. The morning had been disappointing. No one at the gaol would let her see Mr. MacAdam since she was not a relative.

Muttering under her breath, she hung her bonnet and shawl on a peg by the door. She hurried up the back stairs, tying her apron around her waist as she climbed. Knocking briskly, she opened the door immediately without waiting for his summons. "I'm sorry, sir, I was just coming in as the bell . . ." Her voice trailed away.

Draped across the wingback chair, its skirt swept wide, was Ashtaroth's green brocade dress. She clapped her hand to ther mouth as color drained from her face.

Her eyes, brilliant against her white skin, flew to his face. He leaned back against the desk, his arms folded across his chest, his mouth curved in a mirthless grin. "So you do recognize it, Miss Fitch? Or would you prefer that I call you Cassandra?"

She uttered a faint cry and backed away from it. Desperately, she slammed the door behind her and began to run. She could feel the tears starting from her eyes. It was over now. The deception. The least that she could hope for was that she would be thrown out. How horrifying to think that she might be arrested! And poor Mr. MacAdam would be imprisoned forever, or perhaps deported, or worst of all, hanged.

"Cassandra!" Edward Sandron's voice thundered after her.

She did not stop. She dared not stop. Perhaps he would not bother to follow her. She could dash into her room, throw her things into her valise, and leave. She could not run out into the streets as she was.

Her mind darted frantically over the possibilities. He would not expect her to leave immediately. He would expect her to come back to him after she had gotten over her initial terror. He would want her to beg. He would want to dismiss her officially.

Trembling, she flung herself to her knees beside her bed and dragged the valise from beneath it. Haphazardly she jerked the clothes off their pegs and stuffed them into it. Next the drawers. A hollow feeling settled in the pit of her stomach as she tumbled the total of her wordly possessions into one small bag. The tears were falling faster now, stinging her eyes, blinding her. Her sobs tore at her throat.

Then the door burst open. Edward Sandron towered on the threshold. "Cassandra!" he repeated. "Are you Cassandra?"

Alarmed, she sprang up, but her heel caught in her skirt. With a muffled exclamation, she staggered, then toppled over, sprawling across the valise. From that embarrassing position, she looked up the length of his long frame.

Almost casually he bent down. She cringed, but his hand fastened in the top of her wig and pulled. The hairpins caught, scratched her scalp, and brought more tears to her eyes. She gave a cry of protest, but he was inexorable. A final twist left the wig dangling from his hand. He hoisted it up as if it were a trophy, then tossed it aside and bent again.

"No. No, damn you. Stop!" She threw up her arms to shield herself, but he brushed them aside. "Stop it, I say. Don't."

Paying not the slightest attention to her commands, he plucked the pins from her hair and combed through it with ungentle fingers. "Cassandra," he repeated.

"My name is—"

Slipping his hands under her arms, he set her on her feet. "Cassandra," he finished.

"No, Cassie Fitch."

"You called yourself Cassandra Hallowe'en night."

She cowered back, shielding her face. "I just took m'lady's name. I didna mean no harm."

He grinned malevolently as he heard her Scot's brogue broaden. "Accent's quite strong now, Cassandra. It comes and goes, I've observed."

"I dinna ken what ye're talkin' about."

He cursed mildly then. His hard hands wrapped around her upper arms and shook her back and forth. Her head rocked on her shoulders. The red mane tossed wildly. "The truth! I want the truth!" he thundered. In that moment he might have been the true Prince of Darkness and she might have been a damned sinner. "And that is what I will have. I want no more of that humble, self-effacing playacting. Who are you and why are you here?"

"I'm Cassie Fitch," she managed to choke out, though her head was spinning and she thought her neck would snap.

"Then why are you here?"

"I'm a housekeeper. I'm here to keep from starving to death."

"Lies," he growled. "All lies!" He let go her shoulders at the same time he pushed her back toward the end of the narrow bed. "All lies!"

Free of the terrible crushing grip on her shoulders, her own temper roused. She straightened angrily. "No! I don't tell lies."

Fists dug into his hips, he laughed mirthlessly.

"At least not about that." She defended herself breathlessly. "I applied at the employment agency and you hired me as a housekeeper. And I'm good at what

I do," she rallied as he seemed about to speak. "You must admit that I give good service."

"Oh, you give good service, right enough."

She blushed bright red.

He raised an eyebrow when he saw her hands double into fists. "And who is MacAdam?"

"He is . . . was your butler."

"The two of you came to work in my house. Did someone pay you to come to work for me?"

She shook her head violently. Her red hair, shaken completely loose from its moorings, swirled around her shoulders. "If someone else paid us, we would work for him. We came to work for you because you applied with an employment agency. They sent me. Remember?"

"You came to work in the Devil's Palace."

She shook her fists in his face. "I had no choice. When my . . . my employer died, I was turned out of my old place in Scotland. We both were. Can't you understand? I came here to work for you because you advertised that you needed help. You pay me. I work for you. You pay well. I work hard and I'm grateful. I don't want to starve or walk the streets."

A small grin tugged at the corners of his mouth. She was magnificent. The red hair was like living flame, brighter in the light of day than he remembered it. What would her complexion be like without the greasepaint? He cocked his head to one side. "You would probably earn more walking the streets," he observed.

She flushed again. "I cannot answer you as to that."

He put his hand beneath her chin and turned her

face to the light of the window. "Why the disguise if you're innocent?"

"I was afraid that you'd"—she swallowed hard—"do what you did if you knew I was young."

That answer silenced him for a moment. It aroused the memory of the sublime passion, the dark excitement of their coupling. His eyes narrowed. In that minute he became determined that she should not leave here. He only wanted to know one thing more. He aimed one long slender finger at her like a dagger. "Why do you want to kill me?"

"I?" Her mouth gaped in total amazement. "I don't want to kill you. I could have left you lying in the hall outside the chapel. You were almost paralyzed. Left there all night, with no help . . ." She shook her head. "You were very sick. I've never seen anyone so sick."

He shook his head. "Too many things are not right about this . . ."

She gave a small inelegant snort of disgust. "I should think that most things are not right in a gambling casino. Didn't you almost get shot by a poor boy trying to kill himself over his losses? How do you know he didn't intend to shoot you all the time? Maybe he was just threatening suicide to get you to come near him?"

"But . . ."

She picked up her valise. "Listen, I really don't see the point in our continuing this conversation. I need to be on my way if I'm going to find a roof to spend the night under. If you'll just step aside, I'll leave." She started around him.

He blocked her path. "You're not going anywhere."

She blinked at the change in his voice. It had deepened. In the smoky eyes little gold flecks began to move. "I can't stay here as a housekeeper any longer."

He was smiling now, the most malicious smile that any demon of hell ever smiled. "That's right. You can't. I don't intend that you should."

"Then let me pass."

Boldly, he wrested the valise from her hand. "You won't need that."

"Give that back."

He dropped it to the floor behind him. "I have another proposition to make to you Cassie or Cassandra or whatever your name is."

She eyed him narrowly. "What?"

"Obviously, you can't stay here as a housekeeper . . ." he began.

"I don't see what's so obvious about that," she objected, interrupting him. The frown between her eyebrows smoothed out. "Although if you think about it, you'd realize I've given you good service. If I were allowed to stay, I'd keep out of your way. You'd never see me except when I brought your meals. If Mr. MacAdam were allowed to return, he could serve those. You'd never see me again. And I'd work ever so hard."

"As to the hard work, well, we'll have to see. But I very much want to see you again, Cassie."

"You do?"

"Yes."

She looked at him doubtfully.

His face assumed a bland expression. "I want to see all of you. And you won't have to work hard at all. As my mistress you would have plenty of time to lie around. You could sleep as late as you like and your only work would be . . ."

Her heart contracted painfully. The sense of shame made her dizzy. Combined with it was the hurt that he should make her such an offer. It confirmed the difference between women and ladies. If she had behaved as she ought, he would not have dared to make such as offer. That night had ruined her forever. Her only hope was to get as far away from him as possible. Her eyes stung. She blinked rapidly.

He shifted his feet, trying to read her answer in her face. "What do you say, Cassandra?" he prompted at last.

She drew herself up proudly. "I thank you, sir. I am cognizant of the honor you do me." Her voice was heavy with sarcasm. "However, I must decline. I prefer to remain free and independent. A housekeeper's lot is not such a bad one. It is, after all, honest work."

He gaped slightly, then recovered his poise. "You could have an allowance."

Had he no concept of how he insulted her? Her face flamed. "I thank you, sir, but I would rather have a reference."

"No."

Her shoulders slumped. "Then give me my valise and let me pass."

"No. Damn you. I will open a charge account for you at whatever store you like. What about one of those new department stores? Harrod's? or Barker's?" He cursed himself mentally. His voice had a desperate sound. He was actually begging the wench.

He thought he could pay for her like a whore. Her stomach churned. "I thank you, sir, but no."

"Damn you!" He put his hand on her chest and pushed her back against the end of the bed. The valise fell from her hand.

"Wait! What are you doing?" Her eyes flew wide as he did not ease the pressure but with ungentle force tumbled her backward.

"I am going to try to fit together two pieces of the puzzle," he replied cryptically. Even as she attempted to move, he put a knee on the bed, setting it on her skirt.

Her face went quite white, as he straddled her and dragged down a corner of the spread. "Now we'll see what you really look like under that bloody mess."

"Ouch! Don't!" Her nails scored the spread as he roughly wiped away the greasepaint and graphite pencil. "Ow! Stop it! What do you think you're doing?"

"Seeing what you really look like, without the mask."

"I'm just an ordinary girl."

One corner of his mouth lifted in derision. He lifted a lock of her hair. "Of course. An ordinary girl — with skin like milk and hair like flame and eyes like emeralds."

"You sound like a bad novel."

His face darkened as she scored a hit. "Why, so I do! I write them, as you have pointed out."

She swallowed, realizing she had gone too far. The male heat of his thighs on either side of hers was having its effect on her breathing. She must get him off her. Her next request was couched in conciliatory tones. "Please let me up, so I can be on my way."

"You're not going anywhere."

"You've seen what I look like. You've asked me to be your mistress. I've refused. I should think that would be enough. After all, a few minutes ago you were convinced that I had tried to kill you. Think for a minute," she sneered. "You don't want to take a chance on my hurting you."

Ignoring her sarcasm, he leaned above her. "You gave yourself to me the night of the ball."

She looked away from him. He was cruel as the very devil to remind her of such a thing. "To my eternal shame."

"You wanted me. You couldn't get enough of me. You wrapped your beautiful legs around me and begged and moaned . . ."

She closed her eyes tightly. "For God's sake! Don't torment me so."

He laughed softly. "But as you pointed out that night. I am the devil. Does not the devil torment his souls?" He waited for an answer. When none was forthcoming, he shrugged. "I am dismissing you as my housekeeper. You'll get no character from me."

His words hurt. She had really not expected a character, but somehow, deep inside of her, had remained the hope that he would write something. Determined not to show her lacerated feelings, she closed her eyes. "I didn't expect you to give me one."

He grinned as he gripped her chin and turned her face back to him. "You'll get no character from me.

Because I'll make you my mistress." Beneath his ring finger he could feel the pulse skip a beat in the side of her throat.

"Never," she whispered at last.

He tapped her lips with his finger. "Never is a long time. Especially when a woman is as passionate as you are." Insolently, his hand moved over her throat.

She jerked her gaze away, he but took no offense. Instead his clever fingers opened the fastener of the cairngorm jewel at the neck of her dress.

"Don't," she whispered,. "Don't . . ."

With painstaking care, he withdrew the pin and laid the heavy silver brooch on the bed. "I'm going to open your blouse now, Miss Fitch. I already know what beauties I'll find there, but I haven't seen them in the light of day."

"You! You monster!" She slapped at his hand. "Devil!" Simultaneously, she bucked her hips upward. His full weight on her skirts held her as surely to the bed as if she had been strapped down.

He laughed again, a mirthless, hollow sound. She felt the cool rush of air as he peeled back the dress from her throat. Her camisole was gathered across the tops of her breasts by a ribbon threaded through eyelet embroidery. With torturous slowness, he pulled loose the bow.

"No!" She gasped for breath as she twisted and writhed under him. "Leave me alone. Stop!"

"Such a struggle," he mocked. "You did not make such a fuss the other night. I remember your gasps of quite a different nature. Now let me see them."

Suddenly, she stopped struggling. Her breath stilled

as her flesh prickled in dreadful anticipation. "Please," she whispered, her eyes squeezed tightly closed. "Don't do this."

If he heard her, he paid no heed. His face was rigid as he pushed the thin lawn down. They were as beautiful as her hair and her eyes. Creamy white perfection. Each a perfect cone peaked with a delicate pink nipple. A wave of inordinate desire swept through him. Hot blood surged through his veins, arousing his body to a fever pitch.

His muscles humming with tension, he slid one thigh down beside her, lowering his body onto hers, letting her feel his hardness. At the same time he hovered over her. Pursing his lips, he blew gently on the pink tip. Her shudder communicated itself all along his length.

He smiled and drew in a deep breath to blow again.

"Don't."

"Why not? You love it so." He blew again, his lips not a half inch from his goal.

She drew a tiny shallow breath. The nipple moved, brushed like the wing of a moth across his lips. "No . . ." Her voice was a moan of pain. "No . . . I don't love it."

He lowered his head the half inch. "But you do," he whispered. "You do. Your body cries out what you deny." His words branded themselves on her tingling flesh with each syllable he uttered.

"No. Oh, no." She sobbed her denial.

"Shall I kiss you now?"

"No."

"Yes. Now." His tongue laved the pink tip. It hardened miraculously as she cried out. "So sweet. You taste so sweet, Cassandra."

She bucked again, futilely, expending her frail strength. His weight and shape pressed down on her belly where a hot liquid melting curled and writhed. Her hands clutched at the spread beneath her, her nails scored it.

He moved on to the other breast while his thumb and third finger replaced his mouth on the first. "So sweet. Am I giving you pleasure, Cassandra? Cassandra." His other hand grasped her hair. "Like living flame. Like silk. So long." He wrapped a lock around his hand.

"Let go of me," she warned. Her voice was stronger, less breathless.

"Never." Yet something in her voice made him raise his head.

Her desperate hand had found the cairngorm brooch.

"What . . . ?"

She stabbed downward, catching him on the temple less than an inch from the corner of his eye.

He gave a yell and rolled away. At the same time she gave a tremendous push that toppled him off the bed. In the same motion she sprang to her feet. She made to dive for her bag but took only one step before he caught her skirt. Twisting around, she tugged frantically at it, fairly dancing up and down in her terror and determination to be free.

Grimly he held on, wrapping one hand more securely in the stout black wool. The other hand he clapped to his temple, his face contorted with pain.

Silently, she struggled, bracing her legs and pulling at the skirt, but the heavy material resisted her best efforts.

Using her strength against her, he swiveled his body around on the floor. Horrified, she froze at the sight of his face. Blood. His blood that she had shed seeped between his fingers.

Her momentary paralysis was all he needed. He gave a swift jerk that toppled her toward him. With her legs encumbered by the wrappings of the skirt, she fell heavily face downward on the floor. As she rolled over, he pinned her with his body. When she began to writhe again, he clapped the bloody hand on her throat.

His face not six inches away from hers was scarcely recognizable. Blood had trickled into his eye stinging and blinding him. His teeth were bared as if he meant to bite her throat. His chest heaved against hers, his breath sobbed out of his throat.

The last of the fight was out of her. Eyes dilated, face drained of all color, breath labored, she lay limp. He had subdued her at last.

Chapter Fifteen

Edward let his muscles go slack and shifted himself off her body. He could feel the warm trickle of blood down the side of his face and across his cheek. His temple stung like the very devil and his eye twitched involuntarily. Keeping one hand at her throat, he fumbled in his pocket for a handkerchief. Without taking his eyes off her, he clapped it to the wound.

Cassandra drew in a great shuddering breath that ended in a sob. Her eyes remained firmly closed, her brow creased in pain.

The difference between this scene and the scenes in his books struck him forcibly. The heroines cooperated by fainting until a lackey chained them somewhere. The numerous dukes and earl who had tamed women never ended up on the floor with their faces bleeding.

His lips peeled back from his teeth in an animal grin. He had underestimated her determination. Street stories portrayed the rich and aristocratic as weak, easily overcome in hand-to-hand fighting. If this girl were exemplary of the type, the stories were far, far from the truth.

Warily, he released her throat and sat up, mopping at the scratch on his temple. The blood on his handkerchief had already begun to darken. It confirmed his diagnosis of a superficial wound. Nevertheless, he climbed to his feet and made his way slowly to the mirror.

At first glance his face looked to be a mess. Blood streaked and smeared the entire left side, but it was already beginning to clot. "Did you have to be so violent?" he threw over his shoulder as he dipped the handkerchief into the pitcher of water on the chest.

She said nothing. With her face turned away from him, she sat up and began to gather the facings of her dress together. With shaking fingers she fumbled for the ends of the ribbon to draw up her camisole.

The wound was about an inch long, shallow he judged, but deep enough to leave a scar. It continued to bleed sluggishly every time he removed the handkerchief. "The blood's getting on my shirt," he complained, turning to show her. "Come see if you can do something about it."

For the first time she looked at him. Her eyes widened at the sight. Only once before had she seen more blood—when her father died. Sandron's wound was all the more horrible becauses she had shed it herself. Forgotten for the minute was their fight.

Obediently, she climbed to her feet and made her way to her valise. Opening it, she pawed through the tumbled contents until she found another handkerchief. She carried it back to the chest and dipped it into the stained water.

She flinched at the sight of his face so close, then

steadied, a worried frown creasing her forehead as she raised the handkerchief. His eyebrow was caked with blood, as well as the white hairs at his temple. Watching the play of emotion across her face, he endured her ministrations patiently, his forearm on the chest. Despite an occasional tremor, she managed very well. Only when he put his other hand on her hip did she stop. Her eyes flew to her waist where his thumb pressed gently, then back up to meet his steady gaze.

"The wound is closing," she told him, her voice shaking.

"That's good," he murmured. "Will it leave much of a scar?"

Tears started in her eyes then. One overflowed and trickled down her cheek. Despite the involuntary reaction, she managed to put on her sternest face. "I doubt it. If you have a court plaster around, I could cover it for you."

"Leave it. If it's closing of its own accord, those things just complicate matters. I've had much worse than this with never a beautiful lady to clean them up for me."

She dropped her cloth onto the top of the dresser and stepped back, pulling away from his hand. "If that is all then, sir. I'll be going."

He stepped in front of her. "No, you'll not."

"I believe that we've had this conversation before."

"Indeed, to my sorrow. However, I don't intend to argue with you this time."

Her eyes darted to her bag, then back to him as she took another step backward. "What are you going to do?"

He laughed then. The sound was hollow, and his temple hurt where his eye crinkled. "Just like the men in my books, I'm going to let you think over the error of your ways."

She divined his intent but sprang forward too late. "No! Don't lock me in."

The doorknob was in one hand, the key in the other. He jerked the key from the keyhole with the same motion that he pulled the door open. When she tried to follow him, he spun and fended her off with the flat of his hand in the center of her chest. A gentle push sent her staggering back a step. He backed over the threshold and slammed the door behind him. Even as she flung herself against it and twisted at the knob, he turned the key.

"Let me out! Damn you!"

He heard the flat of her hand slapping against the panelling. The knob rattled frantically. "This is for your own good," he called.

"My own good?" she screamed. "My own good!"

"You don't want to go out into the world to be a housekeeper," he advised sarcastically. "You'd be old before your time."

"Everyone gets old. Let me out!"

"As my mistress you'd have a housekeeper to work for you."

"No!"

"Think about it!" He slid the key into his pocket and strode off down the hall.

"Edward Sandron! Let me out of here! I'm not one of your women in one of your filthy books. This is the nineteenth century." Her voice followed him down the hall.

"Edward!" Her voice rose to a piercing shriek as terror struck her, but he did not perceive its tone, muffled as it was by the heavy door.

With a jaunty step he climbed the stairs. How unfortunate that he had no balcony overlooking her room! On the other hand perhaps he really did not want to hear all the things she was calling him. He grinned imagining her choice of words, now muffled by the heavy oak and distance.

He would leave her there for just a couple of hours. Long enough for her temper to cool and her natural practicality to assert itself. Canny Scot that she was, she would come to look with favor on his offer to realize that it was not only generous, but the best solution to her problem.

Then he would bring her supper.

And a piece of jewelry. Sally was extracting jewelry from her admirers. His mother also was especially fond of it. Probably all women liked it. After all, Cassandra had worn a brooch. He would give her a nice bracelet. Definitely, not a brooch. He touched his cheekbone beneath the wound. It felt swollen and very tender.

Back in her room the locked door wreaked its own particular brand of horror on Cassie. Leaving off the futile pounding, she ran to the window and tugged up the stubborn sash. The gust of icy wet air made her hug her arms about her body, but it restored her courage. She was not really locked in so long as she could hang out a window. Claustrophobia was in the mind after all.

"Only in the mind," she whispered to herself. Here in the bright cold air, she could regain her control.

She thrust her head and sucked long calming breaths into her panting lungs. Within just a minute, she was able to look about her. The prospect was not a pleasant one. Although her room was at street level, the steps to the basement went down beneath it. She could not climb out the window without a drop of some twenty feet to stone. With a broken ankle she could not run very far or very fast. Worse, she would be crippled. No one would hire a servant on crutches, always supposing she would be able to get medical aid.

She thought about calling for help, but her room faced the alley where unsavory characters were always passing by. In this section of town, any passerby would think she was a prostitute. She might even manage to get herself arrested as a thief. She turned away but could not bring herself to pull the window down. Stomping across to the bed, she jerked the blanket off it. As she wound it around her shoulders, she cursed her employer virulently for placing her in a position where she would surely have to freeze to death because of her stupid fear.

Cassandra sank down on the bed. A sharp object stabbed the back of her thigh. Twisting around she found the cairngorm brooch. A wave of nausea rose in her throat as she lifted it gingerly. To her surprise, she could find no trace of blood on the silver.

She closed her eyes, then snapped them open as the memory of his face rose before her, torn, his blood streaked across. She stared down at purple stone in its sharp-edged setting. The light glanced and danced off the facets. It represented her pride unstained and unrepentant. She thrust it deep into her pocket with a defiant shake of her head.

Her opening the window had thoroughly chilled the room. She tucked her feet beneath the disordered covers and hunched against the headboard, the pillow clutched in her arms. No matter if he kept her imprisoned for weeks, no matter if he starved her, she would never, never submit to his demands. She would not be his mistress. She would fight him as she had done today. He would get tired of that soon enough. He would get tired before she did.

The longer she sat there, the more relaxed her muscles became. Her head felt too heavy for her neck. She rested her cheek on the pillow. Her eyelids drooped over her burning eyes.

The alarm bell rang in Edward's study. He pushed the pen into the inkwell and frowned. Someone had forced the door to the Devil's Palace. Selecting a burled wood walking stick from the stand, he went down the hall to the entrance at the back of the card room.

The draperies at the two tall windows were tightly drawn, allowing only minimal light to seep in beneath them. The debris left by the police raid had been cleared away. Undamaged chairs and tables had been righted and arranged neatly, awaiting their next occupants. All in here was as it should have been except for the eerie silence and dimness. Moving silently, the thick carpeting muffling his steps, Edward took a firmer grip on the stick. When he reached the archway, he backed against the wall and peeked into the main casino. He relaxed slightly as he recognized the intruder.

His jaw set in a determined line, Fitzwalter crept through the empty salon of the Devil's Palace. He carried a half-open umbrella before him as if he were feeling his way with it. His short, chubby figure tottered slightly as he mounted the steps of the stage. With a nervous glance around him, he thrust aside the edge of the curtain. "Sandron!" he shouted, craning his neck upward.

Edward came forward into the main room, now bare except for the thick carpets. Positioning himself beneath the gas-o-lier, he held his cane across his body at the ready.

"Sandron!" came the shout again.

Edward waited. Sooner or later the little man would get tired of shouting.

"Sandron! I know you're up there. Come down!" The moralist banged with his cane on the proscenium arch. When no answer was forthcoming, he stepped behind it, letting the curtain drop to behind him.

"Baal!" he barked. "Baal! Where are you?"

Edward could picture him cocking his head, his sagging cheeks reddening, their tiny networks of veins turning purple with anger.

"Baal! You devil!" the man shouted.

At this rate the man would have an apoplectic stroke. A sardonic grin turned up the corners of

Edward's mouth. "Here, Fitzwalter!" he called in a deep voice.

A short silence, then something thumped at the curtain, batted at it, and at last pushed it aside. Fitzwalter glared at his adversary then trotted down the steps. "I've come to tell you that your evil schemes are for naught," he announced.

Unperturbed, Sandron noted the spittle collected on the edges of the thick graying moustache. "How interesting!" he replied. "What evil schemes are these?"

The little man thrust his chin out. "Ferris Mac-Adam is on his way back to Scotland. I have paid his bail."

Edward's smile broadened. "You could have saved yourself the money for your League for Moral Uplift or whatever you called the thing? I had planned to do it this afternoon."

Fitzwalter gaped then pointed an accusing finger. "A lie. Everyone know the devil lies."

"Let's be serious, Fitzwalter. There's nobody here but us. We don't have to put on a performance for an audience. You know I'm not the devil."

The red jowls trembled. "You dare to stand here in this—this den—this earthly hell and tell me you are not the devil."

Edward sighed. "Is that all you came for? If you came to tell me that my butler was on his way back to Scotland, thank you for the information. If you came to preach to me about sin, then I'll ask you to leave immediately."

"I'll leave. I'll leave and gladly. As soon as I have

your housekeeper with me."

"Cassie Fitch?"

Fitzwalter hesitated infinitesimally. "Er, yes. Cassie Fitch. She belongs back in Scotland with her own people. Not here in this den of iniquity, this hellhole, this—"

Edward rapped the cane on the floor. "Spare me."

Fitzwalter's mouth snapped to with a gasp. His head jerked backward on his pudgy neck.

Bringing his eyebrows together in a Mephistophelean frown, Edward surveyed the intruder. "What is this? Some new plan to render my home so uncomfortable that I'm forced to give it up? I promise you it won't work. I can always hire more servants . . ."

"Then . . ."

"But I refuse to dismiss an excellent woman because you want to take her away. How do you know she wants to go with you?"

"She will."

"She has a very good job here. The work is not arduous, the hours are not long. She has her own room, time to herself, good food." Even as he rattled off the list, Edward's conscience jibed at him. "She is very happy here."

"No! You're wrong." Fitzwalter's eyes darted about the room. "Let me speak to her. We will speak with her together. You will see."

"I'm afraid that's not possible. She is about her duties."

The moralist twisted the umbrella in his hands. He swallowed hard. "I demand that you summon her."

Edward took a deep breath. "Get out," he said

softly.

"What?"

"You heard aright. Get out. You have broken into my house. If you do not leave immediately, I will send for the police to have *you* arrested."

"On what charge?" Even as he blustered, Fitzwalter took a backward step.

Edward grinned maliciously. The enemy was in retreat. Too often in the slums he had bluffed his way out of a fight by attacking. "Attempted robbery for a start. I caught you breaking into my house, sneaking around to see what you could find to steal."

"That's . . . that's preposterous." The perspiration popped out on Fitzwalter's forehead. He drew his handkerchief from his pocket and wiped at his lips. His high color had faded somewhat.

"Not really. Shall we ask them to check the lock on the front door. Has it been broken?"

"I didn't break it." Fitzwalter protested.

Edward gestured with his cane. "Shall we go and see?"

The man stumbled over his own feet, recovered himself, and threw up his hands. "No! That is, it will not be necessary. You would waste your time to call them. The lock was not broken. The door was open. That is, the lock had not been locked, um, properly."

"We'll see."

Fitzwalter fled. Outside on the steps of the Devil's Palace, he recovered a little courage. "You haven't seen the last of me," he warned.

Edward slashed the cane across the portico like a dueling saber. "Get off. Go find someone else to threaten."

The man leaned back. "At least let me see Lady—that is—Miss Fitch," he begged.

"Get off and don't come back!" Edward closed the door with a resounding slam.

"Miss Fitch. Hsst, Miss Fitch!"

Cassandra sat up on her bed. The light was waning. She must have slept and dozed all afternoon. She had not realized she was so tired. The deception must have exerted a heavier strain on her than she had realized.

"Miss Fitch. Cassandra."

She glanced around bemused. Was she still dreaming? No. Someone was calling her name.

"Miss Fitch." The sound came from directly outside.

Sliding off the bed, she ran to the window. "Mr. Fitzwalter." Tears began to pour down her cheeks at the sight of his dear familiar figure. Frantically, she waved. "Oh, Mr. Fitzwalter. I'm so glad to see you."

He stepped back; his mouth fell slack. "Really?"

"Oh, yes." She held out her arms. "Can you get me out of here?"

He looked to right and left, then up at the windows of the floor above her. "Surely, dear lady. Surely." His voice did not sound convincing. "I'll wait right here while you come out."

"I can't get out," she wailed in exasperation. "He's locked me in this room. I can't get out of my own door."

"That monster! Are you, er, otherwise, um, uninjured?"

Cassie flushed, suddenly remembering her condition. She realized instantly what Fitzwalter must be thinking. One hand pushed ineffectually at her disheveled hair while the other tugged at the rents in her dress. "Yes, I'm all right." Then a sense of dreadful urgency possessed her. "Please . . ."

Fitzwalter gulped. He had already had one confrontation with Edward Sandron. He stared fixedly at the windows above her. Was the owner of the house even now lurking behind one waiting to attack with that cane?

"Hurry. I've been locked in for hours. I don't know when he'll come back. My suitcase is all packed. Hurry! My room's the third door on the right after the kitchen. I'll put on my coat and hat."

Still Fitzwalter hesitated.

"Mr. Fitzwalter . . ." Her voice broke. "I can't stand this a moment longer. The walls of the room are closing round me. I feel as if I'm strangling."

"My dear," his round face was the picture of sympathy. "Whatever is wrong?"

"I've always been like this. I can't tell you how a locked room terrifies me." The tears began to trickle down her cheeks. She held out her arms in supplication.

Sweating, his hand trembling, Fitzwalter drew from his pocket the skeleton key that had opened the front door of the Devil's Palace. After a minute's fumbling, the back door yielded with even less effort. It swung open noiselessly into the kitchen.

The perspiration trickled down his spine and soaked the armpits of his tweed sack coat. If he were discovered . . .

The hallway was dark and deserted. The third door on the right, she had said. He tapped gently on it. "Cassandra?"

"Here, Mr. Fitzwalter."

"One minute." Sandron had left the key in the lock. A quick turn and she was free.

She all but tumbled into his arms. True to her word, however, she had managed to put on her hat and coat. Her carpet bag was clutched in her hand. "Let's hurry." Casting a fearful glance up the stairs, she tucked her hand through his arm and rushed him down the hall.

The night train for Edinburgh left Paddington station at eight o'clock. Fitzwalter had purchased two first-class tickets for them and helped her to tuck her valise into the overhead before settling down. They were the only ones in the car. As the station master came by and closed the door, Cassandra settled back with a sigh of relief.

Fitzwalter faced her, his eyes speculative. As the environs of London disappeared, the interior of the coach was illuminated only by the palest of moonlight. "Do you mind if I ride over beside you, my dear?" he asked after a few minutes. "I get sick if I have to ride backward."

The tone of his voice made Cassandra's skin creep. Suddenly, she realized that to escape from Edward

Sandron, she had placed herself at the mercy of a man whose motives might be highly suspect. Too late she remembered his suggestion that she accommodate him since his wife would not. Somewhere in her mind a voice whispered, *Rather the devil you know, than the devil you don't.*

Without waiting for an answer, her rescuer got up and sat down next to her. "Now. That's better." He patted her arm. "Now don't you worry, my dear. You just settle down for a rest. We'll be in Scotland by tomorrow afternoon."

"Of course," she murmured. Pulling her cloak more firmly around her, she rested her head on the seatback near the window.

"My dear." He patted her knee this time. "Think of me as your father. Lean on me. There is no need to bruise your pretty head."

She struggled with her feelings. Perhaps he did really think of himself as her father. He had always been her father's friend. Still, she hesitated. "I'm quite comfortable the way I am. I don't want to inconvenience you."

"Nonsense. You won't. I insist."

Before she could protest further, he had slipped his arm around her shoulder and gathered her against his side. "Now isn't that more comfortable? Not the least bit chilly. And you'll keep me warm, my dear."

She could not deny that the compartment was cold. She had brought no traveling rug to wrap around her feet. "Won't your arm go to sleep or something?"

Removing his hat and laying it on the seat beside him, he leaned his head against hers. "I would gladly endure such a minor discomfort to smooth the way for my best friend's daughter. You know, Cassandra, I once thought that someday when you grew up, we might be able to forget or overlook the disparity in our ages." His palm cupped the point of her shoulder, hugging her gently.

She frowned tiredly. "Mr. Fitzwalter, please."

Instantly, he pulled the hand away. "Oh, I know. I know. My Sarah was a good choice. She has been a good wife to me over the last fifteen years."

"I remember meeting her," Cassandra agreed eagerly. "She is so gentle."

"Oh, she is." The train swayed rhythmically, its wheels chattering over the rails.

"And you are my dear friend. I will always think of you as such. You are so like a father to me."

The hand dropped back on her shoulder. The other hand sought hers, folded in her lap. "When I think of that devil Sandron imprisoning you, I can hardly contain myself." He clutched her tightly. "He is a fiend incarnate. And you alone in his house. You must never do something so foolish again, Cassandra. You need a good man to take care of you and cherish you." His hand slipped down under her arm. His chubby fingers pressed against the side of her breast.

She tried to shrug him off. "Please, Mr. Fitzwalter . . ."

"No!" His voice rose. "No. You must see reason." Before she knew what he was about, he had thrown his other arm around her and dragged her to him. His thick lips closed wetly over the side of her mouth. One hand slid from the middle of her back to her buttock. "Just consider, Cassandra."

"Mr. Fitzwalter . . ."

"You are a lady, Cassandra. You are to the manner born. You must not work as a common housemaid. I saw you in your dress. All torn. That swine. That devil was pawing you. Wasn't he?" He kissed her again. This time she managed to turn her head so his kiss landed on her ear. "Wasn't he?"

"Mr. Fitzwalter . . . Stop!"

He rooted at her throat, his hands clutching and pulling at her clothing. "I am a good man, Cassandra," he panted. His breath was hot in her ear. He thrust his belly against her, trying to press her back against the seat. "I have always been a God-fearing man. I have been a pillar in the League ever since its founding." His mouth sucked at the curve of her breast through the thicknesses of her clothing. She pounded on his back, but she realized that he did not feel her blows. "You know that I have."

She caught at his thinning greasy hair. "For God's sake, Mr. Fitzwalter, remember your wife."

"But a man has needs," he whined, still slobbering on her clothing. "Even though I'm a God-fearing man, I'm not a priest. A good Protestant needs a warm, willing woman."

"Please . . ."

He left off clutching her buttock to close over her breast, gripping it in alarmingly strong fingers. Feverishly he tried to tug his arm free from between the seat and their bodies.

"Mr. Fitzwalter. Stop this inst—"

He cut her off with a wet, hot kiss. When she

opened her lips to gasp, he thrust his tongue into her mouth, almost strangling her with his force.

For several minutes, they fought a silent battle. He tore at her clothes, she pushed and struggled against him. The wool skirt much abused by Edward's clutch parted from the waistband with a dreadful rip. While she clawed at Fitzwalter's wrist, he managed to get his hammy knee onto the seat between her legs.

Twisting her face away from him, she sucked in air. "Stop! Don't!"

"You don't mean that," he growled. "You've been mauled and doubtless raped by that monster, Baal. I'm a real man, not a monster. Don't fight me. I won't hurt you."

"Let me go." He was much stronger than she. She slapped at his face, but he only ducked his head. The buttons on her dress parted from the buttonholes and he nuzzled at her breast again, sucking and biting this time through only the thin camisole.

Her mind was clear above the pain and fear. She must fight him off and get off this train. With a supreme effort she managed to get her foot up onto the seat and buck outward. At that instant, the train rounded a curve. He tipped off and landed on the floor. Summoning all her strength, she sprang to her feet.

"Mr. Fitzwalter. Stay away from me."

He laughed nastily from his undignified heap between the car seats. "You're infected by the Devil's power. Of course, you don't want a good man. You can't love one until the devil has been driven from you. I'll do that, Cassandra. I'll do that before we reach Scotland." He climbed awkwardly to his feet.

The train was beginning to slow. Cassandra glanced through the window behind him. Light. She could see light.

"You'll arrive in Scotland a new woman. You'll be cleansed of all that sin." Throwing wide his arms, he made a dive for her.

The door to the coach was behind her fingers. The train slowed for a curve. Lights were on the other side of the window. Without thought, without a pause to consider, she thrust open the door and jumped into the dark night.

Chapter Sixteen

An experienced horsewoman who knew how to take a fall, Cassandra tucked herself into a ball. Unfortunately, nothing in her past had prepared her for the shock of hitting the downward slope of a roadbed at twenty miles per hour. Her body burst out of its tuck. Her limbs flapped wildly as she tumbled over and over. Her right arm ended up between her and the rock-lined bottom of the ditch.

A scream of fear ripped from her as the crushing force of more than her own weight snapped her forearm. An instant later the crown of her head struck the opposite side of the ditch. A kaleidoscope of color zigzagged through her vision before the light went out completely.

She recovered consciousness by slow degrees. First, she was aware of blinding pain in her head. At her first attempt to sit up, exquisite agony lanced through her arm. She might have lain on her back paralyzed for hours had not she opened her eyes, unable to see a thing except whiteness.

A heavy fog had settled in the ditch. Impenetrable as a shrouding white blanket, it reawakened her claustrophobia. In her imagination the ghostly smothering stuff filled her nose, her eyes, her throat. Panic superseded pain.

Adrenaline pumping, she began to thrash about convulsively. In less than a minute she had managed to scramble to the top of the ditch and stand upright. Surrounded by a swaying, lapping world, the elevated roadbed stretched like a gangplank above a sea in which she would drown if she fell. Beneath her feet the railroad ties, rising out of the loose rocks, felt comfortingly flat and secure.

The entire world seemed black and white as she squinted against the pain, her arm clutched to her side. Then in the distance to the right, she discerned a light. She stared at the tracks, then at the light. Not for a moment did she consider starting out through the fields in a direct line and perhaps finding her way to help more rapidly. To step off into that smothering sea would have driven her mad.

Grimly, she determined to follow the railroad tracks on relatively level ground with no barrier until they led her roundabout to the light. If by some terrible quirk, they did not lead her to the light, eventually they would lead her to help.

Slitting her eyes and bending her head against the cold wet breeze, she struck out between the tracks. As she walked, she counted grimly to one hundred, each number hissing out between her clenched teeth. Concentrating on keeping her steps even so she could put each foot on a tie, she managed to shut out some part of the pain.

Edward Sandron raged helplessly when he found the door standing wide open, the key still in the lock, and Cassandra gone. "Fitzwalter!" he guessed. "That damned kidnapper!"

Nash grinned mockingly. "Really, Baal. Can't imagine how you work these things about. You are truly a great fiction writer. I'm sure your housekeeper regarded him as a rescuer."

Choosing to ignore that jibe, Edward turned on the publisher, chin thrust out belligerently. "Where are his digs, Nash?"

"Here in London?" The publisher set his face in deceptively mild lines. "Oh, I believe he's got just a small flat out in Clerkenwell."

"The address."

"Come now, Baal, old imp. Don't carry the address of a member of the League of Moral whatever about. Bad for my image, don't y'know?" He leaned against the wall, crossing one leg in front of the other. His pale eyes gleamed with amusement at the sight of Edward Sandron pacing back and forth like a caged tiger. "Doubt if he'll be there," he put in at last. "He only uses it occasionally. Prefers to go home to Scotland when he—"

"To Scotland?" Edward stopped in midstride.

Nash's sandy eyebrows rose. "Ring a bell with you, old chap."

"Of course. That's where they've all gone. Mac-Adam, Cassandra, and him. What town?"

"It's hard to say really. The address of the League for the Uplift of Moral Virtue is Edinburgh. Now *that* I do have written down somewhere. Made a note of it to send them a bill for all the damages. Won't get anything of course . . ."

"Nash . . . !" Edward slapped his palms against the wall on either side of his publisher's head.

"Oh, very well." He raked his index fingers through his vest pockets. "Ah, yes."

"Give it to me."

Nash drew out a small slip of paper folded twice. When Edward made a grab for it, he pulled it back. "Something to do with that red-haired girl, old chap?"

"Everything. She was Miss Fitch."

Nash gaped. "The more-dead-than-alive housekeeper."

"In disguise. She's been working here for me for weeks. Somehow she got hold of a dress and came to the party."

"And you, er, and she . . . ?"

"Nash, mind your own business."

The publisher drew back, a cynical smile curving his lips. "Sorry, old chap. Didn't mean to pry. But you know you can replace a housekeeper. Or a doxy for that matter. Just let her go. You'll forget her before the week's out."

Edward snapped his fingers under the long thin nose. "The address, Nash."

The publisher sighed as he relinquished it. "Not like you to make a fool of yourself."

"I'm not. I'll be back in a few days."

"What about your manuscript?"

"I won't be long. Just pretend it got damaged in the raid and you have to wait for me to rewrite it."

"Mr. Edward Boggan," the butler intoned.

"What can I do for you . . . my God!" Fitzwalter took a step backward, the color draining from his naturally florid face.

Edward strode forward to grasp the extended hand in a travesty of a handshake. "Where is she?"

Fitzwalter hesitated fractionally. "Who?"

"You know who. You knew the minute you saw me."

"No." Fitzwalter tried to free his hand and step back, but Edward held it, tightening his grip, grinding the bones. Fitzwalter's hand was smaller, white, and chubby. It stood no chance in Edward's long-fingered vise. "Ow!"

The butler started forward, alarmed.

Edward drove his hand forward, pushing Fitzwalter's back until he came within inches of the man's chest. "Send him away unless you want this to be spread around as general gossip."

"You're attacking me in my own home." Fitzwalter groaned, grabbing at his wrist with his free hand. "Ow!"

Edward gave the entrapped hand an extra sharp squeeze. "Nonsense. We're just two old acquaintances shaking hands," he contradicted between clenched teeth.

"Shall I summon aid, Mr. Fitzwalter?"

"Tell him 'no,' " Edward grated, his face only inches

from Fitzwalter's. "Unless you'd like a headline like 'Prominent Do-Gooder Abducts Young Woman.' "

Fitzwalter stopped struggling. His face was red, his breath coming in hard swift pants. "Let me go and I'll tell you what I know. You may go, Forsythe. This young man is simply excited. I'll be able to explain everything to his satisfaction."

The butler looked unconvinced. He hesitated, wringing his hands.

Edward Sandron looked over his shoulder. "Get out," he ordered quietly.

The man stumbled backward, closing the door behind him with a loud snap.

"Now. Where is she?"

Fitzwalter hesitated again.

"Damn you." Edward shifted his grip. Viciously, he spun the smaller man around and twisted his fat wrist up behind his back. "Tell me!"

The Scotsman screamed shrilly. His free arm pawed ineffectually at his shoulder where the pain was most severe. "You're a gentleman . . ."

Edward twisted the wrist an extra quarter of an inch. "I'm a tough from the streets. Don't for an second believe that I can't or won't hurt you. Where is she?"

The fat man danced on tiptoe, sweat pouring down his face. "Ow! Stop! I don't know where she is. Ow! No . . . She jumped off the train."

"What?" Edward's hand relaxed.

Fitzwalter slipped from the punishing grip and flung himself across the room, where he dodged behind a heavy library table. "She jumped off the train just after it left Northampton."

Edward stared after him incredulously. "My God! Why?"

The man's face suffused with color. "She . . . she decided she didn't want to go with me."

"But to jump off the train? Was it moving?"

"Yes."

A sick feeling rose in Edward's throat. He shook his head. "Let me get this straight. She jumped off a moving train, and you didn't bother to help her."

Fitzwalter moved uncomfortably. "Well, I thought about it. But it had slowed down. So I'm sure she was all right. Maybe a bit shaken, but quite all right. I decided she'd made her choice. She didn't need my help anymore. I wasn't going to bother her anymore."

Edward towered over him, his face darkened with anger. "Let me get this straight. She jumped off a moving train and you didn't make any effort to stop the train and help her. You just left her lying there, without knowing whether she was injured or"—he swallowed painfully—"dead."

"Well, it was dark . . ."

Edward interrupted him by laying a hand on the man's chubby shoulder. Instantly Fitzwalter cringed. Tears began to trickle down his cheeks. Edward could barely contain his contempt. He dropped his hand immediately. "Just outside of Northampton, you say?"

Fitzwalter dragged a handkerchief from his pocket and mopped at his face. "Right! Couldn't have been more than a half a mile from the station. We were just about to settle down for the night when . . ." He never really saw the fist coming. It connected with the loose flesh on the side of his jaw and laid him flat.

Massaging his knuckles, Edward opened the door to find the butler hovering in the hall. Immediately, the servant shrank back as if the tall man in black might really have been Baal. With a sardonic grin, Edward accepted his hat and stick from the trembling hands. "Tell him when he comes to, that if I don't find the young lady in good condition, I'll come back and beat him to a pulp."

The butler nodded his head. He clasped his hands together tightly. His jaw wobbled. "Yes, sir. I'll tell him."

Cassandra lay on the narrow cot, staring up at the concentric stains left by leaks in the ceiling of the attic room. Her good hand stroked the bare piece of material at the neck of her dress. The manager of the shabby hotel would have turned her away but for the cairngorm brooch. She had plucked it from her pocket with her good hand and placed it on the desk.

The man behind it had held the piece of jewelry up to the light, calculated the weight of the stone, then passed it to a hard-faced woman sitting in a doorway behind him. She had run her fingers over the ornate silver setting. For a moment Cassandra feared she might be turned away. Then the woman had nodded shortly. As she tucked the piece into her pocket, the manager had pulled a key from a hook at the bottom of the board and pointed with it. "Climb them stairs till they ain't no more."

Now she lay on the bed staring up at the ceiling,

the thin covers of the narrow cot pulled up across her breasts. Motion and reason seemed farther away with each passing minute. She did not even have a clear idea of how long she had been there. The last of her strength had been expended when she managed to crawl under the covers of the narrow cot.

She had no money. Believing herself safe with Fitzwalter, she had unwrapped her reticule from her wrist and laid it on the seat beside her. Now what was she going to do?

Setting her teeth against pain, she attempted to sit up in bed. Her effort was a dismal failure. Her head swam dizzily as a weakness rose out of the great hollow feeling in her stomach. Dropping back down with a sigh, she ground her teeth and concentrated on stoking her anger. Damn Edward Sandron! Thanks to him she had been almost forty-eight hours without food. He had locked her in her room before she had even had time for breakfast. In her haste to escape from him, she had insisted Fitzwalter take them directly to the train station. She should have plenty of time to eat when she had gotten safely away.

She had made so many mistakes. Wearily she closed her eyes. Hunger, exhaustion, injuries all combined to defeat her pathetic effort to become angry at her former employer. Perversely, her thoughts of him refused to remain angry. Memories of him dancing with her, kissing her, talking with her in her disguise as Miss Fitch flowed before her eyes. Had she been a fool to try to escape from him? Angrily she rolled her head on the pillow, shaking those weak thoughts from her brain. She must concentrate on getting to her feet and going out to find food.

Her body was hot and aching in every place. With her good hand she tried to assess the extent of the damage. The results added to her depression. Possibly every part of her body above the waist was bruised or broken. Shoulders, ribs, head, most especially her right arm hurt in varying degrees from nagging ache to excruciating throb.

She did not have the courage to get up today. She stared hard at the door. Would the landlord come and check on her? A tiny hysterical chuckle slipped from between her lips as she pictured him coming slowly up the stairs in a couple of weeks to find her dead. Gray and cold. He would wrap the sheet around her and toss her body out onto the refuse heap in back of the hotel.

On the other hand, if he came, what could she ask of him? Not only had she no money with which to purchase food, she had no possessions of value now that the cairngorm was gone. She had no clothing except the pieces on her body. Thank heavens for the six petticoats under the serviceable skirt. Her limbs were in good working order. She could walk well, although the pain in her arm made her light-headed.

If she were to go downstairs now, perhaps there would be some kind of meal. A cold collation. A hot stew. Her mouth began to water. She raised her head again from the pillow. Pain lanced behind her eyes, but it was bearable. The prospect of food gave her strength.

Closing her eyes, she swung her feet over the side of the bed. With that counterbalance she got her left elbow under her and sat up. The room reeled around her. She had to brace her feet to keep from sprawling forward off the bed. With infinite care she gathered her right arm into her lap. She could not imagine that anything would ever hurt her more than it did at that moment. Added to that was the pounding in her head.

No. Vaguely, she realized that the pounding was outside her head. How she wished whoever was doing it would stop. The noise was not easing the throbbing behind her eyeballs.

Abruptly, the pounding stopped, then came again, louder than before.

She winced, put out her left hand. She was staring at the wall. She had gotten up on the side of the bed away from the door. She moved her dry lips to curse her stupidity, but no sound came.

"Cassandra."

Someone was calling her.

"Cassandra."

She looked toward the end of the bed. Edward Sandron stood there. Baal in his black suit, without the red satin cape. Instead, he wore a black overcoat and black top hat. She closed her eyes. She must be imagining all this.

"Cassandra, are you all right?"

She looked at him again. "Are you really there?" Her voice was the barest of hoarse whispers.

"Yes, I'm here." His first impulse was to gather her up in his arms to assure himself that she was all right. Instead he moved gradually closer for fear his presence might frighten her. He had to remember that she had run away from him with just cause. But she looked so pale; even her lips were colorless. The angry bruise on her temple, a hideous red and purple splotch that stained the side of her cheek beneath her eye, presented a starting contrast to the rest of her face.

She extended her left hand palm up. "Edward, I hurt so much . . ." She never felt his warm hand close over hers.

She blinked. She was in the fog again. A thick white fog blocked her vision. She blinked again. It began to clear. She tried to swallow, but her mouth was so dry. Her lips felt stuck together. With some effort she managed to lick her lower lip.

"Water?" a voice asked her.

"Please." She drank greedily from the proffered glass before she looked up. Edward Sandron's dark face hovered above her. Where had he come from? He must have caught up to her and Fitzwalter.

She raised herself off the pillow, stifling a moan, and lifted her chin. "I don't need help." Her effort for more volume and a cold dismissive tone was unsuccessful. "Please leave me."

He looked at her uncertainly. "Shouldn't you have a doctor look at your temple?"

Involuntarily, she lifted her hand to the wound. "A trifle," she lied. "It looks much worse than it really is. I bruise easily."

He was sitting down beside her on the side of the bed next to the door. He replaced the water glass on the tray. "Is that the only place you're hurt?"

She shifted nervously. "You should not be here in this room with me. I shall complain to the hotel keeper."

Edward kept his voice soft. He could guess how her head must be aching from the size of the bruise. "Why should he care? It's none of his business." He put his hand on her shoulder. "Please, Cassandra."

"No." His touch galvanized her into action. Drawing on her last reserves of strength, she pushed herself up to a sitting position. Edward's hand slid down her right arm until it clasped the break. A hoarse gasp was all she could manage before she slumped back unconscious.

She awoke in a different room. It was much more spacious. The bed was infinitely more comfortable. Her right arm was cushioned between two pillows. "Drink this." Baal's deep voice pierced the dream. His long warm hand held her head.

It was water but laced with some spirits that felt like nectar to her raw throat. She drank the glassful. "Thank you."

"Do you want some more?"

"Please."

When she had drunk again, he laid her down. "Sleep or food?"

Her stomach growled its own reply.

He lifted her higher and slipped another pillow behind her back. Then he ladled soup from a covered tureen into a bowl. In silence, he began to feed her.

"I'm sure I can do it myself," she said primly after the first few bites.

"You're right-handed, aren't you?"

She nodded.

"Then you'd probably just make a mess of it." He tore off a piece of bread from a small loaf and dipped it into the rich creamy liquid. "Open up." When she had eaten it all, he set the bowl down and held the glass for her to drink again. "Now. Why don't you go back to sleep?"

"Not with you here."

He regarded her steadily. His smoky eyes looked blacker with the dark circles under them. He had missed some sleep himself recently. "I don't intend to leave, Cassandra."

"I'll scream."

"Don't be ridiculous." He leaned back in the chair and poured himself a small glass of brandy from the decanter on the supper tray. "Scream and you'll get nothing but trouble. You don't want the hotel keeper to burst in on you and find you naked in my bed, do you?"

Despite her pain and utter weariness, she blushed. Frantically, her eyes scanned the length of her body beneath the blankets. "Naked?" she choked.

"As the day you were born." He grinned. "Except you don't look the same way you did the day you were born. You're much longer and curved in different places. Of course, you probably had the same birthmark on your—"

"Please . . ." Tears of embarrassment stood in her eyes.

He regarded her seriously for a moment. "Now that we've got that settled, I suggest you go back to sleep."

"Why did you take my clothes?"

He rose over her and eased the pillow from behind her back. With a gentle touch, he settled her head on the cool pillow below. "Because I didn't want you to do something silly like try to get away in the middle of the night. I've sat up with you now two nights and a day. I'm about dead for sleep." He planted a light kiss on her forehead then turned away.

With a small sigh he flexed his shoulders. For the first time she realized that he wore only a rumpled white shirt and trousers. As she assimilated his appearance, he pulled the shirt from his waistband and unbuttoned the cuffs.

"What—what are you doing?"

"Getting undressed myself."

"In here? With me?"

"In here with you." He tossed the shirt onto the foot of a small cot and reached for the button at the waistband of his trousers.

She closed her eyes, feeling heat suffuse her breasts and creep up her throat into her cheeks.

She heard a soft slap as the trousers joined the shirt. The cot creaked under his weight as he sat down on it to pull off his shoes one by one. She heard him rise and pad across the floor to turn out the light. He padded back and sank onto the cot with a weary sigh.

All was silent for several minutes.

"Are you asleep?" came his soft voice out of the darkness.

"No."

"Tell me who you are."

She hesitated so long that he was afraid she was not going to answer. Finally, she cleared her throat. "Cassandra MacDeramond."

"The name means nothing to me. Why did you use Cassie Fitch?"

She sighed. "You ruined my father."

He made a faint murmur of protest, but she did not allow it to interrupt her. She had not realized how she had longed to tell him the terrible story. Her only regret was that she could not see his face in the dark.

"He gambled and lost, gambled and lost. Until finally he lost everything. Then he committed suicide. I was afraid you might recognize the name." Then bitterness laced the weariness in her voice. "Of course, now I know that you really don't know the names of most of the people who gamble with you. Only someone like that poor boy the other day, someone who almost kills you. Him you'd remember. My father was easy to forget."

She heard the cot creak again as if he had reared up in it. "I swear to you, I never heard the name MacDaermond."

"Mr. Fitzwalter said he lost most of his fortune at the Devil's Palace."

"Then why did you come to work for me?"

"I've already told you. I hadn't been able to get a job anywhere else. Too much competition. But nobody else wanted to go to work for the devil. The devil, I reckoned, would be preferable to starvation. Now I'm bitterly sorry that I didn't just starve to death. At least Mr. MacAdam would be safe."

The bedclothes rustled. "He's free. Fitzwalter bailed him out."

"I know."

There was another silence. Then, "Why did you jump from the train?"

"I'd rather not say."

He chuckled. "Let me guess." His voice was snide. "He believes in Moral Virtue in theory, but in practice he's not one to turn down an opportunity." He waited, but no comment was forthcoming. "He decided that you'd be grateful for his daring rescue of your person from the devil's clutches." He waited. "Cassandra?"

"Good night."

"I'm sorry, Cassandra."

The next morning she opened her eyes to find him fully dressed, combing his hair in front of the beveled glass mirror. He was incredibly handsome and impeccably dressed in his black suit, soft-collared white shirt, and black silk necktie.

Satisfied at last, he turned around. "Good morning."

She shrank back slightly against the pillows. Emotions speeded her heartbeat and quickened her breathing as he came toward her all masculine beauty and dominance. At the same time she remembered her naked helplessness. Fearful of it, she remained silent.

He smiled down into her pale, drawn face. "Feeling better this morning?"

"I believe so."

"Good." He poured her a pale concoction and held it to her lips. When she had finished, he propped another pillow beneath her head. "Now tell me, where you were going with Fitzwalter."

"To Scotland. Mr. MacAdam is ill. I was going to care for him." She glared at him, a little color coming back in her cheeks. "That *is* your fault, you know. You can't deny it."

"Ah, but I do deny it. I didn't murder my valet. The police were well within their rights to pick up the butler. Of course, they might have picked up my housekeeper as well." He grinned significantly.

"Give me back my clothes, so I can get up."

"I think not." He stripped the sheets from his cot. Her green eyes widened in alarm. "What are you going to do?"

"Tie you to the bed."

"No." She sat up, but he knotted two corners together and tossed one across her chest. Efficiently, he looped one end behind the leg at the head of the bed and knotted the two ends together on the right side well out of her reach.

"Damn you! Let me up."

"Now remain there and rest. I'll return when I've made a few arrangements."

"I'll kill you when I'm free. You'll suffer for this." He grinned down at her. "Sticks and stones."

The sheet slipped off her shoulders, exposing the tops of her breasts. "I shouldn't take advantage of you, but I really can't help myself." Putting one knee on the bed, he bent over her. His lips touched her forehead, her eyebrow, the wound on her temple. He moved on to her cheek, then the corner of her lips. She gave a tiny shiver as he slid his tongue across her lips. Gently, firmly, he insinuated it between hers.

Involuntarily, she opened her mouth to him. His kiss deepened until her whole body began to heat. At last he broke the kiss and stepped back. The devil's golden flames were dancing in his eyes.

"Now." He slid into his coat. "Stay there and don't scream for help. You might get more than you really wanted. I'll be back in an hour or less."

Chapter Seventeen

Cassandra lay flat on her back just as Edward had left her. Only the faintest motion of her chest assured him that she breathed. Her lips were pale whereas dark shadows like bruises formed half moons beneath her closed eyes. His gut tightened against unfamiliar emotion he could not name.

Releasing the breath he was unconscious of holding, he bent over the bed. As he did, nerves, strung taut by the pain that would not let her truly rest, perceived him. She opened her eyes. At first their expression was glazed. Then memory returned. With recognition came an angry flash of green fire.

His eyebrows shot up in mock horror. Then his face settled into serious lines. "Can you stand?"

"Not without clothes," she hissed. Like a tigress trapped, she bared her teeth in fury.

His expression did not change. "Let's not waste time," he said matter-of-factly. As if his action were the most normal thing in the world, he unknotted the binding sheet and turned the covers back.

Bright color flooded her face and breasts as her delicate skin revealed her embarrassment. Her left hand fluttered helplessly as she sought unsuccessfully to cover herself. "For pity's sake . . ."

Fearing that in her emotional anguish she might injure herself further yet hating himself for a brute, he caught the fragile wrist in one hand at the same time he slipped the other under her left shoulder. "Let me help you to sit up. Here's your shift or whatever you call it." When she hung back, stubbornly turning her face away, he continued. "Let me remind you that I undressed you. In fact, if memory serves me right, I've undressed you completely, twice." Gently but inexorably, he set her up.

Between gritted teeth, she moaned. The sound scraped across his own nerves, adding to the ache in his gut.

"Bad?" he murmured sympathetically. Then, "My God?" He drew back appalled.

"What is it?" she asked alarmed.

His fingers touched her shoulder, trailed down her shoulder blade. He swallowed.

She shivered involuntarily. "What is it?" she repeated. "For mercy's sake . . ."

"Your back," he muttered. "It's practically a solid bruise. I've never seen anything like it."

She tried to crane her neck to see. "I tumbled over and over."

Even as he held up the undergarment, he shook his head. "If you called for the police, I'd be in gaol for the rest of my life. You look as if you've been flogged." He slipped the chemise over her head and good arm, then set about gingerly working it over the heavy bandage.

She sat silently head bowed as he drew the ribbon through the eyelets and then pulled the white linen snug across the tops of her breasts. His long clever fingers burned her skin where they touched it even as they tied the simple bowknot.

He bent to stare into her face, noting her color had faded to be replaced by an alarming pallor. She shivered. "Cold?" he asked. "I'm sorry, but I can't hurry without hurting you." Instead of making her stand nude from the waist down, he dropped the petticoats over her head one by one until all six were in place. "Now, your modesty is spared."

His proprietary handling of her body, his closeness, his clean masculine scent were all playing havoc with her overcharged senses. As he tied the tapes of her petticoats, she could not take her eyes from the sharp planes of his cheek and jaw stained by the dark shadow of his beard. She could see every detail of his face with stark clarity. A faint curling warmth began at the base of her belly. Beneath the thin fabric of her chemise, she could feel her nipples tingle. Her lips were suddenly dry.

He turned his head in time to see her tongue moistening them. He sucked his breath in sharply. His mouth was only inches from hers. Her eyes had gone soft and green as the sea. The golden flames flickered in his own eyes. He hesitated, fearful she might struggle and hurt herself. Then her lids drooped, her head tilted backward to receive his kiss.

With a sigh he slid his arms around her as emotion unlike anything he had experienced swept over him. Sexual excitement was familiar to him. He had seen it manifested even before he could understand it. From a very young age he had seen his mother entertain her customers. He had seen the act of sex and all that it entailed including the very depths of human depravity. His own sexual awakening had been animalistic.

A very young, very tiny whore with some pitiful notion of romance still about her had seduced the even younger, demon-dark boy. He had acquitted himself nobly or so she had maintained. For a few weeks he had thought himself in heaven. Then she had been dragged away from him by her pimp, who had beaten him savagely and threatened to kill him if he came near her again. The attack had been more in the nature of a man driving away a dog. Not for one minute did the pimp regard the slender youth as a man whose love for a woman would make him want to stay with her.

And in the end he had believed the pimp had been correct. He had told himself she was like his mother and therefore he must not care for her at all.

Later he had seen her from a distance, sad-eyed, bruised, one side of her mouth swollen. Then he had not seen her again. By that time he had found someone else. Then someone else. The emotion of love had never been a part of his life.

The feeling of protectiveness, of possession, that this girl roused in him was different from anything he had ever experienced. He did not understand himself why he had followed her, nursed her, and now kissed her with such exquisite care. He did not think about those things. He only knew that strange emotions poured through his veins until his breath came short against her lips and his fingers trembled against her delicate skin.

After a long minute, he drew away. He did not open his eyes immediately. By keeping them closed, he might conceal and at the same time savor the very private feelings the kiss had aroused.

A heavy thud from the rooms below reminded him of the present. "Can you stand?" His voice was a husky whisper.

"Yes."

When she was dressed as best as he could manage without hurting her arm too severely, he wrapped a blanket around her and began to pin it at the shoulder with her cairngorm brooch.

She did not bother to ask where he had gotten it. Instead, her eyes glittered with a suspicion of tears. "Thank you for retrieving this for me," she whispered.

He ducked his head and fumbled extra long with the catch. "They didn't really want it. They'd much rather've had the cash. More convenient." He shrugged himself into his overcoat, then helped her to stand. "Can you walk downstairs?"

"I think so."

On the top riser he paused. "I would carry you, but the stairs are too narrow."

She swayed dizzily. The steps wavered and rippled as her vision dimmed then brightened. "I can make it. Just go in front of me and let me hold on to you."

"Are you sure? I could get someone up here to help me."

"And be carried down like a load of dirty linen? No, thank you."

She eased back her bruised shoulders and took a deep breath. At the bottom, he turned and lifted her carefully into his arms. The proprietor held the door open for him to carry her out to a hackney coach.

At the station, she waited in it until the train pulled in. Then he placed her in a first-class compartment.

"Drink this." He uncapped a silver flask.

She shook her head, but he insisted, holding it to her lips, his dark form looming above her. Compelled, she took only a sip. The fiery brandy warmed her despite the harsh taste. Stubbornly, she put it aside. The pain would ease of its own accord in a few minutes. It had to. Arranging her features in an impassive mask, she held herself stiffly against the upright seat. He handed in his portmanteau and went away.

Her head and arm throbbed mercilessly. By the time he had attended to last-minute details, she was clenching her teeth. As he leaped in and slammed the door behind him, the train started with a jerk that tore a cry of pain out of her throat.

Instantly, he dropped down beside her and offered her the flask again. This time she drank greedily with hardly a wince. For a while she sat upright, trying to hold herself against the swaying train. He watched her for a few minutes, then with a mild curse, he gathered her into his arms. "You just won't ask for help, will you?"

"I don't really need help. I'll get comfortable in a few minutes."

He ignored that false assertion. Instead he cursed himself mildly. "I should have brought a pillow from the hotel as well as the blanket."

"I can sit alone."

"Be quiet." He held the flask to her lips again.

"You'll get me drunk," she protested when she had swallowed.

"That's the general idea. If you're drunk enough you can't feel anything."

The train swung into a curve that swayed the coach, then rattled up a grade. She found she could not bear so much pressure on her bruised back. She told him so.

"Then lie across my lap," he suggested. Her brain befogged by pain, she allowed herself to be arranged with her waist against his left thigh, her cheek pillowed on his right. He crossed his right ankle loosely over the top of his left knee to accommodate her more comfortably. She stirred awkwardly, but the only place for her left arm was between his thighs. The position might have embarrassed her more had she not been in so much pain.

"Now settle down, Cassandra," he murmured as he rested his right hand lightly on her hip.

She closed her eyes to blot out the unseemly intimacy. Within a few minutes she was asleep in his arms.

She stared at the house through the window of the carriage. "Where are we? Who lives here?"

"We are in Dumfries where MacAdam has taken up residence."

She looked at him incredulously. "Are you sure?"

"As sure as anything can be. It's where his sister, a Mistress Tamsen MacLeon, lives. It stands to reason he'd go to someone who would give him some help. She'd give him a place to heal his wounds."

"How do you know so much about Mr. MacAdam?"

The corner of his mouth twisted. "From your 'rescuer' Fitzwalter, who also rescued Mr. MacAdam. Didn't he tell you?"

She shook her head. "No, he didn't tell me that. I wonder why."

"Probably too busy with other things," came the cynical rejoinder. "Fitzwalter bailed him out of gaol and sent him on his way. For all I know he may even have paid for his ticket."

She touched her bruised temple gingerly. "I don't understand the man at all. Father trusted him. Told me to go to him when I was alone. Only my pride made me seek my own way."

He stared at her silently. "A good thing you did," he said at last.

She grimaced. "Oh, obviously I did the right thing. Look at what a wonderful circumstance I find myself in."

Obstinately, Mrs. MacLeon blocked the entrance to her stone cottage. "I'm not allowing any visitors to be disturbing him. He's not recovered from that terrible time."

"But I'm his friend. I only wish him well. I must reassure myself that he's all right," Cassandra insisted. "I'm"—she swallowed hard—"he's the closest thing I've got to a father in this world."

The woman hesitated. Then, reluctantly, she swung the door wider and ushered them into the kitchen. "Well. Maybe you'll do him a bit of good," she muttered.

Cassandra's heart turned over at the sight of Mr. MacAdam. He sat in a rocking chair beside a glowing iron stove, his hands folded in his lap. At their entrance he glanced up dully. As he recognized his visitors, a light came into his face. "Lassie! Ah, Lassie." He climbed shakily to his feet, his eyes glistening with tears.

"Ah, Lassie, you've come to visit me. You're a good one." He stared over her head at Edward Sandron. "And you too, sir. Most kind."

The sight of her faithful retainer staggered Cassandra to the point of collapse. To all the pain, the loss, the fear that had gone before, she added the destruction of this innocent, good old man. She swayed against Edward. Instantly, his arm banded her waist under the shawl and supported her. "Sit down, MacAdam," he advised. "Don't stand because of us." Pivoting hastily, he called over his shoulder. "Mrs. MacLeon, may we sit on this bench?"

"Of a certainty, sir. Please dinna stand on ceremony. And you, Ferris, reseat yourself. You haven't the strength of a louse and your fever will shoot sky-high." Her soft burr soothed them all.

A prey to her emotions and her physical weakness, Cassandra was scarcely competent to utter a word. Fierce hatred for the man who held her so tenderly burned through her. This swine. This beast. Her rescuer. Her head whirled with the conflict. How could great hate and great love exist together side by side in one body without driving the host mad?

Mrs. MacLeon bustled to the pump, filling a tea-kettle with a gush of water and plunking it on the stove. "Ferris, you must sit," she scolded her brother again. "You know what the doctor told you."

"Mr. MacAdam," Cassandra managed to quaver. "How are you?"

"Now, Lassie, 'tis nought. I fear I was not quite prepared for the rigors of imprisonment." He sank back into the rocker. "Seems I caught a fever . . ."

"Oh, no."

"Ah, 'tis nothing that I won't get over, rest assured."

Not fooled by the sight of the man's condition, Edward remained silent. Against him, he could feel shudders run through Cassandra's whole body.

"Mr. MacAdam will never be able to work again."

Privately, Edward believed her, but he shook his head. "Don't discard him before his time. Prison puts its stamp on men every hour that they're there. Food is inedible, exercise is impossible, sunshine and fresh air become memories. Emotionally and spiritually it drains the very soul out of the body. He's an old man. He'll take longer to recover."

She brushed at the tears on her cheeks. "Do you really think so?"

He shrugged, not quite meeting her eyes. "He needs time to rest and recuperate. I've seen men recover from much worse." He did not add that they were much younger, hardened criminals whom the London streets had toughened until they had the survival instincts of rats.

As the silence lengthened between them, she stirred restlessly. At last she pushed herself up from her chair and made her way gingerly to the window of the hotel room. Clutching her injured arm by the elbow, she stared out at the snow-covered street below.

"I feel as if the whole thing were my fault. He would never have left Scotland if not for me. He didn't want to come to work in the D-Devil's Palace, but he would not desert me." She could not control the tears that thickened the last part of her speech.

"Don't blame yourself," Edward advised reasonably. "No one can blame another person for something he did of his own free choice."

She would not be assuaged. "He didn't choose to go to gaol."

"A person doesn't have to commit a crime to be in a prison."

"Not a decent kind person like Mr. MacAdam."

His mouth drew down in a bitter grimace. "Of course not. Not 'decent, kind Mr. MacAdam.' "

She turned back away from the window to accuse him contemptuously. "You know much of gaols, don't you?"

His face became more austere than ever. The flames of hell danced in the smoky eyes. "I was born there."

She gaped at him. "You were—?"

"Born there," he finished for her. "Who is more innocent than a babe? Yet the very first light I ever saw was filtered through a prison grate. The very first breath I ever drew was a fetid stench. The first bed I ever lay in was—"

"Stop it!" The harsh whisper tore from her throat. "Stop it!"

He sank down in the large wing chair by the fire. His face had turned to stone; his eyes were hard as diamonds. His long hands curved over the chair arms as he surveyed her. "Not to your liking, Lady Mac-Daermond?"

She shook her head, a quick violent shake. "You are to be admired. You have risen far." Fleeting approval in her voice was quickly replaced by biting contempt. "The Devil's Palace is . . . far from 'fetid stench.' "

"I had nothing to do but rise," he countered sarcastically.

"You might have set higher sights than luxurious corruption."

"I am not done living yet." He bit the words out between sharp, even teeth.

Her rigid posture and arrogantly uplifted chin presented a caricature of lady-of-the-manor. Once he would have jeered in her face. Now with perverse pleasure, he remembered his purpose. He should never have spewed forth this most ignoble of beginnings if he had only thought. With her aristocratic birth she would consider him beneath contempt.

And yet why not? He rose, straightening slowly to his full height, using his stature with every inch of theatricality to intimidate her. He noted with pleasure that she had to tilt her head back a bit, quite destroying her arrogant pose. A tiny smile curved his stern mouth. "Lady Cassandra MacDaermond," he inquired formally. "Will you do me the honor to become my wife?"

Her mouth dropped open. She gasped for air, then faltered back a step. "You must be mad." Her voice was reduced to a raspy whisper.

"Do you think so?"

"How could you possibly think that I would marry you?" Wildly she stoked her anger at his affrontery.

"I am a man of means. I make you an honorable offer to marry you, to care for you," he suggested mildly. "I could give you the comfort you have been denied these past months."

"I am a lady, sir. I would not marry a man merely because he could give me 'comfort.'"

"No?" He came closer. "Perhaps you would like to reconsider your answer. You would never have to work again as a housekeeper, scrubbing, mending, polishing." He took her right hand protruding from the sling and turned it over palm up. Gently, he ran his thumb over its roughened surface. "The calluses would gradually fade from your hands."

She stumbled back, conscious of the tingling in her fingers that his touch evoked. "They are honest calluses, sir."

"And I make you an honest offer. Will you marry me? I shall not offer again."

"No!"

He stared at her for a moment, then chuckled. "Too bad. You missed your chance. Then you'll be my mistress."

"Never!" She almost screamed the word in his face. "Never!"

Her vehemence earned her only a raised eyebrow. Again he chuckled. "Since you are no longer my prospective wife, I no longer need to remain standing in your presence." Suiting action to words, he seated himself, crossing one leg indolently over the other. "Sit down, Cassandra," he advised. "You might faint and fall down. Then I'd have to go to the trouble of picking you up."

"I'll not stay and listen to this."

"Poor Mr. MacAdam."

She stopped with her hand on the doorknob. "What do you mean?"

"Simply that Mrs. MacLeon has confided to me that she cannot support her brother since the pittance that Fitzwalter gave him has run out."

She spun around, her tone of voice incredulous. "But you owe Mr. MacAdam money."

"I . . . ?" He flicked a minute piece of lint from the sleeve of his black suit.

She came toward him with her fists clenched. "You know you do."

He stifled a yawn. "I don't owe anything to a former employee whom the police hauled off to gaol."

"But you know he was innocent." She was standing in front of him now, the palm of her left hand thrust into his range of vision in earnest supplication.

"Do I?" He refused to raise his eyes to look at her.

Without thinking what she did, she went down on her knees and turned her face up to his. "You know . . ." she repeated.

He stared at her, savoring the fantasy of the moment. The proud beauty on her knees to crave a boon from the merciless master. "But I can choose not to pay him anything." His words were uttered with utmost gentleness.

Slowly her face changed as she realized the full import of his power and her helplessness. "You . . . you bastard . . ." she gasped.

"Indeed."

She rose to her feet, staggering sideways, so that he shot out a hand to prevent her falling. "Take your hands off me."

He retained his grip until he no longer felt her weight on him, then sat back, his fingers curving around the chair arms once more.

She retreated to the window, her eyes narrowed, her mouth tightly compressed. In the silence she looked around her desperately. A gust of icy wind rattled the pane behind her and drew the fire to leap up the chimney. Suddenly she felt incredibly cold and miserable.

Frustration and pain made her long to tear her hair, to scream, to break something, to fly at the man who regarded her with only a hint of triumph on his demon-dark face. She shuddered as the wind gusted again.

He rose. She watched as he came toward her, standing beside her but facing the window and the street beyond. "You have it all within your power," he murmured silkily.

She shook her head. "I have nothing within my power." Her voice was a dry leaf rasping over ancient stones.

"You can walk out that door and never see me again." He paused. "I will return to London and never trouble you more."

"And you would not pay Mr. MacAdam." It was not a question.

"No."

"And I cannot work with a broken arm."

He nodded deliberately. "I would consider it a deterrent if I were interviewing you."

"But not to a mistress."

"Perhaps at first," he acknowledged with a hint of slyness, "but your incapacity would not result in noticeable neglect. I would be prepared to be . . . patient."

Grimly, she pushed the sling back over her elbow and tested the arm. The resultant pain drained the color from her face. She set her teeth against the humming in her ears.

"Don't be a damned little fool," he snarled. His hand under her left arm, he led her to the chair.

When he had seated her, she raised her head. "I am trying desperately not to be."

"Not to be what?"

"Damned." She leaned her head back. "But I am failing . . . miserably."

He looked down into the green eyes — so deep and green like emeralds under the sea — and drowned. His determination faltered. He despised the devil of perverseness in him that wanted her at any cost. He sighed and thrust his hands into his pockets.

"I will," she whispered.

"What? What did you say?"

She shuddered. Her head fell forward until her chin almost touched her chest. She cradled her right wrist as if it were newly injured. "I will be your mistress."

He stared at the silky red hair, braided and coiled in an intricate design on the crown of her head. As one compelled, he rested his hand on it. The feudal symbolism was not lost to either of them.

Edward shrugged into his greatcoat. "I've given a sum to Mrs. MacLeon with more to come quarterly for MacAdam's care until he is well able to work. I've paid the hotel for a week. Your meals will be served here in the room. A personal maid has been assigned to you for your clothing and your bath. You'll be able to recuperate and regain some of your strength."

Cassandra regarded him coldly. "You've thought of everything then. I should say you've been 'gentlemanly' in your concern."

His face darkened at the word. "Not at all," he returned. "I have been workmanlike." His eyes defied her to comment further. "I'm returning to London to prepare an apartment for you in the Devil's Palace. I shouldn't want you underfoot in all the confusion. After all, you are of little use to me in your present state."

Her fair skin blushed dark, her eyes flashed her hatred. But she managed to control her voice. "I suspect so."

"You know so." He pulled on one gray leather glove and then the other as he strolled across the room.

Insolently, he placed one finger under her chin and turned her mouth up to him. "Kiss me now as a mistress should." When she stubbornly tightened her lips, he chided, "I know you know how."

Helpless, furious heat rising in her face, she watched his mouth come down. She felt his lips on hers; his tongue caressed her lips. His scent, his heat, his touch made her feel weak. As he demanded, her lips parted.

Then he was kissing her hard, thrusting into her mouth. His fingertips felt the increase in the pulsebeat at the side of her throat. He smiled against her mouth and drew away. "I shall return in a week," he promised. "Then we shall go to London together." He strode to the door and turned. "If you think to run away, remember that MacAdam can be safe only so long as you keep your part of the bargain."

Chapter Eighteen

"Your apartments, my dear mistress."

"You're mad!"

"Not at all." Edward swung the great black overcoat from his shoulders and tossed it carelessly over the red, blue, and cream striped divan. The gold flames danced in his dark eyes as he stalked about the room. His polished black boots made no sound on the thick red and blue Turkish carpets. His arms spread wide to encompass it all. "You should be very comfortable here."

"You don't seriously expect me to live here?"

Cassandra stared upward in amazement at the brass gas-o-lier from which four Aladdin lamps jutted toward the four corners of the room. The ceiling was a radiant *trompe l'oeil* desert tent, its painted folds extending to the walls. These in turn were draped from ceiling to floor with great lengths of real fabric hung between poles that jutted out into the room. Thick golden ropes ending in enormous tassels secured the material to each pole.

In the center of the room beside the divan was a nest of carved sandalwood frames supporting ornate brass trays. Edward grinned mischievously as he flung himself down. From a heavy Turkish pot he poured a stream of thick black coffee. "It might take a bit of getting used to," he admitted.

"It's — it's like a . . ." Her face burned bright red. ". . . a harem."

He lifted the demitasse to his lips. "Exactly. A harem for my mistress." With a flourish he drank the brew off, then grimaced. "You may have to make the coffee, however. This brew tastes vile."

She shuddered. "I . . ."

"Come sit beside me." He patted the raw silk. "Or would you rather lie down? You must be exhausted."

She glanced toward the end of the room, then looked away with a shudder. A gigantic bed waited, covered in sapphire blue and piled with cushions of red, blue, and green silk. Golden tassels hung from every corner. Above the bed rose a half canopy also draped with swathes of the same colors and hung with tassels. She closed her eyes. "I think I prefer to sit."

He poured her a cup of coffee and held out a candy dish. "Turkish delight." This time his grin was self-mocking.

Nervously, she sat beside him and accepted the cup but refused the candy. The coffee was thick and slightly bitter. She drank it without a grimace. "I find this to my liking."

He threw her a swift glance from beneath raised black brows. "Beyond this room, there is a smaller dressing room. With clothing," he added.

"Appropriate to my new position," she guessed frostily.

"As a matter of fact, yes. I decided to indulge my fantasy to the fullest."

She glanced upward at the ceiling, shaking her head slightly in wonder. "This must have cost a fortune."

He shrugged. "Actually very little. Many very clever men are very poor gamblers."

"I should have guessed."

Her eyes flashed accusingly, but he faced her down, daring her to say more.

When her eyes dropped, he started up abruptly. "Well, that's that. I suspect you'll want to get settled in. The train ride was a long one." He looked around him, a mocking grin on his face, then back at her.

She rose too, putting her uninjured hand behind her. "I went to see Mr. MacAdam just before you came for me."

"Oh . . . and how was he?"

"Better. Much better."

"I'm glad to hear that. So you have no reason to regret your bargain."

"No, I have no regrets on that score." Her eyes swept the room, finally coming back to his face. "With his mind at ease he can really recover," she said softly. "He blessed you."

Edward Sandron's face darkened. A shutter dropped across his eyes. He bowed hastily. "I'll leave you until suppertime."

Shaking her head, Cassandra closed the door and leaned her forehead against it. Edward Sandron was a strange man. If she had not known him to be an unprincipled monster, she would have thought he blushed.

The dressing room in contrast to the bedroom was quite ordinary. A dressing table and stool with an ormolu mirror occupied an alcove formed by a tall japonaiserie screen. On the other side was a chest of drawers beneath the single window. A huge wardrobe filled all the space on the opposite side of the room.

Despite her wish to remain unmoved, Cassandra could not entirely suppress the little quiver of excitement. She had been forced to make do with old clothing and almost no cosmetics for so many years. At least she would allow herself to look at the contents of the room.

Crossing to the dressing table, she picked up the brush to stare wide-eyed at its back shining with the subdued gloss of sterling silver. Hastily, she put it down beside the comb and hand mirror on a crystal tray rimmed with wrought silver. Arranged beside the tray on a hand-embroidered linen cloth were two delicate crystal jars with silver lids. Opening one, she inhaled the delicate scent of rose sachet.

She sank down on the stool, her finger tracing the Tudor rose design on the lid of the jar. How could the man who called himself Baal have chosen anything of such beauty and elegance? Under other circumstances, she would have been deliriously happy, especially since she had had so little of beauty, much less elegance, in her life. Since her father's gambling debts had become unmanageable, all gifts had ceased except those of a symbolic nature, a bunch of heather, a box of sweets, an embroidered handkerchief.

She dipped her index finger into the pink cream and touched the fast-beating pulse on the side of her throat. She should not appreciate this. She should hate Edward Sandron, for he held her in his power. She should have flung it all to the floor, shattering the lovely glass and scattering the contents across the soft carpets.

She shook her head at the sight of herself in the mirror. Her face was white, but her eyes were shining softly. A half smile curved her lips. She dropped her head, ashamed to look at herself as she acknowledged she was not capable of destroying the beautiful and costly things. What had happened to her resolve to be strong, to resist the devil?

Hastily, she pushed herself up to leave. The huge oak wardrobe dominated the rest of the room. As if a demon whispered in her ear, she imagined its contents billowing out as she opened the door. The same demon controlled her body as she walked slowly across the thick pile of the carpet, her feet making no sound.

At the doors, she pressed her fist tight against her mouth. Then squeezing her eyes shut, she pulled open first one and then the other of the doors. With her eyes still closed, she stood there, her conscience berating her. Temptation was too strong. She opened one eye just a fraction. The sight was as bad as she had known it would be.

The contents astounded her. Worse than ever she had imagined and more beautiful. A whole enclave of dress designers must have gambled and lost every night at the Devil's Palace. Evening costumes of silk taffeta and slipper satin in blue, green, amethyst, and turquoise, her favorite colors, hung on one side. Day gowns of wool and velveteen and linen hung in the other. Two shawls, one of cashmere, the other of velvet, swayed on one door.

Wonderingly, she touched the shimmering garments. They were beyond her wildest dreams. With trembling fingers, she plucked at her old black dress, the costume of Cassie Fitch. What a perfectly evil, wonderful man!

Brokenhearted and thoroughly ashamed of herself, she staggered away to lean against the wall. Her self-control, so strained for so many days, broke completely. She covered her mouth with her hand but could not stifle the sobs. More than anything, she wanted to put on one of those beautiful dresses and make herself up at the lovely dressing table.

Even more a danger to her immortal soul was the realization that she wanted to go down the stairs to the Devil's Palace and dance in the arms of Edward Sandron. Most dangerous of all was the trembling warmth she felt at the thought of coming back to the harem room. He would take her as he had said, indulge his fantasies, treat her exactly as she should be treated, as his mistress. She would be caressed and kissed and carried to heights of shameful ecstasy.

And she loved the thought of it.

She wanted to do all those things desperately. And her conscience tortured her. For the first time she really understood the nature of temptation. Temptation could be resisted only if the person who was being tempted wanted to be saved. To her horror, she realized that she did not want to be saved. She wanted to belong to the devil, even if damnation were the price. She was being tempted by all that she knew to be wrong. And yet she wanted to do what was wrong.

In despair she sank to her knees and huddled in the corner made by the magnificent wardrobe and the wall. Staring fixedly at it for several minutes while she tried to get herself under control, she suddenly realized she was staring at the image of a rose. The wallpapers were decorated with Tudor roses. Her tears started afresh as her conscience and her desires warred with each other.

He had thought of everything, damn him. But she must be strong. She should concentrate on the rules that a lady must follow, on the rules of good manners, on the beliefs that she had been taught all her life. She was a lady. Through her superior mentality and breeding, she would remain cool and unmoved while he used her body for his pleasure. She would not feel pleasure. She was a lady.

Perhaps she fell asleep. Perhaps, the tears emptied her mind of all thought so she believed herself asleep.

At length she raised her head. Something had disturbed her. What?

"Ma'am?" a soft voice called.

Hastily, she climbed to her feet, wiping at her eyes with the back of her hand. "Yes."

"Oh, you're in here." A middle-aged woman in a black dress and spotless white apron stood in the doorway. Cassandra stared at her blankly.

"I'm to keep the house for you, ma'am. Mrs. Smithers is my name."

Cassandra's early training stood her in good stead. Moving across the room to the dressing table, she sat down and picked up the nail buffer. "Yes, Mrs. Smithers?"

"I thought perhaps you'd like me to draw you a nice hot bath." The woman's face was kind and bland. Cassandra's white cheeks were mottled with tears stains, but she did not appear to notice them.

"A bath would be lovely." Cassandra's voice sounded unnaturally hoarse, but the woman did not comment.

"Then it'll be ready in just a few minutes. Before I go, may I help you out of your dress?"

Cassandra put her hand on her broken arm. She still could not manage easily, but her pride would not let her unbend before anyone. Especially not now that she was living with a man to whom she was not married. She could feel a blush of shame rising in her face. "No, thank you. I shall undress by myself, Mrs. Smithers."

For the first time the woman's smooth expression wrinkled into a frown. "If you're sure, ma'am . . ." Her unfinished sentence left a world of doubt.

"I'm sure," Cassandra replied firmly. "Why don't you go straightway and draw the bath and then I'll take tea in . . ." Where? She would die of embarrassment if anyone else saw . . . that . . . harem. But how silly. Of course, the housekeeper had seen the bedroom and obviously she had not died of shocked sensibilities. ". . . in the bedroom when I'm finished."

"Yes, ma'am."

Still Cassandra waited until she heard the bedroom door close before she began to struggle with her buttons.

Her teacup was empty. A half-eaten scone and a smear of honey remained on the plate. She lay back on the divan, her ankles crossed, her eyes half-closed. One minute she was alone, her mind blessedly free, leaning back on the divan, a robe of lavender quilted satin wrapped around her.

The next minute the door opened and Edward strode in. His black and crimson cape swirled around him. Despite her resolve to remain cool and unmoved, she caught her breath as her heart gave a leap.

He stared at her from beneath brows that she realized for the first time had been blackened and drawn into peaks to give him a devilish appearance. "Did you have a warm bath?"

Her heartbeat speeded as a faint blush stained her cheeks. "You shouldn't ask me about my bath."

He dropped down beside her, throwing the hem of the crimson cloak over the back of the divan and leaning over to study her face closely. "Of course I should. I engaged Mrs. Smithers to draw it for you and to bring you tea." Trapped, his hip pressed against her thigh, she dropped her eyes in consternation. He hesitated a few seconds before turning away and helping himself to a bite from her scone. Chewing reflectively, he looked her over. "She was hired to be your personal servant. If there is anything else you need, please tell me."

"I need nothing. I wish you had not engaged her. I feel embarrassed."

He reached for the teapot. "Why?"

"Because . . . because she will know."

One corner of his mouth curved up. "She will not

comment."

"Because you would dismiss her," she whispered bitterly.

He sighed. "No. Because she will not be surprised by our relationship."

"Oh . . . I see . . ." His plain speaking brought the blush to her cheeks.

"Quite." He stared at her frankly now, taking in every detail of her body. "You have not selected a dress to wear this evening."

She stirred uncomfortably and drew the neck of her robe higher, wishing too late that she had donned her old dress, which Mrs. Smithers had taken it away to be cleaned. She had hated to put on any of his dresses, feeling that to do so would acquiesce to his desires too easily and cheapen her in his eyes. At the same time she recognized the emptiness of that defiance since she had become his mistress the night of the Hallowe'en party. Suddenly, she felt stupid and furious all at once. "I supposed you would tell me what to wear," she replied frostily. "I am yours to command."

He grinned then. "Why so you are. I didn't expect that you'd allow me to go so far as to select your clothing." He sprang up with a swish of crimson and made for the dressing room.

Behind him, she gritted her teeth. He was not reacting as she had hoped.

Back in a few minutes, he carried an exquisite dress of rich amethyst taffeta. "I would like to see you in this tonight. With your hair and skin it should become one of your favorite dresses." He waited as if for a comment.

"As you wish."

The silence grew. He cleared his throat, eyeing the robe significantly. "Is everything then to your liking?"

"Yes. Certainly." Her hand shook so that the tea threatened to spill over the side of cup. "I have everything to make me content."

He noted the motion of the liquid. "I see."

"I — that is . . ."

"Cassandra, we made a bargain," he chided her.

She set the teacup down with unnecessary force. "I will keep it."

"And you will come downstairs with me dressed as I request?"

She rose nervously, gesturing toward the window where the draperies were tightly drawn against the night sky. "It's late. I really thought you were going down to the . . . I didn't think you'd . . ." She stopped, took a deep breath, and looked him in the eye. "What schedule shall I follow, sir?"

"My name is Edward."

"What schedule shall I follow, Edward?"

He nodded formally. "Since you no longer have to rise early in the morning, I would prefer that you wait to have supper with me."

"At what time?"

"Ten or so. I'll make my first appearance downstairs at nine. Then come back up for an hour before I revisit the tables. Of course, on the nights of special performances, you may eat when you like."

She glanced at him in some concern. "Do you still do those 'special performances'?"

He shrugged. "Of course. They earn quite a bit of extra money, while they're not really much more trouble than a regular evening."

"I should have thought that after what happened, you would have discontinued them."

"No reason to. No one else was hurt. And I've learned my lesson. I don't drink or eat anything not prepared by my cook." Rising, he strolled to the bed, looking up into the half canopy, flicking a tassel that tied back the hanging. Without thinking, she followed him. When he turned, she was standing at the end of the bed.

The frill of lavender lace at the neck of her robe complimented the creamy whiteness of her throat. Her red hair blazed under the light from the gas-o-lier while her skin had an opalescent quality. Her slender hand fluttered nervously at her neckline.

She was his possession. No matter that he had gotten her by foul means. He was—after all—the devil. Perverse excitement made him clamp his jaw. Then he swallowed hard.

"Come here."

Cassandra's heart skipped a beat as if he had touched her. She retreated a step, clasping her right wrist in her left one. "Sir . . ."

He came round the end of the bed, his crimson-lined cape swinging gently, his eyes watchful. Again her hand rose to her throat. She took another backward step. "Kiss me, Cassandra."

For just an instant her expression was agonized, then she nodded, her voice without inflection. "I won't resist."

He frowned. "That's very well and good. A mistress does more for her man than just be here, Cassandra."

Her cheeks were pink. "You want me to make love

to you, sir?"

"For a start you may call me Edward."

"Do you want me to make love to you, Ed-Edward?"

He shot a swift glance at the little gold clock on its shelf. "That will come later. For now I want you to come when I call. Come here."

Her lips tight, she took a step.

"Closer."

Concentrating on the lion's heads that fastened together the top of his crimson cape, she moved until their bodies were only inches apart.

"Closer, still." He moved his feet apart. "Between my legs."

"Sir . . . Edward," she quavered.

When she touched him from thighs to breasts, he put his arms around her. "Now you may kiss me."

She complied mechanically, her embarrassment tinged with resentment, lifting her face, her eyes closed.

He hesitated briefly, then one hand came to the neck of her robe and began to pull it apart.

Instantly, she clutched at her wrist, "Don't . . ."

"My mistress," he reminded her. His voice seemed to vibrate in her ears. "I want to see what I have bought."

"You've seen me," she reminded him.

"Seeing is part of loving." His hand pushed aside the parted robe and bared her breast, a white conical hill peaked with palest rose. "Your skin is so beautiful," he murmured. "I've never seen skin this fine before."

She pushed against him with her left hand, a futile

exercise that made no difference to him at all. He held her easily in his all pervasive warmth. The crimson satin swirled around their knees. "May I kiss it now?"

She should have screamed no. She should have scratched his face, poked out his eyes, kicked him in the shin. But she did none of these. Instead she stood stockstill. The dark head bowed. Then she felt him take her nipple into his mouth, laving it with his tongue. She moaned softly as an unsatisfied ache began in her loins.

When he teased her hardened flesh, she buried her fingers in his hair and pulled him back against her. This time he suckled more vigorously, a little roughly, a little fast. She shuddered as the ache grew.

At last he straightened, turning his face up toward the ceiling and sucking in a deep breath of air.

She might had hidden her face against his chest. She might have pushed back away from him. She might have fainted dead away with an attack of the "vapors," except that she had no corset on. Instead, she allowed her head to fall back on her shoulders, baring her throat and white breast to the light. When he looked back down, her eyes were closed, but her lips were open. She did not see the dancing devils in his eyes. As he dropped his head and took her mouth, he roughly threaded his hand through her hair and tilted her head back even farther.

His warm, hard kiss went on and on until she whimpered beneath it. At the sound he released her hair and ran his hand down over her shoulder, pushing the robe off. The knot at her waist came loose. She might never have given herself a lecture, so eagerly did her body warm and stretch and sway against the length of his.

Abruptly, he broke off the kiss and stepped back. The lavender satin robe fell open, revealing the left half of her body, the breast with hardened nipple, shimmering and moist still from his kiss, the narrow inward curve of her waist, the smooth outward curve of her hip, and finally the long slender length of her leg. He swallowed hard, noting with pleasure quite apart from his sexual excitement the swollen kissed mouth and the dazed slumbrous eyes. "Now you look like a mistress," he remarked.

Her eyes flew open, catching him staring mockingly at her. She lifted her chin in an automatic gesture of defiance before she glanced down at herself, seeing what he saw. Her face twisted in anguish.

"I can't believe—"

"Believe it." He grinned, a triumphant tone in his voice. "Oh, yes. You'll be the most satisfactory of mistresses." He chuckled softly as he reached out.

She stepped back. "No. Oh, please . . ."

"I only want to close your robe," he reassured her. "I don't have time for any more. Really. See?" He pulled it up over her shoulder and buttoned it beneath the lavender lace.

"How do you feel now?"

She shook her head. "I don't feel any different."

He grinned at her. "I didn't think you did."

Angry at the sight of his mocking face, she spun away from him. Her proud retreat to the divan was spoiled by her stumbling slightly to catch her balance. He caught her around the waist. She pulled at his hands. "Damn you! Let go. You're making fun of me.

I won't have it."

He swept her up in his arms. "And I'll continue to do so until you can be honest with yourself," he promised cruelly. "I've dealt with hypocrites all my life. I'll have none in my bedroom."

"Let me go." She bucked, trying to throw herself out of his arms, and beat at his shoulder with her good arm.

He held her fast and carried her to the bed. There he stretched her out and held her shoulders on the blue silk spread. "You enjoyed everything I did to you. Confess it."

"No. I'm a lady. A lady doesn't—"

"A lady does," he interrupted angrily. "A lady is flesh and blood. The bodies are all the same."

She rolled her head back and forth on the pillow. "They're not."

"We'll see," he sneered, his voice ugly. His hands left her shoulders and caught the lapels of her robe, jerking it open. The button popped at the neck. As she opened her mouth to protest, he closed it with a kiss. At the same time one hand found her breast, the other slid down over her belly to her mound to thread his fingers through her auburn curls.

"If you're not excited," he jeered, "then why are you wet?"

She struck at him then. Her left hand shot up and smacked the side of his face.

He caught her wrist, twisting it behind her. "You can't deny your body," he declared. "Can you?"

"No." She struggled then. "That is, yes. I can deny my body. My mind rules my body." Even as she fought and struck and clawed, she was thinking. This was going to be immeasurably harder than she had ever imagined that it would be. Finally she broke free and scrambled off the bed on the other side.

He stalked her, a sinister smile on his lips as she fled across the room to put the divan between the two of them. "You're being ridiculous."

"No."

"Get back there." He pointed toward the bed.

"No! Stay back." Her hair swirled round her shoulders as she looked around hurriedly for some avenue of escape.

"Don't be silly." He stopped, hands on hips. "You act as if I'm going to hurt you. You know I'm not."

She tried to fend him off. "I can't do this. I suddenly realized I can't."

"Why in hell not?"

She was shivering from head to foot. "I can't go through with this and keep my self-respect."

Suddenly his temper snapped. "Oh! A welcher. We made a bargain. I paid for your friend. You become my woman. That's the way of it, simple and honest."

"I can't do it!"

They squared off against each other, the divan between them. Both were furiously angry. "You can. And you will. I'll respect you a whole lot more if you keep your bargain."

"I can't become a whore!"

"By your definition you already are." His voice was flat and dry. "A whore is someone who does it for pay. I paid for you. I'm still paying for you. Now get in that bed and act like one."

"No. I'll be tricking you. I can't feel anything. I can't. I can't." She was trembling furiously. "You'll be getting a shell of a woman."

He stopped, hands on hips, throwing back his head, laughing cruelly. "Just so I get what I bought. Who says I want anything more?"

"But you must. You . . . you want a mistress. I can't respond."

"Get back on that bed." He pointed to it autocratically.

"No."

She caught up a porcelain ornament, a Buddha, from one of the tables and flung it at his head. Unfortunately, she threw with her left hand and it came nowhere near him. With a loud crash it shattered against the wall, its pieces clattered to the floor.

"Hellion!"

"Don't come any closer. I'll hurt you."

He laughed nastily. His index finger pointed directly at her then at the bed. "I'm telling you to wait for me there."

"And what will you do if I don't?" she dared him.

"You won't like it," he promised.

Chapter Nineteen

Fearfully, she tugged at her bonds. The faint rattle of a key being turned in a lock brought her head around with a sharp snap. An exclamation of terror burst from her lips. The Duke stood outlined in the doorway, the blazing fire leaping behind him. With a muffled cry she redoubled her efforts but to no avail.

Nearer he came and nearer until his shadow fell across her naked form dyed crimson by the firelight. "So, my dear, have you reconsidered the error of your ways. Will you render up your body and your soul to me?"

"No. Never. A thousand times no."

"Your throat is hoarse, my dear. Your screams and cries have proved futile. Have you not learned that there is no help for you?"

"Let me go. You cannot want a woman who does not care for you."

He touched her wrist encased in the black leather strap. "But look where you have hurt yourself. Such terrible bruises on such tender flesh. You cannot escape these bonds. Whether you care for me or no, I will have you."

"No," she moaned as his hand stroked down her arm to the swell of her satiny breast. "Please. You are a gentleman. An aristocrat."

"Such appeals are useless, my dear. The blood of arrogant Vikings flows in my veins. I command the lives of all my people. They obey me without question." His hand closed over her breast. His warm breath fanned her cheek. "Even as I shall command you and you will come to obey me."

"No," she shuddered. "Oh, no . . ."

Edward squeezed the bridge of his nose between his thumb and third finger. How flat. How stale. How self-accusing. Somehow none of this was working out as he had envisaged.

A homily from the street had maintained that all women whether rich and titled or poor and nameless were sisters under the skin. They would all open their legs for a man if the price was right. Furthermore, none of them ever would be faithful.

How Cassandra had fought to disprove their words. Of course, her efforts were doomed to failure. She was after all a woman. All female. And her body betrayed her. Still she resisted to the limits of her will each time he came to her. He would be thoroughly amused if he did not admire and pity her pathetically gallant efforts. He could almost read her mind as she sought to allow him pleasure and deny herself. She would close her eyes and grit her teeth. Then when he caressed her body, she dissolved in flames.

The first night when he returned from his appearance in the Devil's Palace, he had found her lying as if she were a corpse in the harem bed. Determined to play his mistress and still keep her self-respect, she had arranged herself in the exact center of the bed on top of the covers—an offering for the pasha.

She had exchanged her quilted lavender robe for a gown of the same color. She had removed the sling and clasped her hands together at her waist. Her feet were bare, her ankles crossed, her little pink toes pointed. As he bent over her, he could detect the rapid beating of her heart beneath the revealing satin. Feeling like a starving man at a feast, he had stared his fill at every nuance of her exquisite figure lovingly sculpted in shimmering cloth. His blood heated and his body tightened.

He must have made some small sound, for her eyes flew open. She swallowed hard. "I am too tired to go downstairs to eat tonight," she whispered. "I have decided to be fair, however."

"Fair?"

"Yes." She spread her hand palm down across the blue spread in an unconsciously provocative motion. He followed the movement, mesmerized by the knowledge that she could stroke his body as well. "You were right about what you said. I must keep my honor by paying my debt." She looked at him expectantly.

He nodded, his eyes drawn irresistibly to the erect nipples thrusting against the thin satin. "Right," he muttered. "Oh, yes."

The rapt expression on his face disconcerted her. She dragged her eyes away from him to focus upward on the folds of the canopy above her head. "So I've decided that my self-respect must be my problem. I shall do all that you ask of me." She took a deep breath. The movement increased the sweet ache throbbing at the bottom of his belly.

Waiting no longer, he flung off his cape and coat and dropped down beside her on the bed. He opened her lips with a long kiss and thrust his tongue into her mouth. She did not move although he imagined he could feel her muscles tensing.

When at last he drew back to breathe, she still lay with face utterly composed. She might have been a corpse except for a rising flush in her cheeks.

He grinned in spite of himself. So that was to be the way of it. As he stood up to strip off his clothing, he remembered the writhing, passionate woman he had held in his arms the night of the Hallowe'en costume ball. She had been like a wild thing pressing herself against him, demanding that he please her.

Then he had demanded that she take off the mask. Only for a minute had she resisted. How long before she would throw aside this mask and admit to desire?

He stripped off his white shirt. As he did, he ran his palm across the front of his chest. He was sweating, his hot, damp skin testimony to his desire. "Look at me," he commanded as he began to unbutton his trousers.

With eyes carefully blank and unfocused, she turned her head on the pillow just as he freed his manhood from the last buttons. It jutted out at her. His dark eyes watched her face, noted the flush deepening. Her left hand moved, her nails savaging the smooth silk. Her eyes flew to his face, accusing, a hint of pleading in her expression.

"I want you," he informed her needlessly. He sat down on the bed beside her to tug off his boots.

Excruciating waves of desire swept over her, leaving

her helpless, her body trembling. She ran her eyes over his broad back. The muscles were well defined, yet flat over the shoulder blades and ribs. Beneath the ribcage, his waist tapered down to his well-shaped buttocks.

Her fingers itched to touch him. She had to clench her fist to keep from raising her hand.

He turned back and caught her looking at him. "You want me, don't you?"

"No. I'm a lady."

"Lady or whore, a female wants a male," he said softly.

"I'm a civilized person. The animal has been—"

He bent over her then, stopping her mouth with his kiss. It began as a gentle tribute but swiftly turned into a sensual triumph. Without breaking it, he turned his body on the bed until he lay beside her. His right hand roamed freely over the satin-covered body.

As his mouth held her own, he cupped and stroked her breasts, the curve of waist and hips. He clasped her slender thigh, rotating his thumb high in the tender inner skin. At that moment he felt her palm touch his shoulder.

Her touch was light and over instantly, as if his skin were a stove that burned her and made her pull away. He smiled to himself and deepened his kiss. At the same time he drew up the skirt of her gown.

Cassandra set herself to recall the names of the kings of England in chronological order, their queens, the dates of their reigns. Still her body heated, her breasts ached. *Henry IV married Joanna of Navarre.* A warm tight pain curled and writhed at the bottom of her belly until she could not endure it and remain still. *Henry V married Katherine of France.* Sighing into her tormentor's mouth, she drew up one leg. At the same time she rested her hand on his back between his shoulderblades.

Henry VI married . . .

"Put your hand on my chest, mistress mine." Edward broke off the kiss to whisper the instructions into her mouth that gasped for breath.

Like a person in a dream, she slid her damaged arm forward across her waist until her fingers splayed across his midriff. Hard muscle, satiny skin, silky black hair all damp, all warm, all desirable. *Edward IV . . .* "Edward. Edward."

"Yes, Cassandra, yes, my sweet lady."

Somehow he had pulled the gown up to her waist. He began purposefully to stroke her thighs, the soft red curls at the bottom of her belly.

"Edward . . ." She stiffened. Her thighs went rigid. She closed her eyes. *Richard III married Anne of Warwick.*

His index finger slid deep into the soft curls, finding the hot moist nub of pleasure. She moaned helplessly, digging her heels into the yielding mattress, lifting her hips.

"Oh, you like that. Don't you? Don't you?" He nipped her earlobe before running his tongue into her ear, punctuating his questions with caresses.

"N-no-o-oh," she wailed. "No." To prove she lied, both her hands clasped him, her left one pulling him down toward her, her right clawing at his midriff. Unconsciously they demanded what she consciously denied.

His finger moved on, replacing the pressure with his palm while he searched for the opening between her legs, found it, slid inside.

A gasp, a plaintive keening, her thighs would not close against him.

A second and a third finger moved inside her while his thumb rotated more swiftly.

"No, Edward. No. Please." He pressed up on one arm and one knee, looking down into her face, glowing with perspiration, her lower lip caught between her teeth, her eyes slittered, her head thrown back.

"Say please again, Cassandra. Sweet Cassandra."

"N—oh, Please. Please. Please, Edward."

"Yes, Cassandra." With a last hard pressure of his thumb, he pulled his fingers out of her and thrust himself into her moist clasping depths. She cried out with the exquisite pleasure as he stroked deeper into her. Every movement caressed her passage until she twisted and moaned mindlessly.

He set his teeth to ride her long to bring her to supreme pleasure, but he had misjudged her. Another quick thrust and she went rigid beneath him, her breath stopped, her head thrown back. He waited until he felt her sheath begin to relax, then began to move again slowly at first so as not to hurt her, but determined now to reach his own climax.

Cassandra felt the ripples of pleasure, the tension begin to build. Helpless to do more, she grasped his upper arm, digging her fingernails into his bulging muscle. Joy erupted from her in the form of laughing sobs as he stoked her higher, her sensations more heart-stopping than ever.

He heard her. Was he hurting her? God forgive him. He could not stop. He could not . . . he could not . . .

Then he exploded, ramming his body forward into hers, farther than he had ever gone before. Himself so strong that he felt godlike. His shudders of pleasure went on and on. He heard her cry out again, felt her convulse about him. Thank God he had not hurt her too much. He rested his sweaty forehead on her shoulder. Only for a moment. Then he would get up and apologize. Only for a moment.

His body shifted sideways with automatic consideration. His arms drew her into the curve of his body. She turned on her left side, propping the injured arm on a pillow. They slept.

Edward could never forget that night. He stared at the page he had just written. No matter what had happened tonight, or any night in the future, she had belonged to him utterly that night as he had belonged to her. He had poured himself into her and neither one had made an effort to cleanse her body of his seed. Perhaps she was pregnant.

That was his hope. Pregnant, she would marry him for the name of her child. She would never bear a bastard. He thought about asking her to marry him again. Perhaps tonight after dinner when she was fed and rested. Her arm was healing nicely. She carried it in a sling to prevent its aching, but she was beginning to use it with some confidence.

She was settling into her surroundings beautifully. He had come upon her smiling only the other day as she prepared the menus for the cook. She was a treasure, a lady to the manor born.

He broke off his thoughts, looking around him at the books. Shakespeare's *Hamlet* had popped into his mind without his seeking to summon it.

In his library lay the one hope of his being deserving of her love and service. He was not Eddie Boggan any longer. He was Edward Sandron. He held out his hand studying it. It was strong and white. Suddenly, he wondered who his father had been. He had never thought about the man before. Certainly, his mother would not be able to tell him. She did not even know the names of the men she coupled with.

If he knew his father's name, would it make any difference to Cassandra? He shook his head. Once he had fantasized that the drunken gentleman who had taught him to read had been his father. He had been one of his mother's regulars at that time. But not thirty-one years ago.

No. He looked around him at the books. These were his father. His friends, his teachers, his saviors. For years he had read and studied until suddenly he found he could write.

They had lifted him up and made him a human being.

His thoughts were interrupted by a knock at the door.

"Don't bother with that, m'man. I'll walk right in. Man's m'best friend, y'know."

"Nash." Edward raised an eyebrow. "To what do I owe this unexpected visit?"

"Just came by to see if I could catch you not at work, old chap." The publisher handed his coat and stick to the new manservant and selected a cigarette from the box on the desk.

Edward spread his hands above the shuffle of papers. "As you see."

Nash smiled humorlessly. "Ah, yes. The little Scottish bird beginning to bore already?"

Edward shook his head. "As a matter of fact, no. But that's none of your business, is it?"

Nash raised his hand in mock surrender. "Not a bit. Not a bit. Couldn't care less really. Just that Sally's getting a little miffed."

Edward shrugged. "I can't see why she should be. Our relationship has always been strictly business. Neither one of us cares a whit about the other. I don't get miffed when she enjoys herself with someone else." He stared at the publisher meaningfully.

Nash suddenly began to cough in the haze of blue cigarette smoke rising around his head. "Really," he wheezed after a minute. "Can't imagine where I got the idea that you two were, ahem . . ."

"Probably because you would expect a man and a woman from the slums to have only one thing on their minds." Edward's answer was bitter.

Nash smiled cynically. "Actually expect any man and woman from anywhere to have only one thing on their minds."

Edward sat back in his chair. "What did you want to know, Nash?"

The publisher met the hard black eyes, then looked away. Ill at ease, he rose and wandered over to the golden skull. He stared at it as if it had an answer to all the questions in the world. "Well, actually wanted to know what you intend to do with the girl."

Edward looked at him narrowly. "Why? Do you care?"

Nash shifted uncomfortably, still keeping his back to Edward. "Actually, I do. Oh, not about her. Hell, a bird's a bird. And a soiled dove is a cut below the rest." He did not see the writer rise from his chair, his face a mask of anger. "Fact of the matter is . . ."

Whatever the fact of the matter might have been was cut off as Edward swung Nash around, caught him by the lapels, and slammed him back against the bookcase. "Keep your filthy sophistry to yourself."

"For God's sake . . ." The publisher clasped Edward's wrists. "Let me go."

"Not till you understand to keep your mouth off the woman I'm going to marry."

"Marry . . . ?" Nash blinked.

"That's right."

"You've lost your mind."

"Don't say that."

One lapel ripped up the front of the coat. "For God's sake, Eddie . . ."

"I'm going to marry Lady MacDaermond."

"Lady . . . ?"

Edward stepped back. In his anger at Nash's foul insinuations, he had revealed more than he had intended. "Forget that."

The publisher straightened his suit, inspected the lapel, stared at the frayed cloth, then at Edward's back. His gaze turned quizzical. Shrugging his coat more comfortably onto his shoulders, he lowered himself into his chair again. His pale eyes never left the form of the man he had come to hold in high regard.

"Does she want to marry you?" he asked at last, his voice neutral.

He watched the shoulders hunch as if they had received a blow. "She will."

Nash blew out a long plume of blue smoke. "You're living your own novels," he declared positively. "People don't force other people to marry them."

"She will," Edward insisted.

"Marry a woman who doesn't want you and you'll marry misery the rest of your life."

"No. I'll make her happy."

Nash sprang to his feet with uncharacteristic urgency. "But why? Why, for God's sake?"

Edward looked into Nash's thin cynical face. He had no intention of baring his soul to this man. The words *I love her* would draw a shout of laughter. "She's an earl's daughter," he said at last. "I have a chance to marry nobility. Eddie Boggan of Cheapside never even expected to marry. But Edward Sandron can marry well."

"You're bonkers, old chap."

"She said words that amounted to the same thing, but you'll both change your minds." Edward seated himself behind his desk and located his pen in the shuffle of papers. "See you tonight, Nash."

For once Nash had nothing to say. He stubbed out the cigarette and let himself out. Face thoughtful, he slowly descended the stairs to the private drawing room completely closed off from the casino. There he found Cassandra, sitting before a fire, an embroidery frame drawn up before her.

"Good day, Miss . . ." The publisher paused, undecided. ". . . Fitch."

She raised her head. Her natural hair would not lie smooth as the old gray wig had. Instead, dark red wisps formed a nimbus around her oval face. "Good day, Mr. Nash," she replied guardedly.

"I, er, how is your arm?"

"Better. Almost well, actually. I can use it with care, but it gets tired quickly. Fortunately, I seem to heal rapidly."

He looked at her closely. Her skin was almost translucent, pale, milk white, except for the delicate flush of her cheeks. Her eyes were green, fringed with dark brown lashes. Only a certain weariness of expression coupled with smudges beneath the eyes bespoke the unnatural strain circumstances had placed upon her. "Delighted to hear it," he murmured.

She waited a minute, then waved her left hand toward a chair opposite her. "I do forget my manners. Will you have tea?"

He blinked. He could not remember when a lady had offered him tea. The novelty of it tickled him. "Why, yes." He seated himself while she rang. The manservant entered.

She acknowledged his bow with a sweet smile. "Thank you, Barston, we'll have tea and"—she looked inquiringly at Nash—"brandy?"

He nodded, smiling expansively. The manservant bowed and left.

"Were you visiting Mr. Sandron?"

"Yes, but the chap's writing like a good fellow, so I wasted my trip."

"Then you must not leave without some refreshment. The weather—I'm advised—is freezing."

"Correct." Nash studied his boot toes, then leaned

forward to hold out his hand to the fire. Her demeanor put him at a disadvantage. Not only was his purpose unclear in his mind, but it was unpleasant. He was not used to being greeted pleasantly. He cleared his throat as a log spewed resin out along its side in a bubbling hiss.

"Did you wish to say something to me, Mr. Nash?"

He looked over his shoulder at her. The candid green eyes drew him in. If indeed she were an aristocrat, she was no simpering fool. "Yes." He drew back. "Do you wish to leave here, Miss Fitch?"

"Do you know that my name is not Fitch?" She answered a question with a question.

"Yes. Miss MacDaermond, is it not?"

"Yes. Cassandra MacDaermond."

"Lady Cassandra MacDaermond, according to Baal."

She stared into the fire. "That is all behind me forever."

"Baal doesn't seem to think so."

She did not know what to say. She would have died rather than discuss her private life with this man.

"Baal has some rather strange ideas," he continued, watching her. He waited. When she did not answer, he continued. "If you wish to leave here, Miss Mac-Daermond, I can arrange it."

The emerald eyes widened with hope, then the lids dropped over them. She shook her head. "I can't."

"Whyever not? If you want to go, there's no one to stop you." His tone of voice turned nasty. "Unless you're another female looking to Edward to support you?" Although he watched her closely, he could detect no change of expression. "Is that the way of it,

Miss MacDaermond. Are you like so many of the nobility, down on your luck and too proud to work?"

What she might have said was interrupted by the entrance of Barston with the decanter and tea service. They both waited in strained silence while he fussed at arranging the things and serving them. When finally he bowed and departed, Nash spoke again as if to himself, his eyes scanning the bric-a-brac on the mantel. "Of course, you did come here as Edward's housekeeper or upstairs maid, or some such."

"How generous of you to recall it, sir. I would still be if not for a set of circumstances over which I had absolutely no control."

The publisher pursed his lips, his eyes still steadfastly elsewhere. "But fortuitously you were in time to nurse him back to health."

Her mouth tightened. "I fear we are talking at cross-purposes. I was alluding to his bringing me back from Scotland and installing me here. You are speaking of his illness, Mr. Nash, if you have something you wish to accuse me of, perhaps you should take your suspicions to Edward."

He spread his mouth in a vulpine grin. "Wouldn't do a bit of good, Miss, er, milady. Poor chap! He won't hear a word against you."

"Then this conversation appears to be at an end."

"If we had reached an end so swiftly, I would never have begun it."

"Would you be so good as to tell me why you did begin it?"

He nodded briskly. "Capital idea. Hate tiptoeing around a subject m'self. The truth is that I hate to see my friend made a fool of."

The corners of her mouth twitched upward. "How kind! Forgive me if I don't believe you."

Nash tossed off the brandy. "Fact. Someone tried to poison him. Fact. Someone did poison the valet by mistake. Fact. A pair of toughs one with a Scottish name tried to run Edward down in the street and kill him. Fact. The police arrested one man, a Scotsman, as if happens, for questioning, but had to let him go. However, now they're far enough away from the case to forget it." He looked to see if she was following him.

"But the killer is still loose," he continued, "and Edward is surrounded by night and by day with people who don't like him."

He paused to judge her reaction to his summation, but her expression did not reveal guilt. Instead her green eyes appeared to be judging him.

He shrugged. "Suspects. Number one. Mac-Adam — the man they arrested. Apart from the fact that he didn't come to the house until several days later, he had no motive. Number two. Me — his publisher and partner in this venture. No motive again. Actually rather like the chap. He's a bit of all right when he's not being too literary."

"Have you gone to the police with these 'suspects'?"

"Not likely they'd listen to a fellow who owns part interest in a gambling casino, not to speak of the other, ahem, ventures. No." He shook his head. "Just compiled this list for m' own amusement."

"It seems rather short."

"Not complete. Number three. Sally — Ashtaroth. Motive, tricky. He doesn't pay her the attention she'd like. If he were dead, she'd get half instead of a third. On the other hand without him, there's not nearly so much of the pie. Baal is the chief draw in the casino and his books bring in good money. Sally's not one to cut off her own nose to spite her face. Also, poison's not her style. She'd slip a knife below his ribs or a hatpin through his heart. Kind of a violent type, y'know."

Cassandra placed a trembling hand to her forehead. "I don't think —"

"Wait. There's only number four." He paused for effect. "You."

"Me!" She stared at him, unable to believe her ears.

He leaned forward, his vulpine smile stronger than ever. "You, Lady MacDaermond. Fact. You disguise yourself and come to work here just before the crime. Fact. You know Fitzwalter. He's cracked on gambling. How do we know you're not one of his disciples, so to speak? You met him on the street. He helped you to escape. What were you escaping from? If the police searched your background, what would they find?" His pale eyes glittered as they held her own.

She could not suppress her feelings of dismay and distress as she set her teacup down. The untouched tea sloshed into the saucer as it rattled against the tabletop. She could not deny the reasons he put forth. If the police did check into her background and found her father's suicide, they might arrest her. They had certainly arrested Mr. MacAdam on much less motive than that. She looked at Nash coldly. "You have quite a convincing list of reasons. Have you told Edward about them?"

"Not likely. He'd just get all upset with me and probably knock me around some."

"So what do you intend to do with your great

detective work?"

He poured himself another finger of brandy and leaned back. "Don't suppose you'd just panic and run screaming from the house, would you?"

She shook her head slowly. "Not *my* style."

He acknowledged her dry humor with a gesture of his glass. "True. Police won't give a listen. Edward gets upset. I'm gambling that the one person who'd pay attention is you." His eyelids came down to veil his eyes. "Only one more thing to say. How does a couple of hundred pounds sound to you to take you away from here?"

Two hundred pounds would be fine for her, but what about Mr. MacAdam? Moreover, what about her bargain? With real reluctance she shook her head. "I truly wish I could say yes, Mr. Nash."

"Three hundred."

"I made a bargain with Mr. Sandron. I can't go back on my word of honor."

He snorted inelegantly. "Honor . . ."

"If you don't believe I have any, then you shouldn't have offered me money in the first place."

"Five hundred." He rose and stood over her. "That's my last offer."

She looked up into his eyes, her own tinged with real regret. "I can't. I truly can't."

He ground his teeth so tightly that his jaw quivered. "By God, I'll not stand by and see you kill my friend. I'll find a way, I swear—"

The manservant knocked at the door. "Miss Ashtaroth," he announced even as Sally pushed her way into the room.

Her black eyes widened, then narrowed suspiciously. "How interesting. The two of you so close together. Were you getting ready to kiss her? Not enough for you, Miss Fitch, to have Eddie wrapped around your little finger. You've got to have Nasty there too."

Cassandra looked Nash squarely in the eye. "You do see why I couldn't possibly leave this house?" she inquired sweetly. "The society here is so convivial."

Chapter Twenty

My hesitant ring at the gate brought out Marguerite. She locked it after admitting me and led me into a dark passage where her candle stood. Then with her candle in her hand she looked over her shoulder, superciliously saying, "You are to come this way."

The passage was a long one, and at the end she stopped, put her candle down, and opened a door. Here the daylight reappeared, and I found myself in a small paved courtyard. There was a clock in the outer wall of this house, but it had stopped.

We went in at another door into a gloomy room with a low ceiling on the ground floor at the back. In the center of the room Marguerite turned around, holding her candle at shoulder height, and said in a taunting manner, her face close to mine:

"Well?"

"Well, miss?" I had to check myself to keep from bumping into her.

"Am I pretty?"

"Yes, I think you are very pretty."

"Am I insulting?"

"Not so much so as you were last time."

Flushing with anger, she slapped my face. "Now?" said she? "You coarse little monster, what do you think of me now?"

"I shall not tell you."

"Then why don't you cry again, you little wretch?"

"Because I'll never cry for you again," said I which was, I suppose as false . . .

The chiming of the clock on the wall shelf behind him reminded Edward of the approaching dinner hour. He thrust the pen back into the inkwell and put his hands over his eyes. Was he a fool for trying to write a novel of character and substance?

He cast a furtive glance at the door, half expecting Nash to burst in upon him and rip the manuscript to shreds. Except that Nash was not the type to do a violent act. With his rapier wit and tongue, he did not need the battle-ax. A quick shuffle through the pages, the icy eyes skimming the words, and then a pitying sneer.

Edward shuddered. He probably should be writing more of *Memoirs of Lord S—* instead of wasting his time on this romance. He called it a romance, yet it was more than that. And once he had begun it, it fascinated him. Whenever he put it aside to work on the other, the characters and their problems hammered at him until he returned.

In reading back over it, he heard again the sounds and sights of the London street where he had roamed as a child. He recognized the proud, well-born character of the heroine as Cassandra. Moreover, he recognized autobiographical elements in the hero. He could never publish it, of course. It was too revealing. He could not stand naked before the world.

The clock chimed the quarter hour. Hastily, he pushed all the papers into a folder and slid the whole into the tray drawer. His muscles responded as a quiver of excitement tightened them.

He could not relax in the hot bath Barston had drawn for him. His mind, released from the iron discipline he had clamped upon it while he wrote, now hummed with anticipation. This night could very well be the most important of his life. His plans were made, all was in readiness, the events were set in motion. His only uncertainty involved whether he should have invited Nash and Ashtaroth as guests. They were his only friends, yet he worried about their reaction.

"Running late, old chap." Nash hailed him and pressed a glass of sherry into his hand. "Good to see that. Been writing, I hope."

"What else?" Edward took the glass and bowed to Cassandra and Ashtaroth, who sat stiffly on opposite ends of the drawing room sofa obviously avoiding one another with their eyes. "My apologies, ladies." In an uncharacteristic gesture, he stepped forward and brought Cassandra's hand to his lips. "My lady, I beg your pardon." He scanned her face, marveling at its almost impossible fragility accentuated by faint smudges beneath the big green eyes.

The dress she wore was one for which he had carefully selected the material, a pale lime green taffeta. The dressmaker had cut it low over the bosom so that the very tops of her breasts rose above it. Mentally, he drew her up into his arms to press his lips against the velvety, flawless skin.

She smiled uncertainly as he realized he had hovered over her an instant too long. Her fingers twitched as if only by effort could she refrain from pulling her hand away. "We waited upon your pleasure, sir."

"Oh my, yes, indeed we did," Sally sneered from opposite end of the sofa. The direction of Edward's gaze was not lost on her. "We have such precious manners now that we've got a titled aristocrat in the Devil's Palace."

Nash rolled his eyes heavenward. "Sally, old gel, you'd best behave yourself. Can't you see Edward's jaw tensing. He'll be throwing you out if you can't keep a civil tongue in your head."

The dark woman's eyes narrowed angrily. "I own part and parcel of all of this," she reminded him hotly. "And don't any of you blokes forget it." Her speech varied from one sentence to the other, the first cultured in tone, the next the rough accent of the slums.

Cassandra withdrew her hand from Edward's to accept the glass of sherry Nash handed her. She lifted it in tribute to the woman at the end of the couch. "You're much richer than I, Sally. You've struggled and slaved for everything you have. I'm not likely to forget that you own part of the house in which I live. I thank you for your generosity."

The charming speech of gratitude rocked Sally back on her heels. "Well . . . that's good. I don't care who lives here since I've got my own place. I guess Eddie can have whoever he wants to warm his bed."

"That'll be about enough, Sal," Edward murmured.

"Oo-o-oh. I'm so scared."

On the verge of losing his temper, Edward took a step toward her. Hastily, Nash interposed his body between them. "Drink up, old chap. Don't let Sal get on your nerves, Miss MacDaermond. She's just naturally insulting. Can't help it. Result of a bad upbringing. Hates everybody and everything. Eaten alive with jealousy."

"Damn you, Nash . . ." Lunging to her feet, Sally slashed her taloned nails at the air in front of Nash's face. Not drawing back an inch, he raised one eyebrow as he took a sip of sherry.

At that moment Barston opened the doors to the dining room. "Dinner is served."

Sally spun around in a swirl of her magenta taffeta skirts. With a toss of her head, she thrust her arm through Edward's. "I'm starved. I hope the cook has something fit to eat this time. The last time it was awful."

"Different cook, m'dear," Nash supplied easily, offering his arm to Cassandra. "I picked him out myself. Ask for nothing fancy from him and he's aces."

Throughout the meal, Edward took the opportunity to observe Cassandra in the relative privacy of their dining room. Her manners were impeccable, her attention to both Nash and Ashtaroth's conversation all that was polite. Her appetite, however, was depressingly small, seeming to confirm what he had guessed.

Because she would not actively seek him out, he had spent comparatively little time with her since her return from Scotland. Despite their late hours, he rose early to be served breakfast in the library where he wrote. She busied herself around the house where she had hired two more servants including the excellent Barston. She was exquisitively dressed when he came for her at ten. Together they went to the Devil's Palace where they ate among the guests at the buffet. After midnight, they retired sometimes together to the harem room, sometimes she to sleep there alone while he held a "performance" for a select few.

Unaware of Edward's eyes on her, Cassandra concentrated on eating her food and being a hostess to the two guests. Privately, she considered them by far the most unpleasant part of her bargain. The well-seasoned fish tasted like sawdust in her mouth as Ashtaroth's filed tongue deplored the abominable behavior of a gambler who could not bear to lose. Of the two, she much preferred Nash's satiric wit. Tonight, however, he was strangely silent.

Between them opposite her sat Edward, obviously in control of the conversation, a catalyst between them and yet more. He was their leader, the touchstone and foil of their intelligence.

As the fish was removed and a platter of roast mutton offered, her physical condition intruded more and more into her mind. The nausea in the morning, the ever-present lethargy both warned her that she was in trouble. But what could she do?

Veiling her eyes with her lashes, she stole a glance at the head of the table. He was watching her; his black eyes scanned her expectantly. Hastily, she ducked her head and concentrated on her plate. To cover her nervousness, she put a small bite in her mouth. A moment later the strong-flavored meat made her choke.

Edward observed her distress. "More champagne, Cassandra?"

She nodded, one hand touching her napkin to her mouth, the other encircling the stem of her wineglass.

"I'll have some more too, Eddie." Ashtaroth reached for her glass as Barston moved toward the foot of the table. "I really like this stuff. Of course, it's probably old hat to somebody born in a castle. That's where you were born, weren't you, m'lady?" Her voice dripped with scorn. She held the glass over her shoulder for the servant to fill as if daring anyone to comment on her bad manners.

"Better watch it, Sal, old gel." Nash studied the dark woman knowingly, feeling the vibrations of anger emanating from her. "You've already got a bit on."

"I'll get a bit more on before I'm through," she promised, tilting the glass to her mouth.

"Cassandra?" Edward invited, ignoring the comments passed back and forth across the table between them.

She accepted the filled glass gratefully and took a generous sip. With its help she swallowed the mutton and took a deep breath. "I never had champagne until I came to the Devil's Palace," she remarked to the table in general.

All three pairs of eyes stared at her in surprise.

"But you're the daughter of an Earl . . ." Edward began incredulously.

"An impoverished earl by the time I grew old enough to drink." She smiled bleakly. "No, I forgot. Mama let me have a little from her glass at the last party we had before she died. That was such a long time ago, I can scarcely remember it."

"Oh, boo-hoo," Sally sneered coarsely. "Tell her all about your dear old dad, Eddie. Bet you can't 'scarcely remember' him either."

"A toast," Nash announced, drowning out the last of her words. "To better times for us all. Nice to know that we've all come up in the world."

"Here! Here!" Edward murmured, watching closely as Cassandra smiled with some relief at Nash and drank. Her head was buzzing faintly and the candles had a special glow around them.

"Course some of us didn't have very far to go," Sally muttered.

The butler refilled the glasses as the table was cleared.

"A toast," Edward called. "To wealth and all the comforts it can buy."

"Certainly have to drink to that," Nash agreed. Then his eyes narrowed at the sight of a man in clerical garb being ushered into the room behind Cassandra's back. He shot a glance at Edward, who smiled broadly, then at the tipsy Cassandra. He started to comment, then shrugged his shoulders elaborately. Sally, who was no more sober than Cassandra, had not even noticed the man.

"The dessert," Edward called.

This time Mrs. Smithers appeared bearing a small white cake frosted with *sotelties* of spun sugar and crystallized white violets. She placed it in front of Cassandra and stood back smiling while Barston filled the glasses again with champagne.

Cassandra's green eyes, overbright now, glowed at the sight of the exquisite creation. Then she looked inquiringly at Edward.

"It is for you, Cassandra."

She shook her head a little dazedly. "On what occasion?"

"Drink up," he urged, "and you will soon find out. To the Devil's Palace, and all its devotees. May they enjoy the best of health and the poorest of luck."

Cassandra attempted to refuse to drink, but Nash's quick mind had immediately realized what Edward sought to effect. Resigning himself to what he considered to be his friend's stupidity, he tipped the foot of her glass up with a mocking grin. "In for a penny, in for a pound," he chuckled to her.

Edward rose from his place and came around the table to her. Puzzled, she stared up at him. The light from the candles, so much softer than the harsh flame of the gas-o-lier, shone in her eyes. He bent over to take her hand and help her to her feet. "Come, love."

"I'm a little dizzy," she apologized, softly slurring her words. "I don't know what's . . ." She blinked in surprise as Nash rose at her other side. Then Edward passed her hand through his own and guided her over to stand before the cleric.

"Nash, for Gawd's sake . . ." Ashtaroth exclaimed.

He hurried to her side and offered her his arm, his own face darkly resigned. "Seems that we were invited here to be witnesses, old gel. Let's make the best of it, shall we?"

"But . . ."

"Dearly beloved . . ." the minister began.

Cassandra's head was spinning. She should be objecting, but somehow she could not find the strength of character to do so. She should be twisting out of his arms and sweeping haughtily from the room instead she swayed against him. She could not stifle the feeling of peace about her heart. Her child, an Earl's grandson or granddaughter, would have a father. Even as she doubted the future, she blessed the man beside her for granting her the use of his name before a condemning society.

Edward's arm went around her shoulders, his hand gathered hers firmly. "Say 'yes,' sweetheart," he coached.

"I—I—"

"Yes," he urged, his lips against her ear.

She felt a thrill run through her. Suddenly, she wanted him. Despite her best efforts she could not lie quiet and still beneath him. He turned her to fire.

"Yes," he whispered again. His tongue caressed the shell of her ear.

She shivered in response. "Oh, yes."

"Sweetheart." He hugged her against his side. He freed her hands to lay his fingertips on her cheek and turn her head into his shoulder.

The minister droned on for a minute, but Cassandra could not absorb his words. Her senses were full of the warmth and nearness, the clean male smell, the masculine toiletries, the steady beating of his heart.

Then he was tipping her head up and kissing her long, his tongue working its special magic in her mouth until her knees went weak and he had to put both arms around her to hold her up.

She heard a hum of conversation. He turned her to face Nash and Ashtaroth and a pleased Mrs. Smithers. Barston stepped forward with a silver tray. Edward passed one stem of champagne to her, took one of his own, and raised it high. "To my beloved wife."

With a shrug Nash drank.

Sally sneered malevolently. "Got a bun in the oven, Eddie?"

He flushed. "Probably, Sal."

She made a rude sound. "I should have tried that."

"Too late now, Sal, old gal." This from Nash, who stared with calculating eyes at Cassandra's dazed expression. "When's the glad event, old chap?"

"Several months away, I should think," Edward replied softly. He kissed Cassandra's forehead, now wrinkled in a frown as she tried to concentrate on what had been done.

Edward began at the crown of her head, deftly pulling the pins from her hair and letting the glorious red mass tumble down her back. With hands that trembled faintly, he caressed her temples then stroked back through her hair, spreading it over her shoulders. "Beloved."

She swayed forward, her inhibitions dissolved in champagne, her eyes limpid. Her own hands rose to stroke the white wings at his temples. "You have wonderful hair," she murmured. "So beautiful. Beautiful face too."

He kissed her on her forehead, the tip of her nose, her lips, then turned her around. "I shall play lady's maid tonight." Button by button, he unfastened the lime green dress, holding her by the arm to help her out as it pooled around her feet. "You shouldn't be wearing a corset," he scolded softly over her shoulder as he unhooked the contraption. Then he destroyed whatever effectiveness his polemic might have had by nibbling and kissing her neck.

"I couldn't get into my dress without one."

"Then get a larger dress." He cast the corset aside like the shell of a locust. A second later, he stripped off the chemise to run his hands over her ribs, gently massaging the red marks left by the tight bones of the garment. As she sighed, he clasped her breasts, pulling her back against him.

Instead of standing stiffly in his arms as she usually did at this time, she laid her head back on his shoulder and moaned. The nearly unbearable tingling and aching of her breasts was relieved by his hands squeezing them, his thumbs and index fingers tugging at the turgid nipples.

The sweetness of her nature released by the champagne, she turned her head until he could capture her mouth in a long kiss.

"Sit down," he whispered at last, his voice a hoarse unfamiliar croak. She sat while he knelt to pull off her green slippers and white stockings, her drawers and her petticoats.

When she sat naked on the sofa, he rose and stripped off his own clothing. For the first time she watched him, forgetting to be embarrassed. Her eyes wide, a pulse beating in her throat as she stared at the width of his shoulders, the black curling hair, the flat masculine nipples. A shiver ran through her, as he unbuttoned his trousers and stepped out of them and his smallclothes at the same time.

He sat beside her to pull off his boots and socks. She was aware of the warmth of his thigh brushing against her own. Then he went down on his knees before her to put both hands on the tender flesh of her inner thighs and gently pushed them apart. "Sweetheart, kiss me."

Her eyes flickered up to his face, then back at his chest. Hesitantly, she put out her hand. Her fingers touched his nipple, circled the sensitive areola, tugged at the nub, felt it harden.

He gasped as if in pain and stared down at her white hand, such a contrast to his skin. "What are you . . . ?"

"Are you as sensitive as I am?" she murmured, raising her other hand to his other nipple.

"Probably," he groaned, setting his teeth to keep himself from dragging her from the couch and making love to her on the floor. His manhood sprang up like a lance from the black curls at the bottom of his belly. His hands so gentle a minute before now clutched her painfully.

She moaned in turn, edging her body forward. "Do you like this?"

"Yes . . . I . . . Yes." He felt sweat break out on his body. Somehow he had lost control of the lovemaking. Instead of carrying her to their bed as he had planned, he found himself sinking back on his haunches between her thighs, kneeling at her feet while she explored his sensuality with innocent inventiveness.

His head fell back on his shoulders, his torso swayed backward.

Quite naturally, she slipped off the divan, straddling his thighs with her own. Without quite realizing how she did it, she stared down at the rampant manhood touching her belly. Nervously, she clutched at his chest, her nails scoring his nipples. He groaned at the exquisite torment.

She jerked her hands away. "I'm sorry."

"No." He caught her wrists. "It's so good."

"But . . ."

"Please." One hand he guided back to his chest, the other to the organ, hard as metal, between them. "Please."

She allowed him to close her hand around it. As from a long way off, she wondered why she did not die of shock. But the thought died in a shudder of desire as his fingers found and caressed the throbbing nub buried in the red curls between her legs.

"Do you like that?"

"Oh, yes."

"Then it's the same for me." To illustrate his lesson, he rubbed his hand up and down. The tender lips of her gently swelling mound were like silk as his fingers slid between them.

Driven by ecstasy she pressed closer, delighting in the satiny feel of him in her hand, rubbing him against her belly. Her eyes were closed, her lips parted, as she gave herself up to the rushing, pounding tumult of her own blood and the heady feeling of her rapid breathing.

"Stop," he whispered at last. "Stop. If you don't, I'll . . . It's too much . . ."

"I can't stop." The tension in her thighs built until her whole body began to shudder. When he felt her release begin, he pushed his hand harder against her.

She cried out as a kaleidoscope of color burst in her mind. Her head snapped back, her body arched.

Instinctively he thrust himself into her sheath, which welcomed him with exquisite contractions, drawing him farther and farther up into her, while she writhed and moaned.

Together they completed the dance of love, arching rhythmically as their pleasure mounted, peaked, then slid away. Arms about each other they sank onto their sides still joined together, his shoulders beneath her neck cradling her head against him.

When their bodies had cooled and their awareness returned to the harem room, Edward opened his eyes. If he lived to be a hundred, he would never forget the pleasure of his wedding night. He felt exhilarated and at the same time at peace.

His wife lay cradled in his arms. Proprietarily, he slid his hand lightly over her swollen breast to the slight thickening of her waist. Their child lay between them. She might object to her marriage to a commoner, but their child would not be a nameless bastard, forever barred from society.

By his marriage to her, he had given them all status. She was the daughter of an earl, he was her husband. His profession might not be the best in the world, but he was acquiring wealth. Money could buy most things in the latter part of the reign of Victoria. It gave him prospects of better things. He vowed . . .

Cassandra stirred. The prickly surface of the carpet made her shift her hip in an effort to find a more comfortable spot to lie in. The pile of the carpet shifted with her. She moaned in discomfort.

Edward kissed her ear. "I think it's time I moved you to the bed for a good night's rest, wife."

At the last word, her eyes flew open. "I am your

wife," she acknowledged dully.

He kissed her forehead. "I'm sorry I forgot the ring."

"It doesn't matter." She started to sit up, but he forestalled her.

With ease, he picked her up in his arms as he rose and carried her to the bed. Tenderly, he tucked her underneath the covers and climbed in himself. "That was wonderful," he told her, pressing another kiss on her. "Wonderful. I never knew it could be so good."

She closed her eyes in shame. "I was too bold."

"Nonsense. Married people cannot be too bold with each other. Bold with your husband. You made me very happy. What was bold about that?"

"I'm sure I did not behave as a lady should."

He grinned at her. "How can you be sure? Perhaps ladies always make love like that."

"I can't believe it." She covered her face with her hands.

Privately, he very much doubted if most women, whether ladies or no, made love like that, but he had no intention of conveying that information to her. Gently he took her hands and kissed them. "You're upset. You had a little too much champagne and it has made you weepy."

"I never drank so much champagne before," she agreed, her voice weaker.

"But think how good it made you feel." His hands stroked her back. "You must have a good night's sleep."

Obediently, she slid down under the covers and curled on her side, where he could continue stroking her. In measureless content, she closed her eyes. She had refused to marry him and then realized she was pregnant. She had alternatively cursed herself for her foolishness and praised the courage of her convictions. But it had been cold courage. She had begun to worry about how she could go to him with the information and what his reaction would be. She had worried about being cast out and having to bear her child in poverty. Now she did not have to worry any longer. "I feel so relaxed," she purred. "It's probably the champagne."

"Yes," he replied, leaning over to kiss her ear. "You're probably right."

Chapter Twenty-one

"There he is! There he is! Arrest him, Inspector. He kidnapped her."

Edward rose from behind his desk, his lips tight, his black eyebrows drawn together in a frown. Barston spread his hands in wordless apology as Fitzwalter shouldered his way into the library.

"Oh, no." Cassandra stabbed her embroidery needle into her fingertip. She did not see the drop of blood ruin the white linen so possessed was she with the memory of the raid on the gambling casino when Baal had been led away in irons. Pushing aside the embroidery frame, she sprang to her feet, only to stagger and have to hold on to the chair arm as black spots swam before her eyes.

Heedless of her distress, Fitzwalter continued his triumphant denunciation. Brandishing his umbrella like a crusader's sword, he pointed it at Edward Sandron. "He kidnapped her," he repeated positively. "And now he's keeping her drugged so she can't run away."

In the doorway behind Fitzwalter, Inspector Revill appeared to be noting the reactions of the room's occupants.

"How very enterprising of you, Edward!" Nash remarked. The publisher continued to lounge in the other chair beside the fire, his feet on the fender. His lips pulled back from his teeth in a sardonic grin. "Never had the slightest notion you were so very, very evil. What kind of drugs did he give you, Cassandra? Might pass a few of them around if they'd make ladies look like you."

Ignoring Nash's sarcastic remarks, she tried to cross to Edward's side, but Fitzwalter's umbrella drove her back.

"Stay away from him, Cassandra," the little moralist commanded. "Don't get too close. He'll turn vicious when he realizes he's cornered. But you're safe now. Come in, Inspector, and do your duty."

Inspector Revill still stood in the doorway, his bowler hat tucked under his arm military fashion. At last frowning heavily, he pulled his omnipresent little notebook from his pocket and opened it to a new page. "I'll have to take a few statements before I can do anything, Mr. Fitzwalter."

He looked pointedly at Edward, who had subsided in his chair, his face impassive. The measure of his happiness was such that he felt no nervousness at the sight of the policeman. "By all means take a statement, Inspector Revill, but please be quick. I was just completing some work for my publisher before going on a trip."

"Ah-ha!" Fitzwalter pounced on the last few words. "Leaving town. Trying to escape just retribution. Did you hear that? We got here just in time, Inspector."

The inspector nodded. "First, tell me what you have to say to this accusation, Mr. Sandron."

"Perfectly ridiculous, Inspector. If the truth were known, Mr. Fitzwalter actually kidnapped Miss Mac-Daermond from my household and tried to take her to Scotland."

Revill turned his gaze on Fitzwalter. "What about that, sir?"

"That's a lie. A lie!" Fitzwalter all but shouted. His face darkened as his anger built. His little black eyes flitted to Cassandra, daring her to dispute his word. "I rescued her. She was locked in her room. I rescued her and was taking her back to her home. I offered her a home."

The inspector scribbled rapidly, filling the tiny pages. "Perhaps you'd like to make a statement, ma'am," he hinted, "just to corroborate or deny?"

"You were locked in your room. Tell him Cassandra."

"That's true, Mr. Fitzwalter, but—"

"Ah, you see? Inspector, this young woman is a countess by birth, the daughter of my oldest and dearest friend, the Earl of Daerloch. Before he died, he begged me to take care of her. I was trying to do my duty to my friend and to his daughter. This"—he stabbed the umbrella toward Edward—"scum should be hanged. He's not fit to live. A molester of young gentlewomen. That's what he is."

Nash had risen and strolled around to peer over the inspector's shoulder. "M-o-l-e-s-t-e-r," he spelled *sotto voce*. "If you're going to take such copious notes, Inspector, you really should learn to spell."

The burly lawman merely hunched his shoulder to block Nash's view. "I'll take your statement later," he grunted. "Now, Miss MacDaermond . . ."

"Mrs. Sandron," she revealed quietly.

"Mrs.?" the inspector queried.

"Mrs.!" Fitzwalter exclaimed, his umbrella point sagging.

"That's right."

The inspector laid his stub of a pencil between the leaves and closed his notebook.

Edward came round the desk and put his arm around his wife's waist. Cassandra leaned her bright head against his shoulder. "We were married last night, Inspector. Another hour and you would not have found us at home. We are leaving for Brighton for our honeymoon."

The inspector could not restrain a skeptical glance at Nash, who moved unconcernedly to the desk, where he selected a cigarette and lit it.

"My publisher is waiting for me to finish some business, so he can drive us to the train."

"Thought I'd throw a grain of rice and catch the bouquet." Nash smirked as he blew a stream of smoke high in the air above the visitor's heads.

Fitzwalter gaped and choked. His face flushed an unbecoming purple with wrath. "She's been drugged!" he shrieked. He lunged forward, raising his umbrella over his head.

"Here now!" Clapping his hat back on his head, Inspector Revill caught Fitzwalter handily, dragged his arm down, and forced him back against the door. "Calm down."

Unfortunately, the little man was almost beside himself with rage. "Don't you understand? He's done something terrible to her. He's a spawn of Satan. He may even be the devil himself. Downstairs is hell on earth. Hell on earth!"

The inspector managed to wrest the umbrella away. "Mr. Fitzwalter, get hold of yourself. Nothing can be sorted out if you don't remain calm."

Gradually, the man stopped his futile struggling. His black eyes darted from face to face and finally back to the inspector. "He's possessed you too," he accused flatly.

The inspector eased his grip. "I'm just here for the facts," he contradicted flatly.

"I'll report you to your superiors. You can't be a detective if you can't see what he's done. Look at this house, this room." He twisted away from the inspector and hurried across the room to point to the pentagram that surrounded the tiger skin rug on the floor. "Come here. Look at this. Do you know what this is?"

The inspector exchanged a speaking glance with Nash, who grinned maliciously. "That design on the floor, Mr. Fitzwalter?"

"Yes. This abomination is . . ." He paused for effect. "This is a pentagram."

The inspector raised his eyebrows, then looked to

Edward for information.

"A Great Pentacle for summoning the devil," he replied with a perfectly straight face.

Inspector Revill nodded solemnly. "Mr. Fitzwalter, I think I have enough information to write up a report. Will you accompany me to headquarters?"

"Only if we can take Cassandra with us. We can't go without this poor child," the evangelist objected. "You've seen for yourself what a terrible place this is. He did all manner of terrible, vile things to her. You must save her."

The policeman looked over his shoulder at the "poor child" who clasped her hand in her husband's and stared with pitying green eyes at the man he held. Edward Sandron's handsome face was equally grave. The two men's eyes met in perfect understanding.

Inspector Revill took Fitzwalter by the arm. "We'll have to talk to a judge about a writ. Why don't we go somewhere where we can talk this over?" he suggested.

"No. No! We can't leave her. She's not safe . . ."

"Good idea, Inspector," Nash agreed, his harsh voice overriding Fitzwalter's. He stubbed out his cigarette and pulled the door open. "Edward will sign a few more papers and then we'll be on our way. Might be a good idea if someone put Fitzwalter on a train too. I suggest back to Scotland."

"Damn you, Trevor Nash. You'd like to get rid of me too, but—"

Revill nodded, ignoring Fitzwalter's protestations. He turned back to Cassandra. "You are all right, ma'am?"

"Quite all right, I assure you."

"She's not. She's drugged."

"I do apologize for this unpleasant interlude." He held out his hand to Edward, who took it firmly. "Good luck and congratulations."

"Thank you, Inspector."

"Let's go, Mr. Fitzwalter. We'll find a judge for you to talk to."

"You don't understand . . ."

As the door closed behind them, Nash gave a whoop of laughter. "Great show. Fitzwalter had just the right touch of religious fanatic mixed with mildly deranged. I was impressed. Weren't you impressed, Baal, old chap?" He looked over his shoulder. "Oh, very well, if you must."

Edward had turned Cassandra in his arms and was kissing her with determined fervor on the lips. She was kissing him back, her body nestling against his with perfect ease.

Cassandra knew the instant she opened her eyes that she was going to be sick. Her whole being quailed at the thought of stumbling down the hall to the water closet, but her embarrassment would be even worse if she disturbed her sleeping bridegroom by being sick in their chamber.

If she remained on her back and inched herself around on the bed until she could reach the robe draped across the foot, she would be able to work herself into it before she actually sat up.

Then she could run from the room, decently covered. Heaven help her if the facility was occupied. Taking long calming breaths she slid down and to the side in the bed. At the same time, she kept her eyes firmly focused on a spot on the ceiling. "I'm not moving at all, stomach," she whispered. "No need to get upset or excited. Feel. I'm lying perfectly still. It's not time yet." Her fingers touched the edge of the robe, drawing it up across her legs.

"What are you doing?" came a sleepy voice.

Her fingers froze. "Nothing. Go back to sleep."

"Ummph!" Her husband's arm slung out behind him, patted the bed beside him, expecting to find her hip. Instead he patted her face. His fingers explored her cheek, her nose and mouth, her hair. "What are you doing down there?"

"Ssh. Go back to sleep."

The hand went away, then combined with the other one to push him up. He twisted around and stared down at her. "What are you doing down there?" he asked again.

She swallowed convulsively. Her eyes watered. "I'm trying to get my robe."

He twisted around, bouncing the bed as he did so. "I'll get it."

She gave a gurgle as she lost her spot on the ceiling. The bed pitched her toward him. Her stomach heaved. She grabbed the robe and sprang up.

"Here! What's going on?"

Unable to answer, she flung open the door to flee

down the dim hallway, the robe streaming out behind her.

"Cassandra!"

She just managed to slam the water closet door behind her in time. Almost a quarter of an hour later, she made her way back down the hall, trying to convey an air of dignity. She had washed her face and rebraided her hair. Unfortunately, she had had no cosmetics to cover the dark circles beneath her eyes and the pale greenish tinge about her mouth.

Edward was waiting for her, his face stern. "What can I do?" he demanded.

She slumped back on the bed, staring hard at her toes, refusing to meet his eyes. "I must have eaten something last night . . ."

"Cassandra. Cassie." He sat on the edge of the bed beside her and took her hand. "Cassandra, I have sent for tea and toast. Please tell me what this is really all about."

She shuddered. "I'm just upset from traveling. I'm still not over my broken arm."

"Cassandra . . ." He looked at her sadly. A knock sounded at the door. "That will be the maid with breakfast."

He insisted on stretching out beside her. Together they drank the tea and ate the toast. The nausea passed as she knew it would and she felt better. "Ready to take a stroll along the beach," she suggested, in an effort to dispell his suspicions.

"Are you sure?"

"Of course. I feel wonderful. We can take a walk

and then come back and have some real breakfast."

The sea wind was rising as the sun rose. Grayish-white thunderheads piled up and up on the horizon and sailed in toward the town. Behind them the Royal Pavilion rose, shabbily majestic.

"I've never been to the seacoast before," Cassandra confided. "This is my first glimpse of the sea. Isn't that strange? Britain is surrounded on all sides by saltwater and I've never seen it until today."

Edward smiled. "You've seen a lot of strange things in the past six months."

She nodded. "Some I could have done without." She hugged her arms around her as the tide foamed over the rocks. A herring gull dived for his breakfast with a wild shriek.

Edward tried to put an arm around her, but she walked away without seeing his gesture.

Stopping with the toes of her shoes barely an inch from a line of white foam left by the last wave, she bent over, hands on her knees. "Does it really taste like salt?"

He came up behind her, this time succeeding in wrapping both hands over her hipbones. "Taste it and see."

"May I?"

"There's quite a lot of it. No one will miss what little you drink."

She made a face at him. As the next breaker came rolling in, she stretched over with cupped hand, trusting him to steady her. The icy water poured into her palm. "It's certainly cold." She touched her tongue to the tiny pool in her hand. "And very salty."

"So now you know."

She straightened up satisfied. "Can you swim?"

"Yes. I used to swim in the Thames when I was a boy."

"I can't. I should like to learn someday though. Perhaps when . . ." She could not voice her thought. She had been about to say that when he taught their child, he could teach her too. But she had not told him about the child. Somehow the time did not seem right. She wanted him to be pleased about it. How would he react? She looked at him quizzically.

"When what?" he urged.

"Perhaps we could come here in the summer sometime."

"Perhaps so." He backed up a step at a time, guiding her with him. He knew she had been on the brink of telling him but, at the last minute, had resisted. He cursed inwardly. Did she think he was stupid? Any man . . . He stopped himself. Most men perhaps would not know. Only someone reared in the constant company of a gaggle of prostitutes who talked openly and coarsely of all sorts of women's matters would know what was bothering her.

One possibility for her silence was that a woman reared so delicately would not feel free to discuss her condition with anyone. Cassandra was in all things a lady. Another distinct possibility was that perhaps she did not know that her nausea was normal for a woman in the early stages of pregnancy. "Cassandra, about this morning . . ."

She squirmed away from him. "I'm sure it won't happen again. Let's just forget it."

They walked for over a mile before he sat her down to rest on a tuffet of grass surrounded by white sand. Instead of tasting as she had drunk the saltwater, she inhaled great breaths of sea wind and spray. The sky turned from gray to mauve to pink to pearl before the sun burst over the horizon. Then the streaks of bright orange chased all the others colors away until they, too, were absorbed in a magnificent blue.

The waves rolled in, breaking far out then recovering and breaking again and then again into a froth between the rocks along the shore. As swiftly they retreated. Cassandra could not have believed the strength of the undertow had Edward not helped her take her shoes and stockings off. Then barefoot himself, his pantlegs rolled up over his muscular calves, he led her into the surf so she could feel the secret tugging of the waves retreating. "They're just as strong going out as they are coming in," he warned her. "That's why people can drown in a few feet of water in an ocean."

She shivered and tugged at his hand. "Come away then. Let's walk back barefooted. Do you know the names of any of the shells?"

Before he would allow her to lead him where she would, he pulled her hand back across his body and gathered her into his arms. Their eyes locked as he carefully aligned their bodies before bringing their mouths together in a long searching kiss.

They stuffed their stockings into their shoes and carried them each with one hand while they held hands with the other.

"Why haven't you ever seen the sea?"

She smiled up at him, her nose beginning to turn a bit pink. "We couldn't afford to go anywhere."

He looked down at her incredulously. "Tell another one. Your father was an earl."

One corner of her mouth quirked upward in self-mockery. Letting go of his hand, she spread her sea-stained skirt as if it were a ballgown. "Oh, la, yes. And upon his death, the title being unentailed to the male line, I became *the* MacDaermond. A countess, if you please." She made a curtsy, swinging her shoes in front of her.

"Your ladyship." He bowed low over her hand as she stood to receive his kiss.

"Thank you, m'lord." They walked on together for a minute before she spoke again. This time her voice was low and serious. "It's true we lived in the castle when I was a child. We might as well have lived in a cave. More than half the rooms were absolutely unin-habitable. No heat except open fires of peat. No bathrooms. We ate in the kitchen because the dining room was not only too expensive to light with candles but too far away for the food to be carried without getting cold. In the winter there was frost on the *inside* of the windows in my bedroom." She scanned his face to see how he was taking all this information.

"Sounds about like my home, only bigger," was his

bitter comment. His face darkened angrily.

"Exactly. And here you thought you had come up in the world to marry me." Her voice held no trace of bitterness. In fact she chuckled a little. She might have been relating someone's else's story.

"I think now that my father couldn't see the good of putting any money into it. I think he knew that it would be just pouring money down a rat hole. At the same time I think it overwhelmed him. He had been left with a lot of empty words and an worthless inheritance. And he couldn't get rid of it. He couldn't sell it and become a clerk or a farmer. At least he didn't have the courage to. So in the end he just did the things that his friends did, drink and gamble." She looked hard at Edward.

He was staring out toward the sea, one hand thrust deeply in his pocket, the other holding his boots.

"After he had lost all his substance, money, goods, land, when his body was wrecked"—she paused for effect—"he killed himself."

He reached for her arm, but she put out a hand to forestall him. "No, hear me out. He left me to Fitzwalter's tender mercies. I was too proud to go to him. So I came to London."

"And came to work in the Devil's Palace."

"The rest you know."

He shook his head. "No. I don't know everything." He looked her up and down significantly. "Do I?"

She tilted her head to one side with just a suggestion of a smile. "I think you know all you need to know for the moment."

Her cheeks were bright red and the smudges beneath her eyes almost gone by the time they reached the porch of their hotel.

He led her to the door of the breakfast room despite her protests that they should be dressed. "Hot chocolate," he called to the footman. While the drink was being brought, he seated her on a bench in the hall. Kneeling, he took his handkerchief and dusted off the clinging sand. "Slip your stockings and boots back on." Grinning, he performed the same service for himself. "Now we'll go in as we are."

She touched her hand to her disordered hair, then grinned in return. "Why not?" they were after all at Brighton to take the sea air.

"Shall we go to the concert?" Cassandra asked eagerly. "The Chamber Orchestra is playing tonight."

Edward could not conceal a start of alarm. Beyond the walls of the Devil's Palace, he did not mingle with polite society. The streets of London, the vulgar often filthy entertainments of the bawdy houses of Soho, he knew quite well. But to attend a concert? Of chamber music? He frowned. "I don't think—"

"It will be wonderful," she assured him. "Besides. Guess where it is?"

"In the main saloon?"

"No. I doubt if there would be room for the orchestra in the saloon downstairs much less the people who would want to hear it. No. It will be held in the Music Room of the Royal Pavilion." Her eyes were sparkling with anticipation.

"The Royal Pavilion . . ." He cleared his throat. "But . . . isn't it rather old?"

She rushed on, reciting what she had read on the bill. "Sixty years or so isn't old. Besides it was restored only twenty years ago to its original splendor. If you don't want to hear the music, you can walk around and look at the rooms."

She had never asked him for anything for herself. The only time she had ever asked a favor was with regard to MacAdam. He could not refuse her this simple request. "I suppose we could go . . ."

Her exclamation of delight interrupted him. She laid her hand on his wrist and squeezed it hard.

The Music Room like the rest of the Pavilion was a re-creation of the original. Stripped of all its furnishings by Victoria early in her reign, the building had been saved by the Brighton Town Commissioners from destruction. Systematically they had redecorated it, reclaiming many of the original pieces of the furniture while replacing others in the same style. Now it was their concert hall and their banqueting room and their museum by which they maintained the image and prosperity of the town.

To entertain winter visitors from the north, they commissioned special programs.

Dressed in a black suit, his hair combed less theatrically than for his appearance as Baal, Edward shuffled uneasily from one foot to the other. The magnificence of the Music Room was beyond his wildest dreams. The walls were a riot of crimson and gold Oriental landscapes with huge dragons and serpents flying about the ceiling. Above them rose the blue dome of dragon scales from which hung the magnificent blazing gas-o-liers.

While Cassandra was awed by the magnificent portico and rooms, she was perfectly at ease. Her head was high, her smile eager, as she moved among the knots of well-dressed people.

From the moment they entered, Edward felt uncomfortable. He classified the audience as middle-class people, well-dressed and law-abiding with a tradition of moral virtue. They were not the type to frequent the Devil's Palace. Indeed they would shun it. And him if they knew his identity.

Acutely uncomfortable, he expected a hard hand to fall on his shoulder and someone to pitch him out in the street, probably with a vigorous kick on the behind. He dared not look at any of these people. They must have been aware that he did not belong among them. He studied his fingernails, noting at the same time that his hand was trembling, the palm glistening with perspiration. "God help me," he murmured under his breath.

His wife looked up at him, her face shining with excitement. "Did you speak?"

"Just murmuring in amazement," he lied.

"It is incredible, isn't it?"

"Incredible." If he could just stop shaking, he would probably stop trembling.

"Can you imagine hearing Rossini play here?"

He closed his eyes, swaying slightly. He dared not answer. He could not imagine hearing Rossini play because he had not the slightest idea who Rossini was.

"Sir . . ." An usher tapped his shoulder. ". . . we are requesting everyone to take a seat." The light hand felt like a battle-ax. He swung around, his fists raised. He was Eddie Boggan prepared to fight for his life.

"Sir . . ." The man fell back before the blazing threat implicit in the demon-dark face.

"Edward . . ."

"Let's get out of here." He took her elbow and started to lead her away.

"What are you doing?"

"Sir?"

"Don't argue," he snarled under his breath.

"For heaven's sake . . ."

Outside in the cool air, with latecomers hurrying past them, he leaned against one of the pillars supporting the porte cochere. His heart was beating like a trip-hammer and he was so embarrassed he could have wept.

Chapter Twenty-two

"Are you ill?" Cassandra's anxious voice, her gentle hand touching his shoulder mocked him.

"No!" he managed to respond.

"What's wrong?"

Straightening away from the pillar, he pulled a handkerchief from his pocket and wiped his forehead. "Let's go."

"Go?" Cassandra stared up into his closed face. All emotions were under tight rein now. "Why should we go?" she objected. "If you're not ill, then why not go in and take our seats?"

He winced inwardly. Her question was couched in perfectly reasonable terms, but he could not bring himself to give her a reasonable answer. "Come," he said forbiddingly. He even managed to take her arm and lead her down the steps.

Then she stopped stock-still. "What has come over you? Oh, listen, I can hear them applauding. Please, we'll miss it."

"No." He descended another step, but she would not move. When her turned back, their eyes were level.

"I want to hear this concert," she insisted stubbornly.

Over her shoulder he could see ushers closing the doors. The sound of stringed instruments tuning could be heard.

She put one hand on his shoulder. "Please."

That single word sliced like a knife beneath his ribs. He almost let her lead him back into the Pavilion. Then he remembered the curious faces all turned to stare at him. Not even for her would he allow himself to be laughed at. Everyone would look at him and know that he did not belong there. Someone might even order the ushers to throw them out. No, he was saving her from further embarrassment. She did not understand.

He shook his head stiffly. "No."

Cassandra's patience shattered. "Oh, for heaven's sake," she hissed. "Why not?"

He tugged her down the steps and out into the street.

"Let me go," she protested. She was so angry and hurt she could feel tears starting from her eyes. Rather then shed them, she cursed fervently under her breath.

Pretending to ignore her, Edward hurried her along. Head down, eyes front, he led her through the dusk toward the hotel.

Cassandra heard her skirt rip. He had caused her to tear her clothing. He must be insane. All the dark demonic behavior had not been a play. He had told her they might attend, had bought the tickets, had actually taken her into the room, but then had dragged her out. His perversity infuriated her all the more because she could see no reason for it.

On the porch of their hotel, Edward finally stopped. He was sweating now despite the coolness of the night. At his side he could almost feel Cassandra's righteous wrath mounting. Assuming a look of cold implacability, he turned to face her.

She was leaning against the white column, her hand pressed to her side.

Instantly, his facade cracked. "I'm sorry," he began, reaching out to her.

She struck his hand away. "Don't. It's too late for that now. Just take me in." The pain of the stitch in her side was not the main reason for gritting her teeth. Another word from him and she would not be able to control her temper.

He swept a bow toward the door. "After you, madam." In icy silence neither of them looking to left or right, she preceded him through the lobby to their room.

At the door she turned to face him. High color burned on her cheekbones. "I am sure you will want to do other things tonight. I do not wish to be disturbed when you come to bed. Therefore, please take another room."

His face darkened although it remained perfectly void of expression. He bowed again. Then turned on his heel and stalked back down the hall. She did not watch him but closed the door to her room with unnecessary force and turned the key in the lock.

The hotelier's face was stern, obsequious, apologetic, and frightened all at the same time. "Madam, I cannot imagine how this unfortunate accident might have happened. The servant who was assigned to check the lights has been instantly dismissed without reference."

"But my husband . . ." Cassandra could not stop the frightened tears from trickling down her cheeks. With one hand she mopped at them with a handkerchief. With the other she clutched the slight mound of her belly.

"I assure you, he is being attended by the finest physician in Brighton."

"Are you sure he is all right? I must see him, Mr., er—"

"Stykes, madam. I most strongly advise—"

Anger assumed ascendancy over fear. "Damn you, He is my husband. Let me in to see him immediately." Clenching the handkerchief in her fist, she pushed the protesting hotelier aside and flung open the door of Edward's room.

The odor that greeted her made her reel back a step. Although the windows were open wide, the odor of gas was still strong in the air. Mixed with it was the vile odor of vomit.

The tableau at the bedside was—if anything—worse than the stench. One man knelt on the bed supporting Edward's shoulders while a second held a basin. Her husband, his face mottled and blue around the lips, hung limply above it. A third man, better dressed than the other two, turned at her entrance, frowned impatiently, then came toward her motioning her back.

Adroitly she sidestepped him and hurried to the bed. "Edward . . ."

"He is no condition to be bothered, madam." The doctor pursued her, his voice angry. "You will only be in the way."

"How can I be in the way?" she threw over her shoulder. "I am his wife. I have cared for him through worse than this."

Aware of her presence for the first time, Edward managed to turn his head. His eyes, dulled and unfocused, struggled to locate her. "Cassie?" he whispered.

She pushed the attendant with the basin aside and knelt in front of him. "Are you in much pain, sweetheart?"

He managed a negative shake. "Just sick."

"He will be well in a few hours, madam," the doctor boomed over her. He put a firm hand underneath her arm to lift her to her feet. "We will soon have the room cleared of noxious vapors. When he can breathe pure air, his lungs will soon be functioning correctly again. I do not hold with bleeding him to draw away some of the tainted blood. However, if you insist . . ."

"No!" Both Cassandra and Edward spoke at once.

"Good. Stupid practice. No. Fresh air, a light diet stressing liquids, perhaps a little laudanum later for the headache you'll have, my man. You'll be right as rain in twenty-four hours."

With Cassandra's help, the man holding Edward's shoulders laid his patient down on the bed. Her husband's condition made her ache in sympathy. He had not bothered to undress properly. His rumpled shirt and trousers were now fouled and wringing wet with perspiration. Dark shadows blued his chin and encircled his eyes. He clasped her hand weakly as if to satisfy himself that she was there, then wearily closed his eyes.

If she had not locked him out of his room, he would not have had such an accident. Determined to make all right for him, she left his side. "The bed linens are foul and his clothing is soaking. Send for the chambermaid immediately." The hotelier who had been hovering anxiously in the doorway came forward.

The doctor nodded in response to the other man's harried look. "He is out of danger now. Cleaning him up will do him a world of good."

"Better still," Cassandra interposed. "Send a valet with clean garments to this room and a chambermaid to change the sheets on my bed. We'll move him from this sty." Her glance prompted the doctor to confirm her orders as if they had been his own.

"It shall be done. Right away." Clapping his hands, the hotelier motioned to the man who had held the basin. "Hop to it, Rob."

Later while Cassandra held Edward's hand, they listened to Mr. Stykes faltering explanations and apologies. "Never. Never in the history of this establishment. Not since we had the gas lights installed has such a thing happened."

"Obviously, something or someone is at fault here," Cassandra declared. Her expression was fierce. She sat beside Edward's bed, her hand covering his on the counterpane. He had determined to ask his own questions, but the pain in his head, now abating before the laudanum, made concentration difficult. Growing drowsier by the minute, he followed the conversation with only half an ear.

Stykes shook his head. "You do not understand the precautions we have taken to avoid an accident like this. I myself had heard of the tragedies that occurred because people did not understand that the light had to be turned out rather than blown out. To forestall this often fatal accident to a person who did not understand the principle, I have hired men to patrol the halls at regular intervals. They listen at each pipe for the hiss of gas, then if the light is out in the room, they go in and turn it off. If there is no hiss, then there is no danger. You understand."

"Nevertheless, a tragedy almost happened."

The hotel manager leaned forward obsequiously. "Of course, when one is sleepy, a little relaxed by food and, er, wine, one is perhaps a little forgetful or a little careless. By any chance did you get up and bump against the light fixture, Mr. Sandron?"

Edward shook his head drearily. "I am used to late nights, Mr. Stykes. Furthermore, I have gaslights in my own home. Mrs. Sandron retired early, but I went for a walk on the beach. After I came in, I took off my outer garments and my boots and climbed into bed. I didn't get out of it."

Cassandra glanced skeptically at the little gas rod, its nipple shielded by a glass chimney. A man staggering around in the dark would have been most unlikely to bump into it five feet above the floor.

"I cannot imagine how this could have happened," Stykes muttered for the tenth time.

"Perhaps something broke?"

He shook his head. "The cock was open."

"Perhaps the mechanism was faulty."

Stykes was becoming more discouraged by the minute. "If such a thing is possible, we will have to check everything." He heaved a great sigh. "Still the system worked."

"What system?"

"The servant on his early morning rounds heard the gas hiss and came immediately into the room to open the windows. Then he summoned me. Another hour or two and you, sir, would not have awakened."

A sharp cry burst from Cassandra. She caught up her husband's limp hand and carried it to her cheek.

"I am sorry, madam." The hotelier burst into another series of apologies.

At this point Edward heaved himself up on one elbow. "We accept your explanation, sir, and I for one am infinitely grateful for the vigilance of your men. Perhaps I could rest now for a time . . ."

Remembering herself at last, Cassandra squeezed Edward's hand. "Of course, you must rest, sweetheart." She rose. "Edward will take a long nap. In two hours please send a chambermaid up with a pot of tea and some light, tempting foods."

"It shall be done, madam. And again, sir, my sincere, abject apologies."

Locking the door behind him, Cassandra came back to the bedside. "Now I shall sit with you while you sleep."

He looked up at her through half-closed eyes. "Don't sit. Lie. I want you to lie beside me."

"Are you sure I won't disturb you?"

"Oh, you'll probably disturb me," he murmured significantly, "but you won't hurt me."

Obediently, she put aside her robe and slipped beneath the covers. Carefully, as though he might break from rough handling, she gathered him into her arms. "Now will you go to sleep."

"Not until I say something." He hid his eyes against the smooth skin of her throat. "First, I must tell you how sorry I am for the way I behaved last night." He felt her body stiffen, but he rushed on. "You must have thought me mad, and in a way I-I was."

"We don't have to talk about this now."

"Please." His lips moved against the pulse in her neck. "Don't interrupt me. I may never have the courage again. I lost my nerve."

"I don't understand."

"I panicked. Plain and simple. I was afraid they'd laugh at me. I couldn't stand the thought."

Her grip on him tightened. "Why should they laugh at you?"

He shivered. "Because I'm — you know — who I am."

Suddenly, his behavior was clear to her. And she ached for him. Even with her impoverished youth and her father's shameful death, she had never felt ashamed of herself. This man felt truly inferior to polite society. The motives for many things suddenly became clear. The costumes, the playacting, even the blackmail to get a bride.

She hugged him close. "That's nonsense," she whispered gently. "How would they know? You're handsome and aristocratic of bearing. You speak well. Your manners are impeccable. And even if they knew, I doubt if many would care. They'd be more likely to envy you for your talent and initiative."

When he did not reply, she thought he had drifted off to sleep. Cautiously, she began to rearrange the covers over him, so he would not get a chill. "Don't leave," he murmured drowsily. "Don't ever leave me. Please."

While he slept, she thought over the events of the night. Stykes had taken every precaution that an accident with the gas should not happen. What if, indeed, it had not been an accident? The more she went over the events in her mind, the more terrified she became. Had someone tried to murder her husband? She could not be sure. She tried to discard the thought. An accident was bad enough. But murder? As the idea took more horrendous shape in her mind, she began to try to disprove it by logic.

No one in Brighton would have any reason to kill Edward. But had his enemies all been left behind in London? Had someone who had lost money to him seen them in Brighton? She cast this idea aside as more farfetched than the accident to the gaslight. But perhaps someone had followed them down on the train the next day, waited his chance? Who had known they were coming to Brighton?

Nash.

THe publisher's name burned in her brain. Of

course. He had taken them to the train station. What easier way to accomplish his purpose than to take a later train, perhaps the next morning? He could easily have obtained information at the hotel desk. She had not paid any attention to who might have been waiting in the lobby when they came in last night. Had he followed Edward, seen him go into a room alone, and waited until he was asleep? Skeleton keys were easy enough to obtain, if indeed all the doors in the hotel did not open with the same key.

Their confrontation before her marriage now appeared to her a clever smokescreen. How easy to deflect suspicion from himself by pretending to be trying to find the guilty party himself.

Her breathing quickened as she thought of the near miss her husband had sustained. If anyone were brought to account for his death in Brighton, Nash would most certainly have directed the hunt toward herself. Clearly she saw his Machiavellian plan.

She released a long shuddering breath, at the same time cuddling her husband close. She must start her own investigation. Edward must be protected at all costs.

Her husband stirred in her arms, muttered something. His legs twitched. She gathered him closer, stroking his forehead, murmuring love words. Only when he was asleep did she dare to tell him how much she loved him. To do so to his face would give him too much power. As much as she loved him, she did not trust him. His background, his reputation, his occupation, and now his acute vulnerability terrorized her. Likely, he would not be pleased when he realized how much he had revealed to her.

The laudanum was making him sweat.

Gently she disengaged herself from his arms. While she was gone to fetch a pan of water and washcloth, he began to toss and turn, to fumble about the bed, to mumble.

"Poor darling, did you lose your pillow?" she teased softly. "This will make you feel better." As if he were a baby, she washed his face and chest, his hands and his long muscular arms.

As she washed his right hand, his eyes opened. At first they gazed at her without comprehension. Then gradually his sense returned. "Cass . . ." he whispered. His throat was so dry, she winced to hear the word.

Hastily, she poured water into a glass. Slipping her hand beneath his neck, she helped him sit up. When he had drained the glass, she would have left him, but he caught at her.

His expression was almost fearful. "I remember talking to you before I fell asleep." He studied her face intently.

"Well, yes, you did." She had not been unmoved by bathing his shoulders and chest. A tiny wave of desire swept over her, a prickling of her senses.

He plucked at the coverlet. "I want you to know that I'm still sorry."

She bent over him then to kiss his forehead. "It doesn't matter now that I understand why you did it." She clutched at the neck of her robe to keep it from falling open.

One hand wrapped gently around her wrist to pull

her hand away. The other slid down the column of her throat to the slope of her breast above the low neck of her gown.

"Sir, you are taking advantage of a lady's dishabille. I have not had time to dress today for holding and bathing you."

He pushed the gown aside, baring her fully. The nipple was swollen and darkened from her pregnancy. He cupped her breast and squeezed it. "I suppose I should be ashamed," he murmured whimsically. "What if I performed a penance?"

"A penance." Her voice sounded strained. She tried to take a deep breath but failed utterly.

"I could do something to pay for my rudeness. What if I kissed every inch of your breasts?"

She made one last attempt to normalcy. "Edward, remember your condition."

"Ah, yes, my condition . . ." He cupped the firm mound. "In my condition this is probably all I'm capable of."

She responded by releasing her breath in a ragged groan. "Your condition is too precarious to be risked." She kissed his forehead and smoothed the black hair back from it. Meanwhile he pushed the gown off her shoulders and switched his attentions to the other breast.

"You are the most beautiful—"

A knock interrupted his tribute. He cursed feelingly as she jerked out of his arms. Hastily, she caught up her robe from the foot of the bed and shrugged into it. "Come in."

A chambermaid bore in a huge tray of food with a

sprig of holly in a silver bud vase. "Tea, mum," she announced. "Exactly at the time you ordered. Mr. Stykes himself checked to be sure that I was leaving the kitchen at exactly the right time."

As Edward sank back on the pillows muttering, Cassandra smiled sweetly. "A good man is Mr. Stykes. Please put the tray down on the far side of the bed. I will serve Mr. Sandron myself."

"Mr. Stykes said you wanted several tempting foods. Well, Miz Cole prepared her very best chilled cucumber sandwiches, pâté with soda water biscuits, truffles, jelly roll, and—"

"Thank you." Cassandra motioned the woman toward the door. "It all sounds delicious. Give my compliments to Mr. Stykes and to Miz Cole for the special breakfast."

"I'll just wait outside the door, mum, if you should want anything else."

Without meeting Edward's eyes, Cassandra poured his tea. "We have plenty of time," she chided when she finally saw his belligerent expression. "After all they are very worried. You almost died."

He drank the tea in silence. Then he took a bite of pâté on a soda water biscuit. "I'm sure it was an accident."

She looked at him from beneath her lashes. "Are you really?"

He swallowed the bite. "No doubt about it."

She shook her head. She set the teacup down and folded her hands in her lap. "I don't think so, Edward. Frankly, I'm afraid. I can't help but believe that this is too much like the other accident."

"You mean the one where Parks was killed."

"I found you after you'd been poisoned the first time. Whoever did this may not be very brave, but he is very determined."

"Coincidence. Look at the facts. The first time, I just happened to be in the way. Nothing else has happened in months at the Devil's Palace. Then we come down here on our honeymoon. No one knows we're down here."

"Except Nash," she interrupted.

He stared at her blankly for a full minute. A horrendous black shadow swept across his mind. Then he shook his head somberly. "Not Nash, my dear Cassandra. Anyone but Nash and I might give some credence to the idea, but not Nash. Cassandra, you don't know."

"No, I don't. Please tell me."

"He's the best friend I've got. In fact, besides you and Sally, he's the only friend I've got. I wouldn't be anything if not for him."

"You mean he made you into a gambling casino attraction and a writer of filthy novels." She made no effort to conceal the anger and disgust in her voice.

Edward looked down into the teacup, the flush rising in his face. "I—I didn't know you knew about the writing."

"Good grief, how could I not know? The stuff is spread all over your desk and all over the library and in the wastebasket. I'm literate, you know. And I was curious to find out what my employer wrote. I found it out the first week I came to work for you."

He shook his head. "And you married me anyway?"

Her tone was bitter. "What choice did I have?"

"That's true."

The silence grew between them. She took his cup and poured him more tea, placing a rich jelly roll on the saucer beside it. "If you were dead, who would inherit the Devil's Palace?"

He looked nonplussed for a moment as if the thought of his having property to pass on had never occurred to him. "Nash and Sally would divide my share, I suppose." Then he looked at her. "No, now you would get my third."

"I wonder if the murderer thought we were both in that room together. He might have thought to kill us both with one blow. It would look like an accident. No one would even investigate very much. Mr. Stykes would certainly have been happier if I had not questioned him so closely. The perfect crime is easier to commit if the person who did it is the one to demand the investigation."

"But—but Nash doesn't want my share. Besides, he couldn't run it without me," Edward protested lamely.

"Of course he could," she insisted. "He could get anyone to dress up in a black cape and flirt it around the stage. Perhaps Ashtaroth is eager to assume center stage instead of just be your handmaiden?"

"You don't do much for a man's self-confidence."

Again she was silent, hating to hurt his feelings. He was still reeling from the debacle of the previous night. Now to hit him again with her theories seemed too cruel. Still, he had to be made to guard himself. "He didn't want me to marry you."

One black brow shot upward. Instantly, he remembered the conversation between Nash and himself about Cassandra. Had Nash really an ulterior motive for his warning?

Picking her words carefully, she hurried on. "Perhaps with us married the situation might get complicated very rapidly. We could"—she put her hand to her stomach.—"there could be complications."

"Such as?"

"Oh, inheritance problems . . ." she insisted vaguely.

He slumped back on the bed exhausted. "I don't think I care to finish this." He might have meant either the tea or the conversation.

"Shall I take it away?"

"Please. I think I'll rest for the afternoon, if you don't mind."

She had said too much, gone too far. Concealing her hurt along with her very real fear for his life, she made a show of plumping the pillows and smoothing the covers. "Shall I give you another couple of drops of laudanum? The doctor left some."

"No! That is, I hate to take the filthy stuff. I think I can sleep normally, if I'm alone in the room. You do distract me, sweetheart." He tried to smile guilelessly.

She bent over and kissed him. "Then I'll be right across the hall."

When she was gone, he stared up at the ceiling, his brow wrinkled in pain. Had she tried to kill him? And failed? And then tried to divert his suspicions to Nash? He could see no reason for Nash to kill him. The idea that his publisher would kill him for the gambling casino was ridiculous. Of course, Nash had his nasty side. He had probably insulted her. Her pride was the very devil. Of course, she had much to be proud of.

He thought back over his behavior. Always, always, he had coerced her. He covered his eyes with his hand in a vain attempt to shut out the horrible memories. Mistaking her for a prostitute the night of the masquerade, he had manhandled her while threatening to call the police. No amount of hiding behind his hand could dim the memory of tossing her over his shoulder and carrying her up the stairs to one of the rooms provided for gentlemen and their fancy pieces. There he had taken her with brute strength, paying no heed to her pleas or protests.

When he had discovered her identity, he had ripped her clothing, threatened her, and finally locked her in her room without food or water. When she had escaped him, he had hunted her down like an animal and blackmailed her into marriage.

God! What a fool. What a vulgar, bleeding sod!

Poison was too good for him. He should have been drawn and quartered.

Yesterday had been a hiatus, an idyllic time. They had walked and talked. She had talked and held hands. He had held her body with affection and respect. She had begun to relax around him.

Then he had behaved like a madman at the concert, dragging her out, shattering her confidence, undoubtedly shaming and embarrassing her in front of all those people, her peers. Members of the socially elite.

He was not fit to kiss the hem of her dress, much

less lay his hands on her. She was an earl's daughter for all her vivid descriptions of an impoverished childhood. She had no conception of true poverty. Probably it had not been nearly so terrible as she had described. All was relative. Poverty to the well-born would be wealth to the truly poor.

No. She was a delicately bred lady carrying the child he had forced on her. Women became irrational at such times. Undoubtedly, his explosion had been the last straw. Suddenly, she could stand no more. Hatred and disgust had overpowered her. In a moment of hot temper, she had more than merely wished him dead. She had actually acted on her wish.

Sudden tears stood in his eyes. He blinked them away rapidly. He loved her so much, but he dared not tell her so, dared not give her so much power over him. She must hate him out of all reason to deny him the knowledge of his child. Just the thought that she was carrying his child made him weak with wanting.

What to do! He could not let her go. She would have no way to support herself, nowhere to turn. He did not want her or the child to suffer want or hardship. He would give her everything she wanted. He would make her life so comfortable and love their child so much that she would forgive him. Until the birth he would keep a sharp lookout. She would become content after the child was born.

"Cassandra."

He heard the click of her heels across the hall. She opened the door, her face anxious, eager. Her long red hair was brushed smooth and tied back with a lavender ribbon. She had put on a skirt of lavender broadcloth and a blouse with a jabot of ecru lace. Nestled in the lace was her beloved cairngorm brooch.

"Edward, you didn't sleep long."

"I decided I had more important things to do than sleep."

She came to the side of the bed, bent over, and kissed him. "Did you?"

He put his arms around her gently, ever so gently. "I remembered we were on our honeymoon." Their lips met in a long kiss. "Is there anyone waiting outside the door to burst in at a specified time?"

She chuckled, rubbing her nose against the tip of his in negation.

"Then perhaps we should continue where we left off."

Chapter Twenty-three

"Ah, back safe and sound," Nash purred. "Sorry if I'm interrupting something." The air in the library was charged with emotion. With a mirthless grin he selected a cigarette and lit it. "Don't let me bring the conversation to a standstill. Please."

Ashtaroth spun away from the front of the desk and flounced over to a chair. Dropping down into it, she stared sullenly at Edward.

He returned her stare pointedly then shrugged. "Please come in, Nash, and do make yourself right at home. Have a cigarette, but try to refrain from comment unless it is specifically requested."

"Oh, my, we are upset today," Nash sneered. Blowing a cloud of blue smoke toward the ceiling, he strolled over to the embroidery frame where Cassandra sat. "What have you been feeding the man, Cass, old gel? Try a little less red meat and a few more sweets."

"Nash," Edward called. "My wife's name is Cassandra."

"Sorry." He smiled at her, a hint of a threat in his eyes. "Do you mind being called Cass?"

She stared up into the pale eyes. They slanted just a bit. The lashes and brows were sandy, the face narrow almost delicate. Sandy hair and sideburns blended with the skin of his face and cheeks. The lackluster fairness was marked between him and his dark-complexioned business associates. "I have never been called Cass," she said at last.

"Then you don't know how you'll feel about it until you experience it, dear gel." He put his hand on the top of the embroidery frame. The nails were rather long for a man and curved like talons.

"Oh, for God's sake!" Ashtaroth exploded. "What the hell difference does it make what you call her? You're interrupting, Nash. Get out!"

He turned to face her, keeping one hand on the embroidery frame. The other dangled the cigarette. "Wouldn't think of it, Sally, old gel. Piqued m'curiosity, you have." He grinned back at Cassandra. "If you're privy to their spitting and clawing, I should think I could be too."

"I offered to go elsewhere," she informed him mildly.

"No need for anyone to leave." Edward leaned forward elbows on his desk. "Sally, I can't pay any more of your dressmakers' bills." He raised one eyebrow in Nash's direction. "Does that bit of earthshaking news satisfy your curiosity?"

"God. Is that all this is about?" Nash assumed a look of ineffable boredom. "What a terrible disappointment. Hardly worth the climb up the stairs."

"Shut up!" Ashtaroth's face was flushed with anger and embarrassment. Neither man seemed willing to treat this matter seriously. Furthermore, the reason for the whole scene was sitting imperturbably behind her embroidery frame. "Edward, you absolutely cannot do this to me. It isn't fair. You've always paid them. I've always counted on you to pay them. You can't just suddenly not pay them. I'd be in debt for months."

"Sally, be reasonable. You must have realized that I would have much more important things to do with my money now that I'm a married man." He smiled in the direction of his wife.

Cassandra smiled back. "I think you should pay Sally's outstanding bills, Edward. She didn't have any reason to think you wouldn't."

Before Edward could answer, Sally sprang to her feet. Black eyes snapping with bad temper, she bore down on the woman at the embroidery frame. "Who pulled your string?"

Cassandra's fingers faltered. "But I —"

"Keep your charity to yourself, Miss Goody-Goody. I can handle this myself without you butting in. Soften him up with your own tricks."

"I assure you . . ." Cassandra faltered, confused as to why her offer had so angered the other woman. She looked dazedly toward Edward.

Before he could intervene, Nash laughed lazily. "Sally, you are the greatest fool I've ever met."

With a curse, Ashtaroth lunged at him, but he merely stared up at her, his face bland. "Don't you realize that she doesn't have a single reason to offer to pay your bills except her own good manners? Just because you can't bring yourself to do a decent thing because it is a decent thing, don't judge everybody else by yourself."

Edward came round the desk to meet his wife. "If you expect me to get any writing done before the performance, Nash, I suggest you take her out of here." When Sally gave a sharp angry exclamation, he shook his head. "All right. I'll do as Cassandra says and pay your outstanding dressmakers' bills, but—" he pointed his finger at her—"if anything comes in with a date after today you'll have to pay it yourself."

"But . . ."

"And this is all, Sally. We all get the same share of the income from the Devil's Palace. Nash and I manage to feed, clothe, and lodge ourselves. You should too."

Fuming impotently, she stood in the center of the room, her breath coming short, her hands shaped into claws.

Nash came up behind her and put his hand in the small of her back. "Let's go downstairs and have a little drink, old gel. It'll work wonders to get your nerves under control."

"You'll be sorry for this," she threatened. "I'll get you both."

"Ss-sh, Sally." Nash took her by the upper arm. "Don't say a lot of things that you'll regret."

"Ow!" You're hurting my arm. You bastard. Let go." As he hustled her through the door, she caught hold of the door facing. "I'll fix you both. I'll move into the Devil's Palace!" was her parting screech.

Once the pair were down the hall, Edward took Cassandra in his arms. "I'm sure you can see why you have not a reason in the world to be jealous."

"I'm not jealous."

"I see that." He kissed her forehead as a rueful smile curved his lips.

"Would you rather that I were? Ranting and cursing, perhaps throwing things at your head?" She stepped back smiling and clenched her hands into fists. "How about if I hand you a facer?" She feinted for his jaw.

He laughed then. "Handed me a facer? Where did you learn words like that?"

She turned her fist toward her own face and studied it demurely. "When we were eating last night in the supper room, a very hefty gentleman used the expression in between stuffing large numbers of oyster pies into his mouth."

"Did he now? And you knew what it meant?"

"Edward, you persist in thinking that I am some kind of idiot. Of course, I understood what he was talking about."

Frowning darkly, her husband turned away. "I hadn't thought about what language you might hear as we moved among the tables. I never meant for you to be offended . . ."

She came up behind him to put her arms around his waist and lay her head on his shoulder. "Edward, my ears can stand a good deal more than the rather mild expletives that are passed around at the tables. Believe me, everyone down there is behaving in a very civilized manner. They have too much at stake to relax."

"But you're an earl's daughter . . ."

"Yes, so I am. And that earl had a group of rowdy friends who used to come up for the hunting season and get very drunk and disorderly after a day of shooting. The language they used when they were drunk and thought themselves in masculine company exclusively would have shocked you."

"I really doubt that."

She patted him on the shoulder before going back to the embroidery frame. He followed her as she seated herself. His hands were thrust into the pockets of his trousers. He shifted from one foot to the other as he looked out the window at the street beyond. At last he cleared his throat. "I suppose I'd better explain about Sally."

"Not if you don't want to."

"She's not what you think."

Cassandra threaded a needle with a double strand of silk. "I know she's a very beautiful young woman. And most of the time she's very angry."

He looked at her sharply, a little surprised at her perception. "She has plenty of reason to be angry."

"Like you."

"A little more, a little less."

She inserted the needle from beneath the cloth. The point came through precisely in the heart of a flower. She drew it through, held the silk taut, and wrapped the needle point twice times around it. Pushing it through the linen two threads farther on, she made a perfect French knot. "I would like very much for you to tell me about her."

He drew a deep breath; a muscle flickered in his jaw. "She always claimed she knew her father. She said he was a Spanish sailor. When I first met her, she was maybe five years old. I figured I was about ten, twice her age. I was collecting my supper from the back of a public house . . ." Here he looked at Cassandra almost defiantly, but her serene expression did not change. ". . . when she came up behind me and snatched it off my wagon."

"You had a wagon?"

"Just a crate with some skids and a rope. Nothing like a rich kid might have." As Edward talked, his language became less and less precise. He grinned suddenly at the memory, his face looked intensely alive. "She could run like a deer. I thought I was fast, but she'd have gotten clean away from me if she hadn't slipped on a patch of ice. She was going so fast she slid bang! right into a curbstone that give her head a good lick.

"I grabbed m'bread and was reared back ready to give her a kick, just to teach her manners, y'know, when she grabbed m'standin' leg. Damned if I didn't go down on the same ice. Then while I was rollin' around on the ground she bit m'ankle."

"Served you right," Cassandra chuckled.

"Whose side are you on?"

"You shouldn't have kicked the poor little thing while she was down."

"Humph! Sally may get down but she's never out. So I howled and she started tryin' to get away again. I was willin' to let her go. But damn! She made another dive for m'bread. So I fell on her. This time she did get knocked out. I must have weighed twice what she did."

"I understand just how she felt," Cassandra murmured.

He shot her another dark look. "I didn't lie there but a minute before I was up and gettin' m'bread. By this time it was gettin' pretty dark. The snow had started to fall. She was just lyin' there. I kicked her, but she didn't move. I found out later she was playin' dead, hopin' I'd leave her alone. But I didn't know that. I couldn't just leave her there in the streets to freeze to death."

"No, you couldn't." Cassandra smiled as she put a particular emphasis on the "you."

"Well, anyway I hauled her up on the wagon and dragged her home."

"And you've been responsible for her ever since."

"Oh, she's pulled her own weight, believe me. We've taken care of each other. I even taught her to read." The pride in his voice was obvious. "She never did like to though. After I learned, I'd read aloud to her. She'd listen by the hour, but she didn't want to do it herself. When I began to write, she'd copy for me, but she never wanted to do it herself. Then when I met Nash, I insisted . . ." He looked at her again, rather helplessly, as though she would think him a fool.

"You insisted that she come as a partner in the business. You created the part of Ashtaroth for her and bought her clothes. Do you pay for her flat as well?"

"At first, but she really wanted to do it herself after a while."

"And now she doesn't want to give you up."

"But she's not like a woman to me."

"She's your sister," Cassandra told him softly. "She's your baby sister. She's your family. And more important — you're all the family she has. You're her brother and her father and she's afraid I'll make you throw her out."

"She's no kin to me, I told you."

"She's the most important kin there is. She's someone you love."

He shook his head emphatically. "Not her. I don't love her. I don't love any . . . body . ." His voice trailed away. He rubbed his hand across the back of his neck. "I need a drink."

Cassandra stared at her hands clenched tightly together against the slight swell that intruded into her lap. "I think she probably thinks of you as a big brother."

The lip of the decanter clinked against the rim of the glass. "She'd laugh to hear you say that."

"You both have perfected the parts you play."

He took a sip of brandy. "I don't know what you mean."

She stood up abruptly. "I must see to the shopping. I'll leave you with your writing until this evening."

"Cassandra . . ." He spoke to the empty room, his voice in a whisper never meant for her ears. Why had he said that he did not love anyone when he knew it was a lie?

Nash guided Ashtaroth down the backstairs and into the saloon of the gambling casino. At this time of the afternoon, only a single desultory game was going on. One waiter attended to the players, who did not bother to acknowledge the entrance of the two.

"Whiskey, neat, two," Nash ordered.

"I'll not drink that filthy stuff," she snapped.

"Beg pardon," Nash mocked. "What will her ladyship have?"

"Champagne."

"Two."

They stared at each other in hostile silence while the bottle was uncorked. When the champagne was poured, Nash lifted his glass to his lips and toasted her. "To the prize of bitches."

"Damn you." She drew back her glass as if to sling its contents in his face.

"Get this suit dirty and you'll lick it clean," he promised, his eyes like flint.

She hesitated, angry, yet certain he meant what he said.

"Drink it," he advised. "Really, old gel, you shouldn't get yourself so worked up. It's not as if you wanted to marry Baal yourself."

Sally drank most of the champagne in a single swallow. Her eyes were black and unfathomable over the rim of the glass. At last she set it down. "He just wants her because of her damn title."

"Well, of course. Why else should he want her?"

"And because she's so bloody nice." Sally fairly spat the words. She held out her champagne glass. The waiter filled it instantly.

"That too."

"And because she's got such nice manners."

Nash took a sip of his own champagne. "A little too sweet for my taste."

She looked at him sharply. "The champagne."

"That too."

She made a rude noise. "You say that, but what if she'd come to work for you and you'd found her out?"

"Dear gel, I wouldn't have cared whether she was nineteen or ninety. Servants in any shape or form do not interest me." He waved a hand airily. "I lack the common touch, Sally."

She stared at him. Her eyes really saw him for the first time, the slight form, hardly taller than her own, the long curved nails at the end of the slim clever hands, the pale eyes that made their pupils look so black, so piercing. "I despise you," she stated in a dead, flat voice.

He motioned the waiter away when the man sought to refill his glass with champagne. "Really don't suppose I should ask, but why?"

"Nothing bothers you. You don't care about a damn thing. You never lose your temper. I can't stand a cold fish." She leaned forward with a conspiratorial smile. "Fess up, Nash. You really do like the boys, don't you?"

The corners of the thin mouth turned up in a mirthless smile. "Let's see, shall we?" He leaned forward and tilted the glass up to her lips.

A thrill of desire shot through her. It was perverse. It was fearful, but it was shattering. She had to clench her jaw to keep from groaning.

"Drink," he commanded.

With shudders still vibrating through her, she opened her lips. The champagne flowed down her throat, cool wine with no chance to put out the blaze.

"Now." He took the glass away and set it down on the table. Taking both her hands in his, he drew her to her feet and turned her toward the door. When she balked, he slid one arm around her waist and gripped the back of her elbow. "Don't cause a scene, Sally," he warned.

Upstairs she balked again at the door of a private

room. "I don't want this."

He put his arm around her neck this time. His warm breath caressed her ear as his silky voice made her shiver. "Of course, you don't. You'd have to admit that you want a man, that you're not completely independent, a woman untouchable in a man's world. And that's what you don't want. You do want this." He moved so quickly that she could not defend herself.

He spun her into the trap of his arms. One hand fastened in the chignon while the other caught her free hand and twisted it behind her. He kissed her then, hard, rough, long. His tongue took possession of her mouth. At the same time he dragged her into the room. His hand left her hair long enough to slam the door and push her up against it.

"Nash," she gasped.

"The name is Trevor," he snarled. "Use it."

"Trevor, damn you."

He kissed her again, using his strength to bend her back across his arm. "I intend to love you, Sally. And when I get through, you'll know you've been loved."

She twisted in his arms, pushing against his shoulders, writhing, scratching, a fury unleashed. "No man loves me."

Purposefully, he released her, allowing her to twist to the side and escape him. Then, his lips grinning thinly, he pursued her, hedged her right and left, blocked her escape routes to the door, backed her inexorably toward the bed.

She was panting. Her long midnight-black hair fell down her back after his hands and her struggles had loosened it. Anxiously, she cast a glance behind her.

He lunged. His arms encircled her waist as his force carried them both onto the bed in a great creak of springs and frame.

"Nash . . . Trevor . . . no."

"Yes." He kissed her again, then rolled off. Before she could move, he had tossed up her skirts and petticoats. "Damned underwear. Should be a law against it." He clenched his fists in the fine silk and ripped it off.

"Trevor!" She swung her legs away, but not fast enough.

He caught her by the shoulders and held her down so he could look into her eyes. He was panting slightly, his eyes glittering with excitement. "Sally. I'm going to have you. Now we can do this the hard way and you can end up with all your clothes in the condition of your drawers, or we can make this easy. Which will it be?"

She glared at him fiercely. "Let me go! I'll not undress for any man unless he pays me."

He did not even flinch. "Until now, Sal, old gel. I'm going to be the one you undress for and give your beautiful body to because you want to."

"No."

He kissed her hard on her pouting little mouth. "Yes." She squealed as he flipped her over on her stomach. While she kicked and cursed, he bound her hands behind her with strips of French silk. The skirt, bustle, and petticoats were an easy matter. In a matter of seconds she was bare from the waist down to her dark burgundy stockings rolled to just below the knees and her spool-heeled shoes.

"Oh, Sally," he murmured. His hands slid over her

437

buttocks and down the backs of her thighs. "Oh, Sally, what a beautiful sight. What a beautiful sight!"

"Nash," she pleaded.

"Trevor . . ." He bent and kissed her on the cheek of her right buttock.

"Trevor, oh, don't . . . please . . ."

"I'm not embarrassing you, am I?" He slid his hand up the inside of her thigh. "Not hard-talking, hard-drinking Ashtaroth, Baal's handmaiden."

"Stop."

"What beautiful long legs. So slim, so shapely. Sally, running wild in the streets really makes a girl's legs beautiful." His fingers caressed and insinuated themselves into the warm, wetness at the joining of her thighs. He searched with his thumb, then found the spot he sought.

Her back arched and her head came off the pillow, a cry keened from between her teeth. "Ple-e-ease . . ."

"Begging, Sally," he chuckled. "What for, I wonder?"

Conscious of how much of a spectacle she was making of herself, she buried her face in the pillow again. Her body twisted, but his fingers would not be dislodged. He bent to kiss the backs of her knees. A tremor went through her. He could feel her quivering beneath his lips and hands. "Sally?"

She shook her head, burying her face in the pillow.

He kissed the tips of her fingers curled helpless and pale, the black silk knotted around her wrists, its frayed ends with bits of lace still attached lying on the mounds of her buttocks. "Are you ready to surrender, Sal?"

No answer. He moved his thumb in a maddening circle. One by one he took her fingers in his mouth to suckle.

She was on fire, dying and hating herself, dying and hating him. She would not say another word, not one more word.

"Think, Sally. Think how long I can kiss you. You can't get away. You can only move as I allow you to."

She twisted and kicked back suddenly with her heels, aiming for his thigh lying beside her own.

He easily avoided her. "Time to turn you over, Sally, and kiss those pretty breasts."

He took his leisurely time about it all, stroking and petting, kissing and sucking until she thought she would go mad. Midway through the agony with his mouth on her breast and his hand betwen her legs, she could not withhold herself any longer.

Her body pushed against him, conscious thought dissolved into a red mist of pleasure. She exploded, flying off into a brilliant starburst that dissolved into dark warm release.

But when the darkness dissolved, she awoke in Nash's arms, his hand still on her body, his mouth on her breasts. "Oh, no," she begged now, tears flowing from her eyes, trickling into the midnight air spread over the pillow. "Oh, no."

"Oh, yes, sweet, sweet Sally. Sally, who doesn't know herself. Are you ready to say you love me, Sally?" His teeth took her nipple delicately and bore down, increasing the pressure until she writhed with the intensity of her pleasure. "Are you ready to call me lover and master?"

"Swine," she hissed.

"Lovely, lovely, proud Sally." He pulled the bodice and the straps of the corset cover down her arms. His hands ran over the floral designs in the black damask. They followed the path of the whaleboning down to her waist and out over her flat stomach. "Such a cruel device," he murmured as his fingers found the hooks on her left side. When the shell fell away, he broke the narrow straps on the chemise and rolled it down to her waist.

During the entire process, she kept her eyes firmly closed, trying desperately to think of anything to take her far, far away from this terrible man and his knowledgeable hands and mouth.

"You're naked, Sally," he whispered at last, his lips nibbling along her neck. "Naked and oh, so warm and so beautiful."

She turned her face away from his mouth.

"Still not ready to kiss my mouth. Then I think I just must kiss you elsewhere." She stiffened as he slid down her body. He kissed her throat, the valley between her breasts, the arch of her ribs, her navel . . .

"Nash," she wailed. "Trev—"

He lifted her buttocks and brought her up to his mouth. Where his thumb had been, his lips now took possession. His tongue flicked back and forth and round and round. His teeth nipped and scored.

She screamed. She tugged at the silk that bound her hands. She pleaded incoherently. She begged.

He was remorseless, though her torture was not endless. This time she exploded higher than before, her blood pounding through her veins, her breath searing her lungs. Her eyes were wide open as she surged upward with a cry of ecstasy ripping out of her throat. She did not close them as she sank back on the pillow. But she saw nothing.

At last she was aware of Nash's face hanging over her. Astraddle her hips, he took her cheeks between his hands, cuffing her lightly. "Lover and master," he commanded.

Her eyes were black pools where the light came and went through her tears. "Lover and . . ."

". . . master," he probed.

". . . master." The word was only a tiny breath of sound.

He smiled. "Now watch me."

Somehow she was surprised to see that he was still fully clothed except for his coat. She never took her eyes off him as he peeled off his clothing, his vest, his shirt, his undershirt. He put his feet on either side of her hips and stood, towering over her, grinning as he lithely stripped off his trousers, underpants, socks, boots. His manhood stood out rampant in a nest of pale silky curls. Naked he dropped down again, making the bed bounce.

Without bothering to untie her hands he spread her legs and plunged into her. His pleasure was long and slow. Taking his time, he stroked her limp body until it began to respond again, her moans accompanying him to the heights, so she was there when he exploded inside her.

He lay between her legs for a long time, loving the feel of her breasts beneath him, the rise and fall of her chest, the scent of her femininity rising all around him. At last he pushed himself up on his hands and gazed down into her face. "Now," he whispered at last. "Now, I'll have that apology."

Slowly, she opened her eyes. "No."

He rubbed himself against her. "Have you not had enough?"

She gasped in alarm. "No, please, Nash. I've had enough."

"Then apologize."

"I'm sorry," she whispered.

"Lover and master," he prompted, bumping against her.

"L-lover and master." Two tears trickled from the corners of her eyes.

"That's right. Lover and master."

Smiling at her tears, he turned her over on her stomach, untied her hands, kissed her wrists in penance, and drew the covers over their naked bodies. She fell deeply asleep with her face in the hollow of his shoulder.

Chapter Twenty-four

I had told myself I did not care for anything nor anyone. The cloud of caring for nothing, which overshadowed me with such a fatal darkness, was very rarely pierced by the light within me.

And yet I did care something for the streets that environed that house, and for the senseless stones that made their pavements. And something more. I cared for something more. From being irresolute and purposeless, my feet became animated by an intention, and they took me to the same house.

I knocked and was shown up-stairs, and found her at her work alone. She had set an embroidery frame before her and was creating a fanciful picture out of silk thread. Looking at my face in the intercourse of the first few commonplaces, she observed a change in it.

"I fear you are not well!"

"No. But the life I lead is not conducive to health. What is to be expected of, or by, such a wastrel?"

"Is it not — forgive me — a pity to live no better life?"

"God knows it is a shame!"

"Then why not change it?"

Looking gently at me again, her expression changed from surprise to one of ineffable sadness. I was ashamed that she had seen tears in my eyes. There were tears in my voice too when I answered:

"It is too late for that. I shall never be better than I am, I shall sink lower, and be worse."

"That I will never believe . . ."

Edward Sandron stared at what he had written and within him Eddie Boggan shivered. The whole of it, every word, every syllable was a desperate wish. Certainly, the work could never be published. He could not bear that others should see his soul in print. He looked desperately around him at the books on his library shelves, the books that had made him.

Their presence reassured him somehow. Even if he must live with only "one virtue, and a thousand crimes," still he had risen so far. He took a certain pride in that. A swift knock preceded Cassandra's entrance. Hastily, he shoved the papers into the drawer.

She smiled at him. "Don't hide that stuff away, Edward. I really don't mind. I know you're writing it."

He nodded sheepishly, wondering what she would say if she could read what he was really working on in his spare time. "You're looking exceptionally lovely tonight," he observed in an effort to change the subject.

She dropped a deep curtsy. "Thank you, m'lord."

He thought, with a little twinge of pain, that she looked lovelier every time she walked into the room. Her pregnancy had made her positively bloom with health. The thin tightness that he had associated with Miss Fitch and the weight she had lost during her abortive break for freedom had been replaced by a soft becoming fullness in her face and shoulders. Her breasts were larger, of course, and her color higher.

She wore a dress of sapphire blue taffeta shot with copper threads. The skirt was the new slender style with very little bustle. Her red hair was swept back from her cheeks and then allowed to fall down her back in its natural ringlets and waves. Turning sideways, she pretended to check her hair in the oval mirror beside the door. As he came round the desk, he watched her smooth her hands over the thickening at her waistline.

He stared at her, his brows drawn together. When would she tell him she carried his child? How much longer did she think to conceal it?

She frowned. "I suppose I'm ready."

He came up behind her. "You're ready," he agreed. "I've never seen a woman who compliments her clothing as you do."

"Why thank you." She held up her face to be kissed.

When he had accommodated her with special tenderness, he swung the black cape round his shoulders, adjusted the high collar, and clipped the edges to his wrists.

She watched him with a smile. "Very satanic!"

As he opened the door, Barston, the manservant, stood poised to knock. "Beg pardon, sir, but there's a person downstairs at the back. She says she must see you, sir."

"She?"

"Insists upon it. I've tried to turn her off, but she

refuses absolutely. I'm sorry, sir." He took in their dress. "I realize you're dressed to go down to the club, but . . ."

A pang shot through Edward's belly. He dreaded what lay ahead. "Will you excuse me, Cassandra?"

"Why don't I come with you and save you a trip back up the stairs?"

He shook his head, his frown black. "I don't know what this could be, but it might be sticky."

"So long as I'm living here, I shall just have to get used to being sticky, won't I?"

They descended together, Barston leading the way. Before he opened the kitchen door, he paused, looking from one to the other. About to speak, he changed his mind. "I asked her to wait in here, sir."

Cassandra was the first to see the figure of a woman sitting facing the great stove. Her hands, white and swollen, were stretched out toward its heat. Rings glittered on every finger. She had tossed back a short black cape to bare a dress of magenta satin, wrinkled and not particularly clean. A large magenta toque with bedraggled dyed feathers came down over her ear and concealed the side of her face.

She did not hear them enter, but as the door closed, she turned her face toward them. Cassandra distinctly heard Edward groan. The face was a cracked mask of white lead. The gaunt cheeks were rouged in a triangle that made no attempt at naturalness. Thick black mascara lined the eyes and turned the eyebrows into startling bats' wings in the white face.

The eyes were frighteningly familiar. Edward's eyes, steel gray and piercing. Baal's eyes that had looked into hell.

"Eddie!" The woman's voice was a gin-soaked bass. Catching up a striped taffeta parasol that must have been a good four feet long, she rose and planted the tip firmly on the floor in front of her. Both hands crossed over the brass knob at the top. Her chin jutted out stiffly.

"What do you want?"

The hard expression did not change. The defiant stance did not change. Like a grand dame she faced him with a shrug. "What else?"

"Goddammit!"

"Eddie," she snapped. "Clean up yer mouf . . ." She peered at Cassandra, who instinctively had taken a step backward out of the range of fire. "And who might this'n be? Nice bit of mutton. Y've moved up in the world from Sally?"

"She's none of your business." He caught Cassandra's arm and led her to the door. "Please leave us. If you'll wait in the hall . . . or Barston can escort you . . ." He ran his hand over the lower half of his face. "Barston, please escort her back upstairs."

"Bloody shame." The gin-soaked voice came nearer. The ferrule on the parasol tapped once, twice as the owner crossed the kitchen. "Yer gonna made this'n climb all the way up them bleedin' stairs when she's already seen me. Why y'wanta send 'er off? She ain't faintin' and fallin' down. Bloody shame."

Edward spun round, snarling, thrusting his face within an inch of the woman's. Two sets of volcanic eyes blazed at each other. "Will you clean up your language?"

The woman laughed low in her throat. "Ow-o-o-oh," she mocked. "Clean up m'langidge. Wot'll y' give me t' clean it up?" She winked lewdly at Cassandra. "Y've got 'im on the ropes right and proper."

"Cassandra, please leave." His voice was desperate.

"Miss," Barston interposed. "I'll really be happy to escort you anywhere you want to . . ."

The parasol thumped the floor. "No. Maybe she'd like t' stay and 'ear what's bein' said. Might be news t' 'er?"

"For God's sake!"

The woman dug an elbow into Edward's ribs by way of pushing him aside to confront Cassandra. "I'm so very pleased to make yer acquaintance," she sneered, her accent improving markedly. "I don't s'pose Ed-ward has told you 'bout me. So neglectful of 'im. I'm 'is mother."

Cassandra nodded coolly. "I had assumed as much. Good evening."

Again the hoarse moo. " 'Ow'd y' figger that one out?" She looked over her shoulder at her son, whose face had gone quite gray around the mouth. "Been braggin' on yer mum t' yer fancy bit?"

Edward closed his eyes as the world reeled around him. Vainly he wished for all the powers of hell to crack open the floor and swallow her.

There was a long silence. Then the woman shrugged. Moving slowly, the parasol thumping rhythmically, she made her way back to the bench and sat down heavily. "I'm temporarily busted, Eddie."

"What happened to the funds for this quarter?"

For the first time, the woman looked embarrassed. Eyelids, heavy with mascara and shadow, dropped over her eyes as one swollen hand waved vaguely. "A friend come by an' needed a stake."

"Any chance the friend might be Bagchock?"

"Eddie . . ." The white masque creased in a anguish; the hand came out in supplication.

"Damn it all! When will you drive that louse off?"

"Well, yer not down there to 'elp me now and again," she accused. "Bagchock still 'ooks a mean left. For which y' owe 'im, I might add."

Cassandra could see Edward's hands trembling as he ran them through the white wings at his temples. "Not one cent more for that parasite," he groaned.

The woman tapped the parasol on the floor authoritatively. "I don't think y' 'eard me clear, Eddie. Y' owe 'im."

"I don't owe Bagchock a thing." His features might have been set in stone.

"Beggin' yer pardon, but y' do. 'E done y' a right friendly turn. Didn't y' ever wonder wot 'appened to a certain *Jock* and 'is friend?"

"Jock?"

"An' a certain lorry driver."

Edward looked at his mother, then back at Cassandra. His expression altered perceptibly. "Bagchock 'ad a talk' with them?"

She nodded, her smile malevolent. "They won't never see Scotland again."

Edward folded his arms tightly across his chest. His jaw set stubbornly. "Bagchock wasted his trouble. He'll never be my friend."

" 'E ain't yer enemy neither."

Edward turned to Cassandra. "Will you please wait outside?"

Again his mother intervened. With a toss of her head she addressed the witness to their argument.

"Don't suppose 'e told y' somebody tried t' do 'im in over on Notting Gate Hill?"

Cassandra bowed her head. "I know he's in danger. Someone tried to poison him on our honeymoon."

The woman's mouth twisted. "Didn't get 'im though. Eddie's tough. Tough as old boots." She laughed. One beringed hand rested on the broad shoulder only for a moment. Her son stiffened under her touch. Instantly, the hand was removed. The moment of affection, if it had been one, was over. When the voice came again, it was a querulous whine. "C'mon, Eddie, be a sport. Can't I 'ave an advance on me quarterly?"

His face grim, he nevertheless shrugged. "Very well, Barston, please help Mrs. Pilkington . . ." He looked at her for confirmation of the name.

She nodded grandly. The peacock feathers fanned gently.

". . . Mrs. Pilkington to the chamber, third door on the right upstairs. Rouse Mrs. Smithers. Have her draw a bath."

The woman smiled archly at Cassandra. "Eddie does have lovely 'ot water and warm towels."

"Yes, he does," she replied softly.

"I'll get some money from the club. Wait for me, Cassandra." Throwing another furious look at his mother, Edward hurried from the room.

The woman rose, staggering a little this time as if she had relaxed and no longer tried to put up a front. " 'e's generous to a fault," she confided. "Jus' like me. Can't say no."

Cassandra watched the woman gather her black cape around her shoulders. She recognized in some surprise that it was Persian lamb.

"Eddie's a good man," the woman mused. "I'm the only woman I know of whose children'll even speak to 'em. The woman who takes up with 'im and treats 'im square'll be set for life. 'E never forgets 'is friends."

"I intend to treat him square," Cassandra agreed softly.

Mrs. Pilkington stared at the younger woman. Then her glance wavered.

Barston held the door open. "Mrs. Pilkington."

She belched. "Oh, I know m'way. Goodness, ain't we fancy?"

Cassandra listened to the parasol thumping rhythmically on its way up the stairs. Alone in the kitchen, she looked around with a shiver. Without thinking, she moved closer to the stove.

At last Baal entered. His face white, the darkened black brows a startling contrast, he stopped dead still in the doorway. Cassandra faced him in her silk dress of sapphire shot taffeta. Across the dim kitchen he searched her face.

"Oh, but I'm glad you're back," she exclaimed, hurrying to take his arm. "I'm starved. Let's hurry before those gamblers eat all the curried crab." She almost giggled at the look of amazed relief on his face.

In the early morning hours, Edward began to toss and turn. His occasional moan became a groan. He fought the bedclothes, twisted and pounded them. The scream of agony and anger he sought to utter came from his throat as a muffled wail. Still he fought.

Cassandra hurried to the connecting door. She had never opened it before, never gone to his side. She grasped the knob, then pressed her ear to the panel. Perhaps the nightmare was over.

Again the anguished sound followed by a terrible groan.

She pushed open the door to find him tottering to his feet. His eyes were open, his arms sawing the air wildly. She ran to him, caught him by the arm, but he shrugged her off.

Again the groan. "Coming!" he called. "Coming!"

Light was just breaking through the windows, dim yet enough for her to see. She waved her hand in front of his eyes. He did not blink.

"Edward," she whispered.

He took a tottering step. His free hand batted the air. "Coming!"

"This way." She managed to turn him and guide him around the bed. Once on the other side, she pushed him back, but he resisted her efforts, still struggling in the grip of his nightmare. "You're tired now," she soothed, stroking his shoulder and chest. "You're so tired. Lie down and rest."

At last with a deep sigh, he closed his eyes and sank back on the bed.

She worked the covers out from under his heavy limp body. They were twisted every which way with a great rent down one side of the top sheet. His nightmare had been terrifying indeed.

Now his breathing was even. Nevertheless, as she worked over him, he occasionally gave a faint sigh. The horrid dream still crouched at the edge of his consciousness.

A faint smile twitched at the corners of her mouth as she remembered the first time she had played this scene with him. How vividly she recalled the night he had been poisoned. Then he had been too sick to leave alone. Now he was too troubled.

Certainly no harm could come to her tonight, barring the possibility that he became violent again. In his sleep he might swing an arm and hit her, but she had no fear of sleeping with him. Besides the room, particularly the floor, was cold.

Hesitating no more, she lifted the covers and slid in beside him, eagerly seeking his warmth. He cooperated instantly, wrapping his arms around her, cuddling her against his body. When she sought to tuck her head into his shoulder, however, he would have none of it. Instead, he placed his mouth firmly on her temple, his face buried in the swirl of her hair.

Despite the warmth and coziness of his bed, she did not become drowsy. The turmoil of her own thoughts kept her awake. The sight of that terrible woman had effected a change in her attitude toward her husband. Now she wanted him awake to tell about it. Throughout dinner and their rounds of the casino, she had found no opportunity for important revelations.

He stirred beside her, pushed the covers back, and rolled over on his stomach. Grunting softly, he burrowed beneath the pillow. She trailed her fingers over the broad back in the fine cambric nightshirt. His skin was warm through the fabric.

Desire curled in her stomach. He was her husband, the father of her child. What better occasion to inform him of his impending fatherhood than when he awoke and found her beside him! She could imagine his surprise, perhaps a bit of uneasiness at the prospect, a moment or two of doubt. Not for a minute did she believe that he would not want the child.

Any man who had adopted a street waif of the temperament of Sally Atkins would welcome a sweet baby. After he got used to the idea that they were having a baby, or perhaps after she had actually produced the child some six months hence, she would tell him she loved him and let him laugh if he would. By that time she would be strong enough to withstand a little ridicule.

Her hand continued its stroking of his back, now caressing his neck, now patting his firm buttock. He had such beautiful buttocks. Over and over, her hand memorized their shape. Suddenly her gown felt scratchy and stuffy. Daring gently, she worked the nightdress off over her head.

The warmth of the bed and the smoothness of the sheets felt infinitely better to her skin. She slid her leg up and down the side of his, enjoying the rasp of his hair against her calf.

He murmured something. His breath stilled but then went on evenly.

She raised herself on one elbow beside him and began rotating her palm on his shoulder blade. Gradually, she worked down to his narrow waist and then to his buttock.

By the light of dawn, she noticed how his hair curled to one side on the back of his neck. He had a cowlick. It made him seem infinitely young and vulnerable. Lovingly she kissed his neck, then inhaled his scent, the shaving soap he used, his shampoo, his own warm body. Emboldened to experiment, she put out her tongue to lick the spot.

His taste was like an aphrodisiac. Desire curled tighter in her stomach. She could feel herself growing warm and damp between her legs. Without thinking, she rubbed her leg over the back of his thighs, pushing up his nightshirt. How warm and right her thigh felt pressed tightly against the lower curve of his buttocks.

She licked again, this time the sensitive spot behind his earlobe, kissing it, licking it again, then taking the earlobe between her teeth. Was it her imagination? Did she feel his shoulders hunch beneath her?

No, he still slept soundly. She nestled her bare breasts against his shoulders, so his deep breathing would caress them. They were so swollen that they ached, the nipples hard and tingling.

His whole body was so warm and exciting. She had never thought about a man's body as being beautiful or desirable. She had never even seen one until she had seen her husband's. At the thought of his dark smooth skin, an itch began between her legs. Involuntarily, she rubbed herself against his hip.

She had not imagined his movement then. He had actually heaved his buttocks upward, then dropped them back down on the bed. She froze, not wanting to disturb him, her confidence wavering. What if he found her pressed against him? Would he think her wanton?

Was she wanton? Was this desire, this ache, this itch, wantonness? Again her conscience railed at her, but faintly. She was married to this man. If she was not acting like a lady, so be it. She was in love with her husband and he was a very sensual man. Instinctively, she knew that to be awakened like this would give him pleasure.

The first rays of the morning sun shot between the edges of the draperies. The man beneath her moaned and stirred.

Daring greatly, she put her mouth against his ear. "Good morning."

He stiffened, then relaxed. "Good morning." He had to clear his throat twice before he could bring the words out.

"I . . ." She could not think what to say. "I got in bed with you in the middle of the night."

He turned on his side, careful not to disarrange her legs. "I see you did."

"Yes." She felt a little breathless. He had caught the hand with which she had absentmindedly been caressing his buttock and brought it around to his chest. When she had tried to pull back a little, he had pulled her wrist tighter so that her breasts pressed more securely against his back. "I . . . I didn't want you to get cold."

"That's very good of you." He began to move his buttocks against her belly. "This is very good of you too."

She gasped at the sensation. "You were walking in your sleep," she explained. "Your feet were cold by the time I guided you back to bed, so I got in bed to warm you up."

"Um-hm."

"What are you doing?" she gasped.

"Do you mind?"

"N-no. I just didn't know I was supposed to . . . Is that *nice?*"

"For you to touch me there is the nicest thing I know of."

"But, I mean . . ." She was blushing fiery red at the hard object he was rubbing her palm against.

He edged over onto his back. His free hand cupped her breast now nestled against his chest. "Your nipples are so hard," he murmured. "So hard and swollen."

She arched her back, pressing herself against him all along his side. "They ache. I can't . . ." She shuddered uncontrollably. Somehow she had managed to thrust her hips forward until her crotch was pressed against the top of his thigh. Or had he bent his leg? She could not remember which. It seemed unimportant. Another interminable spasm shook her.

Suddenly, she had to kiss him. Had to. Pushing up on her elbow, her hand gripping the rod he had pressed into her palm, her sex pressed against his thigh, she kissed him. Kissed him with her mouth open, thrusting her tongue in to couple with his tongue, shaking her head back and forth as she drove deeper, unconsciously tightening her grip at the same time she rubbed herself tighter against him.

He groaned. His hands clutched at her bare buttocks and lifted her onto him.

"Edward," she demanded, her voice a hoarse moan. "Edward."

"Yes."

"Edward, I want . . . please . . ."

His hands clutched her to him, rocked her from side to side. The staff of his manhood hurt her belly. "What do you want?"

Desperately, she placed both hands on his chest and pushed herself away. "I can't say it."

"You can say it. Tell me what you want?"

"I want . . ."

"Say it!" he hissed.

"I want you." The words came in a rush. "I want you to make love to me. I ache. Oh, Edward, I ache so much."

"What, sweetheart? Tell me what aches."

"My breasts. They ache. And—and between my legs."

"Here."

"Oooh, yes."

"And what do you want me to do about it?" He was teasing her now. He was a monster. A devil.

"Make love to me!" Her excitement brimmed over. "Make love to me. Damn you!"

"Why don't you make love to me?"

"Me? Can I?"

"Very easily." He lifted her then, guided her. "Put your knees on either side of my hips. Now. Your hands on my chest as you have them. Now."

She thought she would die in that minute when he filled her. But she did not. Instead, she waited, uncertain what to do until she could stay still no longer. Even as he had pleased her with his strokes, she realized she could do the same for him. By pushing up and down on his chest, she could slide her pelvis up and down around him.

As her movement became surer, he began to groan as if she was hurting him. "Oh, sweetheart. Oh, Cass. Cassie. Cassie."

Her body burned, her breasts bobbed, their weight no longer painful, but wonderful. With each contact with his belly, she rubbed herself against him, creating the most exquisite sensations.

She had never imagined in her whole life that anything could feel so good. It felt so wonderful. So complete. Nothing would ever feel this good again, but at least she had had this. The tears started in her eyes. She threw back her head.

He stiffened beneath her, thrusting up as she came down. His rod pierced her to the quick. Her whole being shuddered as release flowed through her. She screamed and collapsed, her red hair covering their arms and shoulders with a silken curtain.

She lay spent for several minutes. When she could think again, she remembered the reason she had wanted to wake him up, the thing she had wanted to tell him.

Slowly, she managed to raise her head. "Edward."

He moaned. His storm-gray eyes flickered open.

She swallowed. She must tell him quickly before she lost her nerve. "Edward, I have something important to tell you."

"Yes?"

"I'm having your baby."

The smile on his face restored all her confidence. "Clever, dear girl."

"Is that all you have to say?" She was a little bit hurt.

"What do you want me to say? That I'm glad? That I'm proud? That I'm excited?" He punctuated each question with a kiss. "Or that I've known it for weeks?"

She rolled off his body and bobbed up on her knees. "You haven't. How could you?"

He shrugged. "Remember I'm not your proper

Scottish lord. I've been reared among women who consider that the second greatest fear."

She stared at him speechless, flooded by the realization that he probably knew more about her bodily functions than she knew herself. It made her position undeniably weaker.

But did strength or weakness in this case really matter?

While she was musing, he pulled her down and reared up over her. "Kiss me," he demanded. "I haven't got enough of you yet."

Chapter Twenty-five

"Your mother is gone," Cassandra reported incredulously. "Mrs. Smithers said she didn't even stay the night. She just took a bath and left."

"She likes to take a bath in the warm bathroom," Edward told his wife drily. "Otherwise she wouldn't even have gone upstairs. She doesn't come for long visits. When she gets what she wants—chiefly money—she goes on her way."

Cassandra cleared her throat, not knowing what to say. She had been shocked by the woman's appearance, which so clearly bespoke her profession.

"She's a whore, Cassie. She goes out and drinks every night until she finds herself a john. Then she takes him back to her bed-sitter and entertains him." He took her by the shoulders. "I'd give everything I own if you didn't know about her."

"But you're supporting her, aren't you?"

He hesitated. "I give her a quarterly allowance," he muttered.

"Then why . . . ?"

"Why is she still out walking the streets? And giving her money to pimps? That's why Bagchock used to

461

be—her pimp."

"Good lord, yes, But why would any woman . . . ?"

"Because she's a prostitute. It's the way she's always made her living. It's the way of things." His voice was low

"I just can't understand." She looked around her incredulously. "She could be warm and comfortable all the time. You're generous, aren't you? You don't give her just a token amount, do you?"

He shrugged. "I give her enough." Turning away from her, he poured himself a brandy although it was early in the day. Leaning back against the liquor cabinet, he tossed it off. His dark eyes met hers defiantly as he lowered the glass. "No, you can't. You can't understand a woman like her, or a man like me for that matter. And you never will. As they say in the religious tracts, you've fallen in with evil companions, Lady MacDaermond."

She looked at him strangely. "I don't know. I'm confused."

"Nothing to be confused about," he mocked. "Just keep the facts in front of you. I'm a gambler and a writer of filthy novels. I take men's money and drive them to lecherous acts that despoil womankind." He lowered his voice to a menacing growl.

"You married a penniless crippled waif and gave her a home. You support your mother as well as an old butler in Scotland. You care for your friends."

"My mother is a whore. My friends are the dregs of society. I'm scum. And perhaps the worst thing as far as you're concerned is that I'm the father of your child. As I said, Lady MacDaermond. You've fallen in with bad companions. You're liable to acquire some very bad habits from your association with them."

She stared at him, reading correctly that he was not watching his language because he expected her to fly at him perhaps cursing and condemning. She could see no point in arguing with him. Instead to defuse his anger, she smiled. "I certainly have. Look what I did last night."

He frowned trying to recall, then grinned. "I would like to look at it over and over. Can you do it every night?"

"How would you know? You were asleep."

"I was awake most of the time."

"Oh, what a lie. The devil always tells lies."

"I felt you take off your gown and push your leg up under my rear and . . ."

"Hush!"

He set the glass down and held out his arms. She went into them naturally and he held her close. A sudden burst of emotion made him swing her up high on his chest and whirl her around. "We're going to have a baby!"

"Careful," she squealed. "Or we'll have it right here and now."

He stopped moving instantly, but continued to hold her tightly in his arms. He set his lips to her forehead. "When will she be here?"

"She?"

"Absolutely. A little girl just like you." He kissed her red hair.

She tilted back her head. "Well, she was conceived on All Hallows' Eve, so I suppose she'll get here at the end of July."

"Wonderful." He kissed her again. "I'm so glad you told me. I was beginning to get worried."

"Why?"

"I was afraid you might not know you were increasing. You're pretty stupid about some things, you know."

"What!" She struck him on the shoulder. "Put me down."

"No."

"Put me down," she repeated in mock anger. "You persist in thinking that I'm some sort of dullard. I'll have you know aristocrats have babies too."

His grip tightened round her momentarily, then he set her down as if she would break at the slightest jar. "I'm sure they do," he soothed.

"We even have libraries," she continued, sweeping her arm in a circle. "Although the library at Daerloch was not so fine as this one, I managed to get an education."

"Do you think this is a good library?" He was watching her closely.

She walked over to the shelves where books were shelved double by author. "Obviously, one of the best. Was it here when you and Nash bought the house?"

Her innocent question bothered him. "No." Again the defiant look crept into his eyes. "It's mine."

This time she did gape, first at him, then at the books, then back at him. The silence grew between them as she adjusted her thinking. "Tell me about it," she begged at last.

He pulled a slender volume off a shelf where books were not shelved double. The blue silk back was stained and warped, the pages rippled, but he cradled it as if it were an old friend. "Fell at my feet," he remarked offhandedly. "Thrown out in an alley. This one and all the rest of these." He ran his hand across their spines. The touch of his long strong fingers was as gentle as when he had caressed her body. His mouth curved in a tender smile. "I learned to read from these."

She moved closer. The titles were eclectic. Chaucer's *Canterbury Tales*, Jonathan Swift's *Gulliver's Travels*, *Tom Jones* and *Clarissa Harlowe*, translations of *Candide* and *Don Quixote* shelved between copies of *Lyrical Ballads* and *Frankenstein*. *Prometheus Unbound* and *Samson Agonistes*.

"What do you have there?"

"*The Corsair.*"

"And you've read them all?"

He looked incensed.

"I'm sorry. I didn't mean to be insulting. It's just that we had a small library, as I told you, but I don't recall ever seeing my father open a book. I just thought . . ." she finished lamely.

"Well, perhaps you are right to think so." He opened *The Corsair*. "You could only think that this was a show to gild my utter foulness. '. . . by Nature sent to lead the guilty — guilt's worse instrument.' "

She looked away from his self-scorn. Her own fingertip traced the titles. "*An Essay on Human Understanding* by John Locke. I haven't read this. Father's library did not run to philosophy."

He reshelved *The Corsair* and drew forth Locke. "Then by all means you must read anything you like."

She took the book from his hand, purposefully closing her hand over his to touch him. He had withdrawn himself, refusing to let her get close. "Will I find the secret of you in these books?" she asked.

He drew a deep breath. "I have no secrets, Cassandra. I am clear as crystal. You have always seen the real me. This is a bad place to work, but you had no choice. I am a bad person to marry, but you had no choice. My friends are bad friends, but you had no choice."

When she would have spoken, he shook his head. He drew himself up like a soldier for inspection, his arms straight at his sides. "I can understand your hatred of me. I can recognize hatred and its motives."

In a protesting movement, she put her hand on his chest. "I don't hate you."

He relaxed, smiling slightly. "You are right to hate me, just so you do not dwell on your hatred and turn it against her." He put his arm around her shoulders and placed his hand on her abdomen.

"I do not hate you, Edward Sandron."

"My true name is Eddie Boggan."

She put her hand over his lips. "Husband," she said firmly, "I do not hate you."

"Well, perhaps right now you can't generate enough emotion for a good hate. You wore yourself out this morning," he teased her. "But you'll get your strength back."

Nash knocked once, then pushed the door open. "How precious," he mocked. "You two billing and cooing in the middle of the morning. I may be sick."

"Then take yourself off," Edward advised. He did not release Cassandra and step back as she had expected, but merely dropped his hand from her belly.

"Have some important news to report. Sally should

be along in a minute. Surprised she's not here already."

"Perhaps I should leave," Cassandra suggested.

Nash shrugged. "Not necessary, Cass, old gel. Just sit yourself down over there at the embroidery frame and keep still as a mouse. We're not going to discuss a thing unfit for virgin ears." He laughed softly. "Strange to see what we've come to, Edward, old chum. Think we're civilizing down in the most amazing way. Imagine two old reprobates like us worried about our language." He lit a cigarette and inhaled deeply.

"Am I late?" Ashtaroth stood in the doorway. Her dress was the very latest fashion with the bustle arranged lower to show off her tiny waist and sleek hips. The skirt of maroon taffeta was knife-edge pleats with a maroon paisley overskirt tied back in French apron fashion *en tablier*. Under a tiny plumed hat her black hair was elaborately styled with soft bangs curled on her forehead. From her small ears dangled garnet earrings set in gold. She posed in the doorway with a long-handled maroon taffeta parasol furled and handled like a cane.

Edward merely shook his head. "You're in good time, Sally. Nash just burst in upon us." He looked critically at the dress, obviously new, but made no comment.

"Come in," Nash called affably. "Sit down and hear what I have to tell you."

Sally entered with little mincing steps. Cassandra realized that the other woman's skirt was so taped up that she had only limited room around her knees. She realized in another minute that something else was different about her.

Sally was smiling, really smiling. During their association, during many meals, during many evenings in the Devil's Palace, Sally had never managed more than a cynical twist of the lips. Her habitual expression was a sultry stare that most frequently turned into a frown or a sneer depending on whether she was displeased or amused.

She also had eyes only for Trevor Nash. Although she did not cross to his side, she took a seat rather close to him. Her hands trembled slightly as she stripped off the black kid gloves and folded them demurely in her lap.

Nash opened his grip and drew out papers. "First, the repairs are at last completed on the casino. And the receipts have been such that we should completely recoup our losses by the first of March." He chuckled cynically. "The raid did us more of a favor than harm. A certain raffish element of the population decided it was rather a lark to be caught in one. So they've brought friends with them in hopes that we'll be raided again. With those new customers along with our regulars, we're doing more business than ever before."

Cassandra only managed to conceal her astonishment at this bit of news. How could people be so contemptuous of the law! But then her own father had borrowed money from people that he had no intention of repaying as well as taken goods on credit that he had no money to pay for.

"A couple of investments have done exceedingly well," Nash continued, putting down one file of papers and picking up another. "The distillery that we supported is paying back dividends. Our broker informs me that the corn futures we purchased in America have paid back handsomely. We have received hefty checks from these. Edward, your latest book has been reprinted in French, Danish, and German, so its royalties are forthcoming. In fact, the forces of evil and vice seem to be winning all over the world."

"Anything good to report on that investment in the electric company?" Edward asked sarcastically.

Nash grinned cynically. "Everyone is entitled to one mistake. Fear I may have made one there. However, it should relieve everyone's mind to know that it is behind us. If everyone is entitled to one, then I have made mine."

"What is an electric company?" Cassandra wanted to know.

"Don't ask," Edward advised. "Just one of Nash's deals that cost us a lot of money but didn't bring any returns."

"It didn't cost so much money," Nash complained. "And if it had worked out, then we could have all been rich. Still could be."

Edward snorted. "The reason it cost so little to invest in it is that it was worthless."

"Long odds make a more exciting game."

"We are all gamblers," Ashtaroth inserted neutrally.

Edward shot an incredulous glance at her. "Are you feeling all right?"

She shifted uncomfortably. "Of course. After all, we are getting a lot of money on his investments."

"From the looks of your clothes, you'll need a lot."

"I-I did not put this dress on your account."

Nash snapped his grip together. "Well, must dash.

Tonight a group of American gamblers will be in the club. Uncouth, noisy, but very rich. They will be in London for the rest of the week. On Saturday next we will stage a Black Sabbat for them. Understand some of them are buying your last book at two guineas a copy, illustrated, of course. Can't get good stuff like that in America, they say."

He rose and offered his arm to Ashtaroth with exaggerated politeness. "Going my way, Sally, old gel?"

She looked up into his face, her expression eager. "Thank you, yes." She put her arm in his and let him lead her out.

Edward watched them go with a puzzled expression on his face. "Last time he had to drag her out," he observed.

"They may have reached an understanding," Cassandra hazarded. "I'll leave you to your writing. Mrs. Smithers is accompanying me to Harrod's. They have a new department with everything for baby."

"Damnedest thing I've every seen. Old Scratch in a red cape yelling at us to gamble. Sure sets a man to thinking."

"Yeah, but not very long." The man who spoke threw a twenty-guinea chip onto the roulette table, letting it lie where it rolled. When the wheel stopped spinning, the croupier raked the chip in with a bland smile.

"With your luck, Roscoe, you'll be losing your gold teeth before the night's out."

With a wild satanic laugh and a swirl of crimson

satin, Baal descended and took Ashtaroth's arm. She stepped a little closer than necessary to his side. "Don't leave me," she whispered. "These American savages are about to tear me to pieces."

Edward patted her hand thoughtfully. Was Sally feeling all right? He could never remember her asking for help before. "They are rather a rambunctious lot," he agreed.

A man, sporting ferocious handlebar moustaches, made a low awkward bow in front of Ashtaroth. "We don't have a thing to beat you, gal," he declared. "Hey, Devil, okay if I take her and let her blow a little luck my way. I can be as devilish as you can."

Baal shook his head. "Sorry not now, old man. She has to make the rounds with me. Part of the script, you know."

Ashtaroth's face remained cold and remote. "Damn Trevor for setting this party up. He doesn't have to put up with all this patting and pinching. How will we ever get through a Black Sabbat for these people?"

Baal shrugged. "We'll begin it. If the party gets too wild, we'll just call the whole thing off and give everyone his money back."

Ashtaroth shook her head. "I wish I could believe you, but you know how Trevor is about money."

"Trevor?" He looked down at her quizzically.

She pinched her lips together. "Nash."

"When did you begin to call him Trevor?"

Before she could answer, a man called from a dice table. "Hey, Devil, is all your luck this bad?"

Edward smiled saluted the man who had spoken. "Certainly hope so, old chap. After all, you wouldn't expect to win in the Devil's Palace." He motioned to a demon-waiter. "More champagne for the loser. Sweeten your luck or drown your sorrows."

"Most likely drown," came the morose comment.

"Cassandra! Cassandra!"

Someone—a man other than her husband—was in the harem room. She exchanged a startled look with Mrs. Smithers before reaching for her robe.

"Shall I summon Barston?" the woman asked.

"That might be wise." Hastily, Cassandra threw on her robe and opened the door a crack.

"Cassandra, where are you?"

Cassandra pushed the door closed and pressed herself against it. The very thought of this man in her apartments filled her with disgust and not a little terror.

"Cassandra." His voice was more insistent, nearer.

She was trapped. She took a deep steadying breath. Still, her voice shook as she whispered. "We must get out of this dressing room, Mrs. Smithers. I'll face him. You leave me immediately and bring back Mr. Barston." She pulled the ends of her gown tighter at the throat. "Perhaps you'd better send Mr. Barston and go for Mr. Sandron as well."

"Oh, lord, ma'am . . ."

"Just do as I say."

"Cassandra . . ."

"Maybe he'll go away . . ." Mrs. Smithers suggested. The knob to the door of the dressing room rattled. It opened a crack despite Cassandra's weight on it.

Hastily, she rammed her shoulder against it. "Just a

minute, Mr. Fitzwalter. I'm getting dressed," she called, striving for a normal sound.

"Sorry to intrude, my dear. But I must speak to you." The pressure on the door ceased. "Please come out."

"Very well. Just a minute." Cassandra straightened away from door. She flexed her hands nervously, then reach for the doorknob.

"Oh, ma'am, should you go in there?"

"I've no choice," she whispered with a wan smile. "Perhaps I'll be all right. He was my father's best friend, after all. Just hurry and get Barston."

"Yes, Mrs. Sandron . . ."

Before she lost her nerve entirely, Cassandra opened the door. "Mr. Fitzwalter, you shouldn't be in here, but I'm so glad you've come back."

He had stationed himself in the middle of the room, next to the divan. His heavy body had held regally erect. "I've come to speak to you, Cassandra, for the salvation of your immortal soul."

She winced. "Mr. Fitzwalter, I don't think this is the proper surrounding for you to be discussing my soul with me. Mrs. Smithers will show you to the drawing room downstairs, and I'll be down as soon as I dress."

Fitzwalter dismissed the housekeeper with a violent sweep of his cane. He waited momentarily while she hurried out, then allowed his eyes to slide round the bedchamber. "You poor child."

The hypocrisy of his pity made Cassandra shiver. She could not forget that this man, a self-styled moralist with a faithful and loyal wife, had sought to make her his mistress.

He tilted his head back to stare at the harem

draperies, represented on the *trompe l'oeil* ceiling. His face was bright red in the light from the gas-o-lier. "What a horror your imprisonment has been!"

She followed his gaze, remembering her shock when she had seen it for the first time. "This room does take a bit of getting used to," she admitted neutrally. How had he found her apartment, she wondered frantically. A lock and a guard were going to have to be placed on that entrance on Margaret Street. If Fitzwalter had found his way to the harem room, she might very well come in to go to bed one night and find it very occupied.

His inspection done, he reached out to take her hands. "My dear girl, I've come to take you back to Scotland with me."

Repressing a shudder at the memory of his hot, moist palms, she stepped back. "We've been through this before, Mr. Fitzwalter. I'm not prepared to be your mistress any more now than I was then."

"But surely my cleanly presence would be preferable to this . . . this ordure. . . . Be advised, Cassandra. I run a great risk to take you damaged as you are. I will not take you when he is through with you."

"Mr. Fitzwalter, you don't understand. I am not Edward Sandron's mistress. I am his wife. I cannot and will not leave my husband."

"Hush, my child. Your marriage vows were obtained under duress. No wedding under those conditions is legal. I can offer you freedom from all that. I can guess at the terrible bargain you struck with Baal. A devil's bargain. Am I right? You may tell me about it."

Cassandra felt her stomach heave again. This man

was blind to all but his own narrow version of things. How had her liberal father been able to love and trust him? She could remember when he had dandled her on his knee. The thought made her ill.

"Cassandra," he prompted. The bland cherub's face looked somehow hollow, its jowls sagging. The dapper black suit was no longer buttoned tightly across a rounded belly. The little black eyes glittered out of dark circles.

She took another step back. Ironically, this man looked more demonic than Baal had ever been. Carefully, she chose her words. "Mr. Fitzwalter, you know so much. It is true that I struck a bargain with him. He gave money for Mr. MacAdam's care. He took me back and gave me a home when my arm was broken and I could no longer work. He married me in honorable fashion. I am indebted to him in so many ways. I must pay the debt."

"Never." Fitzwalter pursued her and bent to take her hand. When she laced her fingers together, he satisfied himself by taking both her hands between his. "You do not have to honor a bargain like that. You were ill, weak. God will understand and forgive."

She sighed at the introduction of religion into the conversation. The man was impossible to reason with when his mind was set firmly on his moral beliefs. "Mr. Fitzwalter, I am sure God understands why I am living here now. Believe me, I am happy here with my husband." She could scarcely control the irritation in her voice.

His pleading smile disappeared. His slack lips pursed. He clutched her hands tightly in a grip reminiscent of the one she had jumped from the train to escape. "You don't know what you're saying, my dear. You are the Countess of Daerloch. Your fine skin must crawl with revulsion when that common guttersnipe puts his filthy hands on you."

She threw an agonized glance at the door as he began to stride up and down the room. Where was Barston? Where was Mrs. Smithers? Where was her husband? "Mr. Fitzwalter . . ."

He paid no attention. His tongue rattled on and on, spewing out the hateful words from his lips. Flecks of foam gathered at the corners of his mouth. "He is a viper, a fiend incarnate, a demon who lures men to their deaths. And he has put his hands on your pure, white body. Sullied it. Oh, what a fall. What a fall!"

"Mr. Fitzwalter!" Only by shouting could she choke off the monologue.

His eyes flickered vaguely, then searched for and found her. He wiped a trembling hand across his mouth.

"Mr. Fitzwalter. I am a respectable married woman with a fine husband who works for a living. He is well educated and cultured. He is the care and support of his mother and his sister." Here she stretched the truth a little, but she reckoned Sally Atkins to be a truer sister than most. "I could ask for no better husband were he a belted earl."

"But—but he is a gambler and a writer of filthy obscene works that lead the minds of men to terrible acts."

She held up a hand. "I don't care about that. I am married to him and soon we will have a child."

Fitzwalter's red face paled, then twisted obscenely.

"You . . ." He spluttered when he could speak. "You are having a child. God forgive you! It will be a child of the devil." He pointed to her stomach, which appeared perfectly normal beneath the folds of her robe.

Involuntarily, she put one hand in front of her waist to shield the baby from his wrath. She was very close to panic. Her voice rose shrilly. "I must ask you to leave, Mr. Fitzwalter. My husband will be here any minute to fetch me to supper."

Fitzwalter stared toward her, his face contorted, his hands outstretched.

At that instant Barston thrust open the bedroom door. With a gasp of relief, Cassandra hurried toward him. "Mr. Fitzwalter is leaving now," she cried. "Please see that he is escorted out."

"Yes, ma'am." The butler placed himself between her and her unwanted guest.

"Get out of my way," Fitzwalter hissed.

Barston thrust out his chest. "I'll show you out, sir."

"You've no right to interfere here."

The butler pressed his left fist into the palm of his right hand. "This way, sir."

Fitzwalter's face contorted until it was unrecognizable. "Your immortal soul is damned, Cassandra MacDaermond." He raised his stick to strike.

Barston caught the smaller man's arm in a hammerlock. At the same time he grabbed a handful of the man's sack coat at the back. "This way, sir."

Fitzwalter began to struggle and shout as the butler forced him out into the hall and down the stairs. "The demon Baal has possessed your soul and your body. I pity you above all others. For you are your father's daughter and he was my best friend."

"What's going on here?" Edward Sandron waited in the lighted foyer, his crimson satin cape swirling around him, the collar surrounding his head like the points of a web.

"She's damned," Fitzwalter cried again. "Damned."

"Keep your mouth shut," Edward commanded, his face dark. "You're not to malign my wife."

"Your wife." Fitzwalter began to shriek with laughter. "She's the whore of Babylon."

Cassandra came to head of the stairs. "Don't hit him, Edward! He's mad," she cried too late.

"Bloody swine!" Edward's left fist connected with the side of Fitzwalter's jaw as Barston leaped back out of the fray. The blow brought the man to his knees.

"Edward!" Cassandra shrieked again.

The evangelist crouched on all fours, shaking his head dizzily.

Edward stood over him, his fists clenched. "Get out and don't ever come back," he snarled.

The man's body trembled, then he slumped back on his haunches. His mouth contorted hideously. "I'm going. I'm going," he grunted. "I've done all I can for her. She's the evil one now. I was mistaken. She lured me back here." He laughed eerily. "I was mistaken in her. I did not realize what she intended when she came here. You were right not to tell me, Cassandra MacDaermond, for I would have tried to prevent you from destroying him. For Scotty's sake."

Cassandra stared at the crouching man, her arms crossed tightly across the front of her body. "I don't know what you're talking about."

Fitzwalter chortled, a horrible sound. Pink fluid

sprayed from between his slack lips. "You sought his death. You! You did the murder for which your poor gullible servant was imprisoned. You are the one trying to kill this evil man." He looked up at Baal. The triumph in his face was ugly to behold. "You deserve each other. God works in mysterious ways. He uses us all. The good and the evil. Set a thief to catch a thief." He pointed accusing fingers at them both, his arms wide spread out on either side of his shoulders as if he were crucified.

Cassandra could only stare incredulously, trying to control the nausea that threatened to overcome her.

"My, my! What have we here? Prayer meeting in the hall. A bit out of place for the Devil's Palace." Nash had stepped through a sliding panel at the back of the foyer. Smiling nastily, he kept his hand on the mechanism while Ashtaroth followed him through.

Chapter Twenty-six

"Oh, Nash. And Ashtaroth." Cassandra's face flamed at the sight of her husband's business partners, witnesses to this debacle. Embarrassed to the bottom of her soul, she nevertheless gathered the rags of her self-possession to her. "I must apologize for keeping you wondering where we were. Mr. Fitzwalter had detained us, but he was just leaving." With an icy hand she motioned to the butler.

As Barston helped the man to his feet, Edward's stormy gaze never wavered.

The evangelist put a hand to his bruised cheek, touched the side of his mouth with his fingertips. He stared at the bloodstain with a pleased smile. Then he thrust his hand out before him. "See!" he cried. "See! I have shed blood on the side of right."

"Get out of here," Edward snarled, "or you'll shed more."

"I shall be only too happy to leave this den of iniquity."

Ashtaroth laughed suddenly. "But you'll be back

soon, won't you, Fitzy?"

Fitzwalter froze. His hand flew to hide his face; the chubby fingers splayed over his eyes. He all but peeked between them.

Ashtaroth swayed toward him, her taffeta skirts rustling. "The light's a little dim in here, but I recognize you, Fitzy. Just love those little scenes in the chapel, don't you?"

He shuddered. His shoulders hunched. Then he took a deep breath and dropped his hand. "Woman, you have me confused with someone else."

"No, I don't." She chuckled. "No, I don't. You come here every time there's a special performance. Better get your ticket for next week's show. With those Americans in town, they're going fast."

Fitzwalter backed away as she advanced. "I'm not interested."

Nash pounced eagerly upon the tormented man. "Good for you, Fitzwalter, old chum. Glad to hear you're not interested. That streak of bad luck you had a few months ago was enough to wipe out a man's whole quarter earnings."

Fitzwalter fell back against the wall, shaking his head back and forth. The florid jowls trembled. "I don't know what you're talking about. You're all mad."

"I'll tell you who's mad," Ashtaroth sneered. "Madame Audray down on Church Street. She's mad enough to kill. You took out one of her birds last month and didn't pay the full fee. Nikolai is looking for you."

"No!"

"Oh, say it's not Nikolai, Ashtaroth, old gel." Nash threw up his hands to heaven in mock pleading. "Seven feet tall. Fists like boulders. Good God, poor Fitzy doesn't stand a chance."

"Lies. Lies!"

"If you'll just step away from door, sir," Barston murmured, "I'll open it. It's a bit stubborn sometimes. Takes a knack."

Fitzwalter spun away, hugging the wall. He crashed into the umbrella stand, sending the heavy brass cylinder rolling across the floor. The contents scattered around his feet, tripping him in a welter of black silk and ribs and curved Prince of Wales handles. His nerves broke completely. He began to blubber, ugly gulping sounds struggling out of his throat.

Barston swung the door open wide.

Fitzwalter reeled around the jamb and out into the night. His noisy crying ended in a hoarse shout as he slid down on the wet street, where a thin layer of ice was just beginning to form.

Cassandra started forward, but Edward, his expression fierce, caught her arm and pulled her back. Barston closed the door and turned the lock firmly.

Nash put a casual arm around Ashtaroth's waist, pressing her against him for an instant. "Bit of a good thing, Sally, old gel, your recognizing him. Usually better m'self at putting two and two together. Must be slipping. Hadn't realized that he'd come here and harass me on the nights of the Sabbats, then stay around and participate."

Cassandra leaned against the wall, her face white. "I can't believe that Mr. Fitzwalter would do such things. Are you sure you're not mistaking him for someone else?"

Ashtaroth shook her head. "Not a chance. He's been hanging around here for years. He comes and goes. Trevor will tell you."

Nash was still cursing himself. "Damn! I could have got rid of the bloody Moral Virtue League long ago. Saved us all a lot of time and money. Bloody hypocrite! Sorry, Cass, if he was a friend of yours, but he's a bad actor."

"He can't even get into the Lowther Rooms anymore. The last time he was there, he got mad and hurt one of the girls," Ashtaroth continued.

Cassandra shook her head drearily. "I can't take all this in."

Nash turned to Edward, who had been silent since Fitzwalter left. "Classic case, right, Eddie, old top? Hates it, but can't live without it. Blames everybody else for his problems."

The deep frown smoothed out of Edward's face until his expression was properly blank. "Yes, a classic case. Thanks for getting rid of him. Thanks to you too, Barston. I was afraid I was going to have to hit him again."

"My pleasure, sir."

Trevor dropped a kiss on Ashtaroth's cheek. "You handled that a bit of all right, Sal. Really sent him running howling with his tail between his legs."

She blushed, suddenly uncomfortable with the unaccustomed praise. She looked very young and very pleased with herself.

There was a moment's silence in the foyer. Barston left them with a silent bow. The oddness of their grouping suddenly impressed itself upon them. Ashtaroth and Nash stood virtually locked in each other's arms, but Edward had abandoned Cassandra after he had kept her from running after Fitzwalter. Now she stood leaning against the wall, her arms wrapped protectively around her waist. He took care to avoid looking at her.

At last Edward cleared his throat. "Did you need me for something, Nash?"

"Not a thing, old chap. Sal just wanted a respite from the clients tonight. She found them a bit wilder than she likes."

Ashtaroth glanced from Edward to Cassandra, taking in their closed faces. "Yes, well, perhaps we'd better get back to the casino, Trevor," she suggested with uncharacteristic sensitivity. "Those Americans are better gamblers than you gave them credit for. Some of them are actually winning a little."

"God forbid! Get back and distract them, you gorgeous wench. With you to look at, they won't be able to tell a knave from a king."

They left by the sliding panel, the same way they had come.

Suddenly, the foyer seemed much larger, with miles of space between its occupants. The silence stretched between them.

"How did he get into your bedroom?" Edward asked

at last, his voice a deep growl.

She shook her head. "I have no idea how he found it, but I imagine he came in through the Margaret Street entrance. Mrs. Smithers and I heard him together," she added.

"And you entertained him in the bedroom in your dressing gown."

"Who told you that?"

"Mrs. Smithers sent for me after she called Barston. She was afraid you couldn't handle the man." His voice took a sarcastic tone.

"Then if she sent for you, she knew I sent Fitzwalter down to the drawing room almost immediately." She pushed herself proudly away from the wall. "What are you trying to imply by all this?"

"Were you his mistress before you were mine?"

"What?"

"Were you his mistress before you were mine?" he repeated calmly. He might have been inquiring after her health, so lightly were the words spoken.

She dropped her hands to her sides. "If you have to ask that, why did you marry me?"

He shook his head. "I consider it a perfectly logical question. I never asked what your life had been before. The night of the masquerade you came into my arms without a murmur. The only bit of hesitation was taking off the mask. I know you were no virgin."

She put her hands to her face. "Does it matter so much to you? Can you not trust me?"

He made a cutting motion with his hand. The

485

crimson satin attached at his wrist rippled and swirled. "At least deal honestly with me. I have always dealt honestly with you." His voice was hoarse.

She moved so that the light shone full in her face. "If you believe a madman's accusations, how can you believe the defense of a sane woman?"

"Has he been coming secretly to your rooms when I have been working in the casino? Is that how he knew where to come? Did he come too early tonight, before you had dismissed Mrs. Smithers?"

Cassandra clenched her fists in front of her. "Damn you! You are infamous. What wildness is going on in your brain? You married me. I'm carrying your child. Do you think so little of me, of yourself, that you believe I would betray you?"

"You might be regretting your choice of me over him."

"I had no choice."

"All the more reason to take back your first lover. Did you and he have a lover's quarrel? Is that why you jumped off the train?"

She spun on her heel. "I'm leaving!"

"You're going nowhere." He caught her wrist and jerked her back. Off balance, her heel caught in her skirt and she went down on one knee with a thump.

"Monster!" So angry she could have wept, she glared up at him. "You're ruining everything. Everything."

"What am I ruining? What? A servant reports to me that my wife is entertaining an old male friend in her bedroom. What am I ruining that has not already been ruined?"

Twisting her wrist out of his hand, she climbed to her feet, scorning his help when he put his hand under her arm. "I never invited him here. He came because he's a fanatical old man. He feels guilty because of my father's death and because he thinks my being here may be his fault."

"Is it?"

"Of course, it isn't. I'm here because I wanted to earn my own living. I succeeded too until your problems intruded into my existence."

"My problems?"

"Someone murdered your valet . . ."

"Fitzwalter said you did it."

"Do you believe him?"

He hesitated a minute too long.

Then she screamed at him. Her eyes blasted green fire as she called him a name she had heard her father use when the groom had lamed his best hunter. Spinning on her heel, she fled for the stairs.

"Wait!"

The blood was roaring her ears, when halfway up she felt him tug the skirt of her dress. So furious she could barely breath, she spun around. Her nails scoring the bannister, she faced him.

"I never really believed him, Cassandra," he began lamely. "I was just—"

The rage in her face stopped him. He backed down a step raising his hands, remembering as he did so that whatever she was, she was carrying a baby. This upset could not be good for her.

"You impugned my honor," she panted. "Instead of laughing at the whole thing, or at least thinking this through and considering the source, you've believed him. This whole bloody marriage was about honor to begin with. Mine! You reminded me of my honor. You used it like a sword against me to force me to marry you and save Mr. MacAdam. Now you stand there and maintain that I have no honor. Either I do or I don't. Make up your mind!"

"Cassandra . . ."

"Stay back! You believed him when he said I could let Mr. MacAdam take the blame for murder. A murder that he accused me of committing."

"You didn't even defend yourself."

"I had no defense. I had never had to make a defense. I did not do it. And neither did Mr. Mac-Adam. When that incompetent Inspector Revill arrested him, I did everything I could for Mr. MacAdam, including marrying you. Yet you've accused me of murder. You've believe me capable of poisoning a man." Suddenly, her eyes widened. "You think I tried to kill you."

"I can understand . . ." he began.

Her rage turned cold and deadly. She pushed herself away from the bannister. Straight up she stood, her hands clenched at her side. "You think I turned on the gas jet in your room in Brighton. That's why you didn't take me seriously when I tried to make a case against Nash. You already had your mind made up."

"You were furious with me, just as you are right

now."

"I've been furious with a great many people who are still alive. Many of them I cared less about than I do you."

He held out a hand to steady her as she swayed. "I was beneath you," he tried to explain. "I had behaved like an idiot at the Pavilion."

"If I wanted you dead, pray tell me why I didn't leave you lying in the back hall that night. Why did I practically pick you up on my back and carry you into the bathroom and work over you while you vomited and —"

He held up his hand. "Please, I beg you. I know what you did for me."

She leaned down until she was within an couple of inches of his face. "And do you also know that when you were chilled to the bone in your cold bed, shaking like a leaf, no more sense in your brain than a baby, I climbed into your bed with you and warmed you with my body? I fell asleep and the next morning you rewarded my care by using my virgin body as if it were a harlot's." She spat the last word in his face. Then catching up her skirt, she turned and ran up the stairs.

He heard her footsteps running down the upstair's hall as he reeled back. Only his grip on the bannister kept him from falling.

His memory of that morning damned him by confirming her words. He had climbed out of bed naked, brown smears on his thighs. Suddenly, he had the answer to so many questions. Why she had seemed so strangely familiar the night of the masquerade. Why he had felt that he had known her before. Later he had decided that he had only recognized Miss Fitch.

Now he knew the truth, the full sweep of her humanity. She had done everything possible to save him, including the ultimate sacrifice of placing her body in his hands.

And to his shame, his base-born nature had overcome him and he had raped a gentle lady. No wonder she despised him. He despised himself. In the foyer he caught sight of himself in the oval mirror. The crimson web of Baal's cape framed his face, white with strain, the makeup darkening his eyebrows. He looked monstrous. Ugly, evil. Hurling a vitriolic curse at the image, he lunged for the spring that opened the panel. As it slid open, he almost dived through it, sending himself back where he belonged. Baal returning to Hell.

"I've never seen Eddie so upset."

Her face pale and still as stone, Cassandra listened to Sally's description of the night before in the Devil's Palace. When the dark woman looked accusingly at her, Cassandra lifted the teacup to her lips.

"You're not going to give an inch, are you?"

Cassandra set the cup down and blotted her lips with the tiny Madeira napkin. "I don't have anything to give."

"The hell you don't."

Her temper flared. "The hell I do."

"He's your husband."

"He thinks I tried to kill him."

One corner of Sally's mouth curled upward in a grimace. "Well, did you?"

"Of course not. I'm his wife."

"Where we come from that doesn't mean a thing." Sally selected an eclair from the tray and stared at it. "Look here." She leaned forward and bared her teeth at Cassandra. The eyetooth on the right side of her mouth was crooked and badly chipped in the bargain. Her polished accent had been replaced by the sounds of the streets. "I think m' ma did that to me."

Cassandra grimaced and shook her head.

"Y'know why I said, 'I think,' don't y'?"

"Because you don't know for sure who your mother was?"

"Right." Sally drew back and took up the eclair. Carefully, she bit into it, savoring the rich chocolate, the vanilla filling. "From the time I was a little thing, the only sure thing in my life was Eddie Boggan. I might get mad enough to kill him sometime, but y'bet yer bloomin' buttons, I'd never do it. And I'd sure as hell kill to keep him from bein' hurt."

Cassandra hid her face in her hand. "But why could he possibly believe that I would even *want* to kill him, much less actually make two attempts on his life?"

"Because yer the best thing that's ever happened to him, and he can't believe he deserves you."

"Last night he implied that I had dishonored him. Why if he believed that, he might believe that this child was not his."

"He doesn't believe that. I can tell you. I kidded him about it the night you got married. You didn't catch on to what was being said but he admitted it."

Cassandra raised her eyebrows. "Everybody knew that I was increasing? I can't believe—"

"Believe me." Sally chuckled. "I asked if you had a bun in the oven and Nash told me to shut up, but Eddie just grinned, pleased as punch and said yes."

"But why did he marry me, if he believed that I had tried to kill him? And why take me into his home and give me . . . everything, if he believed I tried to kill him on our honeymoon?"

Sally looked at her pityingly. "Eddie Boggan's always going out on a limb for the folks he cares about. And he cares about you and about that baby. He'd never let his child grow up illegitimate, even if he'd have to risk his life."

Cassandra shivered. "And me?"

"Why it sounds to me as if he's too jealous to think straight. When that message came that there was a man in your bedroom, he almost knocked a man down getting out of the casino."

"But he has no reason to be jealous. I . . ." Cassandra hesitated, fearful of telling this mercurial woman too much although Sally had behaved differently the last week. She was gentler, softer. Still Cassandra did not know her. "I care very much for him. Very, very much."

"Have you told him how you feel about him?"

She drew in her breath in a kind of gasp. "No."

"I don't think he'll ever get the nerve to tell you first."

"No, I suspect you're right." Cassandra let out her breath slowly. In the ensuing silence she poured her guest another cup of tea. "I'd better tell him." The two women stared at each other in perfect accord.

When Cassandra opened the door of the library, she found her husband in conversation with Inspector Clive Revill.

The visitor rose to his feet and bowed respectfully. "Afternoon, Mrs. Sandron."

"Good afternoon, Inspector."

"Please sit down, Cassandra." Edward came to lead her to a chair. "The inspector has come in search of Fitzwalter."

She shook her head. "In search of Mr. Fitzwalter? Surely you mean at his behest."

"No, ma'am. We're trying to locate him for questioning."

Her eyes flew to her husband's face. *"Fitzwalter?"*

Edward put his hand on her shoulder. "Cassandra, don't get excited. Please try to keep calm."

"Fitzwalter. My father's best friend. Mr. Fitzwalter!"

Inspector Revill stared at her. "I don't quite see—"

"My wife is very fond of the gentleman. He is an old friend of her family. He has been to visit her several times."

"Might be a good idea if you didn't let him in next time he comes by, ma'am. We've got quite a case built

493

against him. Seems your valet Parks was a member of the League for"—he consulted his notebook—"for the Uplift of Moral Virtue."

Cassandra put up her hand to cover her husband's where it rested on her shoulder. "But this is awful."

"Yes, ma'am. He also used to work for Mr. Fitzwalter, before he came to work for your husband."

"But Parks was poisoned. Why would Fitzwalter poison his own servant?" Edward asked reasonably.

"We think it might have been an accident. The valet might have been in your house to pick up bits of information about your business dealings. A valet has the opportunity to see a man's private papers. And he was the only servant in the house for a while. I understand from Mr. Nash that many of your investments have gone sour in the past six months. Then after the valet's death, everything seemed to move on as before."

"Yes, but—"

"Mr. Nash also told us about another accident that took place before any of your present staff including Ferris MacAdam were engaged. He told us Mr. Sandron took a bad fall."

"Good Lord!"

"Right outside the valet's chamber."

Cassandra could remain seated no longer. Rising, she slipped her arms around her husband's waist and pressed her head against his shoulder. "Mr. Fitzwalter knew we were going to Brighton," she reminded them.

Inspector Revill threw her a sharp look before pulling out his notebook. "Did something out of the ordinary happen in Brighton?"

"Someone tried to kill Edward at the hotel. The gas jet was turned on in his bedchamber. If the hotel manager hadn't had men checking at intervals during the night, Edward would have died."

Revill noted the information. "Do you have any idea where he might be?"

"He was here a couple of nights ago, making a nuisance of himself and cursing my wife."

"What state of mind was he in when he left?"

"Very upset," Edward supplied.

"Furiously angry," Cassandra added.

Revill turned a page and made a notation. "Did he try to attack either one of you? Make any threats?"

"He accused my wife of terrible things, including Parks's murder. I knocked him down."

The inspector shot Cassandra a piercing glance. "Peculiar sort of friend you've got there, Mrs. Sandron. Might be a good idea to place a guard at your house."

Edward drew back, his expression incredulous. "A policeman at the Devil's Palace!"

Revill allowed the tiniest of smiles to crack his stern face. "We'll make it a man in street dress. Wouldn't want to alarm anyone unduly.

"He's probably on his way back to Scotland," the man continued. "I've telegraphed all the details to the office up there. His home will be watched. We'll pick him up soon."

Cassandra tightened her grip around her husband's waist. "You will be careful of him, won't you? He's an old man, mentally disturbed. He came here with the idea of saving me from my husband, whom I love very much."

A tiny thrill shot through her as she felt the swift indrawn breath swell her husband's torso.

Another little smile played about the inspector's mouth. He bowed with extra courtesy.

"That's why I especially appreciate the guard being assigned to our home," she hastened to add. "I want to feel sure that my loved ones are safe — my husband, our friends, our" — she swallowed hard, then continued, flying in the face of propriety — "little one who will soon be born."

The inspector noted the blush rising in her cheeks. He cleared his throat. "I'll assign the man personally, ma'am." Bowing again, he took his leave.

Edward did not move, nor did Cassandra. Beneath her cheek, she could feel his heartbeat and the rise and fall of his chest. His arm encircled her shoulders. He tipped her head back. "That was a very pretty speech." His eyes searched her face.

"I wanted the inspector to be sure that the Devil's Palace is more than a gambling casino."

"I'm sure he went away with that impression."

She smiled sweetly. "I was a bit embarrassed, of course, but he had to know that I love you."

Again the quick indrawn breath. The stormy eyes closed, then opened again. "I . . . I don't know what to say."

Placing her palm along his cheek, she raised herself on tiptoe. "I love you, Edward Sandron." Her mouth was less than an inch from his. On his name she closed the distance. Her tongue touched his lips, slid between them, found his.

His arms tightened around her, hurting her with their strength, but she did not draw back. She welcomed it, pressing herself impossibly closer. Her other hand slid up his back to the nape of his neck. Her fingers slid into the thick black hair.

He made a small sound of pleasure, then another as the kiss went on. The hardness of his aroused flesh pressed against her belly. She twisted her hips from side to side.

"Stop!" He tore his mouth away.

"Why?" she murmured in a dazed voice.

"Because . . . because . . ."

"I love you." She reached for his mouth again.

"No." He jerked his head back. "You can't love me."

She locked her fingers together at the back of his head and drew him inexorably down to her. "Kiss me."

"But—"

She sealed his mouth.

His hands slid up and down her back, at last cupping her buttocks. Her legs trembled as her body heated. The deep sweet ache of her own arousal made her weak with need.

When he pulled away again to breathe, she pushed against him. The edge of the desk caught his legs. He sat down. Swiftly, she insinuated herself between his thighs. "Are you going to make love to me?"

Her question seared through him. "Yes." Suddenly,

he was all male, dominating her with his strength, drawing from her compliance. He turned her around and seated her on the desk. He locked the library door and came back to her, stripping off his coat and vest as he came.

"Here?"

"Yes." His eyes glittered. He took her face between his hands and kissed her deeply. "Do you really love me?"

"I really love you."

"I won't ask how or why. When things fall into your lap, you don't question them. You take them with both hands." Suiting his action to his words, he tossed up her skirts, covering her to her chin in a froth of petticoats.

"Shouldn't I take these off?"

"No time," he said and laughed, his fingers busy at the tapes of her drawers.

"But . . . a-a-aah."

"Is that right?" His palm covered her mound, his fingers sliding into her. Her body twisted luxuriantly beneath his hand. She locked her legs around his hips and tried to pull him forward.

"I'm afraid I'll hurt you," he protested.

"I can't believe that you would ever hurt me."

"But the child."

"It can't be very big. I feel so empty. I want you so badly. Please, love."

Her pleading gave him license. Unbuttoning his trousers, he replaced his fingers with himself. His hesitancy tantalized them both. Trying to be careful, he slid into her with agonizing slowness while she gasped and twisted, her thighs tensing. Slowly, slowly, he stroked her, his body trembling with strain, perspiration dripping down his temples.

She began to sob. The whole exquisite length of her sheath felt him sliding along it like satin. She knew she could not bear it. Such beauty, such pleasure was beyond her capacity, and yet she did.

He did not ask if her tears were discomfort. His own delirious pleasure convinced him that she was enjoying the loving. He felt like crying himself. Unfortunately, it could not last long. Their highly charged emotions urged their bodies on.

Her sheath began to ripple around him. Her mouth fell open; her head slipped back on the desk. A wordless cry burst from her impelled by the exquisite feel of him inside her. At that instant, she clasped him, every muscle tight around him.

He surrendered. All his love, his cherishing, his honor to her body, he poured into her. In that moment he gave her himself to do with as she willed forever.

Chapter Twenty-seven

A cold silvery mist had veiled the afternoon, and the moon was not yet up to scatter it. I could trace out where every part of the old house had been. I was looking along the desolate garden walk when I beheld a solitary figure in it. It faltered as if much surprised, and uttered my name, and I cried out:

"Marguerite!"

"I am greatly changed. I wonder you know me."

The freshness of her beauty was indeed gone, but its indescribable majesty and its indescribable charm remained. We sat down on a bench that was near, and I said:

"After so many years, it is strange that we should meet again here where our first meeting was! Do you often come back?"

"I have never been here since. And you," she said, in a voice of touching interest to a wanderer, "you live abroad still?"

"Still."

"I have often thought of you," said Marguerite.

"Have you?"

"Of late, very often. There was a long hard time when I kept far from me the remembrance of what I had thrown away when I was quite ignorant of its worth. Now, I have given it a place in my heart."

"You have always held your place in my heart," I answered.

"I must leave you," she said at length. "Once you said, 'God bless you, God forgive you!' Would you say that to me again, so I might remember that we are friends."

"We are friends."

"And will continue friends apart."

I took her hand in mine and we went out of the ruined place, and in all the broad expanse of tranquil light the evening mists showed to me no shadow of another parting from her.

Edward read and reread the last passage of the book. The triumph of it made him determined to publish it. The desire to tell the world what he had been able to say in the pages of the manuscript overruled the shy censorious part of his nature. He was a writer. He knew what he had written was good. The compulsion to publish was uppermost in his mind. Therefore he would, he must, publish.

All the while he bound up the manuscript, disparate voices clamored in his mind. Fearful of meeting Nash with the package tucked under his arm, he went down the hidden staircase in his bedroom and out through the Devil's Palace, deserted at ten o'clock on a winter's morning.

At the door to the offices of Messrs. Chapman and Hall, Publishers, Ltd., his nerve almost failed him. He walked past them, studied the contents of a shop window. He walked past again and stood on the street corner reading with painstaking thoroughness the notices on a public bulletin board until his feet were numb in his boots.

Finally, cursing himself for a cowardly idiot afraid of being rejected, he entered. The whole procedure was so anticlimactic as to be laughable. A cool assistant editor took his name and address, logged the manuscript, and promised to post him a letter within sixty days. In a remarkably short time, he was again standing on the sidewalk.

He thought of a thousand things he had not said, not demanded, not requested, too late. He stared at the door. A gust of wind swirled snow down upon his top hat from a roof. He tightened his muffler around his neck and headed home.

His wife was in the kitchen, her hands floury as she demonstrated to the cook a special shortbread. Edward signaled to the man, who grinned equably and took himself off to market.

"Now you see the success of this receipt is not so much in the ingredients as in the kneading. What—?"

Edward threw his arms around her waist and hugged her to him, growling ferociously in her ear.

Cassandra screamed and slapped at him, sprinkling flour in his hair and over his black coat, until she realized who had her. "You fiend." She laughed, turning in his arms and relaxing against him. "I might have thrown this whole batch all over you."

"So long as it tastes good, I don't care." He kissed her mouth, her forehead getting a smear of flour on his lips, her cheeks. As he hugged her tighter, his secret almost bubbled out of him, but he withheld it. Better to present her with a contract than a faint hope.

When he let her loose for air, she leaned her head back and smiled at him. "This is for your supper tonight. You'd better let me get it together."

He released her regretfully. "A late, late supper, I'm afraid it will have to be. Tonight is the Black Sabbat for the Americans."

"Oh, I had forgotten." She frowned. "Just be sure you don't eat anything there."

"I'm not likely to. I'll eat something sweeter right now and it will keep me satisfied." He made to grab her again, but she held him off.

"I think Nash is upstairs in the library. Probably crouched there thinking up nasty things to say to chastise you because you aren't writing."

He made a face in her direction. "He doesn't have to think up nasty things. He just opens his mouth and out they fly."

Cassandra drew her bathrobe more tightly around her. The back stairs were clearly lighted. All the dark shadows had been dispelled since Edward had added the extra light halfway up. Still, she could not get rid of the little niggling fear. Barston had chosen to take a room on the main floor on the other side of the bathroom. He claimed he was not superstitious but preferred to be near the street entrances.

Staring up the long narrow flight of stairs, she shivered. At certain times of the night, this portion of the Devil's Palace frightened her. She could see herself climbing these stairs with Edward delirious, reeling in her arms. She could still recall the thrill of terror as she fled back and forth along the back hall like a silent ghost trying to find help when he was lying near death from poison. Later she had been horrified to learn that she had been searching for a dead man accidentally poisoned before the poison had been administered to his employer. And in the basement, in the black and crimson chapel, masked men and women did . . .

With one foot on the landing, she stopped dead. Ice water flowed through her veins, a scream bubbled in her throat. The door to Parks's room swung open. The black rectangle yawned like a vault.

As she stared, paralyzed with horror, Fitzwalter lunged out of the door. She screamed, a thin frail sound, cut off by his hand fastened around her throat. The other grabbed her arm. The sleeve of her robe tore away and for a dreadful instant both of them teetered on the top step.

Then he flung himself back, toppling her with him away from the danger. Down the hall toward their suite of rooms, he dragged her. Wildly, she fought, clawing at his wrists, his face, kicking, flinging herself from side to side trying to twist from his grasp. Her robe fell open, her gown ripped, but she could not stop him. He twisted her arm up behind her and forced her down the hall.

He did not stop in the library but pulled her into Edward's bedroom. His eyes burning fanatically, he dragged her to the wardrobe. "Still afraid of being locked in a room, Cassandra," he sneered. "You begged me so beautifully that day. You were like a sinner begging for forgiveness."

Weak with horror, she struggled against him as he pulled the mirror door open. I've locked the door to the stage. You'll be trapped inside the passage when I close this door. No one can hear your screams."

"You're mad," she managed to whisper when his hand released her throat.

"If I am, you have made me that way. You tempted me with your beautiful face and flaming hair." He fastened a hand in it, at the same time keeping a tight grip on her wrist. "Flaming hair."

"Mr. Fitzwalter, you must get control of yourself." She tried to make her voice calm. "The police are looking for you for questioning. You must go to them and clear yourself."

"Ah, yes. But they'll never convict me. Everyone who knew anything at all about me is dead. Those stupid churls who tried to run him down in the streets . . ."

"But *they* attempted to murder Edward. And besides, you didn't kill them. A man named Bagchock did."

"A pimp. A known pimp." Fitzwalter fairly spat the word from his mouth.

"But the fact is you didn't kill them. You can clear yourself."

"You are forgetting the valet." Fitzwalter's smile was horrible to behold.

"The valet . . ." She gasped hoarsely. In that minute she recognized her own death sentence. If he confessed this to her, then he must not intend to let her live. A black cloud of horror threatened to render her senseless, but she forced it back. "Then you must escape," she urged. "Don't waste a minute."

"Oh, I shall, my dear. But I'm not going to leave this pesthole behind. I must atone for the sins I've committed. God has spoken to me. He has told me he will forgive Parks's unfortunate death if I will rid London of this horrible rotten borough."

"Oh, no," she cried. "Oh, no. That is"—her voice sank to a calm tone—"I'm sure the valet died by accident. The police will forgive that too."

"He ate the poisoned cake, my dear." Fitzwalter's voice was most gentle. "Fool! To eat food not intended for him. Ah! Gluttony is a deadly sin."

Despite the pain in her shoulder, Cassandra managed to twist around to see Fitzwalter's face. It was bland, the expression as beatific as she could ever remember it. The countenance was fallen and darkened, even more so than it had been a week ago, but the look was horribly devoid of guilt. The black eyes, farsighted by age, squinted at her, trying to read her reaction.

She tried one more time. "You killed him by accident," she whispered.

He shook his head sorrowfully. "I'm afraid the police won't take that liberal a view of the incident, Cassandra."

"You could escape . . ."

"Oh, I intend to. And I'd take you with me if you hadn't denied me to the police inspector. You have been against me from the beginning. If you had only joined my cause, we could go away together." His face creased in an angry frown. "But you didn't. Instead you married"—he made the word an obscenity—"with that monster. Your father was my best friend, you know. He would die of shame."

"Mr. Fitzwalter, you mustn't do this."

Her words might never have been uttered for all the impression she made. He was dead to her protests. "But I must, my dear. Don't you see? I'll save myself and at the same time I'll send this whole terrible establishment and all those in it back to hell."

"No. You mustn't."

"Fire, my dear. Fire is the only thing that will cleanse the city of London as it needs to be cleansed. Centuries ago fire cleansed the city of the black plague. Now it must cleanse it of another plague. And it will begin here in the Devil's Palace, the heart of the houses of sin. All around here, they are. In Margaret Street, in Soho Square, in Piccadilly, and in Leicester. I shall cleanse them all."

Cassandra went for his eyes then, ducking her head and driving it into his chin while clawing at his face. As she dragged her nails down his cheeks, he cursed, then brutally twisted the arm he held in his grasp. The pain drove a scream from her throat before she fainted.

Fitzwalter swung open the doors to the wardrobe, then opened the sliding panel at its back. Cassandra stirred feebly, her eyes half open. Grunting, he went down on his knee beside her. Hauling her by her arm into a sitting position made her moan. The cloud of flame-red hair had come down from its loose knot and fallen over his arm. He touched it sorrowfully. "The devil's flame-haired bride," he mused. "Ah, Cassandra. I am sorry."

He tried then to gather her into his arms, but her weight overbalanced him. Abandoning that idea, he began to drag her by her shoulders. Panting and groaning, he barely managed to stuff her into stairwell before he felt her struggle feebly.

As she uttered a little whimper, he pulled the props out from the panel. It slid closed with a thud to be followed immediately by a sharp cry from her. Instantly, her fists began to pound. "Mr. Fitzwalter. Please. Please."

He did not answer her. Instead, he pulled out a pocket knife. Sweat from his exertions stung his eyes as he sawed through the cord that held the weight that made the door slide open on the spring. As it parted, the heavy lead dropped with a thud. The panel would never move until it was replaced.

Through the thickness of the wall, he could hear her terrified sobs and the scratching of her fingernails as she fumbled for the mechanism. He heard the lever rattle back and forth uselessly, then her subsequent cry of horror. His heart was pounding so hard against his chest that he could not find the breath to tell her what he had done. He would have liked to do that, but he had to move quickly. He had much to do before the Black Sabbat began in the basement chapel.

Black spots whirled in front of his eyes as he staggered out of the wardrobe. His heart was skipping beats, racing furiously, then slowing. It made him dizzy. He staggered to the bed and pitched backward across it. A moment only, then he would be away. Cassandra's sobs had ceased. He wondered if the poor dear had fainted, or if she was trying to make her way down the stairs in the darkness.

Her fear of closed places would add to her punishment on earth. He had forgotten to exhort her to spend her time praying for her soul. His breathing had slowed somewhat. Wearily, he climbed to his feet. One more effort, then he would leave London forever.

The crimson satin behind the altar glowed like flame. The lights from the gold sconces bathed the huge African mask in a red glow.

"Baal! Baal! Baal!"

Edward Sandron stared down at the blond whore who writhed so seductively on the black velvet altar. She really had a very common face. A heavy jaw and slack loose lips. Her breast were saggy also, not the firm perfect mounds of his wife. He felt perspiration trickling down his back between his shoulderblades. He really must get rid of all those candles. Thirteen were far too many. Seven would be more than enough and reduce the heat in here by a half.

"Baal! Baal! Baal!"

Nash's voice had a hoarse quality tonight. Did he have a cold?

Ashtaroth came forward with the wine. He lifted it to his lips, his eyes meeting hers over the rim of the cup.

"What's she up there for?" came a puzzled drunken question.

"She's part of the show, Roscoe. She's probably his assistant, sort of an acolyte."

"Well, is he gonna get 'em both?"

"Baal! Baal! Baal!"

Edward ripped the first and second veils away with one tug. The audience applauded loudly, not realizing he had made a mistake. With a flourish of his cape, he flung them in the general direction of Nash's voice.

His hand fastened in the third veil, a piece of saffron yellow chiffon, and paused for effect. A heavy cane swung out of nowhere and struck him a glancing blow on the side of the head. Only his quick reflexes that made him duck automatically saved him from a broken skull. Still the blow knocked him off the stage.

Fitzwalter flung his arms wide above the altar. "Sinners, your day of damnation has come! I am the Angel of Purification sent to rid this city of evil . . ."

"What the bloody hell!" Nash's voice broke through the monologue.

"Say, what's going on?"

"You shall burn eternally. Burn! Burn!" Screaming the words maniacally, Fitzwalter jerked the cloth off the altar spilling the blond girl into the arms of the closest devotees.

"Hey! This is some show!"

"Baal, how bad are you hurt?" Sally was kneeling beside him, lifting his head.

"Wha—?" He could not manage the words. He licked his lips and tried again.

"It's Fitzwalter. He's gone crazy."

"Burn!" Turning his back on the room, he held the black velvet altar cloth in the candle flames. It caught immediately. "Burn!" He threw it down on the altar and began to rip down the crimson satin. It, too, ignited.

"Hey, he's settin' the place on fire."

"Fire!" a man shrieked. In another instant, panic erupted as the guests began to scream and fight their way to the exits.

"Bloody bastard!' Nash screamed. He launched himself at Fitzwalter, even as the man jumped from the altar. The panic-stricken audience separated them immediately, sweeping Fitzwalter along with it toward the door.

"Trevor!" Astaroth shrieked.

"Cassandra," Edward muttered, staggering to his feet and supporting himself with one hand on the stage.

Trevor Nash stood up on the stage and began to rip down the crimson satin, but the effort was clearly wasted. He staggered back as the heat intensified and the black cloth-covered walls behind the altar began to smolder. He turned, looking down at Edward and Sally, his face pasty white. "It's going to go up like tinder," he shouted. "We've got to get out."

Flames had already blocked the exit behind the altar. Most of the people had already managed to get out of the basement and were running screaming up the stairs.

"Fire! Fire!" echoed through the casino above.

A few demons came running down with buckets of water, but the fire raced across the ceiling on the black cloth, dropping fire literally on their heads as ashes and sparks fell.

"Shut the door!" Nash screamed. "Maybe it'll suffocate it."

Ashtaroth grabbed the arm of a demon. "Run for the fire brigade!" she yelled. The man dashed off.

Upstairs in the casino, the rooms were fast filling with smoke. Guests had dived through windows and out through the doors and were gathering in the street to watch the spectacle if one developed.

"Get away from there!" screamed one man. "The gas will explode."

His warning caused some of them to hurry away and drove others back to a safe distance.

Edward swept aside the curtain and plunged behind the stage. The quickest way to his apartments was through the secret staircase. He pressed the panel, but nothing happened.

"You're both doomed!" Fitzwalter screamed behind him.

Swinging around, Edward sprang to the edge of the stage. His face contorted. Fitzwalter stood in the center of the ballroom floor, wisps of smoke curling upward around his ankles. Wisps of smoke also curled upward from the stage floor. Edward shook his fist at the madman. The crimson cape billowed from his wrists. "Where is she?"

"She's locked in!" Fitzwalter yelled, jumping up and down and waving his hands above his head. His frenzied laugh was cut off by a cough. "You'll never get her out in time. You'll both die."

At that moment Nash launched himself full force into the pudgy back. They fell together, Nash on top, but Fitzwalter rolled away, kicking at the publisher's stomach and groin. Punching and gouging, Fitzwalter cursed at the top of his lungs. The two wrestled furiously under the great gas-o-lier. The fat man easily outweighted Nash by seventy-five pounds. His solidly backed punches bloodied his enemy's face.

Edward sprang from the stage and sprinted for the back of the building. The floor was heating under his feet. The smoke almost choked him. He flung the crimson satin cape around his head.

"Trevor!" Ashtaroth screamed. She sprang forward to catch Fitzwalter's wrist as he drew back to slam a fist into the side of Nash's head.

The evangelist glared at her, his eyes wild, his mouth spread in a ferocious grin. Lashing her slight body back and forth as she tried to keep him from hitting Nash, he slung her down on the floor.

"Sally!" Nash yelled. "Get the hell out of here."

"No!" she screamed, struggling to get up. "No!"

"Let me help you, ma'am." A demon bent over her and pulled her to her feet.

"No! Trevor! No!"

Disregarding her struggles, the waiter dragged her across the smoking floor and out the door.

Dimly Edward could hear the clamor of the fire brigade. Thank God, they were on their way. He jerked open the door to the back hall. Like the floor of hell, the little tongues of flames leaped upward between the boards. The heat was terrific, but he swaddled his head in his cape and dashed for the stairs.

Fear of what he would find when he reached his apartments gave him wings. He tore down the hall and through the library. In his bedroom, the wardrobe was standing open. Unhesitatingly, he flung his shoulder against it and toppled it over on its face. It fell with a thundering crash that shook the room.

"Cassandra! *Cassandra!* Are you in there?" Even as he shouted the question, he knew the answer. The removal of the wardrobe had exposed the ruined pulley mechanism to the light.

He could hear the fire bells but also the roaring of the fire. It must have burst up into the floors below.

No chance to knock down the panel, especially since she was probably crouched behind it. Setting his hands against the edge of the wall that framed the secret door, he pulled outward. Molding and wallpaper tore away, exposing the ends of boards beneath. Sweat poured down his face and into his eyes. His muscles burned. Smoke filled his lungs.

Again he set his fingers to the edge of the board and heaved. The nails began to come from their holes. He could see a crack. Then the board came loose. Like a madman he snapped it away at the next stud.

"Cassandra!"

He heard her cough. Above the noise in the streets, and the roaring of the wind, and the pounding of blood in his ears, he heard her cough.

"Cassandra!"

"Edward . . . ?" He grabbed hold of the wallboard below the one that had come loose. It, too, came away. And the next. He strove for no more. His hands were mutilated, but he had opened a window large enough to get her out.

Her tear-streaked face appeared at the opening for a second. Then she thrust out her hands and arms, then head and shoulders through. He caught her around the chest and dragged her out, scraping her skin savagely where her torn gown and robe did not cover.

He hugged her to him, too filled with joyful thanksgiving to try to ascertain if she was all right. He could feel her sobbing, her body heaving with the force. He kissed her violently on the mouth. "We have no time," he exclaimed.

"I didn't think you'd find me," she gasped. "Our baby. Our baby would have died with me."

"I'll always find you." He kissed her again hard. Heavy gray smoke was pouring out of the hole and into his bedroom. He took her hand and led the way into the library. His feeling of infinite relief at having her with him was marred as he spared one glance around him. The gold lettering on the spines of the volumes was fast dimming as the smoke rose around them. Tears filled his eyes. She caught the look. Her hand tightened in his grasp. She reached toward the shelf.

Sternly, he pulled her away. He could not save them all.

The hallway was so full of smoke that he could no longer see his way. "The Margaret Street entrance!"

he yelled. "It's our only chance." One hand groped for and found the wall; the other clasped hers in a deathgrip.

Together they ran down the hall. He dragged her by the seventh panel. In panic he crashed against the eighth. Then recovering he tried the one next to it. As he pulled them through it, Cassandra looked back. The hall was empty. Then suddenly there was no floor as an explosion blew it away and flames leaped up through the hole.

"Hurry!" He threw his arm around her shoulder and practically carried her down the last flight of stairs. They burst out into the street as a gigantic explosion tore the roof off the Devil's Palace. Flames and burning debris shot upward in a fountain toward the sky.

Edward jerked off his cape and draped it around Cassandra's shaking shoulders. "Let's get around to Regent Street. We can find help there. I've got to get you some clothes and a place to lie down and rest."

Together they hurried through the crowds of curious onlookers standing in the street to watch the spectacle.

At the front of the house they found Ashtaroth in hysterics.

Edward caught her by the shoulders. "Are you hurt, Sally? Are you burned?"

She was crying so hard she could not speak intelligibly at first. "No." She shook her head and gulped. "No! Trevor! Trevor!"

She pointed toward the shell of the house that had collapsed on itself. The gas explosion had blown the fire away, leaving only a smoldering pile of timbers.

"Nash!" Edward spun around, staring with horrified eyes. "Nash didn't make it out."

Sally dropped to her knees in the snow. "He was fighting with that bloody bastard Fitzwalter when the gas-o-lier exploded. Oh, Eddie, they were right under it."

Cassandra came up on the other side of the girl and lifted her out of the snow. Together the three of them clung together as the fire brigade pumped more water onto the wreckage.

Chapter Twenty-eight

Cassandra lifted the edge of the crimson cape and draped it around Sally Atkins's shaking shoulders. The black eyes flashed momentarily as she resisted the sympathetic overture. Then her eyes closed, tears squeezed out underneath them, and she hid her face against Cassandra's bosom.

Leaving the two women, Edward sought out the leader of the fire brigade, who was talking earnestly with Barston. The man's face was sickly white beneath the soot and grime. ". . . total loss. Worse, Thom found a body half submerged in the basement. Badly burned. Who's unaccounted for?"

Barston threw up his hands in relief at the sight of his employer limping toward him. "Mr. Sandron!" he exclaimed, running to clasp his hands. "Oh, Mr. Sandron, are you and the lady . . . ?"

"We're fine, a bit smoky and definitely singed, but otherwise in good shape."

"Thank the good Lord, sir. When I heard the commotion, I roused Mrs. Smithers. She went immediately to Mrs. Sandron's rooms, but she couldn't find her, then to your rooms. She was frantic. I assure you, sir, I had to drag her out. She kept screaming that her lady was in the house somewhere."

Edward flinched at his own negligence. He had not taken time to show Barston the secret passages. If the man had known, would he have been able to rescue Cassandra sooner? "We're both safe, Barston, and I thank you more than I can say. You and Mrs. Smithers both. You'll never want for anything that I can provide for you."

The director of the fire brigade joined them. "Glad to hear you and the missus escaped, sir. At least one poor blighter didn't. Could you give us some idea as to who he might be? The debris is still too hot to get into. Face down in the water, he is. Legs on a sort of a raised platform. Great heavy beam crushing the middle of his back." He shook his head wearily. "Bloody shame, sir. Damned bloody shame."

"Only one man?" Edward asked sharply.

"It's the only one we could see. Could be more. God forbid. Bloody shame." The man bowed his head.

"Bloody shame," Barston agreed, his eyes on the smoking hulk.

Edward stared bleakly at the ruin. "Yes," he murmured softly. *Nash. Damn you, Nash. Too many things left unsaid. You kept surprising me. Just a little bit better than you should have been in every way.*

Inspector Clive Revill approached them. His face grave. He clutched his notebook in his hand. "What happened?"

"We've located a body in basement," the fireman volunteered.

"Good God," Revill breathed, opening it to a fresh

page. "Who could it be?"

"The killer I hope," Edward told him bitterly.

"Fitzwalter."

"And my best friend, Trevor Nash," came the smothered addendum.

"Two?" The inspector broke the point of his pencil. He stared for confirmation at the fireman.

The man shrugged. "Very probably. One's certain. The water's a couple of feet deep in the basement and fearful mucky."

Edward had to clamp down on his jaw to keep his teeth from chattering. "If there's one, the other must be beside him. They fell together when the floor of the ballroom collapsed. Fitzwalter had just boasted that he had locked my wife in a wardrobe in my bedroom and left her there to burn."

The inspector's composure cracked. "My God, man. Say you got the precious lady out all right?"

"As you see." He led the inspector over to the two women.

Sally had recovered herself sufficiently to dry her eyes. One of the waiters had thoughtfully given her a wrap and she'd moved away from Cassandra's warmth to stand alone. Her black eyes glistened as she stared at the ruin.

"Ma'am." Inspector Revill took Cassandra's hand. "Ma'am, I can't tell you how much I regret what's happened. We did our best to find Fitzwalter."

Cassandra looked tiredly at the round face with the pugnacious jaw, but what she might have said was interrupted.

"Best! Best! Y'stupid copper! Idiot!" Sally pushed

her way between them. "Look at that. That's what all of us have worked and slaved over for years. It's all gone. Where's yer bloody guard that was supposed to catch him?"

Revill reeled back before her fury. He looked futilely around him for support. Forming a circle around him were the accusing faces of the employees of the Devil's Palace. "The guard was knocked out," he stammered. "We found him bound in the alley."

"Some guard. What was he? An old ginhead on half pay?" Sally sneered.

"I assure you, young woman . . ."

"Sally." Cassandra touched her arm. "Don't get so upset. It won't help anything."

With a violent twist, Sally shrugged her off. "Hell, no. Nothin'll ever help anything. Callin' this copper a bloody bastard to his face won't help a bit. Nash is dead. Nash!" She screamed his name in the inspector's alarmed face. "Trevor Nash. Put that in your bleedin' notebook." She turned her anguished face up to the heavens. "Nash!"

"Sally, old gel. No need to carry on so."

She spun, her eyes drinking him in. He was almost unrecognizable. What remained of his singed hair was plastered to his head. His eyebrows were gone and the skin of his face was burnt and begrimed. Despite the smoldering garments on his shoulders and arms, he managed a cheeky grin. His lips split back from his teeth, making them appear startlingly white in his face.

"Nash," she whispered. "Oh, Nash."

"Trevor," he reminded her, holding out one arm.

Sooty water dripped from the sleeve of the jacket.

She flew into his arms, hugging him, kissing his face over and over, sobbing. She thrust her hands beneath his coat and felt his body, assuring herself that he was real. "You're soaking wet," she sobbed. "How did you get so wet?"

"Hush," he chided, kissing her hard on the lips, then groaning as she hugged him too tightly. "Don't fuss. Never have known such a woman for finding things to complain about."

"Nash!" Edward exclaimed delighted. "My God, I'm glad to see you. Where'd you come from?"

"From the basement, old chum," Nash coughed wearily. "Sally, could we sit down a minute? Still a bit shaky on m'pins."

While Sally put her arms around his waist, Edward hurried to take his right arm. "Careful there, both of you. I'm singed."

Together the four of them made their way to the bench under the streetlight. Nash all but toppled over, so shaky were his legs. Refusing to relinquish her hold on him, Sally sat beside him. The leader of the fire brigade draped a blanket over his shoulders. The others including Revill gathered around him.

"Can you give us any of the particulars?" the inspector begged.

"I swear I don't know how it happened," Nash explained. He cradled his right arm as he shot a irrepressible glance at Edward. "Except maybe the devil taking care of his own."

Noting his injuries, Cassandra knelt before him and scooped snow over the huge blisters rising on the back of his hand. "You must leave this on to take the burn away," she admonished him.

He smiled down at her. "A lady kneeling at my feet."

"What happened, Nash?" Edward urged.

He sighed, then smiled at Sally. "One minute I was rolling back and forth with that damned blubbery hulk crushing me and the next there was this terrific explosion. I looked up to see the whole ceiling burst into flames. Then I was falling. Don't remember anything for a minute. Then I was choking and icy water was pouring in all around me."

Revill looked at him narrowly. "You fell through the floor into the basement while you were fighting Fitzwalter. His body must have struck the stage. Then a beam that supported the floor must have come crashing down." He made a note on his pad. "Anyone else in that basement?"

Nash shrugged, then winced as he caused himself pain. "Can't help you there. Sorry, Inspector. Went out like a light. I can show you where I was down in there."

Revill put his hand gently on the man's shoulder. "That won't be necessary. We can handle it from here. I'll post guards around the place until morning. Then when the basement cools off, we'll send the forensic department in to get the body out and see what they can find."

Sally began to tremble. "We need to get inside out of the cold." She could feel Nash shivering in his wet clothes. "I've got room in my flat for all four of us. It's near here." Taking charge, she looked expectantly at

Revill. Sally Atkins, the screaming street urchin, had disappeared to be replaced by Ashtaroth, the high priestess whose slightest wish was law. "Inspector, you will provide us your transport, won't you?"

He tipped his hat, politely. "Gladly, ma'am." He went away to make arrangements.

Edward turned to Barston. "Take Mrs. Smithers and check yourselves into the nearest hotel. I'll contact you just as soon as I can. Don't stint yourself. I'll pay the bill."

Barston bowed stiffly. "No need to pay that expense, sir. My brother works in a house in Soho. I shall find welcome there, as will Mrs. Smithers. We shall contrive without inconvenience until matters can be brought under control."

Edward shook the man's hand. "Remember," he insisted. "You are my man. Don't hire out to anyone no matter how much he wants to pay you. And Mrs. Smithers too."

"No, sir."

The clop of horses' hooves signaled the arrival of Revill's cab. The demon waiters had departed to their homes. The onlookers had drifted away. Revill was stationing policemen at intervals around the smoking ruin until morning. Snow began to drift down in huge silent flakes.

Edward stared up at the skeleton of the second story. It could have been so much worse. So very much worse. And yet suddenly his loss seemed insupportable.

The books. The books. Why did he feel as if a part of his flesh had been torn away from him? God forgive him. He had not been able to save his old friends that had made him what he was. And yet they were only books, for heaven's sake!

Why did he feel sick to his stomach at the thought of the words lost? The bindings of blue silk and leather, the pages and pages of print.

He looked down at the grimy trampled snow. God! Was he going to cry like a child?

Cassandra put her hand on his shoulder. "We'll replace them, my love."

He ducked his head, trying to hide the tears in his eyes. "The old Devil's Palace. Of course, no problem. House was only leased anyway. We'll move into something else on Regent Street. Replace the gambling equipment . . ."

She put her hand over his lips. "I meant the books."

He looked at her. "It's silly." He made a harsh snubbing sound and clutched her to him, hiding his face in her smoke-stained hair. "But I feel as if I left them there to burn."

"I felt the same thing. Do you remember? If you had said the word, we would have carried them out together. Because they were your teachers and your parents and your friends. All the wonderful things you are, the values that you live by, came to you through them. They gave you to me."

He drew back to stare at her incredulously. "Do you really mean that?"

"Of course. And we'll replace them. Every single one and have fun doing it."

"First," he agreed.

"Even if we couldn't replace them, they'd still be

with us. Their words are immortal — forever in your mind."

She kissed him as she turned him away from the Devil's Palace. Their arms around each other, they walked together toward the cab through the gently falling snow.

Epilogue

"Lord S—knelt beside her in the silken prison he had created to keep her. "My lady, say you will forgive me. I beg you. Elsewise I shall never draw breath again in this life."

She turned her pale face from the wall and looked into his dark visage, that was once so savage. Worry and despair had softened its cruel lines. When she wearily raised her hand to touch him, he caught it between both of his and raised it to his lips.

"Say you will forgive me," he repeated. "I will make restitution of everything I have taken from you. I will raise your poor father to his former level of society. I will rebuild the castle that I caused to be torn down." He bowed his head on the velvet coverlet. "Only say you will forgive."

"You are as great as in your good as you were in evil," she whispered, her eyes glowing.

"Your courage and devotion have reformed me. I love you although I can never, never be worthy of your love, *nor can I expect that you will love me."*

She took his face between her soft white hands. "But I can. Now that you are changed, I can love you."

"My dearest, neither Hell nor Heaven shall . . ."

"Not our usual style," Nash remarked, reading over Edward's shoulder. He took up the page and read it through again. "No, not what our readers are expecting at all. Still we might start a new style. This might be the time to start a new line, broaden our readership so to speak."

Edward looked at him skeptically.

"No, I mean it. We'll move the old presses to a respectable area of town. Somewhere where people won't associate it with the old stuff. I'll change the name. Create a whole new image. What do you think?"

"I think it sounds like another of your electric light company ideas," Edward remarked. "But take the manuscript anyway. It's finished."

At the sound of the door opening behind them, the occupants of the room turned. Edward shoved the finished book into Nash's hands and rose. "Cassie, love, is it time for our walk in the park?"

She smiled at him, her eyes warm as the sunlight throwing patterns on the floor. Framed in profile in the doorway, she stood with one hand resting on the handle of an elegant black baby carriage. "Absolutely. Nap time's over and the Green Park beckons."

Edward felt the tears start in his eyes as he went

toward her, his hands outstretched. As he towered over her, she tilted back her head to receive his tribute on her lips. As they touched, a soft cooing sound and the tiny jingle of silver beads in a rattle made his heart contract. He hugged her tighter than usual to master his emotion, then bent over the carriage.

The cooing sound turned to a gurgle of recognition and more jingling of the beads. Still keeping his arm around Cassandra's waist, Edward chucked his son under the chin. "Of course you're ready, Scotty boy? You want to the see the leaves and the trees and the ducks . . . ?"

"Obviously far gone." Nash threw up his hands in mock disgust. "Cassie, why don't you just get a larger pram and wheel them both around together? They seem of an age."

Cassandra smiled serenely at Nash, her husband's clasp warming her so that even the publisher's sarcasm could not touch her.

Somewhat disappointed by their lack of response, Nash turned back to Sally, who sat quietly, her hands clasped demurely in her lap. "What do you think of my idea for publishing, old gel? At least give me a sane answer in the midst of all this sweetness and light."

The dark woman exchanged a knowing look with Cassandra. Then she smiled. "I think we should go for a walk with them, Trevor. It's time we get in practice for ourselves."

Her words wiped away the sarcastic smile. The freckles stood out on his face as color drained from it.

"Sally . . ." he gasped incredulously. "Sally." The distance across the carpet seemed a lifetime until he could drop down on one knee and gather her in his arms.

Author's Note

The author has borrowed quite shamelessly from *Great Expectations* and *Tale of Two Cities* in the opening passages of Chapters 20, 24, and 27. Furthermore, she has taken the liberty of having Edward Sandron carry his manuscript to Messrs. Chapman and Hall, Charles Dickens's own publishers, who first commissioned the monthly serial that became the immortal *Pickwick Papers*. Although Dickens's childhood was impoverished, he was never in the dire straits that Eddie Boggan found himself, nor was he forced to write pornography for a living. At no time did this author plan to write a thinly disguised biography. All characters and events in this novel are strictly fictitious.

Deana James
Dallas, Texas